Praise for Jo Nesbø's

The Snowman

"*The Snowman* is strung together with great care, playful in certain stretches, grisly in others, all of it highly readable."
—*Newsweek*

"The writer most likely to take the ice-cold crown in the critically acclaimed—and now bestselling—category of Nordic noir."
—*Los Angeles Times*

"The brilliance of Nesbø: He takes the simple and cozy, and transforms it into the terrorizing. . . . The characters are marvellous, the plot is tight and the setting perfect—just at the edge of a Norwegian winter—and the concept original."
—Margaret Cannon, *The Globe and Mail*

"Many authors know how to make the hairs on the back of your neck stand up. Jo Nesbø's one of the few who keeps them there."
—Linwood Barclay

"This is reading as you experienced it in childhood, without any gap between eye and mind, but with the added pleasures that adult plots and adult characters can bring. . . . Unputdownable. *The Snowman* is probably the most terrifying and certainly the most addictive book in the whole series."
—*Slate*

"This is crime writing of the highest order, in which the characters are as strong as the story, where an atmosphere of evil permeates, and the tension begins in the first chapter and never lets up."   —*The Times* (UK)

"Spine-chilling. . . . This most ambitious of Nesbø's crime novels banishes any fears that the omniscient serial killer scenario has been exhausted."
—*The Independent* (UK)

"Macabre and disturbing. . . . Deft plotting, strong characterization, adrenaline-fuelled action sequences and a whole raft of social issues raised along the way make this book a spectacularly good example of how a tried and tested (and often tired) formula can be made exhilarating and fresh."   —*The Guardian* (UK)

"Hole is all a fictional detective should be."
— *The Times Literary Supplement* (UK)

"[*The Snowman*] is a book as fathomless as the snow, as luminous and abstract as Beethoven's Late String Quartets and a very jarring and unique literary experience. It exists on a recognizable plane of propulsive energy undercut with the irony that molds all kinds of fiction, including my own."   —James Ellroy

JO NESBØ

The Snowman

Jo Nesbø's books have been translated into forty-seven languages. He is the author of the Harry Hole series, as well as *Headhunters*, *The Son*, and several children's books. He has received the Glass Key Award for best Nordic crime novel. He is also a musician, songwriter, and economist and lives in Oslo.

www.jonesbo.com

The Snowman

The Snowman

JO NESBØ

Translated from the Norwegian by Don Bartlett

Seal Books

Seal Books and colophon are registered trademarks of
Penguin Random House Canada

THE SNOWMAN
Seal Books/published by arrangement with Random House Canada
Vintage Canada edition published 2011
Random House Canada edition published 2010

Library and Archives of Canada Cataloguing in Publication is
available upon request.

ISBN: 978-1-4000-2677-7

The Snowman is a work of fiction. Names, characters, places and
incidents are products of the author's imagination or are used
fictitiously. Any resemblance to actual events or locales or persons,
living or dead, is entirely coincidental.

Printed and bound in the USA

Seal Books are published by Penguin Random House Canada.
"Seal Books" and the portrayal of a seal are the property of
Penguin Random House Canada.

www.penguinrandomhouse.ca

10 9 8 7 6 5 4 3 2 1

Penguin
Random
House

For Kirsten Hammervoll Nesbø

Part One

I

The Snowman

It was the day the snow came. At eleven o'clock in the morning, large flakes had appeared from a colorless sky and invaded the fields, gardens and lawns of Romerike like an armada from outer space. At two, the snowplows were in action in Lillestrøm, and when, at half past two, Sara Kvinesland slowly and carefully steered her Toyota Corolla SR5 between the detached houses on Kolloveien, the November snow was lying like a down duvet over the rolling countryside.

She was thinking that the houses looked different in daylight. So different that she almost passed his driveway. The car skidded as she applied the brakes, and she heard a groan from the backseat. In the rearview mirror she saw her son's disgruntled face.

"It won't take long, my love," she said.

In front of the garage there was a large patch of black pavement amid all the white, and she realized that the moving van had been there. Her throat constricted. She hoped she wasn't too late.

"Who lives here?" came from the backseat.

"Just someone I know," Sara said, automatically checking her hair in the mirror. "Ten minutes, my love.

I'll leave the key in the ignition so you can listen to the radio."

She went without waiting for a response, slithered in her slippery shoes up to the door she had been through so many times, but never like this, not in the middle of the day, in full view of all the neighbors' prying eyes. Not that late-night visits would seem any more innocent, but for some reason acts of this kind felt more appropriate when performed after the fall of darkness.

She heard the buzz of the doorbell inside, like a bumblebee in a jam jar. Feeling her desperation mount, she glanced at the windows of the neighboring houses. They gave nothing away, just returned reflections of bare black apple trees, gray sky and milky-white terrain. Then, at last, she heard footsteps behind the door and heaved a sigh of relief. The next moment she was inside and in his arms.

"Don't go, darling," she said, hearing the sob already straining at her vocal cords.

"I have to," he said in a monotone that suggested a refrain he had tired of long ago. His hands sought familiar paths, of which they never tired.

"No, you don't," she whispered into his ear. "But you want to. You don't dare any longer."

"This has nothing to do with you and me."

She could hear the irritation creeping into his voice at the same time as his hand, the strong but gentle hand, slid down over her spine and inside the waistband of her skirt and tights. They were like a pair of practiced dancers who knew their partner's every move, step, breath, rhythm. First, the white lovemaking. The good one. Then the black one. The pain.

His hand caressed her coat, searching for her nipple under the thick material. He was eternally fascinated by her nipples; he always returned to them. Perhaps it was because he didn't have any himself.

"Did you park in front of the garage?" he asked with a firm tweak.

She nodded and felt the pain shoot into her head like a dart of pleasure. Her sex had already opened for him. "My son's waiting in the car."

His hand came to an abrupt halt.

"He knows nothing," she groaned, sensing his hand falter.

"And your husband? Where's he now?"

"Where do you think? At work, of course."

Now it was she who sounded irritated. Both because he had brought her husband into the conversation and it was difficult for her to say anything at all about him without getting irritated, and because her body needed him, quickly. Sara Kvinesland opened his fly.

"Don't . . . ," he began, grabbing her around the wrist. She slapped him hard with her other hand. He looked at her in amazement as a red flush spread across his cheek. She smiled, grabbed his thick black hair and pulled his face down to hers.

"You can go," she hissed. "But first you have to fuck me. Is that understood?"

She felt his breath against her face. It was coming in hefty gasps now. Again she slapped him with her free hand, and his dick was growing in her other.

He thrust, a bit harder each time, but it was over now. She was numb, the magic was gone, the tension had dissolved and all that was left was despair. She was losing him. Now, as she lay there, she had lost him. All the years she had yearned, all the tears she had cried, the desperate things he had made her do. Without giving anything back. Except for one thing.

He was standing at the foot of the bed and taking her

with closed eyes. Sara stared at his chest. At first she had thought it strange, but after a while she had begun to like the sight of unbroken white skin over his pectoral muscles. It reminded her of old statues on which the nipples had been omitted out of consideration for public modesty.

His groans were getting louder. She knew that soon hewould let out a furious roar. She had loved that roar. The ever-surprised, ecstatic, almost pained expression as though the orgasm surpassed his wildest expectation each and every time. Now she was waiting for the final roar, a bellowing farewell to this freezing box of a bedroom, divested of pictures, curtains and carpets. Then he would get dressed and travel to a different part of the country, where he said he had been offered a job he couldn't say no to. But he could say no to this. This. And still he would roar with pleasure.

She closed her eyes. But the roar didn't come. He had stopped.

"What's up?" she asked, opening her eyes. His features were distorted, all right. But not with pleasure.

"A face," he whispered.

She flinched. "Where?"

"Outside the window."

The window was at the other end of the bed, right above her head. She heaved herself around, felt him slip out, already limp. The window above her head was set too high in the wall for her to see out. And too high for anyone standing outside to peer in. Because of the already dwindling daylight all she could see was the double-exposed reflection of the ceiling lamp.

"You saw yourself," she said, almost pleading.

"That was what I thought at first," he said, still staring at the window.

Sara pulled herself up onto her knees. Got up and looked into the yard. And there, there was the face.

She laughed out loud with relief. The face was white, with eyes and a mouth made with black pebbles, probably from the driveway. And arms made of twigs from the apple trees.

"Heavens," she gasped. "It's only a snowman."

Then her laugh turned into tears; she sobbed helplessly until she felt his arms around her.

"I have to go now," she sobbed.

"Stay for a little while longer," he said.

She stayed for a little while longer.

As Sara approached the garage she saw that almost forty minutes had passed.

He had promised to call her now and then. He had always been a good liar, and for once she was glad. Even before she got to the car she saw her son's pale face staring at her from the backseat. She pulled at the door and found to her astonishment that it was locked. She peered in at him through steamed-up windows. He opened it only when she knocked on the glass.

She sat in the driver's seat. The radio was silent and it was ice-cold inside. The key was on the passenger seat. She turned to him. Her son was pale, and his lower lip was trembling.

"Is there anything wrong?" she asked.

"Yes," he said. "I saw him."

There was a thin, shrill tone of horror in his voice that she couldn't recall hearing since he was a little boy jammed between them on the sofa in front of the TV with his hands over his eyes. And now his voice was changing, he had stopped giving her a good-night hug and had started being interested in car engines and girls. And one day he would get in a car with one of them and also leave her.

"What do you mean?" she said, inserting the key in the ignition and turning.

"The snowman . . . "

There was no response from the engine and panic gripped her without warning. Quite what she was afraid of she didn't know. She stared out the windshield and turned the key again. Had the battery died?

"And what did the snowman look like?" she asked, pressing the accelerator to the floor and desperately turning the key so hard it felt as though she would break it. He answered, but the response was drowned by the roar of the engine.

Sara put the car in gear and let go of the clutch as if in a sudden hurry to get away. The wheels spun in the soft, slushy snow. She accelerated harder, but the rear of the car slid sideways. By then the tires had spun their way down to the pavement and they lurched forward and skidded into the road.

"Dad's waiting for us," she said. "We'll have to get a move on."

She switched on the radio and turned up the volume to fill the cold interior with sounds other than her own voice. A broadcaster said for the hundredth time today that last night Ronald Reagan had beaten Jimmy Carter in the American election.

The boy said something again, and she glanced in the mirror.

"What did you say?" she said in a loud voice.

He repeated it, but still she couldn't hear. She turned down the radio while heading toward the main road and the river, which ran through the countryside like two mournful black stripes. And gave a start when she realized he had leaned forward between the two front seats. His voice sounded like a dry whisper in her ear. As if it were important no one else heard them.

"We're going to die."

2

Pebble-Eyes

Harry Hole gave a start and opened his eyes wide. It was freezing cold, and from the dark came the sound of the voice that had awoken him. It announced that the American people would decide today whether their president for the next four years would again be George Walker Bush. November. Harry was thinking they were definitely heading for dark times. He threw off the duvet and placed his feet on the floor. The linoleum was so cold it stung. He left the news blaring from the clock radio and went into the bathroom. Regarded himself in the mirror. November there, too: drawn, grayish pale and overcast. As usual, his eyes were bloodshot, and the pores on his nose large black craters. The bags under his eyes, with their light-blue alcohol-washed irises, would disappear after his face had been ministered to with hot water, a towel and breakfast. He assumed they would, that is. Harry was not sure exactly how his face would fare during the day now that he had turned forty. Whether the wrinkles would be ironed out and peace would fall over the hunted expression he woke with after nights of being ridden by nightmares. Which was most nights. For he avoided mirrors after he left his small, spartan apartment on Sofies Gate and transformed into Inspector Hole of the Crime Squad at the Oslo Police HQ. Then he stared into others' faces to find their pain, their Achilles' heels, their nightmares, motives and reasons for self-deception, listening to their fatiguing lies and trying to find a meaning in what he did: imprisoning people who were already imprisoned inside themselves. Prisons of hatred and self-contempt he recognized all too well. He ran a hand over the shorn bristles of blond hair that grew precisely seventy-five inches above the frozen soles of his feet. His collarbone stood out under his skin like a clothes hanger. He had trained a lot since the last case. In a frenzy, some maintained. As well as cycling he had started to lift weights in the fitness room in the bowels of the Police HQ. He liked the burning pain, and the repressed thoughts. Nevertheless, he just became leaner. The fat disappeared and his muscles were layered between skin and bone. And while before he had been broad-shouldered and what Rakel called a natural athlete, now he had begun to resemble the photograph he had once seen of a skinned polar bear: a muscular but shockingly gaunt predator. Quite simply, he was fading away. Not that it actually mattered. Harry sighed. November. It was going to get even darker.

He went into the kitchen, drank a glass of water to relieve his headache and peered through the window in surprise. The roof of the building on the other side of Sofies Gate was white and the bright reflected light made his eyes smart. The first snow had come in the night. He thought of the letter. He did occasionally get such letters, but this one had been special. It had mentioned Toowoomba.

On the radio a nature program had started and an enthusiastic voice was waxing lyrical about seals. "Every summer Berhaus seals collect in the Bering Strait to mate.

Since the males are in the majority, the competition for females is so fierce that those males that have managed to procure themselves a female will stick with her during the whole of the breeding period. The male will take care of his partner until the young have been born and can cope by themselves. Not out of love for the female, but out of love for his own genes and hereditary material. Darwinist theory would say that it is natural selection that makes the Berhaus seal monogamous, not morality."

I wonder, thought Harry.

The voice on the radio was almost turning falsetto with excitement. "But before the seals leave the Bering Strait to search for food in the open sea, the male will try to kill the female. Why? Because a female Berhaus seal will never mate twice with the same male! For her this is about spreading the biological risk of hereditary material, just like on the stock market. For her it makes biological sense to be promiscuous, and the male knows this. By taking her life he wants to stop the young of other seals competing with his own progeny for the same food."

"We're entering Darwinian waters here, so why don't humans think like the seal?" another voice said.

"But we do, don't we! Our society is not as monogamous as it appears, and never has been. A Swedish study showed recently that between fifteen and twenty percent of all children born have a different father from the one they—and for that matter the postulated fathers—think. Twenty percent! That's every fifth child! Living a lie. And ensuring biological diversity."

Harry fiddled with the radio dial to find some tolerable music. He stopped at an aging Johnny Cash's version of "Desperado."

There was a firm knock on the door.

Harry went into the bedroom, put on his jeans, returned to the hall and opened up.

"Harry Hole?" The man outside was wearing blue overalls and looking at Harry through thick lenses. His eyes were as clear as a child's.

Harry nodded.

"Have you got fungus?" The man asked the question with a straight face. A long wisp of hair traversed his forehead and was stuck there. Under his arm he was holding a plastic clipboard with a densely printed sheet.

Harry waited for him to explain further, but nothing was forthcoming. Just this clear, open expression.

"That," Harry said, "strictly speaking, is a private matter."

The man gave the suggestion of a smile in response to a joke he was heartily sick of hearing. "Fungus in your apartment. Mold."

"I have no reason to believe that I do," said Harry.

"That's the thing about mold. It seldom gives anyone any reason to believe that it's there." The man sucked at his teeth and rocked on his heels.

"But?" Harry said at length.

"But it is."

"What makes you think that?"

"Your neighbor's got it."

"Uh-huh? And you think it may have spread?"

"Mold doesn't spread. Dry rot does."

"So then . . . ?"

"There's a construction fault with the ventilation along the walls in this building. It allows dry rot to flourish. May I take a peep at your kitchen?"

Harry stepped to the side. The man powered into the kitchen, where at once he pressed an orange hair-dryer-like apparatus against the wall. It squeaked twice.

"Damp detector," the man said, studying something that was obviously an indicator. "Just as I thought. Sure you haven't seen or smelled anything suspicious?"

Harry didn't have a clear perception of what that might be.

"A coating like on stale bread," the man said. "Moldy smell."

Harry shook his head.

"Have you had sore eyes?" the man asked. "Felt tired? Had headaches?"

Harry shrugged. "Of course. For as long as I can remember."

"Do you mean for as long as you've lived here?"

"Maybe. Listen . . . "

But the man wasn't listening; he'd taken a knife from his belt. Harry stood back and watched the hand holding the knife being raised and thrust with great force. There was a sound like a groan as the knife went through the plasterboard behind the wallpaper. The man pulled out the knife, thrust it in again and bent back a powdery piece of plaster, leaving a large gap in the wall. Then he whipped out a small penlight and shone it into the cavity. A deep frown developed behind his oversize glasses. Then he stuck his nose deep into the cavity and sniffed.

"Right," he said. "Hello there, boys."

"Hello there who?" Harry asked, edging closer.

"*Aspergillus,*" said the man. "A genus of mold. We have three or four hundred types to choose among and it's difficult to say which one this is because the growth on these hard surfaces is so thin it's invisible. But there's no mistaking the smell."

"That means trouble, right?" Harry asked, trying to remember how much he had left in his bank account after he and his father had sponsored a trip to Spain for Sis, his little sister, who had what she referred to as "a touch of Down syndrome."

"It's not like real dry rot. The building won't collapse," the man said. "But you might."

"Me?"

"If you're prone to it. Some people get ill from breathing the same air as the mold. They're ailing for years, and of course they get accused of being hypochondriacs since no one can find anything and the other residents are fine. And then the pest eats up the wallpaper and the plasterboard."

"Mm. What do you suggest?"

"That I eradicate the infection, of course."

"And my personal finances while you're at it?"

"Covered by the building's insurance, so it won't cost you a krone. All I need is access to the apartment for the next few days."

Harry found the spare set of keys in the kitchen drawer and passed them to him.

"It'll just be me," the man said. "I should mention that in passing. Lots of strange things going on out there."

"Are there?" Harry smiled sadly, staring out of the window.

"Eh?"

"Nothing," Harry said. "There's nothing to steal here anyway. I'll be off now."

The low morning sun sparkled off all the glass on the Oslo Police HQ, standing there as it had for the last thirty years, on the summit of the ridge by the main street, Grønlandsleiret. Although this had not been exactly intentional, the HQ was near the high-crime areas in east Oslo, and the prison, located on the site of the old brewery, was its closest neighbor. The police station was surrounded by a brown withering lawn and maple and linden trees that had been covered with a thin layer of gray-white snow during the night, making the park look like a deceased's shrouded chattels.

Harry walked up the black strip of pavement to the main entrance and entered the central hall, where Kari Christensen's porcelain wall decoration with running water whispered its eternal secrets. He nodded to the security guard in reception and went up to the Crime Squad on the sixth floor. Although it had been almost six months since he had been given his new office in the red zone, he still often mistakenly went to the cramped, windowless one he had shared with Officer Jack Halvorsen. Now Magnus Skarre was in there. And Jack Halvorsen had been interred in the ground of Vestre Aker cemetery. At first the parents had wanted their son to be buried in their hometown, Steinkjer, as Jack and Beate Lønn, the head of Krimteknisk, the Forensics Unit, had not been married; they hadn't even been living together. But when they found out that Beate was pregnant and Jack's baby would be born in the summer, Jack's parents agreed that Jack's grave should be in Oslo.

Harry entered his new office. Which he knew would be known as that forever, the way the fifty-year-old home ground of the Barcelona football club was still called Camp Nou, Catalan for "New Stadium." He dropped into his chair, switched on the radio and nodded good morning to the photos perched on the bookcase and propped against the wall. One day in an uncertain future, if he remembered to buy picture hooks, they would hang on the wall. Ellen Gjelten and Jack Halvorsen and Bjarne Møller. There they stood in chronological order. The Dead Policemen's Society.

On the radio Norwegian politicians and social scientists were giving their views on the American presidential election. Harry recognized the voice of Arve Støp, the owner of the successful magazine *Liberal* and famous for being one of the most knowledgeable, arrogant and entertaining pundits in the country. Harry turned up the volume until the voices bounced off the brick walls, and grabbed his Peerless handcuffs from the new desk. He practiced speed-cuffing the table leg, which was already splintered as a result of this new bad habit of his. He had picked it up in the FBI course in Chicago and perfected it during lonely evenings in a lousy apartment in Cabrini-Green, surrounded by arguing neighbors and in the company of Jim Beam. The aim was to bang the cuffs against the arrestee's wrist in such a way that the spring-loaded arm closed around the wrist and the lock clicked on the other side. With the right amount of force and accuracy you could cuff yourself to an arrestee in one simple movement before he had a chance to react. Harry had never had any use for this on the job and only once for the other thing he had learned over there: how to catch a serial killer. The cuffs clicked around the table leg and the radio voices droned on.

"Why do you think Norwegians are so skeptical about George Bush, Arve Støp?"

"Because we're an overprotected nation that has never fought in any wars. We've been happy to let others do it for us: England, the Soviet Union and America. Yes, ever since the Napoleonic Wars we've hidden behind the backs of our older brothers. Norway has based its security on others taking the responsibility when things got tough. That's been going on for so long that we've lost our sense of reality and we believe that the earth is basically populated by people who wish us—the world's richest country—well. Norway, a gibbering, pea-brained blonde who gets lost in an alley in the Bronx and is now indignant that her bodyguard is so brutal with muggers."

Harry dialed Rakel's number. Aside from Sis's, Rakel's telephone number was the only one he knew by heart. When he was young and inexperienced, he thought that a bad memory was a handicap for a detective. Now he knew better.

"And the bodyguard is Bush and the U.S.A.?" the host asked.

"Yes. Lyndon B. Johnson once said that the U.S. hadn't chosen this role, but he had realized there was no one else, and he was right. Our bodyguard is a born-again Christian with a father complex, a drinking problem, intellectual limitations and not enough backbone to do his military service with honor. In short, a guy we should be pleased is going to be re-elected president today."

"I assume you mean that ironically?"

"Not at all. Such a weak president listens to his advisers, and the White House has the best, believe you me. Even though from that laughable TV series about the Oval Office one may have formed the impression that the Democrats have a monopoly on intelligence, it is on the extreme right wing of the Republicans, surprisingly enough, that you find the sharpest minds. Norway's security is in the best possible hands."

"A girlfriend of a girlfriend has had sex with you."

"Really?" said Harry.

"Not you," Rakel said. "I'm talking to the other guy. Støp."

"Sorry," Harry said, turning down the radio.

"After a lecture in Trondheim. He invited her up to his room. She was interested, but drew his attention to the fact that she'd had a mastectomy. He said he would give that some thought and went to the bar. And came back and took her with him."

"Mm. I hope expectations were fulfilled."

"Nothing fulfills expectations."

"No," Harry said, wondering what they were talking about.

"What's happening this evening?" Rakel asked.

"Palace Grill at eight is fine. But what's all this garbage about not being able to reserve tables in advance?"

"It gives the whole place cachet, I suppose."

They arranged to meet in the bar area first. After they had hung up, Harry sat thinking. She had sounded pleased. Or bright. Bright and cheery. He tried to sense if he had succeeded in being pleased on her behalf, pleased that the woman he had loved so much was happy with another man. Rakel and he had had their time, and he had been given chances. Which he wasted. So why not be pleased that she was well, why not let the thought that things could have been different go, and move on with his life? He promised to try a bit harder.

The morning meeting was soon over. As head of the Crime Squad, Politioverbetjent—POB for short—Gunnar Hagen ran through the cases they were working on. Which were not many, as for the time being there weren't any fresh murder cases under investigation, and murder was the only thing that got the unit's pulse racing. Thomas Helle, an officer from the Missing Persons Unit of the uniformed police, was present and gave a report on a woman who had been missing from her home for a year. Not a trace of violence, not a trace of the perpetrator and not a trace of her. She was a housewife and had last been seen at the day-care center where she had left her son and daughter in the morning. Her husband and everyone in her closer circle of acquaintances had an alibi and had been cleared. They agreed that the Crime Squad should investigate further.

Magnus Skarre passed on regards from Ståle Aune—the Crime Squad's resident psychologist—whom he had visited at Ullevål University Hospital. Harry felt a pang of conscience. Ståle Aune was not just his adviser on criminal cases; he was his personal supporter in his fight against alcohol and the closest thing he had to a confidant. It had been more than a week since Aune had been admitted with some vague diagnosis, but Harry had still not overcome his reluctance to enter hospitals. Tomorrow, Harry thought. Or Thursday.

"We have a new officer," Gunnar Hagen announced. "Katrine Bratt."

A young woman in the first row stood up unbidden, but without offering a smile. She was very attractive. Attractive without trying, thought Harry. Thin, almost wispy hair hung lifelessly down both sides of her face, which was finely chiseled and pale and wore the same serious, weary features Harry had seen on other stunning women who had become so used to being observed that they had stopped liking or disliking it. Katrine Bratt was dressed in a blue suit that underlined her femininity, but the thick black tights below the hem of her skirt and her practical winter boots invalidated any possible suspicions that she was playing on it. She let her eyes run over the gathering, as if she had risen to see them and not vice versa. Harry guessed that she had planned both the suit and this little first-day appearance at the Police HQ.

"Katrine worked for four years at the Bergen Police HQ, dealing mainly with public-decency offenses, but she also did a stint at the Crime Squad," Hagen continued, looking down at a sheet of paper Harry presumed was her CV. "Law degree from University of Bergen 1999, the police academy and now she's an officer here. For the moment no children, but she's married."

One of Katrine Bratt's thin eyebrows rose imperceptibly, and either Hagen saw this or he thought this last scrap of information was superfluous, because he added, "For those who may be interested . . . "

In the oppressive and telling pause that followed, Hagen seemed to think he had made matters worse; he coughed twice with force and said that those who had not yet signed up for the Christmas party should do so before Wednesday.

Chairs scraped and Harry was already in the corridor when he heard a voice behind him.

"Apparently I belong to you."

Harry turned and looked into Katrine Bratt's face. Wondering how attractive she would be if she made an effort.

"Or you to me," she said, showing a line of even teeth but without letting the smile reach her eyes. "Whichever way you look at it." She spoke Bergen-flavored standard Norwegian with moderately rolled *r*'s, which suggested, Harry wagered, that she was from Fana or Kalfaret or some other solidly middle-class district.

He continued on his way, and she hurried to catch up with him. "Seems the Politioverbetjent forgot to inform you."

She pronounced the word with a slightly exaggerated stress on all the syllables.

"But you should show me around and take care of me for the next few days. Until I'm up and running. Can you do that, do you think?"

Harry eased off a smile. So far he liked her, but of course he was open to changing his opinion. Harry was always willing to give people another chance to wind up on his blacklist.

"I don't know," he said, stopping by the coffee dispenser. "Let's start with this."

"I don't drink coffee."

"Nevertheless. It's self-explanatory. Like most things here. What are your thoughts on the case of the missing woman?"

Harry pressed the button for Americano, which, in this machine, was as American as Norwegian ferry coffee.

"What about it?" Bratt asked.

"Do you think she's alive?" Harry tried to ask in a casual manner so that she wouldn't realize it was a test.

"Do you think I'm stupid?" she said and watched with undisguised revulsion as the machine coughed and spluttered something black into a white plastic cup. "Didn't you hear the Politioverbetjent say that I worked at the Sexual Offenses Unit for four years?"

"Mm," Harry said. "Dead, then?"

"As a dodo," said Katrine Bratt.

Harry lifted the white cup. He pondered the possibility that he had just been allocated a colleague he might come to appreciate.

Walking home in the afternoon, Harry saw that the snow was gone from the streets, and the light, flimsy flakes whirling through the air were eaten up by the wet sidewalk as soon as they hit the ground. He went into his regular music shop on Akersgata and bought Neil Young's latest even though he had a suspicion it was a stinker.

As he unlocked his apartment he noticed that something was different. Something about the sound. Or perhaps it was the smell. He pulled up sharp at the threshold to the kitchen. The whole of one wall was gone. That is, where early this morning there had been bright flowery wallpaper and plasterboard, he now saw rust-red bricks, gray mortar and grayish-yellow studwork dotted with nail holes. On the floor was the mold man's toolbox and on the countertop a note saying he would be back the following day.

He went into the sitting room and slipped in the Neil Young CD, then glumly took it out again after a quarter of an hour and put on Ryan Adams. The thought of a drink came from nowhere. Harry closed his eyes and stared at the dancing pattern of blood and total blindness. He was reminded of the letter again. The first snow. Toowoomba.

The ringing of the telephone interrupted Ryan Adams's "Shakedown on 9th Street."

A woman introduced herself as Oda, said she was calling from *Bosse* and it was nice to talk to him again. Harry couldn't remember her, but he did remember the TV program. They had wanted him to talk about serial killers, because he was the only Norwegian police officer to have studied with the FBI, and furthermore he had hunted down a genuine serial killer. Harry had been stupid enough to agree. He had told himself he was doing it to say something important and moderately qualified about people who kill, not so that he could be seen on the nation's most popular talk show. In retrospect, he was not so sure about that. But that wasn't the worst aspect. The worst was that he'd had a drink before going on the air. Harry was convinced that it had been only one. But on the program it looked as if it had been five. He had spoken with clear diction; he always did. But his eyes had been glazed and his analysis sluggish, and he hadn't managed to draw any conclusions, so the show host had been forced to introduce a guest who was the new European flower-arranging champion. Harry had not said anything, but his body language had clearly shown what he thought about the flower debate. When the host, with a surreptitious smile, had asked how a murder investigator related to flower arranging, Harry had said that wreaths at Norwegian burials certainly maintained high international standards. Perhaps it had been Harry's slightly befuddled, nonchalant style that had drawn laughter from the studio audience and contented pats on the back from the TV people after the program. He had "delivered the goods," they said. And he had joined a small group of them at Kunstnernes Hus, had been indulged and had woken up the next day with a body that screamed, demanded, it had to have more. It was a Friday and he had continued to drink all weekend. He had sat at Schrøder's and shouted for beer as they were flashing the lights to encourage customers to leave, and Rita, the waitress, had gone over to Harry and told him that he would be refused admission in the future unless he went now, preferably to bed. On Monday morning Harry had turned up for work at eight on the dot. He had contributed nothing useful to the department, thrown up in the sink after the morning meeting, clung to his office chair, drunk coffee, smoked and thrown up again, but this time in the toilet. And that was the last time he had succumbed; he hadn't touched a drop of alcohol since.

And now they wanted him back on the air.

The woman explained that the topic was terrorism in Arab countries and what turned well-educated middle-class people into killing machines. Harry interrupted her before she was finished.

"No."

"But we would so much like to have you. You are so . . . so . . . rock 'n' roll!" She laughed, with an enthusiasm whose sincerity he could not be sure of, but he recognized her voice now. She had been with them at Kunstnernes Hus that night. She had been good-looking in a boring, young way, had talked in a boring, young way and had eyed Harry hungrily, as though he were an exotic meal she was considering; was he *too* exotic?

"Try someone else," Harry said and hung up. Then he closed his eyes and heard Ryan Adams wondering, "Oh, baby, why do I miss you like I do?"

The boy looked up at the man standing beside him at the kitchen counter. The light from the snow-covered yard shone on the hairless skin drawn tightly around his father's massive skull. Mommy had said that Dad had such a big head because he was such a brain. He had asked her why she said he *was* a brain and not that he *had* a brain, and when she had laughed, she had stroked his forehead and said that was the way it was with physics professors. Right now the brain was rinsing potatoes under the tap and putting them straight into a pan.

"Aren't you going to peel the potatoes, Dad? Mommy usually—"

"Your mother isn't here, Jonas. So we'll have to do it my way."

He hadn't raised his voice, yet there was an irritation that made Jonas cringe. He never quite knew what made his father so angry. Or, now and then, even *whether* he was angry. Until he saw his mother's face with the anxious droop around the corners of her mouth, which seemed to make Dad even more irritable. He hoped she would be there soon.

"We don't use them plates, Dad!"

His father slammed the cupboard door and Jonas bit his bottom lip. His father's face came down to his. The square, paper-thin glasses sparkled.

"It's 'those' plates, not 'them' plates," his father said. "How many times do I have to tell you, Jonas?"

"But Mommy says—"

"Mommy doesn't speak properly. Do you understand? Mommy comes from a place and a family where they're not bothered about language." His father's breath smelled salty, of rotten seaweed.

The front door banged.

"Hello," she sang out from the hall.

Jonas was about to run to her, but his father held him by the shoulder and pointed to the unlaid table.

"How good you are!"

Jonas could hear the smile in her breathless voice as she stood in the kitchen doorway behind him while he set out glasses and cutlery as quickly as he could.

"And what a big snowman you've made!"

Jonas turned in surprise to his mother, who was unbuttoning her coat. She was so attractive. Dark skin, dark hair, just like him, and those gentle, gentle eyes she almost always had. Almost. She wasn't quite as slim as in the photos from the time she and Dad got married, but he had noticed that men looked at her whenever the two of them took a stroll in town.

"We didn't make a snowman," Jonas said.

"You didn't?" His mommy frowned as she unfurled the big pink scarf he had given her for Christmas.

Dad went over to the window. "Must be the neighbors' boys," he said.

Jonas stood up on one of the kitchen chairs and peered out. And, sure enough, there on the lawn in front of the house was a snowman. It was, as his mother had said, big. Its eyes and mouth were made with pebbles and the nose was a carrot. The snowman had no hat, cap or scarf, and only one arm, a thin twig Jonas guessed had been taken from the hedge. However, there was something odd about the snowman. It was facing the wrong way. He didn't know why, but it ought to have been looking out onto the road, toward the open space.

"Why—" Jonas began, but was interrupted by his father.

"I'll talk to them."

"Why's that?" Mommy said from the hall, where Jonas could hear her unzipping her high black leather boots. "It doesn't matter."

"I don't want that sort roaming around our property. I'll do it when I'm back."

"Why isn't it looking out?" Jonas asked.

In the hall, his mother sighed. "When will you be back, love?"

"Tomorrow sometime."

"What time?"

"Why? Have you got a date?" There was a lightness of tone in his father's voice that made Jonas shiver.

"I was thinking I would have dinner ready," Mommy said, coming into the kitchen, going over to the stove, checking the pans and turning up the temperature on two of the burners.

"Just have it ready," his father said, turning to the pile of newspapers on the countertop. "And I'll be home at some point."

"OK." Mommy went over to Dad's back and put her arms around him. "But do you really have to go to Bergen tonight?"

"My lecture's at eight tomorrow morning," Dad said. "It takes an hour to get to the university from the time the plane lands, so I wouldn't make it if I caught the first flight."

Jonas could see from the muscles in his father's neck that he was relaxing, that once again Mommy had managed to find the right words.

"Why is the snowman looking at our house?" Jonas asked.

"Go and wash your hands," Mommy said.

They ate in silence, broken only by Mommy's tiny questions about how school had been and Jonas's brief, vague answers. Jonas knew that detailed answers could evoke unpleasant questions from Dad about what they were learning—or not learning—at the "excuse of a school." Or quick-fire interrogation about someone Jonas mentioned he had been playing with, about what his parents did and where they were from. Questions that Jonas could never answer to his father's satisfaction.

When Jonas was in bed, on the floor below he heard his father say good-bye to his mother, a door close and the car start up outside and fade into the distance. They were alone again. His mother switched on the TV. He thought about something she had asked. Why Jonas hardly ever brought his friends home to play anymore. He hadn't known what to answer; he hadn't wanted her to be sad. But now he became sad instead. He chewed the inside of his cheek, feeling the bittersweet pain extend into his ears, and stared at the metal tubes of the wind chime hanging from the ceiling. He got out of bed and shuffled over to the window.

The snow in the yard reflected enough light for him to make out the snowman down below. It looked alone. Someone should have given it a cap and scarf. And maybe a broomstick to hold. At that moment the moon slid from behind a cloud. The black row of teeth came into view. And the eyes. Jonas automatically sucked in his breath and recoiled two steps. The pebble-eyes were gleaming. And they were not staring into the house. They were looking up. Up here. Jonas drew the curtains and crept back into bed.

3

Cochineal

Harry was sitting on a bar stool in the Palace Grill reading the signs on the walls, the good-natured reminders to clientele not to ask for credit, not to shoot the pianist and to be good or be gone. It was still early evening and the only other customers in the bar were two girls sitting at a table frenetically pressing the buttons of their mobile phones and two boys playing darts with practiced refinement of stance and aim, but poor results. Dolly Parton, who Harry knew had been brought back in from the cold by arbiters of good country-and-western taste, was whining over the loudspeakers with her nasal Southern accent. Harry checked his watch again and had a wager with himself that Rakel Fauke would be standing at the door at exactly seven minutes past eight. He felt the crackle of tension he always did at seeing her again. He told himself it was just a conditioned response, like Pavlov's dogs starting to salivate when they heard the bell for food, even when there wasn't any. And they wouldn't be having food this evening. That is, they would be having food, but *only* food. And a cozy chat about the lives they were leading now. Or, to be more precise: the life she was leading now. And about Oleg, the son she had had with her Russian ex-husband, from when she

had been working at the Norwegian embassy in Moscow.
The boy with the closed, wary nature whom Harry had
reached, the boy with whom he had gradually developed
bonds that in many ways were stronger than those Oleg
had with his own father. And when Rakel had, in the end,
been unable to tolerate any more and had left, he didn't
know whose loss had been greater. But now he knew. For
now it was seven minutes past eight and she was standing
by the door with that erect posture of hers, the arch of her
back he could feel on his fingertips and the high cheek-
bones under the glowing skin he could feel against his. He
had hoped she wouldn't look so good. So *happy*.

She walked over to him and their cheeks touched. He
made sure he let go first.

"What are you looking at?" she asked, unbuttoning
her coat.

"You know," Harry said, and heard that he should have
cleared his throat first.

She chuckled, and the laughter had the same effect on
him as the first swig of Jim Beam; he felt warm and relaxed.

"Don't," she said.

He knew exactly what her "Don't" meant. Don't start,
don't be embarrassing, we're not going there. She had
said it softly, it was practically inaudible, yet it felt like a
stinging slap.

"You're thin," she said.

"So they say."

"The table . . . "

"The waiter will come and get us."

She sat down on the stool opposite him and ordered
an aperitif. Campari, it went without saying. Harry used
to call her "Cochineal" after the natural pigment that
gave the spicy, sweet wine its characteristic color. Because
she liked to dress in bright red. Rakel had herself claimed

that she used it as a warning, the way animals use strong colors to tell others to keep their distance.

Harry ordered another Coke.

"Why are you so thin?" she asked.

"Fungus."

"What?"

"Apparently it's eating me up. Brain, eyes, lungs, concentration. Sucking out colors and memory. The fungus is growing, I'm disappearing. It's becoming me, I'm becoming it."

"What are you babbling on about?" she exclaimed with a grimace meant to denote disgust, but Harry caught the smile in her eyes. She liked to hear him talking, even when it was just gobbledygook. He told her about the mold in his apartment.

"How are you doing?" Harry asked.

"Fine. I'm good. Oleg's fine. But he misses you."

"Has he said that?"

"You know he has. You should keep tabs on him better."

"Me?" Harry looked at her, dumbfounded. "It wasn't my decision."

"So?" she said, taking the drink from the bartender. "Just because you and I are not together doesn't mean that you and Oleg don't have an important relationship. For you both. Neither of you finds it easy to commit to people, so you should nurture the relationships you do have."

Harry sipped his Coke. "How's Oleg getting on with your doctor?"

"His name's Mathias," Rakel said with a sigh. "They're working on it. They're . . . different. Mathias tries hard, but Oleg doesn't exactly make it easy for him."

Harry experienced a sweet tingle of satisfaction.

"Mathias works long hours as well."

"I thought you didn't like your men working," Harry replied, and regretted it the moment he had said it. But instead of getting angry, Rakel sighed sadly.

"It wasn't the long hours, Harry. You were obsessed. You *are* your job, and what drives you isn't love or a sense of responsibility. It's not even personal ambition. It's anger. And the desire for revenge. And that's not right, Harry—it shouldn't be like that. You know what happened."

Yes, thought Harry. I allowed the disease to enter your house as well.

He cleared his throat. "But your doctor is driven by . . . the right things, then?"

"Mathias used to do the night shift at the emergency room. Voluntarily. At the same time as lecturing full-time at the Anatomy Department."

"And he's a blood donor and a member of Amnesty International."

"B negative is a rare blood group, Harry. And you also support Amnesty—I know that for a fact."

She stirred her drink with an orange plastic stick that had a horse on top. The red mixture swirled around the ice cubes. Cochineal.

"Harry?" she said.

Something in her inflection made him tense up.

"Mathias is going to move in with me. Over Christmas."

"So soon?" Harry ran his tongue over his palate in an attempt to find moisture. "You haven't known each other for long."

"Long enough. We're planning to get married in the summer."

Magnus Skarre studied the hot water running over his hands and into the sink. Where it disappeared. No.

Nothing disappeared—it was just somewhere else. Like these people about whom he had spent the past few weeks collecting information. Because Harry had asked him. Because Harry had said there might be something in it. And he had wanted Magnus's report before the weekend. Which meant that Magnus had been obliged to work overtime. Even though he knew that Harry gave them jobs like this to keep them busy in these feet-on-desk times. The uniformed division's tiny Missing Persons Unit of three refused to delve into old cases; they had more than enough to do with the new ones.

In the deserted corridor on his way back to his office Magnus noticed that the door was ajar. He knew he had closed it, and it was past nine, so the cleaners had finished long before. Two years ago they had had problems with thieving from the offices. Magnus Skarre pulled the door open with a vengeance.

Katrine Bratt was standing in the middle of the room and glanced at him with a furrowed brow, as if it were he who had burst into her office. She turned her back on him.

"I just wanted to see," she said, casting her eyes over the walls.

"See what?" Skarre looked around. His office was like all the others except that it didn't have a window.

"This was his office, wasn't it?"

Skarre frowned. "What do you mean?"

"Hole's. This was his office for all those years. Even while he was investigating the serial killings in Australia?"

Skarre shrugged. "I think so. Why?"

Katrine Bratt ran a hand over the desktop. "Why did he change offices?"

Magnus walked around her and plopped down on the swivel chair. "It hasn't got any windows."

"And he shared the office, first with Ellen Gjelten and then Jack Halvorsen," Katrine Bratt said. "And both were killed."

Magnus Skarre put his hands behind his head. This new officer had class. A league or two above him. He bet her husband was the boss of something or other and had money. Her suit seemed expensive. But when he looked at her a bit closer, there was a little flaw somewhere. A slight blemish he couldn't quite put his finger on.

"Do you think he heard their voices? Was that why he moved?" Bratt asked, scrutinizing a wall map of Norway on which Skarre had circled the hometowns of all the missing persons in Østland, eastern Norway, since 1980.

Skarre laughed but didn't answer. Her waist was slim and her back willowy. He knew she knew he was ogling her.

"What's he like, actually?" she asked.

"Why do you ask?"

"I suppose everyone with a new boss does, don't they?"

She was right. It was just that he had never thought of Harry Hole as a boss, not in that way. OK, he gave them jobs to do and led investigations, but beyond that all he asked was that they keep out of his way.

"He is, as you probably know, somewhat infamous," Skarre said.

She shrugged. "I've heard about his alcoholism, yes. And that he has reported colleagues. And that all the heads wanted him booted out, but the previous POB protected him."

"His name was Bjarne Møller," Skarre said, looking at the map, at the ring around Bergen. That was where Møller had been seen last, before he disappeared.

"And that people at HQ don't like the media turning him into a kind of pop idol."

Skarre chewed his lower lip. "He's a damn good detective. That's enough for me."

"You like him?" Bratt asked.

Skarre grinned. He turned and looked straight into her eyes.

"Like, dislike," he said. "I don't think I could say one or the other."

He pushed back his chair, put his feet on the desk, stretched and gave a semi-yawn. "What are you working on so late at night?"

It was an attempt to gain the upper hand. After all, she was only a low-ranking detective. And new.

But Katrine Bratt just smiled as if he had said something funny, walked out the door and was gone.

Disappeared. Speaking of which. Skarre cursed, sat up in the chair and went back to his computer.

Harry woke up and lay on his back, staring at the ceiling. How long had he been asleep? He turned and looked at the clock on his bedside table. A quarter to four. The dinner had been an ordeal. He watched Rakel's mouth speaking, drinking wine, chewing meat and devouring him as she told him about how she and Mathias were going to Botswana for a couple of years; the government had a good setup there to fight HIV but was short of doctors. She asked whether he was seeing anyone. And he answered that he had seen his childhood pals Øystein and Tresko. The former was an alcoholic, taxi-driving computer freak; the latter an alcoholic gambler who would have been the world poker champion if he had been as good at maintaining his own poker face as he was at reading others'. He even began to tell her about Tresko's fatal defeat in the world championships in Las Vegas before he realized he had told her before. And it wasn't true that he had seen them. He hadn't seen anyone.

He noticed the waiter pouring booze into the glasses on the adjacent table and for one crazy moment he thought about tearing the bottle out of his hands and putting it to his mouth. Instead he agreed to take Oleg to a concert the boy had begged Rakel to let him see. Slipknot. Harry had omitted telling her what kind of band she was letting loose on her son, since he fancied seeing Slipknot himself. Even though bands with the obligatory death rattle, satanic symbols and speeded-up bass drum usually made him laugh, Slipknot was in fact interesting.

Harry threw off the duvet now and went into the kitchen, let the water from the tap run cold, cupped his hands and drank. He had always thought water tasted better like that, drunk from his own hands, off his own skin. Then he suddenly let the water run into the sink again and stared at the black wall. Had he seen anything? Something moving? No, not a thing, just movement itself, like the invisible waves underwater that caress the sea grass. Over dead fibers, fingers so thin that they can't be seen, spores that rise at the smallest movement of air and settle in new areas and begin to eat and suck. Harry switched on the radio in the sitting room. It had been decided. George W. Bush had been given another term in the White House.

Harry went back to bed and pulled the duvet over his head.

Jonas was awoken by a sound and lifted the duvet off his face. At least he thought it had been a sound. A crunching sound, like sticky snow underfoot in the silence between the houses on a Sunday morning. He must have been dreaming. But sleep would not return even when he closed his eyes. Instead fragments of the dream came

back to him. Dad had been standing motionless and silent in front of him with a reflection in his glasses that
lent them an impenetrable, icelike surface.

It must have been a nightmare, because Jonas was
scared. He opened his eyes again and saw that the chimes
hanging from the ceiling were moving. Then he jumped
out of bed, opened the door and ran across the corridor.
By the stairs to the ground floor he managed to stop himself, looking down into the darkness, then didn't pause
again until he was in front of his parents' bedroom and
pressing down the handle with infinite caution. Then he
remembered that his dad was away, and he would wake
his mom whatever he did. He slipped inside. A white
square of moonlight extended across the floor to the undisturbed double bed. The numbers on the digital alarm
clock were lit up: 1:11. For a moment Jonas stood there,
bewildered.

Then he went out into the corridor. He walked toward
the staircase. The darkness of the stairs lay there waiting
for him, like a vast open void. Not a sound could be heard
from down below.

"Mommy!"

He regretted shouting the moment he heard his own
terror in the brief, harsh echo. For now *it* knew, too. The
darkness.

There was no answer.

Jonas swallowed. Then he began to tiptoe down the
stairs.

On the third step down he felt something wet under
his feet. The same on the sixth. And the eighth. As if
someone had been walking with wet shoes. Or wet feet.

In the living room the light was on, but there was no
Mommy. He went to the window to look at the Bendik-
sens' house. Mommy occasionally went over to see Ebba.
But all the windows were dark.

He walked into the kitchen and over to the telephone, successfully keeping his thoughts at bay, not letting the darkness in. He dialed his mother's mobile phone number. And was jubilant to hear her soft voice. But it was a message asking him to leave his name and wishing him a nice day.

And it wasn't day, it was night.

On the porch he stuffed his feet into a pair of his father's large shoes, put on a padded jacket over his pajamas and went outside. Mom had said the snow would be gone by tomorrow, but it was still cold, and a light wind whispered and mumbled in the oak tree by the gate. It was no more than a hundred yards to the Bendiksens' house, and fortunately there were two streetlamps on the way. She had to be there. He glanced to the left and to the right to make sure there was no one who could stop him. Then he caught sight of the snowman. It stood there as before, immovable, facing the house, bathed in the cold moonlight. Yet there was something different about it, something almost human, something familiar. Jonas looked at the Bendiksens' house. He decided to run. But he didn't. Instead he stood feeling the tentative, ice-cold wind go right through him. He turned slowly back to the snowman. Now he realized what it was that had made the snowman so familiar. It was wearing a scarf. A pink scarf. The scarf Jonas had given his mother for Christmas.

4

The Disappearance

By the middle of the day the snow had melted in Oslo city center. But in Hoff there were still patches on lawns on both sides of the road as Harry Hole and Katrine Bratt drove along. On the radio Michael Stipe was singing about a sinking feeling, about what was bringing it on, knowing that something had gone wrong and about the boy in the well. In the middle of a quiet estate on an even quieter street Harry pointed to a shiny silver Toyota Corolla parked by the fence.

"Skarre's car. Park behind him."

The house was large and yellow. Too big for a family of three, Harry thought as they walked up the gravel path. Everything around them dripped and sighed. On the lawn stood a snowman with a slight list and poor future prospects.

Skarre opened the door. Harry bent down to study the lock.

"No signs of a break-in anywhere," Skarre said.

He led them into the living room, where a boy was sitting on the floor with his back to them watching a cartoon channel on TV. A woman got up off the sofa, shook hands with Harry and introduced herself as Ebba Bendiksen, a neighbor.

"Birte has never done this type of thing before," she said. "Not as long as I've known her, anyway."

"And how long's that?" Harry asked, looking around. In front of the TV were large pieces of heavy leather furniture and an octagonal coffee table of darkened glass. The tubular steel chairs around the dining table were light and elegant, the type Rakel liked. Two paintings hung on the walls, both portraits of bank-manager-like men staring down at him with solemn authority. Beside them, modernist abstract art of the kind that had succeeded in becoming unmodern and so very modern again.

"Ten years," said Ebba Bendiksen. "We moved into our house across the road the day Jonas was born." She nodded toward the boy, who was still motionless, staring at careering birds and exploding coyotes.

"I understand it was you who called the police last night?"

"Yes, that's right."

"The boy rang the bell at about a quarter past one," Skarre said, looking down at his notes. "Police were phoned at one-thirty."

"My husband and I went back with Jonas and searched the house first," Ebba Bendiksen explained.

"Where did you look?" Harry asked.

"In the cellar. In the bathrooms. In the garage. Everywhere. It's very odd that anyone would do a runner like that."

"Do a runner?"

"Disappear. Vanish. The policeman I spoke to on the phone asked if we could take care of Jonas, and said we should call everyone Birte knew and who she might be staying with. And then wait until early today to find out if Birte had gone to work. In eight out of ten cases, he explained, the missing person reappeared after a few hours. We tried to get hold of Filip—"

"The husband," Skarre interjected. "He was in Bergen lecturing. He's a professor of something or other."

"Physics." Ebba Bendiksen smiled. "However, his mobile phone was switched off. And we didn't know the name of the hotel where he was staying."

"He was contacted in Bergen this morning," Skarre said. "He should be here soon."

"Yes, thank God," Ebba said. "So when we called Birte's workplace this morning and she hadn't turned up at the customary time, we called you back."

Skarre nodded in confirmation. Harry signaled that Skarre could continue his conversation with Ebba Bendiksen, went over to the TV and sat down on the floor beside the boy. On the screen, a coyote was lighting the fuse on a stick of dynamite.

"Hello, Jonas. My name's Harry. Did the other policeman tell you that things like this almost always turn out fine? People disappear and then they turn up of their own accord?"

The boy shook his head.

"But they do," Harry said. "If you had to guess, where do you think your mother would be now?"

The boy shrugged. "I don't know where she is."

"I know you don't know, Jonas. None of us does right now. But what's the first place that would occur to you if she wasn't here or at work? Don't think about whether it's likely or not."

The boy didn't answer, just stared at the coyote desperately trying to throw away the stick of dynamite that had got stuck to his hand.

"Is there a cabin or something like that where you go?"

Jonas shook his head.

"A special place where she likes to go if she wants to be on her own?"

"She doesn't want to be on her own," Jonas said. "She wants to be with me."

"Just with you?"

The boy turned and looked at Harry. Jonas had brown eyes, like Oleg. And in the brown Harry saw the horror he had been expecting and the anger he had not.

"Why did they go?" the boy asked. "The ones who come back?"

Same eyes, Harry thought. Same questions. The important ones.

"For all sorts of reasons," Harry said. "Some got lost. There are various ways of getting lost. And some only needed a break and went off to get some peace."

The front door slammed and Harry saw the boy start.

At that moment the dynamite exploded in the coyote's hand, and behind them the living-room door opened.

"Hello," a voice said. Sharp and controlled at the same time. "What's the latest?"

Harry turned in time to see a man of around fifty wearing a suit stride toward the coffee table and pick up the remote control. The next moment the TV picture imploded to a white dot as the set hissed in protest.

"You know what I've said about watching TV during the day, Jonas," he said with a resigned tone, as if to tell the others in the room what a hopeless job raising children was nowadays.

Harry stood up and introduced himself, Magnus Skarre and Katrine Bratt, who until now had merely stood by the door observing.

"Filip Becker," the man said, pushing his glasses although they were already high up his nose. Harry tried to catch his eye, to form the crucial first impression of a potential suspect, should it ever come to that. But his eyes were hidden behind the reflection from his glasses.

"I've spent my time calling everyone who might conceivably have been in contact, but no one knows anything," Filip Becker said. "What do you know?"

"Nothing," said Harry. "But the first thing you can do to help us is to find out if any suitcases or clothes are missing, so that we can formulate a theory." Harry studied Becker before continuing. "As to whether this disappearance is spontaneous or planned."

Becker returned Harry's searching gaze before nodding and going upstairs.

Harry crouched down beside Jonas, who was still staring at the black TV screen.

"So you like roadrunners, do you?" Harry asked.

The boy shook his head mutely.

"Why not?"

Jonas's whisper was barely audible: "I feel sorry for Wile E. Coyote."

Five minutes later Becker came back down and said that nothing was missing, neither travel bags nor clothing, apart from what she was wearing when he left, plus her coat, boots and a scarf.

"Mm." Harry scratched his unshaven chin and glanced across at Ebba Bendiksen. "Can you and I go into the kitchen, Herr Becker?"

Becker led the way, and Harry signaled to Katrine to join them. In the kitchen the professor immediately began to spoon coffee into a filter and pour water into the machine. Katrine stood by the door while Harry went over to the window and looked out. The snowman's head had sunk between its shoulders.

"When did you leave last night and which flight did you take to Bergen?" Harry asked.

"I left at around nine-thirty," Becker said without hesitation. "The plane took off at eleven-oh-five."

"Did you have any contact with Birte after leaving home?"

"No."

"What do you think could have happened?"

"I have no idea, Inspector. I really don't."

"Mm." Harry glanced out into the street. Since they had been there, he hadn't heard a single car pass. A really quiet neighborhood. The peace and quiet alone probably cost half a million in this area of town. "What sort of marriage do you and your wife have?"

Harry heard Filip Becker stop what he was doing, and he added, "I have to ask because spouses do sometimes simply get up and leave."

Filip Becker cleared his throat. "I can assure you that my wife and I have a perfectly good marriage."

"Have you considered that she may be having an affair, unbeknownst to you?"

"That's out of the question."

" 'Out of the question' is pretty strong, Herr Becker. And extramarital relationships are pretty common."

Filip Becker gave a weak smile. "I'm not naïve, Inspector. Birte's an attractive woman and a good deal younger than I. And she comes from a relatively liberal family, it has to be said. But she's not the type. And I have a relatively good perspective on her activities, if I may put it like that."

The coffee machine rumbled ominously as Harry opened his mouth to pursue the point. He changed his mind.

"Have you noticed any mood changes in your wife?"

"Birte is not depressed, Inspector. She has not gone into the forest and hanged herself or thrown herself into the lake. She's out there somewhere, and she's alive. I've read that people disappear all the time, and then they turn up again with a natural and fairly banal explanation. Isn't that so?"

Harry nodded slowly. "Would you mind if I had a look around the house?"

"Why's that?"

There was a brusqueness to Filip Becker's question that made Harry think he was a man who was used to being in control. To being kept informed. And that argued against his wife having left without a word. Which, for that matter, Harry had already excluded in his mind. Well-adjusted, healthy mothers do not abandon ten-year-old sons in the middle of the night. And then there was all the rest. Usually they used minimal resources at such an early stage of a missing-persons case, unless there were indications that suggested something criminal or dramatic. It was "all the rest" that had made him drive up to Hoff himself.

"Sometimes you don't know what you're looking for until you find it," Harry answered. "It's a methodology."

He caught Becker's eyes behind the glasses now. They were, unlike his son's, light blue and shone with an intense, clear gleam.

"By all means," Becker said. "Go ahead."

The bedroom was chilly, aroma-free and tidy. On the double bed was a crocheted quilt. On one bedside table a photograph of an elderly woman. The similarity led Harry to assume this side of the bed was Filip Becker's. On the other bedside table was a photograph of Jonas. There was a faint scent of perfume in the wardrobe containing ladies' clothing. Harry checked that the corners of the clothes hangers hung with equal distance from one another, as they would if they had been allowed to hang undisturbed for a while. Black dresses with slits, short sweaters with pink motifs and glitter. At the bottom of the wardrobe there was a drawer section. He pulled out the top drawer. Underwear. Black and red. Next drawer. Garter belts and stockings. Third drawer. Jewelry placed in holes in bright red felt. He noticed a large gaudy ring with precious stones that glittered and sparkled. Everything here was a bit Vegas. There were no empty gaps in the felt.

The bedroom had a door leading into a newly decorated bathroom with a steam shower and two steel washstands.

In Jonas's room, Harry sat down on a small chair by a small desk. On the desk there was a calculator with a series of advanced mathematical functions. It looked new and unused. Above the desk there was a poster with a picture of seven dolphins inside a wave and a calendar for the whole year. Several of the dates were circled and had tiny reminders added. Harry noted birthdays for Mommy and Grandpa, vacation in Denmark, dentist at ten o'clock and two July dates with doctor above. But Harry didn't see any football matches, trips to the movies or birthday parties. He caught sight of a pink scarf lying on the bed. A color no boy of Jonas's age would be seen dead wearing. Harry lifted the scarf. It was damp, but he could still smell the distinctive fragrance of skin, hair and feminine perfume. The same perfume as in the wardrobe.

He went back downstairs. Stopped outside the kitchen and listened to Skarre holding forth on procedures regarding missing-persons cases. There was a clink of coffee cups inside. The sofa in the living room seemed enormous, perhaps because of the slight figure sitting there reading a book. Harry went closer and saw a photo of Charlie Chaplin in full regalia. Harry sat down beside Jonas.

"Did you know that Chaplin was a sir?" Harry asked. "Sir Charlie Chaplin."

Jonas nodded. "But they chucked him out of the U.S.A."

Jonas flicked through the book.

"Were you ill this summer, Jonas?"

"No."

"But you went to the doctor's. Twice."

"Mom wanted to have me examined. Mom . . . " His voice suddenly failed him.

"She'll be back soon, you'll see," Harry said, putting a hand on his narrow shoulders. "She didn't take her scarf with her, did she? The pink one on your bed."

"Someone hung it around the snowman's neck," Jonas said. "I brought it in."

"Your mother didn't want the snowman to freeze, then."

"She would never have given her favorite scarf to the snowman."

"Then it must have been your dad."

"No, someone did it after he left. Last night. The person who took Mom."

Harry nodded slowly. "Who made the snowman, Jonas?"

"I don't know."

Harry looked through the window to the yard. This was the reason he had come. An ice-cold draft seemed to run through the wall and the room.

Harry and Katrine drove down Sørkedalsveien toward Majorstuen.

"What was the first thing that struck you when we went in?" Harry asked.

"That the couple living there were not exactly soul mates," Katrine said, steering through the tollbooth without braking. "It may have been an unhappy marriage, and if so, she was the one who suffered more."

"Mm. What made you think that?"

"It's obvious." Katrine smiled, glancing in the mirror. "Clash of taste."

"Explain."

"Didn't you see the dreadful sofa and the coffee table? Typical eighties style bought by men in the nineties. While she chose a dining table in white oiled oak with aluminum legs. And Vitra."

"Vitra?"

"Dining-room chairs. Swiss. Expensive. So expensive that with what she could have saved by buying slightly more reasonably priced copies, she could have changed all the damn furniture."

Harry noticed that "damn" didn't sound like a regular swear word in Katrine Bratt's mouth; it was a linguistic counterpoint that merely underlined her class affiliation.

"Meaning?"

"That big house, at that Oslo address, means it's not money that's the problem. She isn't *allowed* to change his sofa and table. And when a man with no taste, or no apparent interest in interior design, does that kind of thing, it tells me something about who dominates whom."

Harry nodded, mostly as a marker for himself. Her first impression had not been mistaken. Katrine Bratt was good.

"Tell me what *you* think," she said. "It's me who should be learning here."

Harry looked out the window at the old, traditional, though never particularly venerable café Lepsvik.

"I don't think Birte Becker left the house of her own free will," he said.

"Why not? There were no signs of violence."

"Because it was well planned."

"And who's the guilty party? The husband? It's always the husband, isn't it?"

"Yes," said Harry, aware his mind was wandering. "It's always the husband."

"Except that this one had gone to Bergen."

"Looks like it, yes."

"On the last plane, so he couldn't have come back and still managed to catch the first lecture." Katrine accelerated and raced across the Majorstuen intersection on yellow. "Had Filip Becker been guilty he would have taken the bait you set for him anyway."

"Bait?"

"Yes. The bit about her mood swings. You suggested to Becker that you suspected suicide."

"And so?"

She laughed. "Come on, Harry. Everyone, including Becker, knows that the police don't commit resources to a case resembling suicide. In a nutshell, you gave him the chance to espouse a theory that, if he'd been guilty, would have solved most of his problems. However, he replied that she was as happy as a lark."

"Mm. So you think the question was a test?"

"You test people all the time, Harry. Including me."

Harry didn't answer until they were well down Bogstadveien.

"People are often smarter than you think," he said, and then said nothing until they were in the Police HQ parking lot.

"I have to work on my own for the rest of the day."

And he said that because he had been thinking about the pink scarf and had come to a conclusion. That he urgently needed to go through Skarre's missing-persons report and he urgently needed to have his nagging suspicion confirmed. And if it was what he feared, he would have to go to POB Gunnar Hagen with the letter. That damn letter.

5

NOVEMBER 4, 1992

The Totem Pole

When William Jefferson Blythe III came into the world on August 19, 1946, in the little town of Hope, Arkansas, exactly three months had passed since the death of his father in a traffic accident. Four years later William's mother remarried and William took his new father's surname. And on a November night in 1992, forty-six years after his birth, white confetti fell like snow onto the streets of Hope in celebration of their own hope and hometown boy, William—or just Bill—Clinton, after he had been elected America's forty-second president. The snow falling on Bergen that same night did not reach the streets but melted in the air, as usual, and turned to rain over the town. This had been happening since mid-September. But as the following morning unfolded there was a nice sprinkling of sugar on top of the seven peaks guarding this beautiful town. And Inspector Gert Rafto had already arrived on the highest of them, Ulriken. He was breathing in the mountain air with a shiver, hunching up his shoulders around his broad head, his face so covered with folds of skin that it seemed to have been punctured.

The yellow cable car that had brought him and three

Crime Scene officers from Bergen Police HQ up the 2,110 feet above the town was swaying gently from the solid steel wires, waiting. The service had been discontinued as soon as the first tourists who had dismounted onto the popular mountaintop that morning had sounded the alarm.

"Out and about," one of the crime scene officers let slip.

The town's tourism slogan had become such a parody of Bergen Norwegian that Bergensians had almost stopped using it. But in situations where fear prevails, your innermost lexicon takes over.

"Yes, out and about," Rafto repeated sarcastically, his eyes shining from behind the pancake batter of skin folds.

The body lying in the snow had been cut into so many pieces that it was only thanks to a naked breast that they had been able to determine the gender. The rest reminded Rafto of a traffic accident in Eidsvågneset the year before, when a truck coming around a bend too fast had lost its load of aluminum sheeting and had literally sliced up an oncoming car.

"The killer murdered her and carved her up right here," one of the officers said.

The information seemed somewhat superfluous to Rafto since the snow around the body was spattered with blood and the thick streaks to the side suggested that at least one artery had been cut while the heart was still beating. He made a mental note to find out when it had stopped snowing last night. The last cable car had left at five in the afternoon. Of course, the victim and the killer may have taken the path that wound up beneath the cable cars. Or they could have taken the Fløyen funicular up to Fjelltoppen beside it and walked from there. But they were demanding walks and his gut instinct told him: cable car.

There were two sets of footprints in the snow. The small prints were undoubtedly the woman's, even though there was no sign of her shoes. And the others had to be the killer's. They led to the path.

"Big boots," said the young technician, a hollow-cheeked coastal man from Sotra. "At least size thirteen. Guy must have been pretty beefy."

"Not necessarily," Rafto said, sniffing the air. "The print is uneven and yet the ground here is flat. That suggests the man's foot is smaller than his boot. Perhaps he was trying to fool us."

Rafto felt everyone's eyes on him. He knew what they were thinking. There he went again, trying to dazzle, the star of bygone times, the man the media had adored: big mug, hard face and driving energy to match. In short, a man made for headlines. But at some point he had become too grand for them, for all of them, the press and his colleagues. Indirect jibes had begun to circulate that Gert Rafto was thinking only about himself and his place in the limelight, that in his egotism he was treading on a few too many toes and over a few too many dead bodies. But he hadn't taken any notice. They didn't have anything on him. Not much, anyway. The odd trinket had disappeared from the crime scenes. A piece of jewelry or a watch belonging to the deceased, things you assumed no one would miss. But one day one of Rafto's colleagues had been searching for a pen and had opened a drawer in his desk. At least that was what he said. And found three rings. Rafto had been summoned to the POB and had explained himself, and had been told to keep his mouth shut and his fingers to himself. That was all. But the rumors had started. Even the media had picked up on it. So perhaps it was not so surprising that when charges of police brutality were leveled against the station, there was one man against whom concrete evidence was soon found. The man who was made for headlines.

Gert Rafto was guilty of the accusations; no one was in any doubt about that. But everyone knew that the inspector had been made a scapegoat for a culture that had permeated the Bergen police for many years. Just because he had signed a number of reports on prisoners—most of them child molesters and dope dealers—who had fallen down the ancient iron stairs to the remand cells and bruised themselves here and there.

The newspapers had been remorseless. The nickname they had given him, "Iron" instead of "Gert," was not exactly original, but nonetheless appropriate. A journalist had interviewed several of his long-standing enemies on both sides of the law and of course they had taken the opportunity to settle old scores. So when Rafto's daughter came home crying from school, saying she was being teased, his wife had said enough was enough, he couldn't expect her to sit and watch while he dragged the whole family through the mud. As so often before, he had lost his temper. Afterward she had taken their daughter with her, and this time she didn't return.

It had been a tough period, but he had never forgotten who he was. He was Iron Rafto. And when the quarantine period was over, he had gone for broke, worked day and night to regain lost ground. But no one was in a forgiving mood, the wounds were too deep, and he noticed the internal resistance to letting him succeed. Of course they didn't want him to shine again and remind them and the media of what they were so desperately trying to put behind them: photographs of battered bodies in handcuffs. But he would show them. Show them that Gert Rafto was not a man to let himself be buried before his time. That the town below belonged to him, not to the social workers, to the cream puffs, to the smooth talkers sitting in their offices with tongues so long they could lick the assholes of both the local politicians and the pinko journalists.

"Take a few snaps and get me an ID," Rafto said to the technician with the camera.

"And who'll be able to identify this?" The young man pointed.

Rafto didn't care for his tone. "Someone has reported or will soon report this woman missing. Just get on with it, junior."

Rafto went up to the peak and looked back across what Bergensians call *vidden*—the plateau. His gaze swept the countryside and stopped at a hill and what seemed to be a person on the summit. But, if so, he wasn't moving. Perhaps it was a cairn? Rafto squinted. He must have been there hundreds of times, walking with his wife and daughter, but he couldn't recall seeing a cairn. He went down to the cable car, spoke to the operator and borrowed his binoculars. Fifteen seconds later he established that it wasn't a cairn, just three large balls of snow that someone must have piled one on top of the other.

Rafto didn't like the sloping district of Bergen known as Fjellsiden, with its oh-so-picturesque, crooked, uninsulated timber houses with stairs and cellars, situated in narrow alleys where the sun never shone. Trendy children of rich parents frequently paid millions to own an authentic Bergen house, then did them up until there wasn't an original splinter left. Here, you no longer heard the sound of children's running feet on the cobblestones; the prices had driven young Bergensian families into the suburbs on the other side of the mountains a long time ago. Now it was as quiet and deserted as a barren row of shops. Nonetheless he had the feeling he was being observed as he stood on the stone steps ringing the bell.

After a while the door opened and a pale, anxious woman's face looked out at him with a startled expression.

"Onny Hetland?" Rafto queried, holding up his ID. "It's about your friend Laila Aasen."

The apartment was tiny and the layout baffling: the bathroom was located behind the kitchen and between the bedroom and living room. Amid the patterned burgundy wallpaper in the living room Onny Hetland had just managed to squeeze a sofa and a green and orange armchair, and on the little floor space that remained there was a pile of weekly magazines and heaps of books and CDs. Rafto stepped over an upturned dish of water and a cat to reach the sofa. Onny Hetland sat on the armchair, fidgeting with her necklace. There was a black crack in the green stone in the pendant. Maybe a flaw. Or perhaps it was meant to be like that.

Onny Hetland had learned about her friend's death early that morning, from Laila's husband, Bastian. But still her face displayed several dramatic changes as Rafto mercilessly spelled out the details.

"Dreadful," whispered Onny Hetland. "Bastian didn't say anything about that."

"That's because we didn't want to publicize it," Rafto said. "Bastian told me you were Laila's best friend."

Onny nodded.

"Do you know what Laila was doing up on Ulriken? Her husband had no idea, you see. He and the children were with his mother in Florø yesterday."

Onny shook her head. It was a firm shake. One that should not have left any doubt. It wasn't the shake that was the problem. It was the hundredth of a second's hesitation before it started. And this hundredth of a second was all Gert Rafto needed.

"This is a murder case, Frøken Hetland. I hope you appreciate the gravity of it and the risk you run by not telling me everything you know."

She shot the policeman with the bulldog face a perplexed look. He smelled prey.

"If you think you're being considerate to her family, you have misunderstood. These things will come out anyway."

She swallowed. She looked frightened, had already looked frightened when she opened the door. So he gave her the final nudge, this actually quite trifling threat that still worked so amazingly well on the innocent as well as the guilty.

"You can tell me now or come to the station for questioning."

Tears welled up in her eyes, and the barely audible voice came from somewhere at the back of her throat. "She was meeting someone there."

"Who?"

Onny Hetland inhaled with a tremble. "Laila told me only the first name and profession. And that it was a secret; no one was to know. Especially not Bastian."

Rafto looked down into his notebook to hide his excitement. "And the first name and profession were?"

He noted down what Onny said. Peered at his pad. It was a relatively common name. And a relatively common profession. But since Bergen was a relatively small town, he thought this would be enough. He knew with the whole of his being that he was on the right track. And by "the whole of his being" Gert Rafto meant thirty years of police work and a knowledge of humanity based on general misanthropy.

"Promise me one thing," Rafto said. "Don't tell what you have just told me to a soul. Not to anyone in the family. Not to the press. Not even to any other police officers you might talk to. Do you understand?"

"Not to . . . police officers?"

"Definitely not. I'm leading the investigation, and I must have full control over this information. Until I tell you anything different, you know nothing."

At last, thought Rafto, standing outside on the step again. Glass glinted as a window swung open farther along the alley, and again he had the feeling he was being watched. But then so what? Revenge was his. His alone. Gert Rafto buttoned up his coat, hardly noticing the pissing rain as, in silent triumph, he strode down the slippery streets to the Bergen town center.

It was five o'clock in the afternoon, and the rain trickled over Bergen from a sky with a blown gasket. On the desk in front of Gert Rafto was a list of names he had requested from the professional organization. He had started looking for candidates with the right first name. Just three so far. It was only two hours since he had been with Onny Hetland, and Rafto was thinking that soon he would know who had killed Laila Aasen. Case solved in less than twelve hours. And no one could take that away from him—the honor was his, and his alone. Because he was going to inform the press in person. The country's major media had flown in over the mountains and were already besieging the Police HQ. The chief constable had given orders that no details about the body were to be released, but the vultures had already scented a bloodbath.

"There must have been a leak," the chief had said, looking at Rafto, who hadn't answered, or formed the grin that yearned to surface. They were sitting out there now, ready to file their reports. And soon Gert Rafto would be king of the Bergen Police HQ again.

He turned down the radio from which Whitney Houston had insisted all autumn that she would always love you, but before he could lift the telephone, it rang.

"Rafto," he said with irritation, impatient to get going.

"It's me you're looking for."

The voice was what immediately told the discredited detective that this was not just a hoax or a crank. It was cool and controlled with clear, businesslike diction, which excluded the usual nuts and drunks. But there was something else about the voice, too, which he couldn't quite place.

Rafto coughed aloud, twice. Took his time, as if to show that he had not been taken aback. "Who am I talking to?"

"You know."

Rafto closed his eyes and cursed silently and roundly. Damn, damn, damn, the killer was going to turn himself in. And that would not have anywhere near the same impact as if he, Rafto, arrested the perpetrator.

"What makes you think I'm looking for you?" the policeman asked between clenched teeth.

"I just know," said the voice. "And if we can do this my way, you'll get what you want."

"And what do I want?"

"You want to arrest me. And you'll be able to. Alone. Are you listening now, Rafto?"

The officer nodded before he could gather himself to say yes.

"Meet me by the totem pole in Nordnes Park," the voice said. "In exactly ten minutes."

Rafto tried to think. Nordnes Park was by the aquarium; he could get there in under ten minutes. But why meet there, of all places, in a park at the end of a headland?

"So that I can see if you come alone," the voice said, as if in answer to his thoughts. "If I see any other police or you're late, I'll be gone. Forever."

Rafto's brain processed, calculated and drew a conclusion. He would not be able to organize an arrest team in time. He would have to explain in his written report why he had been forced to undertake the arrest on his own. It was perfect.

"OK," said Rafto. "What happens now?"

"I'll tell you everything and give you the conditions for my surrender."

"What sort of conditions?"

"I don't want to wear handcuffs at the trial. The press will not be allowed in. And I serve my time somewhere where I don't have to mix with other prisoners."

Rafto almost choked. "OK," he said, looking at his watch.

"Wait, there are more conditions. TV in my room, all the books I might wish for."

"We'll arrange that," Rafto said.

"When you've signed the deal with my conditions, I'll go with you."

"What about—?" Rafto began, but an accelerated *beep-beep-beep* told him that the other person had hung up.

Rafto parked his car by the Bergen shipyard. It wasn't the shortest route, but it meant he would have a better view of Nordnes when he went in. The big park was on undulating terrain with well-trodden paths and hillocks of yellow withered grass. The trees pointed with black gnarled fingers to heavy clouds sweeping in from the sea behind the island of Askøy. A man hurried away behind a nervous Rottweiler on a taut lead. Rafto felt the Smith & Wesson revolver in his coat pocket as he strode past the Nordnes seawater pool; the empty white basin looked like an oversize bath by the water's edge.

Beyond the bend he could make out the thirty-three-foot-high totem pole, a two-ton gift from Seattle on the occasion of Bergen's nine hundredth anniversary. He could hear his own breathing and the squelch of wet leaves beneath his shoes. It started to rain. Small, pinlike droplets drove into his face.

A solitary figure stood by the totem pole, facing Rafto as if the person had known that Rafto would come from that direction and not the other end.

Rafto squeezed the revolver as he walked the last few steps. Six feet away, he stopped. Pinched his eyes against the rain. It could not be true.

"Surprised?" said the voice he could place only now.

Rafto didn't answer. His brain had started processing again.

"You thought you knew me," the voice said. "But it was just me who knew you. That was how I guessed you would try to do this alone."

Rafto stared.

"It's a game," the voice said.

Rafto cleared his throat. "A game?"

"Yes. You like playing games."

Rafto closed his hand around the stock of the revolver, held it in such a way he could be sure it would not snag on his pocket if he had to draw quickly.

"Why me, particularly?" he asked.

"Because you were the best. I only play against the best."

"You're crazy," Rafto whispered, regretting it immediately.

"Of that," the other said with a tiny smile, "there is little doubt. But you're also crazy, my man. We're all crazy. We're restless spirits that cannot find their way home. It's always been like that. Do you know why the Indians made these?"

The person in front of Rafto banged the knuckle of a gloved index finger against the tree; the carved figures perched on top of one another stared across the fjord with large, blind, black eyes.

"To watch over the souls," the person continued. "So that they don't get lost. But a totem pole rots. And it should rot—that's part of the point. And when it's gone, the soul has to find a new home. Perhaps in a mask. Perhaps in a mirror. Or perhaps in a newborn child."

The sound of hoarse cries came from the penguin run at the aquarium.

"Will you tell me why you killed her?" Rafto said, and noticed that he, too, had gone hoarse.

"Shame the game's over, Rafto. It's been fun."

"And how did you find out that I was on your trail?"

The other person raised a hand, and Rafto automatically stepped back a pace. There was something hanging from it. A necklace. At the end there was a green tear-shaped stone with a black crack. Rafto felt his heart pounding.

"In fact, Onny Hetland wouldn't say anything at first. But she allowed herself . . . how shall I say it? . . . to be persuaded."

"You're lying." Rafto said it without breathing and without conviction.

"She said you instructed her not to tell your colleagues. That was when I knew you would accept my offer and come here alone. Because you thought this would be the new home for your soul, your resurrection. Didn't you."

The cold, thin rain lay like sweat on Rafto's face. He

had placed his finger on the trigger of his revolver and concentrated on speaking slowly and with restraint.

"You chose the wrong place. You're standing with your back to the sea and there are police cars on all the roads out of here. No one can escape."

The person facing him sniffed the air. "Can you smell it, Gert?"

"What?"

"Fear. Adrenaline has quite a distinctive smell. But you know all about that. I'm sure you smelled it on the prisoners you beat up. Laila smelled like that, too. Especially when she saw the tools I would use. And Onny even more. Probably because you told her about Laila, so she knew what would happen to her. It's quite a stimulating smell, don't you think? I've read that it's the smell some carnivores use to find their prey. Imagine the trembling victim trying to hide, but knowing that the smell of its own fear will kill it."

Rafto saw the other's gloved hands hanging down, empty. It was broad daylight, close to the center of Norway's second-largest city. Despite his age, after the last years without alcohol he was in good physical shape. His reflexes were fast, and his combat techniques were more or less intact. Drawing the revolver would take a fraction of a second. So why was he so frightened that his teeth were chattering in his mouth?

6

Cellular Phone

Police Officer Magnus Skarre leaned back in his swivel chair and closed his eyes. And the image that immediately appeared to him wore a suit and stood facing the other way. He opened his eyes again in a flash, and checked his watch. Six. He decided that he deserved a break since he had been through the standard procedure for locating missing persons. He had called all the hospitals to hear if they had admitted a Birte Becker. Called two taxi firms, Norgestaxi and Oslo Taxi, and checked the trips they had made near the Hoff address the previous night. Spoken to her bank and received confirmation that she had not taken out large amounts from her account before disappearing, nor were there withdrawals registered for the previous evening or today. The police at Gardermoen Airport had been allowed to see passenger lists for last night, but the only passenger named Becker they found was her husband, Filip, on the Bergen flight. Skarre had also spoken to the ferry companies sailing to Denmark and England, although she could hardly have gone to England if her husband kept her passport and had shown it to them. The ambitious officer had sent the usual security fax to all the hotels in Oslo and Akershus, and finally instructed all operational units, including the patrol cars, in Oslo to keep their eyes peeled.

The only thing left was the question of the mobile phone.

Magnus called Harry and informed him of the situation. The inspector was out of breath, and in the background he heard the shrill twittering of birds. Harry asked a couple of questions about the mobile before hanging up. Then Skarre got up and went into the corridor. The door to Katrine Bratt's office was open and the light was on, but no one was there. He climbed the stairs to the cafeteria on the floor above.

No food was being served, but there was warmish coffee in a thermos and crispbread and jam on a cart by the door. Only four people were sitting in the room, but one of them was Katrine Bratt, at a table by the wall. She was reading documents in a ring binder. In front of her was a glass of water and a lunch box containing two open sandwiches. She was wearing glasses. Thin frames, thin glass—you could hardly see them against her face.

Skarre poured himself some coffee and went over to her table.

"Planned to do some overtime, did you?" he asked, taking a seat.

Magnus Skarre thought he heard a sigh before she looked up from the sheet.

"How I guessed?" He smiled. "Homemade sandwiches. You knew before you left home that our cafeteria would close at five and you would be working late. Sorry, but that's how you get when you're a detective."

"Do you?" she said, without batting an eyelid, as she sought to return to the pages in her file.

"Yep," Skarre said, slurping his coffee and using the occasion to get a good look at her. She was leaning forward and he could see the lace trim of her bra down the front of her blouse. "Take this missing-persons case today. I don't have any information that anyone else hasn't got. Yet I'm sitting here and thinking that she might still be in Hoff. Perhaps she's lying under snow or foliage somewhere. Or perhaps in one of the many small lakes or streams there."

Katrine Bratt didn't answer.

"And do you know why I think that?"

"No," she answered in a monotone, without raising her eyes from the file.

Skarre stretched across the table and placed a mobile phone directly in front of her. Katrine raised her face with a resigned expression.

"This is a mobile phone," he said. "You think, I assume, it's a pretty new invention. But back in April 1973 the father of the mobile phone, Martin Cooper, had the first conversation on one, with his wife at home. And, of course, he had no idea that this invention would become one of the most important ways in which we in the police force can find missing persons. If you want to become an OK detective, you have to listen and learn these things, Bratt."

Katrine removed her glasses and looked at Skarre with a small smile that he liked, but couldn't quite interpret. "I'm all ears."

"Good," said Skarre. "Because Birte Becker is the owner of a mobile phone. And a mobile phone sends out signals that can be picked up by base stations in the area where it is located. Not only when you ring, but in fact when you carry a phone on you. That's why the Americans called it a cellular phone from the very start. Because it is covered by base stations in small areas—in other words, cells. I've checked with Telenor, and the base station covering Hoff is still receiving signals from

Birte's phone. But we've been through the whole house, and there's no phone. And she could hardly have lost it by the house—that would be too much of a coincidence. Ergo"—Skarre raised his hands like a conjurer after pulling off a trick—"after this coffee I'm going to contact the Incident Room and send out a search party."

"Good luck," Katrine said, passing him the mobile phone and turning the page.

"That's one of Hole's old cases, isn't it?" Skarre said.

"Yes, that's right."

"He thought a serial killer was on the rampage."

"I know."

"Do you? So perhaps you know that he was wrong as well? And it wasn't the first time. He's morbidly obsessed with serial killers, Hole is. He thinks this is the U.S.A. But he still hasn't found his serial killer in this country."

"There have been several serial killers in Sweden. Thomas Quick. John Ausonius. Tore Hedin . . . "

Magnus Skarre laughed. "You've done your homework. But if you'd like to learn a couple of things about proper crime detection, I suggest you and I go for a beer."

"Thank you, I'm not—"

"And maybe a bite to eat. It wasn't a big lunch box." Skarre finally caught her eye and kept it. Her gaze had a strange gleam, as if deep inside there was a fire smoldering. He had never seen a gleam like that before. And he thought he was responsible for it; he had lit the fire and through the conversation he had moved up into her league.

"You could view it as . . . ," he began, and pretended to be searching for the right word. "Training."

She smiled. A broad smile.

Skarre felt his pulse racing; he was hot, thinking he could already feel her body against his, a stockinged knee against his fingertips, the crackle as his hand slid upward.

"What do you want, Skarre? To check out the new skirt in the unit?" Her smile became even broader and the gleam even fiercer. "To fuck her as soon as you can, the way boys spit on the biggest slices of birthday cake so they can enjoy them in peace before the others?"

Magnus Skarre had a feeling his jaw had dropped.

"Let me give you a few well-intentioned tips, Skarre. Keep away from women at work. Don't waste your time drinking coffee in the cafeteria if you think you've got a hot lead. And don't try to tell me you can call the Incident Room. You call Inspector Hole, and he's the one who decides whether a search party will be set up. And then he'll call the Emergency Operations Center, where there are people ready, not just a team from here."

Katrine scrunched up the waxed paper from her sandwiches and lobbed it toward the garbage can behind Skarre. He didn't even need to turn to know that she hadn't missed. She packed her file and stood up, but by then Skarre had managed to collect himself to some degree.

"I don't know what you're imagining, Bratt. You're a married slut who maybe doesn't get enough at home and so you're hoping a guy like me can be bothered . . . can be bothered to . . . " He couldn't find the words. Shit, he couldn't find the words. "I'm just offering to teach you a thing or two, you whore."

Something happened to her face—it was like a curtain being drawn aside to allow him to see into the flames. For a moment he was convinced that she would hit him. But nothing happened. And when she spoke again, he realized that everything had happened in her eyes alone; she hadn't lifted a finger and her voice was totally under control.

"I beg your pardon if I've misunderstood you," she said, although her facial expression suggested she considered that highly improbable. "By the way, Martin Cooper did not call his wife; he called his rival, Joel Engel at Bell Laboratories. Do you think that was to teach him a thing or two, Skarre? Or to brag?"

Skarre watched her leave, watched her suit rubbing against her backside as she wiggled toward the cafeteria door. Shit, the woman was off her rocker! He felt like getting up and throwing something at her. But he knew he would miss. Besides, he didn't want to move; he was afraid his erection was still visible.

Harry felt his lungs pressing against the inside of his ribs. His breathing was beginning to settle. But not his heart, which was running like a hare in his chest. His training clothes were heavy with sweat as he stood at the edge of the forest by the Ekeberg restaurant. The functionalist restaurant built between the wars had once been Oslo's pride and joy, towering above the town on the precipitous ridge face in the east. But as customers had stopped taking the long trip up from the city center to the forest, the place had become unprofitable; it had declined and become a peeling shack for over-the-hill dance fiends, middle-aged drinkers and lonely souls on the lookout for other lonely souls. In the end, they had closed the restaurant. Harry had always liked driving up here above the town's layer of yellow exhaust fumes and running along the network of paths on the steep terrain that provided a challenge and caused the lactic acid to burn in his muscles. He had liked to stop by the crumbling beauty of a restaurant, sitting on the rain-wet, overgrown terrace overlooking the town that had once been his, but which was now emotionally bankrupt, all assets transferred, an ex-lover with new affections.

The town lay below in a hollow with ridges on all sides

and a sole retreat via the fjord. Geologists said that Oslo was a dead volcanic crater. And on evenings like this Harry could imagine that the town's lights were perforations in the earth's surface with the glowing lava shining through. From Holmenkollen ski jump, which lay like an illuminated white comma on the ridge on the opposite side of the town, he tried to work out where Rakel's house was.

He thought about the letter. And the telephone call he had just received from Skarre about the signals transmitted by Birte's missing phone. His heart was beating slower now, pumping blood and transmitting calm, regular signals to the brain that there was still life. Like a mobile phone to a base station. Heart, Harry thought. Signal. The letter. It was a sick thought. So why hadn't he already dismissed it? Why was he already calculating how long it would take him to run to the car, drive to Hoff and check which of them was sicker?

Rakel stood by the kitchen window looking across her property to the spruce trees blocking her view of the neighbors. At a local residents' meeting she had suggested that some of the trees might be cut down to let in more light, but the unspoken absence of enthusiasm that greeted her was so obvious that she didn't even ask for a vote. The spruce trees prevented people from looking in, and that was how they liked it on Holmenkollen Ridge. The snow still lay on the ground here, high above the town, where BMWs and Volvos gently threaded their way up through the bends on their way home to electric garage doors and dinners on tables, prepared by fitness-center-slim housewives taking their career breaks with just a little help from nannies.

Even through the solid floors of the wooden house she had inherited from her father, Rakel could hear the music from Oleg's room above. Led Zeppelin and the Who. When she was eleven years old, it would have been unthinkable to listen to music from her parents' generation. But Oleg had been given these CDs by Harry and he played them with genuine love.

She thought about how thin Harry had become, how he had shrunk. Just like her memory of him. It was almost frightening how someone you have been intimate with can fade and vanish. Or perhaps that was why; you had been so close to each other that afterward, when you no longer were, it seemed unreal, like a dream you soon forgot because it had happened only in your head. Perhaps that was why it had been a shock to see him again. To embrace him, to smell his aroma, to hear his voice, not on the telephone, but from a mouth with those strangely soft lips in that hard and ever more lined face of his. To look into those blue eyes with the gleam that varied in intensity as he talked. Just like before.

Yet she was glad it was over, that she had put it behind her. That this man had become a person with whom she would not share her future, a person who would not bring his grubby reality into their lives.

She was better now. Much better. She looked at her watch. He would be here soon. For, unlike Harry, he tended to be on time.

Mathias had suddenly appeared one day. At a garden party under the auspices of the Holmenkollen Residents' Association. He didn't even live in the neighborhood— he had been invited by friends—and he and Rakel had sat talking almost the entire evening. Mostly about her, in fact. And he had listened attentively, a bit like doctors do, she had thought. But then he had called her two days later and asked her whether she would like to see an exhibition at the Henie Onstad Art Center in Høvikodden. Oleg was welcome to join them, because there was a children's exhibition, too. The weather had been terrible, the art mediocre and Oleg fractious. But Mathias had managed to lift the mood with his good humor and acid comments about the artist's talent. And afterward he had driven them home, apologized for his idea and promised with a smile never to take them anywhere ever again. Unless they asked him to, of course. After that Mathias had gone to Botswana for a week. And had called her the evening he came home to ask if they could go out again.

She heard the sound of a car shifting down to tackle the steep driveway. He drove a Honda Accord of older vintage. She didn't know why, but she liked the idea of that. He parked in front of the garage, never inside. And she liked that, too. She liked the fact that he brought a change of underwear and a toilet kit in an overnight bag he then took away with him the next morning. She liked him asking her when she wanted to see him again and taking nothing for granted. That might change now, of course, but she was ready for it.

He stepped out of the car. He was tall, almost as tall as Harry, and smiled to the kitchen window with his open, boyish face, even though he must have been dead on his feet after the inhumanly long shift. Yes, she was ready for it. For a man who was present, who loved her and prioritized their little trio above everything else. She heard a key being turned in the front door. The key she had given him the previous week. Mathias had looked like one big question mark at first, like a child who had just received a ticket to a chocolate factory.

The door opened, he was inside and she was in his arms. She thought even his woolen coat smelled good. The material was soft and autumn-cold against her cheek, but the secure warmth inside was already radiating out to her body.

"What is it?" He laughed in her hair.

"I've been waiting for this for so long," she whispered.

She closed her eyes, and they stood like that for a while.

She released him and looked up into his smiling face. He was a good-looking man. Better-looking than Harry.

He freed himself, unbuttoned his coat, hung it up and walked over to the slop sink, where he washed his hands. He always did that when he came from the Anatomy Department, where they handled real bodies during the lectures. As indeed Harry always had when he came straight from murder cases. Mathias opened the cupboard under the sink, emptied potatoes from the bag into the kitchen sink and turned on the tap.

"How was your day, darling?"

She thought that most men would have asked about the previous night; after all, he knew she had met Harry. And she liked him for that, too. She talked while looking out the window. Her gaze ran across the spruce trees to the town beneath them, where lights had started to twinkle. He was down there somewhere now. On a hopeless hunt for something he had never found and never would. She felt sorry for him. Sympathy was all that was left. In truth, there had been a moment last night when they were both silent and their eyes had held each other's, unable to free themselves right away. It had felt like an electric shock, but it had been over in an instant. Completely over. No lasting magic. She had made her decision. She stood behind Mathias, put her arms around him and rested her head on his broad back.

She could feel muscles and sinews at work under his shirt as he peeled the potatoes and put them in the saucepan.

"We could do with a couple more," he said.

She became aware of a movement by the kitchen door and turned.

Oleg was standing there looking at them.

"Could you fetch some more potatoes from the cellar?" she said and saw Oleg's eyes darken.

Mathias turned. Oleg was still there.

"I can go," Mathias said, taking the empty bucket from under the sink.

"No," said Oleg, stepping forward two paces. "I'll go."

He took the bucket from Mathias, turned and went out the door.

"What was that about?" Mathias asked.

"He's just a bit frightened of the dark," Rakel sighed.

"I thought so, but why did he go anyway?"

"Because Harry said he should."

"Should do what?"

Rakel shook her head. "The things he's frightened of. And doesn't want to be frightened of. When Harry was here, he used to send Oleg down to the cellar all the time."

Mathias frowned.

Rakel put on a sad smile. "Harry's not exactly a child psychiatrist. And Oleg wouldn't listen to me if Harry had given his opinion first. On the other hand, there are no monsters down there."

Mathias turned a knob on the stove and said in a low voice, "How can you be so sure of that?"

"Mathias?" Rakel laughed. "Were *you* afraid of the dark?"

"Who's talking about *was*?" Mathias grinned mischievously.

Yes, she liked him. This was better. A better life. She liked him, yes she did, she did like him.

Harry pulled up in front of the Beckers' house. He sat in the car staring at the yellow light from the windows spilling onto the yard. The snowman had shrunk to a dwarf. But its shadow still extended to the trees and right over to the picket fence.

Harry got out of the car. The lament of the iron gate made him wince. He knew he ought to have called first; a yard was as much private property as a house was. But he had neither the patience nor the inclination to discuss anything with Professor Becker.

The wet ground was springy. He crouched down. The light reflected off the snowman as if it were matte glass. The thaw during the day had made the tiny snow crystals hook together into larger crystals, but now that the temperature had fallen again, the water vapor had condensed and frozen onto other crystals. The result was that the snow, which had been so fine, white and light this morning, was now coarse, grayish white and packed.

Harry raised his right hand. Clenched his fist. And punched.

The snowman's crushed head rolled off its shoulders and down onto the brown grass.

Harry punched again, this time from above and down through the neck. His fingers formed a claw and bored their way through the snow and found what they were searching for.

He pulled out his hand and held it up triumphantly in front of the snowman, the way Bruce Lee did, to show his adversary the heart he had just torn out of his chest.

It was a red and silver Nokia mobile phone. It was still switched on.

But the feeling of triumph had faded. For he already knew that this was not a breakthrough in the investigation, just a minor scene in a puppet show with someone else pulling invisible strings. It had been too simple. They had been meant to find it.

Harry walked to the front door and rang the bell. Filip

Becker opened up. His hair was disheveled and his tie askew. He blinked hard several times as though he had been sleeping.

"Yes," he answered Harry's question. "That's the kind of phone she's got."

"Could I ask you to call her number?"

Filip Becker disappeared into the house and Harry waited. Suddenly Jonas poked his face out of the porch doorway. Harry was about to say hi, but at that moment the red phone began to play a children's tune: *"Blåmann, blåmann, bukken min."* And Harry remembered the next line from his school songbook: *Tenk på vesle gutten din.* Think about your little boy.

And he saw Jonas's face light up. Saw the inexorable process of reasoning in the boy's brain, the immediate bewilderment and then the joy of hearing his mother's ringtone fade into intense, naked fear. Harry swallowed. It was a fear he knew all too well.

As Harry let himself into his apartment he could smell the plaster and the sawdust. The plasterboard forming the corridor walls had been taken down and lay piled up on the floor. There were some light stains on the brick wall behind. Harry ran a finger over the white coating that had drifted onto the parquet floor. He put a fingertip into his mouth. It tasted salty. Did mold taste like that? Or was it just salt bloom, the structure sweating? Harry flicked a lighter and leaned over to the wall. Nothing to smell, nothing to see.

When he had gone to bed and was staring into the room's hermetically sealed blackness, he thought about Jonas. And his own mother. About the smell of illness and her face slowly fading into the pillow's whiteness. For days and weeks he had played with Sis, and Dad had gone quiet and everyone had tried to act as if nothing were happening. He thought he could hear a faint rustle outside in the hall. As if the invisible puppet strings were multiplying, lengthening and sneaking around as they consumed the darkness and formed a faint shimmering light that quivered and shook.

Hidden Statistics

The frail morning light seeped through the blinds in the POB's office, coating the two men's faces in gray. POB Hagen was listening to Harry with a pensive furrow over bushy black eyebrows that met in the middle. On the huge desk stood a small plinth bearing a white knuckle bone that, according to the inscription, had belonged to the Japanese battalion commander Yoshito Yasuda. In his years at the military academy, Hagen had lectured about this little finger, which Yasuda had cut off in desperation in front of his men during the retreat from Burma in 1944.

It was just a year since Hagen had been brought back to his old employer, the police, to head the Crime Squad, and, as a lot of water had passed under the bridge in the meantime, he listened with relative patience to his veteran inspector holding forth on the theme of missing persons.

"In Oslo alone, more than six hundred people are reported missing every year. After a couple of hours only a handful of these are not found. As good as none remain missing for more than a couple of days."

Hagen stroked a finger over the hairs on the bridge of

his nose. He had to prepare for the budget meeting in the chief constable's office. The theme was cutbacks.

"Most missing persons are escapees from mental institutions or elderly people suffering from dementia," Harry continued. "But even the relatively compos mentis who have run off to Copenhagen or committed suicide are found. Their names appear on passenger lists, they withdraw cash from an ATM or wash up on a beach."

"What's your point?" Gunnar Hagen said, looking at his watch.

"This," Harry said, tossing a yellow file that landed on the POB's desk with a smack.

Hagen leaned forward and flicked through the stapled documents. "My goodness, Harry. You're not normally the report-writing type."

"This is Skarre's work," Harry said, wasting no words. "But the conclusion is mine, and I'll give it to you now, orally."

"Make it brief, please."

Harry stared down at his hands, which he had placed in his lap. His long legs were stretched out in front of the chair. He took a deep breath. He knew that once he had said this out loud, there was no going back.

"Too many people have disappeared," Harry said.

The right half of Hagen's eyebrow shot into the air. "Explain."

"You'll find it on page six. A list of missing women aged between twenty-five and fifty from 1994 until today. Women who in the last ten years have never been found. I've been talking to the Missing Persons Unit, and they agree. It's simply too many."

"Too many in relation to what?"

"In relation to before. In relation to Denmark and Sweden. And in relation to other demographic groups.

Married and cohabiting women are hugely overrepresented."

"Women are more independent than they used to be," Hagen said. "Some go their own way, break with the family, go abroad with a man, maybe. That has some bearing on statistics. So?"

"They've become more independent in Denmark and Sweden, too. But they find them again there."

Hagen sighed. "If the figures are so divergent from the norm, as you claim, why has no one discovered this before?"

"Because Skarre's figures are valid for the whole country, and usually the police look only at those missing in their own district. There is a national missing-persons register at Kripos that has eighteen hundred names, but it's for the last fifty years and includes shipwrecks and disasters like the Alexander Kielland oil rig. The point is that no one has looked at countrywide patterns. Not until now."

"Fine, but our responsibility is not for the country, Harry. It's for the Oslo Police District." Hagen smacked both palms down to indicate that the audience was over.

"The problem," Harry said, rubbing his chin, "is that it's come to Oslo."

"What *it*?"

"Last night I found Birte Becker's mobile phone in a snowman. I don't know quite what *it* is, boss. But I think we need to find out. Quickly."

"These statistics are interesting," Hagen said, absentmindedly taking Battalion Commander Yasuda's little finger and pressing his thumb into it. "And I also appreciate that this latest disappearance is grounds for concern. But it's not enough. So tell me: What was it that actually made you ask Skarre to write this report?"

Harry looked at Hagen. Then he pulled a dog-eared envelope from his inside pocket and passed it to Hagen.

"This was in my mailbox after I did the TV show at the beginning of September. Until now I had thought it was a madman's work."

Hagen took out the letter, and after reading the six sentences, shook his head at Harry. "The snowman? And what is/are the Murri?"

"That's exactly the point," Harry said. "I'm afraid this is the *it.*"

The POB looked nonplussed.

"I hope I'm wrong," Harry said, "but I think we have some hellishly dark days ahead of us."

Hagen sighed. "What do you want, Harry?"

"I want an investigation team."

Hagen studied Harry. Like most other officers at the Police HQ, he regarded Harry as a self-willed, arrogant, argumentative, unstable alcoholic. Nevertheless, he was glad they were on the same side and that he wouldn't have this man snapping at his heels.

"How many?" he asked at length. "And for how long?"

"Ten detectives. Two months."

"Two weeks?" said Magnus Skarre. "And four people? Is *that* supposed to be a murder investigation?"

He looked around with disapproval at the other three squeezed into Harry's office: Katrine Bratt, Harry Hole and Bjørn Holm from Krimteknisk, the Forensics Unit.

"That's what Hagen's given me," Harry said, tipping back on his chair. "And this is not a murder investigation. For the moment."

"What is it, actually?" Katrine Bratt asked. "For the moment?"

"A missing-persons case," Harry said. "But one that bears a certain similarity to other recent cases."

"Housewives who one day in late autumn suddenly up and run?" asked Bjørn Holm with remnants of the rural Toten dialect he had added to the goods he had removed from the village of Skreia, along with an LP collection consisting of Elvis, hard-core hillbilly, the Sex Pistols, Jason & the Scorchers, three hand-sewn suits from Nashville, an American Bible, a slightly undersize sofa bed and a dining-room suite that had outlived three generations of Holms. All piled up on a trailer and towed to the capital by the last Amazon to roll off the 1970 Volvo assembly line. Bjørn Holm had bought the Amazon for 1,200 kroner, but even at that time no one knew how many miles it had gone because the odometer went up only to 100,000. However, the car expressed everything Bjørn Holm was and believed in; it smelled better than anything he knew, a mixture of imitation leather, metal, engine oil, sun-faded rear dash, Volvo factory and seats impregnated with "personality perspiration," which Bjørn Holm explained was not common body perspiration but a select veneer of all the previous owners' souls, karma, eating habits and lifestyles. The furry dice hanging from the mirror were original Fuzzy Dice, which expressed the right mix of genuine affection for and ironical distance from a bygone American culture and aesthetic that perfectly suited a Norwegian farmer's son who had grown up with Jim Reeves in one ear and the Ramones in the other, and loved both. Now he was sitting in Harry's office with a Rasta hat that made him look more like an undercover narcotics cop than a forensics officer. Two immense fire-engine-red cutlet-shaped sideburns framing Bjørn Holm's plump, round face emerged from the hat, and his slightly protruding eyes gave him a fishlike expression

of constant wonderment. He was the only person Harry
had insisted on having on his small investigation team.

"There's one more thing," Harry said, reaching out
to switch on the overhead projector between the piles of
paper on his desk. Magnus Skarre cursed and shielded his
eyes as blurred writing suddenly appeared on his face. He
moved, and Harry's voice came from behind the projector.

"This letter landed in my mailbox exactly two months
ago. No address, postmarked Oslo. Produced on a standard inkjet printer."

Before Harry could ask, Katrine Bratt had pressed the
light switch by the door, plunging the room into darkness. A square of light loomed up on the white wall.

They read in silence.

*Soon the first snow will come. And then he will appear
again. The snowman. And when the snow has gone,
he will have taken someone else. What you should ask
yourself is this: "Who made the snowman? Who makes
snowmen? Who gave birth to the Murri?" For the
snowman doesn't know.*

"Poetic," mumbled Bjørn Holm.

"What's the Murri?" Skarre asked.

The monotonous whir of the projector fan was the answer.

"The most interesting part is who the snowman is,"
Katrine Bratt said.

"Obviously someone who needs his head examined,"
Bjørn Holm said.

Skarre's lone laughter was cut short.

"The Murri was the nickname of a person who is now
dead," Harry said from out of the darkness. "A Murri is

an Aborigine from Queensland in Australia. While this Murri was alive he killed women all over Australia. No one knows for certain how many. His real name was Robin Toowoomba."

The fan whirred and buzzed.

"Serial killer," said Bjørn Holm. "The one you killed."

Harry nodded.

"Does that mean you think we're dealing with one now?"

"As a result of this letter, we can't rule out the possibility."

"Whoa there. Hold your horses!" Skarre raised his palms. "How many times have you cried wolf since you became a celeb because of the Aussie stuff, Harry?"

"Three times," Harry said. "At least."

"And still we haven't seen a serial killer in Norway." Skarre glanced at Bratt as if to make sure she was following. "Is it because of that FBI course you took on serial killers? Is that what's making you see them everywhere?"

"Maybe," Harry said.

"Let me remind you that apart from that nurse fellow who gave injections to a couple of old fogies who were at death's door anyway, we haven't had a single serial killer in Norway. Ever. Those guys exist in the U.S.A., but even there usually only in films."

"Wrong," said Katrine Bratt.

The others turned to face her. She stifled a yawn.

"Sweden, France, Belgium, Britain, Italy, Holland, Denmark, Russia and Finland. And we're talking only solved cases here. No one utters a word about hidden statistics."

Harry couldn't see Skarre's flushed face in the dark, just the profile of his chin jutting forward aggressively in Bratt's direction.

"We haven't even got a body, and I can show you a drawer full of letters like this one. People who are a lot nuttier than this . . . this . . . snowguy."

"The difference," Harry said, getting up and strolling over to the window, "is that this head case is thorough. The name Murri was never mentioned in the papers at the time. It was the nickname Robin Toowoomba used when he was a boxer with a traveling circus."

The last of the daylight leaked out through a crack in the cloud cover. He looked at his watch. Oleg had insisted on going early so that they could take in Slayer as well.

"Where we gonna begin, then?" Bjørn Holm mumbled.

"Eh?" Skarre said.

"Where are we going to begin, then?" Holm repeated with exaggerated diction.

Harry went back to the desk.

"Holm goes over Becker's house and yard as if it were a murder scene. Check the mobile phone and the scarf in particular. Skarre, you make a list of ex-murderers, rapists, suspects in—"

"—comparable cases and other scum on the loose," Skarre said.

"Bratt, you go through the missing-persons reports and see if you can spot a pattern."

Harry waited for the inevitable question: What type of pattern? But it was not forthcoming. Katrine Bratt just gave a brief nod.

"OK," Harry said. "Get going."

"And you?" Bratt asked.

"I'm going to a gig," Harry said.

When the others had left the office, he looked down at his pad. At the only words he had jotted down. *Hidden statistics.*

*   *   *

Sylvia ran as fast as she could. She ran toward the trees where they were most dense, in the growing murk. She was running for her life.

She hadn't tied up her boots, and now they were full of snow. She held the little hatchet in front of her as she burst through layer after layer of low, leafless branches. The blade was red and sleek with blood.

She knew the snow that had fallen yesterday had melted in town, but even though Sollihøgda was barely half an hour's drive away, the snow could lie on the ground until spring up here. And right now she wished they had never moved to this godforsaken place, to this bit of wilderness by the town. She wished she were running on black pavement, in a city where the noise drowned out the sounds of escape and she could hide in the secure mass of humanity. But here she was completely alone.

No.

Not completely.

8

Swan Neck

Sylvia ran into the forest. Night was on the way. Usually she hated the way November evenings drew in so early, but today she thought the night couldn't come soon enough. She sought the darkness in the depths of the forest, the darkness that could erase her footprints in the snow and conceal her. She knew her way around here; she could find her bearings so that she didn't run back to the farm or straight into . . . into *its* arms. The problem was that the snow had changed the landscape overnight, covered the paths, the familiar rocks, and leveled out all the contours. And the dusk . . . everything was distorted and disfigured by the blackness. And by her own panic.

She stopped to listen. Her heaving, rasping breathlessness rent the tranquillity; it sounded as if she were tearing the waxed paper wrapped around her daughters' packed lunches. She managed to bring her breathing under control. All she could hear was the blood pounding in her ears and the low gurgle of a stream. The stream! They usually followed the stream when they were picking berries, setting traps or searching for chickens that in their heart of hearts they knew the fox had taken. The stream led down to a gravel road, and there, sooner or later, a car would pass.

She no longer heard any footsteps. No twigs cracking, no crunching of snow. Perhaps she had escaped? With her body hunched over, she moved swiftly toward the gurgling sounds.

The stream looked as though it were flowing over a white bedsheet.

Sylvia trampled straight in. The water, which reached mid-ankle, soon penetrated her boots. It was so cold that it froze her leg muscles. Then she began to run again. In the same direction as the water flowed. She made loud splashes as she lifted her legs for long, ground-gaining strides. No tracks, she thought triumphantly. And her pulse slowed, even though she was running.

That had to be a result of the hours she had spent on the treadmill at the fitness center last year. She had lost fifteen pounds and ventured to maintain that her body was in better shape than those of most thirty-five-year-olds. That was what he said, anyway, Yngve, whom she had first met at the so-called inspiration seminar last year. Where she had been all too inspired. My God, if only she could turn back the clock. Back ten years. All the things she would have done differently! She wouldn't have married Rolf. And she wouldn't have had an abortion. Yes, of course, it was an impossible thought now that the twins had come into the world. But before they were born, before she had seen Emma and Olga, it would have been possible, and she wouldn't have been in this prison that she had constructed around herself with such care.

She swept away the branches overhanging the stream, and from the corner of her eye she saw something, an animal, react with a startled movement and disappear into the gray gloom of the forest.

It went through her mind that she would have to be

careful swinging her arms so that she didn't hit her leg with the hatchet. Minutes had passed, but it felt like an eternity since she had been standing in the barn slaughtering chickens. She had cut off two heads and had been about to cut off a third when she heard the barn door creak behind her. Of course she had been alarmed; she was alone and hadn't been aware of either footsteps or a car in the yard. The first thing she had noticed was the strange apparatus, a thin metal loop attached to a handle. It looked like the snares they used to catch foxes. And when the holder of this instrument began to talk, it slowly dawned on her that she was the prey, she was the one who was going to die.

She had been told why.

And she had listened to the sick but limpid logic as the blood slowed in her veins, as if it were already coagulating. Then she had been told how. In detail. And the loop had begun to glow, first red, then white. That was when she had swung her arm in horror, felt the recently sharpened hatchet blade cut through the material under the raised arm, seen the jacket and sweater open as if she had unzipped them and seen the steel slice a red line through the bare skin. As the figure had staggered backward and fallen onto the floorboards slippery with chickens' blood, she had raced to the door at the back of the barn. The one leading into the forest. Into the darkness.

The numbness had spread over her knees, and her clothes were soaked up to her navel. But she knew she would soon be on the gravel road. And from there it was no more than fifteen minutes to the nearest farm if she stayed at a run. The stream turned. Her left foot kicked something protruding from the water. There was a crack, as if someone had grabbed her foot, and the next moment Sylvia Ottersen was falling headlong. She landed on her stomach, swallowed water tasting of earth and rotten leaves, then pushed herself into a kneeling position. Once she knew she was still alone, and the first panic had passed, she discovered that her foot was trapped. She groped with her hand under the water, expecting to find entwined tree roots around her foot, but instead her fingers felt something smooth and hard. Metal. A metal ring. Sylvia's gaze scoured around for what she had kicked. And there on the snowy bank she saw it. It had eyes, feathers and a pale red cockscomb. She felt her terror mounting again. It was a severed chicken's head. Not one of the heads she had just cut off, but one of the ones Rolf used. As bait. After writing to the local council that a fox had killed sixteen chickens last year, they had been given permission to set a limited number of fox traps—so-called swan necks—at a certain radius around the farm, well off the beaten track. The best place to hide traps was underwater with the bait sticking up. After the fox had taken the bait, the trap snapped shut, breaking the neck of the animal and killing it instantly. At least in theory. She felt with her hand. When they had bought the traps at Jaktdepotet in Drammen, they had been told the springs were so strong that the jaws could break the leg of an adult, but she couldn't feel any pain in her frozen foot. Her fingers found the thin steel wire attached to the swan neck. She wouldn't be able to force open the trap without the lever, which was in the farm toolshed, and anyway they usually tied the swan neck to a tree with steel wire so that a half-dead fox, or anything else, would not be able to run off with the expensive equipment. Her hand traced the wire through the water and up onto the bank. There was the metal sign bearing their names, as per regulations.

She stiffened. Wasn't that a twig she heard breaking in the distance? She felt her heart pounding again as she stared into the dense murk.

Numb fingers followed the wire through the snow as she crawled up onto the bank of the stream. The wire was fastened around the trunk of a solid young birch tree. She searched for and found the knot under the snow. The metal had frozen into a stiff, unyielding lump. She had to open it, had to get away.

Another twig cracked. Closer this time.

She leaned against the trunk, on the opposite side to where she had heard the sound. Told herself not to panic, that the knot would come loose after she had yanked at it for a while, that her leg was intact, that the sounds she heard coming closer were made by a deer. She tried pulling at one end of the knot and didn't feel the pain when a fingernail broke down the middle. But it was no use. She bent over and her teeth crunched as she bit into the steel. Shit! She could hear light, quiet footsteps in the snow and held her breath. The steps paused somewhere on the other side of the tree. She might have been imagining things, but she thought she could hear it scenting the air, inhaling the smell. She sat utterly motionless. Then it began to move again. The sounds were softer. It was going away.

She took a deep, quivering breath. Now she would have to free herself. Her clothes were soaked and she would certainly freeze to death at night if no one found her. At that moment she remembered. The hatchet! She had forgotten the hatchet. The wire was thin. Put it on a stone, a couple of well-aimed blows and she would be free. The hatchet must have fallen in the stream. She crawled back into the black water, put her hands down and searched the stony bottom.

Nothing.

In despair, she sank to her knees, scanning the snow on both banks. And then she caught sight of the blade poking up out of the water six feet in front of her. And already she knew, before she felt the wire jerk, before she lay down flat in the water with the melted snow gurgling over her, so cold that she thought her heart would stop, stretching like a desperate beggar for the hatchet, already she knew that it was a foot too far. Her fingers curled around air a foot and a half from the handle. Tears came, but she forced them back; she could cry afterward.

"Is this what you're looking for?"

She had neither seen nor heard a thing. But in front of her sat a figure, crouched down. *It.* Sylvia scrambled back, but the figure followed with the hatchet held out to her.

"Just take it."

Sylvia got to her knees and took the hatchet.

"What are you going to do with it?" the voice asked.

Sylvia felt the fury surge up inside her, the fury that always accompanies fear, and the result was ferocious. She lunged forward with the hatchet raised and swung low with an outstretched arm. But the wire tugged at her; the hatchet just sliced the darkness and the next moment she was lying in the water again.

The voice chuckled.

Sylvia fell onto her side. "Go away," she groaned, spitting pebbles.

"I want you to eat snow," the voice said, getting up and briefly holding the side where the jacket had been slashed open.

"What?" Sylvia exclaimed, in spite of herself.

"I want you to eat snow until you piss yourself." The figure stood slightly outside the radius of the steel wire, tilted its head and watched Sylvia. "Until your stomach is so frozen and full that it can't melt the snow any longer. Until it's ice inside. Until you've become your true self. Something that can't feel."

Sylvia's brain perceived the words, but could not absorb the meaning. "Never!" she screamed.

A sound came from the figure and blended into the gurgle of the stream. "Now's the time to scream, dear Sylvia. For no one will hear you again. Ever."

Sylvia saw it raise something. Which lit up. A loop formed the outline of a red, glowing raindrop against the dark. It hissed and smoked as it came into contact with the surface of the stream. "You'll choose to eat snow. Believe me."

Sylvia realized with a paralyzing certainty that her final hour had come. There was only one possibility left. In the past minutes night had fallen quickly, but she tried to focus her gaze on the figure between the trees as she weighed the hatchet in her hand. The blood tingled in her fingers as it streamed back, seeming to know that this was the last chance. They had practiced this, she and the twins. On the barn wall. And every time she had thrown and one of them had pulled the hatchet out of the fox-shaped target, they had cheered with jubilation: "You killed the beast, Mommy! You killed the beast!" Sylvia put one foot slightly in front of the other. A one-step run-up, that was the optimum to get the right combination of power and accuracy.

"You're crazy," she whispered.

"Of that," the figure said, and Sylvia thought she could discern a little smile, "there is little doubt."

The hatchet whirled through the thick, almost tangible darkness with a low hum. Sylvia stood perfectly balanced with her right arm pointed forward and watched the lethal weapon. Watched it whistle through the trees. Heard it cut off a thin branch. Watched it disappear into the darkness and heard the dull thud as the hatchet buried itself in the snow somewhere deep in the forest.

She leaned back against the tree trunk and slowly slumped to the ground. Felt the tears come without attempting to stop them this time. Because now she knew. There would be no afterward.

"Shall we begin?" the voice said softly.

9

The Pit

"Was that *great* or what?"

Oleg's enthusiastic voice drowned out the spitting fat in the kebab shop, which was crowded with people after the concert at the Oslo Spektrum. Harry nodded to Oleg, who was standing in his hoodie, still sweaty, still moving to the beat as he prattled on about the members of Slipknot by name, names Harry didn't even know since Slipknot CDs were sparing with personal data, and music magazines like *MOJO* and *Uncut* didn't write about bands like that. Harry ordered hamburgers and looked at his watch. Rakel had said she would be standing outside at ten o'clock. Harry looked at Oleg again. He was talking nonstop. When had it happened? When had the boy turned eleven and decided to like music about various stages of death, alienation, freezing and general doom? Perhaps it ought to have worried Harry, but it didn't. It was a starting point, a curiosity that had to be satisfied, clothes the boy had to try on to see if they fit. Other things would come along. Better things. Worse things.

"You liked it, too, didn't you, Harry?"

Harry nodded. He didn't have the heart to tell him the concert had been a bit of an anticlimax for him. He couldn't put his finger on what it was; perhaps it just wasn't his night. As soon as they had joined the crowd in the Spektrum, he had felt the paranoia that used to regularly accompany drunkenness but that during the last year had come when he was sober. And instead of getting into the mood, he had had the feeling he was being observed, and stood scanning the audience, studying the wall of faces around them.

"Slipknot rules," Oleg said. "And the masks were übercool. Especially the one with the long, thin nose. It looked like a . . . sort of . . . "

Harry was listening with half an ear, hoping Rakel would come soon. The air inside the kebab shop suddenly felt dense and suffocating, like a thin film of grease lying on your skin and over your mouth. He tried not to think his next thought. But it was on its way, had already rounded the corner. The thought of a drink.

"It's an Indian death mask," a woman's voice behind them said. "And Slayer was better than Slipknot."

Harry spun around in surprise.

"Lots of posing with Slipknot, isn't there?" she continued. "Recycled ideas and empty gestures."

She was wearing a shiny, figure-hugging, ankle-length black coat buttoned up to her neck. All you could see under the coat was a pair of black boots. Her face was pale and her eyes made up.

"I would never have believed it," Harry said. "You liking that kind of music."

Katrine Bratt managed a brief smile. "I suppose I would say the opposite."

She gave him no further explanation and signaled to the man behind the counter that she wanted a Farris mineral water.

"Slayer sucks," Oleg mumbled under his breath.

Katrine turned to him. "You must be Oleg."

"Yes," Oleg said sulkily, pulling up his army trousers

and looking as if he both liked and disliked this attention from a mature woman. "How d'ya know?"

Katrine smiled. " 'How d'ya know?' Living on Holmenkollen Ridge as you do, shouldn't you say 'How do you know?'? Is Harry teaching you bad habits?"

Blood suffused Oleg's cheeks.

Katrine laughed quietly and patted Oleg's shoulder. "Sorry, I'm just curious."

The boy's face went so red that the whites of his eyes were shining.

"I'm also curious," Harry said, passing a burger to Oleg. "I assume you've found the pattern I asked for, Bratt. Since you've got time to come to a gig."

Harry looked at her in a way that spelled out his warning: Don't tease the boy.

"I've found something," Katrine said, twisting the plastic top off the Farris bottle. "But you're busy, so we can sort it out tomorrow."

"I'm not *so* busy," Harry said. He had already forgotten the film of grease, the feeling of suffocation.

"It's confidential and there are a lot of people here," Katrine said. "But I can whisper a couple of key words."

She leaned closer, and over the fat he could smell the almost masculine fragrance of perfume and feel her warm breath on his ear.

"A silver Volkswagen Passat has just pulled up outside. There's a woman sitting inside trying to catch your attention. I would guess it's Oleg's mother . . . "

Harry straightened up with a jolt and looked out the large window toward the car. Rakel had wound down the window and was peering in at them.

"Don't make a mess," Rakel said as Oleg jumped into the backseat with the burger in his hand.

Harry stood beside the open window. She was wearing a plain, light blue sweater. He knew that sweater well. Knew how it smelled, how it felt against the palm of his hand and cheek.

"Good gig?" she asked.

"Ask Oleg."

"What sort of band was it, actually?" She looked at Oleg in the mirror. "Those people outside are a bit oddly dressed."

"Quiet songs about love and so on," Oleg said, sending a quick wink to Harry when her eyes were off the mirror.

"Thank you, Harry," she said.

"My pleasure. Drive carefully."

"Who was that woman inside?"

"A colleague. New on the job."

"Oh? Looked as if you knew each other pretty well already."

"How so?"

"You . . . " She stopped in midsentence. Then she slowly shook her head and laughed. A deep but bright laugh that came from down in her throat. Confident and carefree at the same time. The laugh that had once made him fall in love.

"Sorry, Harry. Good night."

The window glided upward; the silver car glided off.

Harry walked the gauntlet down Brugata, between bars with music blaring out of open doors. He considered a coffee at Teddy's Softbar, but knew it would be a bad idea. So he made up his mind to walk on by.

"Coffee?" repeated the guy behind the counter in disbelief.

The jukebox at Teddy's was playing Johnny Cash, and Harry passed a finger over his top lip.

"You got a better suggestion?" Harry heard the voice that came out of his mouth; it was familiar and unfamiliar at the same time.

"Well," said the guy, running a hand through his oily, glistening hair, "the coffee's not exactly fresh from the machine, so what about a freshly pulled beer?"

Johnny Cash was singing about God, baptism and new promises.

"Right," Harry said.

The man behind the counter grinned.

At that moment Harry felt the mobile phone in his pocket vibrate. He grabbed it quickly and greedily, as though it were a call he had been expecting.

It was Skarre.

"We've just received a missing-persons call that fits. Married woman with children. She wasn't at home when the husband and children returned a few hours ago. They live way out in the woods in Sollihøgda. None of the neighbors have seen her and she can't have left by car because the husband had it. And there are no footprints on the path."

"Footprints?"

"There's still snow up there."

The beer was banged down in front of Harry.

"Harry? Are you there?"

"Yes, I am. I'm thinking."

"What about?"

"Is there a snowman there?"

"Eh?"

"Snowman."

"How should I know?"

"Well, let's go and find out. Jump in the car and pick me up outside Gunerius shopping center, on Storgata."

"Can't we do this tomorrow, Harry? I've got some action lined up for tonight, and this woman is only missing, so there's no immediate hurry."

Harry watched the foam coiling its way down the outside of the beer glass like a snake.

"Actually . . . ," Harry said, " . . . there's one hell of a hurry."

Amazed, the bartender looked at the untouched beer, the fifty-krone note on the counter and the broad shoulders making off through the door as Johnny Cash faded out.

"Sylvia would never have simply left," said Rolf Ottersen.

Rolf Ottersen was thin. Or, to be more precise, he was a bag of bones. His flannel shirt was buttoned all the way up, and from it protruded a gaunt neck and a head that reminded Harry of a wading bird. A pair of narrow hands with long, scrawny fingers that continually curled, twisted and twirled protruded from his shirtsleeves. The nails of his right hand had been filed long and sharp, like claws. His eyes, behind thick glasses in plain, round steel frames, the type that had been popular among seventies radicals, seemed unnaturally large. A poster on the mustard-yellow wall showed Indians carrying an anaconda. Harry recognized the cover of a Joni Mitchell LP from hippie Stone Age times. Next to it hung a reproduction of a well-known self-portrait by Frida Kahlo. A woman who suffered, Harry thought. A picture chosen by a woman. The floor was untreated pine, and the room was lit by a combination of old-fashioned paraffin lamps and brown clay lamps, which looked as if they might have been homemade. Leaning against the wall in the corner was a guitar with nylon strings, which Harry took to be the explanation for Rolf Ottersen's filed nails.

"What do you mean, she 'would never have left'?" Harry asked.

In front of him on the living-room table Rolf Ottersen had placed a photograph of his wife with their twin daughters, Olga and Emma, ten years old. Sylvia Ottersen had big, sleepy eyes, like someone who had worn glasses all her life and then started wearing contact lenses or had laser eye surgery. The twins had their mother's eyes.

"She would've said," Rolf Ottersen explained. "Left a message. Something must've happened."

In spite of his despair his voice was muted and gentle. Rolf Ottersen pulled a handkerchief from his trouser pocket and put it to his face. His nose seemed abnormally big for his narrow, pale face. He blew his nose in one single trumpet blast.

Skarre poked his head inside the door. "The dog patrol's here. They've got a cadaver dog with them."

"Get going, then," Harry said. "Have you spoken to all the neighbors?"

"Yep. Still nothing."

Skarre closed the door, and Harry saw that Ottersen's eyes had become even bigger behind the glasses.

"Cadaver dog?" Ottersen whispered.

"Just a generic term," Harry said, making a mental note that he would have to give Skarre a couple of tips on how to express himself.

"So you use them to search for living people as well?" From his intonation, the husband appeared to be pleading.

"Yes, of course," Harry lied, rather than tell him that cadaver dogs sniffed out places where dead bodies had been. They were not used for drugs, lost property or living people. They were used for deaths. Period.

"So you last saw her today at four," Harry said, looking down at his notes. "Before you and your daughters went to town. What did you do there?"

"I took care of the shop while the girls had their violin lessons."

"Shop?"

"We have a small shop in Majorstuen selling hand-made African goods. Art, furniture, fabric, clothes, all sorts of things. They're imported directly from the artisans, and the artisans are paid properly. Sylvia is there most of the time, but on Thursdays we're open late, so she comes back home with the car and I go in with the girls. I'm at the shop while they have violin lessons at the Barrat Due Institute of Music from five until seven. Then I pick them up, and we come home. We were home a little after seven-thirty."

"Mm. Who else works in the shop?"

"No one."

"That must mean you're closed for a while on Thursdays. About an hour?"

Rolf Ottersen gave a wry smile. "It's a very small shop. We don't have many customers. Almost none until the Christmas sales, to be honest."

"How . . . ?"

"NORAD. They support shops and our suppliers as part of the government's trade program with Third World countries." He coughed quietly. "The message it sends is more important than money and shortsighted gain, isn't it?"

Harry nodded, even though he wasn't thinking about development aid and fair trade in Africa but about the clock and driving time in Oslo. From the kitchen, where the twins were eating a late snack, came the sound of a radio. He hadn't seen a TV in the house.

"Thank you. We'll carry on." Harry got up and went outside.

Three cars stood parked in the yard. One was Bjørn
Holm's Volvo Amazon, repainted black with a checkered
rally stripe over the roof and trunk. Harry looked up at
the clear, starry sky arching over the tiny farm in the forest clearing. He breathed in the air. The air of spruce and
wood smoke. From the edge of the wood he heard the
panting of a dog and cries of encouragement from the
policeman.

To get to the barn Harry walked in the arc they had
determined so as not to destroy any clues they might be
able to use. Voices were emanating from the open door.
He crouched down and studied the footprints in the
snow in the light from the outside lamp. Then he stood
up, leaned against the frame and tugged out a pack of
cigarettes.

"Looks like a murder scene," he said. "Blood, bodies
and overturned furniture."

Bjørn Holm and Magnus Skarre fell silent, turned and
followed Harry's gaze. The big open room was lit by a
single bulb hanging from a cable wrapped around one of
the beams. At one end of the barn there was a lathe and,
behind it, a board with tools attached: hammers, saws, pli-
ers, drills. No electric gadgets. At the other end there was
a wire fence and behind it chickens perched on shelves in
the wall or strutted around, stiff-legged, on the straw. In
the middle of the room, on gray, untreated, bloodstained
floorboards, lay three headless bodies. Harry poked a cigarette between his lips without lighting it, entered, taking
care not to step in the blood, and squatted down beside
the chopping block to examine the chicken heads. The
beam from his flashlight focused on matte-black eyes.
First he held half a white feather that looked as if it had
been scorched black along the edge, then he studied the
smooth severing of the chickens' necks. The blood had

coagulated and was black. He knew this was a quick process, not much more than half an hour.

"See anything interesting?" asked Bjørn Holm.

"My brain has been damaged by my profession, Holm. Right now it's analyzing chickens' bodies."

Skarre laughed and painted the newspaper headlines in the air: "SAVAGE TRIPLE CHICKEN MURDER. VOODOO PARISH. HARRY HOLE ASSIGNED."

"What I can't see is more interesting," Harry said.

Bjørn Holm raised an eyebrow, looked around and began to nod slowly.

Skarre looked at them skeptically. "And that is?"

"The murder weapon," Harry said.

"A hatchet," Holm said. "The only sensible way to kill chickens."

Skarre sniffed. "If the woman did the killing, she must have put the hatchet back in its place. Tidy types, these farmers."

"I agree," Harry said, listening to the cackle of the chickens, which seemed to be coming from all sides. "That's why it's interesting that the chopping block is upside down and the chickens' bodies scattered around. And the hatchet is not in its place."

"Its place?" Skarre faced Holm and rolled his eyes.

"If you can be bothered to take a peek, Skarre," Harry said without moving.

Skarre was still looking at Holm, who nodded toward the board behind the lathe.

"Shit," said Skarre.

In the empty space between a hammer and a rusty saw was the outline of a small hatchet.

From outside came the sound of a dog barking and whimpering, and then the policeman's loud shout, which was no longer encouraging.

Harry rubbed his chin. "We've searched the whole barn, so for the moment it looks as if Sylvia Ottersen left the place while slaughtering the chickens, taking the hatchet with her. Holm, can you take the body temperatures of these chickens and estimate the time of death?"

"Yup."

"Eh?" Skarre said.

"I want to know when she ran off," Harry said. "Did you get anything from the shoe prints outside, Holm?"

The forensic officer shook his head. "Too trampled, and I need more light. I found several of Rolf Ottersen's boot prints. Plus a couple of others going *to* the barn, but none *from* the barn. Perhaps she was carried out of the barn?"

"Mm. Then the prints of the carrier would have been deeper. Shame no one stepped in the blood." Harry peered at the dark walls outside the range of the bulb. From the yard they heard a dog's pitiful whine and a policeman's furious curses.

"Go and see what's up, Skarre," Harry said.

Skarre went, and Harry switched the flashlight back on and walked toward the wall. He ran his hand along the unpainted boards.

"What's . . . ," Holm began, but stopped when Harry's boot hit the wall with a dull thud.

The starry sky came into view.

"A back door," Harry said, staring at the black forest and the silhouette of spruce trees against the dome of dirty-yellow light from the town in the distance. He shone the flashlight on the snow. The beam immediately found the tracks.

"Two people," Harry said.

"It's the dog," Skarre said on his return. "It won't budge."

"Won't budge?" Harry lit up the trail of footprints.

The snow reflected the light, but the trail vanished in the darkness beneath the trees.

"The dog handler doesn't understand. He says the dog seems petrified. At any rate it refuses to go into the forest."

"Perhaps it can smell fox," Holm said. "Lots of foxes in this forest."

"Foxes?" Skarre snorted. "That big dog can't be afraid of foxes."

"Perhaps it's never seen a fox," Harry said. "But it knows it can smell a predator. It's rational to be afraid of what you don't know. The dog that isn't won't live long." Harry could feel his heart begin to quicken. And he knew why. The forest. The dark. The type of terror that was not rational. The type that had to be overcome.

"This is to be treated as a crime scene until further notice," Harry said. "Start work. I'll check where this trail leads."

"OK."

Harry swallowed before stepping out the back door. It had been more than thirty years ago. And still his body bristled.

He had been staying at his grandparents' house in Åndalsnes during his autumn vacation. The farm lay on a hillside with the mighty Romsdal Mountains towering above. Harry had been ten and had gone into the forest to look for the cow his grandfather was searching for. He wanted to find it before his grandfather, before anyone. So he hurried. Ran like a maniac over hills of soft blueberry bushes and funny, crooked dwarf birch trees. The paths came and went as he ran in a straight line toward the bell he thought he had heard among the trees. And there it was again, a bit farther to the right now. He jumped over

a stream and ducked under a tree and his boots squelched
as he ran across a marsh with a rain cloud edging toward
him. He could see the veil of drizzle beneath the cloud
showering the steep mountainside.

And the rain was so fine that he had not noticed the
darkness descending; it slunk out of the marsh, it crept
between the trees, it spilled down through the shadows
of the mountainside like black paint and collected at the
bottom of the valley. He looked up at a large bird circling
high above, so dizzyingly high he could see the mountain
behind it. And then a boot got stuck and he fell. Face-
down and without anything to grab. Everything went
dark, and his nose and mouth were filled with the taste
of marsh, of death, decay and darkness. He could *taste*
the darkness for the few seconds he was under. And then
he came up again, and discovered that all the light had
gone. Gone across the mountain towering above him in
its silent, heavy majesty, whispering that he didn't know
where he was, that he hadn't known for a long time. Unaware that he had lost a boot, he stood up and began to
run. He would soon see something he recognized. But
the landscape seemed bewitched; rocks had become
heads of creatures growing up out of the ground, bushes
were fingers that scratched at his legs and dwarf birch
trees were witches bent with laughter as they pointed the
way, here or there, the way home or the way to perdi-
tion, the way to his grandparents' house or the way to
the Pit. Because adults had told him about the Pit. The
bottomless swamp where cattle, people and whole carts
vanished, never to return.

It was almost night when Harry tottered into the
kitchen and his grandmother hugged him and said that
his father, grandfather and all the adults from the neighboring farm were out looking for him. Where had he
been?

In the forest.

But hadn't he heard their shouts? They had been calling Harry; she had heard them calling Harry all the time.

He didn't remember it himself, but many times later he had been told that he had sat there trembling with cold on the wooden box in front of the stove, staring into the distance with an apathetic expression on his face, and had answered: "I didn't think it was them calling."

"Who did you think it was, then?"

"The others. Did you know that darkness has a *taste*, Grandma?"

Harry had walked barely a few yards into the forest when he was overtaken by an intense, almost unnatural silence. He shone the flashlight down on the ground in front of him because every time he pointed it into the forest, shadows ran between the trees like jittery spirits in the pitch black. Being isolated from the dark in a bubble of light didn't give him a sense of security. Quite the opposite. The certainty that he was the most visible object moving through the forest made him feel naked, vulnerable. The branches scraped at his face, like a blind man's fingers trying to identify a stranger.

The tracks led to a stream whose gurgling noise drowned his quickened breathing. One of the trails disappeared while the other followed the stream on lower ground.

He went on. The stream wound hither and thither, but he wasn't concerned about losing his bearings; all he had to do was retrace his steps.

An owl, which must have been close by, hooted an admonitory *to-wit-to-woo*. The dial on his watch glowed green and showed that he had been walking for more than fifteen minutes. Time to go back and send in the team with proper footwear, gear and a dog that was not afraid of foxes.

Harry's heart stopped.

It had darted past his face. Soundless and so fast that he hadn't seen anything. But the current of air had given it away. Harry heard the owl's wings beating in the snow and the piteous squeak of a small rodent that had just become its prey.

He slowly let out the air from his lungs. Shone the flashlight over the forest ahead one last time and turned to go back. Took one step, then came to a halt. He wanted to take another, two more, to get out. But he did what he had to do. Shone the light behind him. And there it was again. A glint, a reflection of light that should not be there in the middle of the black forest. He went closer. Looked back and tried to fix the spot in his mind. It was about fifty feet from the stream. He crouched down. Just the steel stuck up, but he didn't need to brush away the snow to see what it was. A hatchet. If there had been blood on it after the chickens were killed, it was gone now. There were no footprints around the hatchet. Harry shone the flashlight and saw a snapped twig on the snow a few yards away. Someone must have thrown the ax here with enormous strength.

At that moment Harry felt it again. The sensation he had had at the Spektrum earlier that evening. The sensation that he was being observed. Instinctively, he switched off the flashlight, and the darkness descended over him like a blanket. He held his breath and listened. Don't, he thought. Don't let it happen. Evil is not a thing. It cannot take possession of you. It's the opposite; it's a void, an absence of goodness. The only thing you can be frightened of here is yourself.

Harry switched on the flashlight and pointed it toward the clearing.

It was her. She stood erect and immobile between the trees, looking at him without blinking, with the same large, sleepy eyes as in the photograph. Harry's first thought was that she was dressed like a bride, in white, that she was standing at the altar, here, in the middle of the forest. The light made her glitter. Harry breathed in with a shiver and grabbed his mobile phone from his jacket pocket. Bjørn Holm answered after the second ring.

"Cordon off the whole area," Harry said. His throat felt dry, rough. "I'm calling in the troops."

"What's happened?"

"There's a snowman here."

"So?"

Harry explained.

"I didn't catch the last part," Holm shouted. "Poor coverage here . . . "

"The head," Harry repeated. "It belongs to Sylvia Ottersen."

The other end went quiet.

Harry told Holm to follow the footprints and hung up.

Then he crouched against a tree, buttoned his coat right up and switched off the flashlight to save the battery while he waited. Thinking he had almost forgotten what it tasted like, the darkness.

Part Two

10

Chalk

It was three-thirty in the morning and Harry was exhausted as he finally unlocked the door to his apartment. He undressed and went straight into the shower. Tried not to think as he let the burning jets of water numb his skin, massage his stiff muscles and thaw his frozen body. They had spoken to Rolf Ottersen, but the formal questioning would have to wait until the morning. At Sollihøgda they had quickly wrapped up the door-to-door inquiries with the neighbors; there weren't so many to ask. But the Crime Scene officers and the dogs were still at work and would be the whole night. They had a brief window of time before the evidence would become contaminated, melted or covered by snow. He turned off the shower. The air was gray with steam, and when he wiped the mirror a new layer of condensation immediately settled. It distorted his face and blurred the contours of his naked body.

Harry was brushing his teeth when the telephone rang. "Harry."

"Stormann, the mold man."

"You're up late," Harry said in surprise.

"Reckoned you were at work."

"Oh?"

"It was on the late-night news. Woman in Sollihøgda. Saw you in the background. I've got the results back."

"And?"

"You've got fungus. A hungry bugger, too. *Aspergillus versicolor.*"

"Which means?"

"That it can be any color. If and when it's seen. Apart from that, it means I'll have to take down more of your walls."

"Mm." Harry had a vague sense that he ought to show more interest and concern, or at least ask more questions. But he couldn't be bothered. Not at this hour.

"Feel free."

Harry hung up and closed his eyes. Waited for the ghosts, for the inevitable, just as long as he stayed away from the only medicine he knew for ghosts. Perhaps it would be a new acquaintance this time. He waited for her to come out of the forest, stumping along toward him on a huge white body without legs, a misshapen bowling ball with a head, black sockets with crows pecking at the remainder of her eyeballs, teeth bared after the foxes had helped themselves to the lips. Hard to know if she would come; the subconscious was unpredictable. So unpredictable that when Harry slept, he dreamed that he was lying in a bath with his head underwater listening to a deep rumble of bubbles and women's laughter. Sea grass grew on the white enamel, stretching out for him like green fingers on a white hand seeking his.

The morning light cast rectangles over the newspapers lying on POB Gunnar Hagen's desk. It lit up Sylvia Ottersen's smile and the headlines on the front pages.

KILLED AND DECAPITATED, DECAPITATED IN THE FOREST
and—the shortest and probably the best—DECAPITATED.

Harry's head had ached from the moment he woke
up. Now he was holding it gingerly in his hands, thinking that he might as well have had a drink last night—it
wouldn't have made the pain any worse. He wanted to
close his eyes, but Hagen was staring straight at him.
Harry noticed that Hagen's mouth kept opening, twisting and closing—in short that he was formulating words
that Harry was receiving on a badly tuned frequency.

"The conclusion . . . ," Hagen said, and Harry knew
it was time to prick up his ears, "is that this case has top
priority from now on. And that means, of course, that we
will increase the size of your investigation team immediately and—"

"Disagree," Harry said. Just articulating a single word
invoked a sense that his cranium was exploding. "We can
requisition more people as and when, but for the moment I don't want anyone else at the meetings. Four is
enough."

Gunnar Hagen looked dumbfounded. In murder
cases, even the straightforward ones, investigation teams
always comprised at least a dozen people.

"Free thinking functions best in small groups," Harry
added.

"Thinking?" Hagen burst out. "What about standard
police work? Following up forensic evidence, questioning, checking tips? And what about the coordination of
information? A total of—"

Harry held up a hand to stem the flow of words.
"That's just the point. I don't want to drown in all that."

"Drown?" Hagen stared at Harry in disbelief. "I'd
better give the case to someone who can swim, then."

Harry massaged his temples. Right now there was no

one in the Crime Squad apart from Inspector Hole who could lead a murder case such as this one, and both Hagen and Harry knew it. Harry also knew that giving the case to the central investigation bureau, Kripos, would be such a huge loss of prestige for the new POB that he would rather sacrifice his extremely hirsute right arm.

Harry sighed. "Normal investigation teams fight to stay afloat in the stream of information. And that's when it's a *standard* case. With decapitations on the front pages . . . " Harry shook his head. "People have gone mad. We received more than a hundred calls just after the news item last night. You know, drunks slurring and the usual nuts, plus a few new ones. People telling you that the murder was described in the Book of Revelation, that sort of thing. So far today we've had two hundred calls. And just wait until it emerges that there may be several bodies. Let's say we have to set aside twenty people to take care of the calls. They check them out and write reports. Let's say that the team leader has to spend two hours every day physically going through the incoming data, two hours coordinating it and two hours assembling everyone in groups, updating them, answering their questions, and half an hour editing the information that can be revealed at the press conference. Which takes forty-five minutes. The worst part is"—Harry put his forefingers against his aching jaw muscles and grimaced—"that in a standard murder case this is, I suppose, a good use of resources. Because there will always be those out there who know something, who have heard or seen something. Information that we can painstakingly piece together or that enables us to magically solve the whole case."

"Exactly," Hagen said. "That's why—"

"The problem is," Harry continued, "this is not that kind of case. Not that kind of killer. This person has not

confided in a friend or shown his face in the vicinity of the
murder. No one out there knows anything, so the calls
that come in won't help us, they'll just delay us. And any
possible forensic clues we uncover have been left there to
confuse us. In a nutshell, this is a different kind of game."

Hagen had leaned back in his chair and pressed his fingertips together, and, immersed in thought, he was now
observing Harry. He blinked like a basking lizard, then
asked: "So you see this as a game?"

As he nodded, Harry wondered where Hagen was going.

"What sort of game? Chess?"

"Well," Harry said, "blindfold chess, maybe."

Hagen nodded. "So you envisage a classic serial killer,
a cold-blooded murderer with superior intelligence and a
proclivity for fun, games and challenges?"

Now Harry had an idea where Hagen was going.

"A man straight from the serial killings you profiled
in that FBI course? The kind you met in Australia that
time? A person who"—the POB smacked his lips as if he
were tasting the words—"is basically a worthy opponent
for someone of your background."

Harry sighed. "That's not how I think, boss."

"Don't you? Remember, I've taught at the military
academy, Harry. What do you think aspiring generals
dream about when I tell them how military strategists
have personally changed the course of world history? Do
you think they dream about sitting around quietly hoping
for peace, about telling their grandchildren that they just
lived, that no one would ever know what they might have
been capable of? They might say they want peace, but
inside they dream, Harry. About having one opportunity.
There's a strong social urge in man to be *needed*. That's
why generals in the Pentagon paint the blackest scenario

as soon as a firecracker goes off anywhere in the world. I think you *want* this case to be special, Harry. You want it so much that you can see the blackest of the black."

"The snowman, boss. You remember the letter I showed you?"

Hagen sighed. "I remember a madman, Harry."

Harry knew he ought to give in now. Put forward the compromise suggestion he had already concocted. Give Hagen this little victory. Instead he shrugged. "I want to have my group as it is, boss."

Hagen's face closed, hardened. "I can't let you do that, Harry."

"Can't?"

Hagen held Harry's gaze, but then it happened. Hagen blinked; his eyes wandered. Just for a fraction of a second, but it was enough.

"There are other considerations," Hagen said.

Harry tried to maintain an innocent expression as he twisted the knife. "What sort of considerations, boss?"

Hagen looked down at his hands.

"What do you think? Senior officers. The press. Politicians. If we still haven't got the murderer after three months, who do you think will have to answer questions about the unit's priorities? Who will have to explain why we put four people on this case because small groups are better suited to"—Hagen spat out the words like rotten shrimps—"free thinking and games of chess? Have you considered that, Harry?"

"No," Harry said, crossing his arms on his chest. "I've thought about how we'll catch this guy, not about how I'm going to justify not catching him."

Harry knew it was a cheap shot, but the words hit home. Hagen blinked twice. Opened his mouth and shut it again, and Harry instantly felt ashamed. Why did he always have to instigate these childish, meaningless wall-

pissing contests, just to have the satisfaction of giving
someone else—anyone at all—the finger? Rakel had once
said that he wished he'd been born with an extra middle
finger that was permanently sticking up.

"There's a man in Kripos called Espen Lepsvik,"
Harry said. "He's good at leading large investigations. I
can talk to him, get him to set up a group that reports to
me. The groups will work in parallel and independently.
You and the chief superintendent take care of the press
conference. How does that sound, boss?"

Harry didn't need to wait for an answer. He could see
the gratitude in Hagen's eyes. And he knew he'd won the
pissing contest.

The first thing Harry did when he was back in his own
office was to call Bjørn Holm.

"Hagen said yes, it's going to be as I said. Meeting in
my office in half an hour. Will you call Skarre and Bratt?"

He put down the phone. Thought about what Hagen
had said about hawks wanting their own war. And pulled
out the drawer in a vain hunt for an aspirin.

"Apart from the footprints, we haven't found a single
trace of the perp at what we assume is the crime scene,"
Magnus Skarre said. "What's harder to understand is
how we haven't found a trace of the body, either. After all,
he cut off the woman's head—there ought to have been
masses of evidence left behind. But there was nothing.
The dogs didn't even react! It's a mystery."

"He killed and decapitated the woman in the stream,"
Katrine said. "Her footprints came to an end farther up
the stream, didn't they? She ran in the water so as not to
leave prints, but he caught up with her."

"What did he use?" Harry asked.

"Hatchet or a saw—what else?"

"What about the burn marks around the skin where he cut?"

Katrine looked at Skarre and they both shrugged.

"OK, Holm, check that out," Harry said. "And then?"

"Then maybe he carried her through the stream down to the road," Skarre said. He had slept for two hours and his sweater was on back to front, but no one had had the heart to tell him. "I say *maybe* because we've found nothing there, either. And we should have. A streak of blood on a tree trunk, a lump of flesh on a branch or a shred of clothing. But we found his footprints where the stream flows under the road. And beside the road there were imprints in the snow of what might have been a body. But, for Christ's sake, the dogs didn't pick it up. Not even the damn cadaver dog! It's a—"

"Mystery," Harry repeated, rubbing his chin. "Isn't it pretty impractical to cut off her head while standing in a stream? It's just a narrow ditch. You wouldn't have enough elbow room. Why?"

"Obvious," Skarre said. "The evidence is carried away with the water."

"Not obvious," retorted Harry. "He left her head, so he's not worried about leaving any traces. Why there's no trace of her on the way down to the road—"

"Body bag!" said Katrine. "I've just been wondering how he managed to carry her so far in that terrain. In Iraq they used body bags with straps like a rucksack."

"Mm," Harry said. "That would explain why the cadaver dog didn't pick up a scent by the road."

"And why he could risk letting her lie there," Katrine said.

"Lie there?" Skarre queried.

"The imprint of a body in the snow. He put her there while he went to fetch his car. Which was probably parked somewhere near the Ottersen farm. That would've taken half an hour—don't you agree?"

Skarre mumbled a grudging "Something like that."

"The bags are black, look like run-of-the-mill garbage bags to anyone passing in a car."

"No one drove past," Skarre said sourly, stifling a yawn. "We've spoken to everyone up in that damn forest."

Harry nodded. "What should we think about Rolf Ottersen's story about him being in his shop between five and seven?"

"The alibi isn't worth shit if there weren't any customers," Skarre said.

"He might've driven there and back while the twins were having their violin lessons," Katrine said.

"But he's not the type," Skarre said, leaning back in the chair and nodding as if to corroborate his own conclusion.

Harry was tempted to make a sweeping statement about the prevailing assumption on the part of the police that they could tell a murderer when they saw one, but this was the phase when everyone was supposed to say what he or she thought without fear of contradiction. In his experience, the best ideas originated from flights of fancy, half-baked guesswork and erroneous snap judgments.

The door opened.

"Howdy!" sang out Bjørn Holm. " 'Pologies all around, but I've been on the trail of the murder weapon."

He pulled off his waterproof jacket and hung it on Harry's coatrack, which was tilting wildly. Underneath he was wearing a pink shirt with yellow embroidery and a legend on the back proclaiming that Hank Williams—despite all evidence that he died in the winter of 1953—

was alive. Then he flung himself down on the last free chair and looked at the others' upturned faces.

"What's up?" He smiled, and Harry waited for Holm's favorite one-liner. Which was not long in coming. "Someone die?"

"The murder weapon," Harry said. "Come on."

Holm grinned and rubbed his hands together. "I was wondering of course where the burn marks on Sylvia Ottersen's neck came from. The pathologist didn't have a clue. She just said that the small arteries had been cauterized, the same way you stop amputations from bleeding. Before the leg's sawn off. And when she talked about sawing, that made me think of something. As you know, I grew up on a farm . . . "

Bjørn Holm leaned forward, his eyes alight, reminding Harry of a father about to open a Christmas present, a big train set he has bought for his newborn son.

"If a cow was calving, and the calf was already dead, sometimes the carcass was too big for the cow to force out unaided. And if, on top of that, it was lying crooked, we couldn't get it out without risking injury to the cow. In that case the vet would have to use a saw."

Skarre grimaced.

"It's a sort of very thin, flexible blade-type thing you can put inside a cow, kind of around the calf, like a noose. And then you pull and wriggle the blade to and fro, and cut through the body." Holm demonstrated with his hands. "Until it's in two parts, and you can take out half the carcass. And then as a rule the problem's solved. As a rule. Because the blade sometimes cuts the mother too as it goes to and fro inside her, and the mother bleeds to death. So a couple of years ago some French farmers came up with a practical gadget that solved the problem. A looped electric filament that can burn through flesh.

There's a plain plastic handle with a dead thin, super-strong metal wire attached to each end of the handle, forming a loop you can put around whatever you want to cut off. Then you switch on the heat. The wire is white hot in fifteen seconds, and you press a button on the handle and the loop begins to tighten and cut through the body. There's no sideways movement and thus less chance of cutting the mother. And if you should cut her, there are two further advantages—"

"Are you trying to sell us this instrument or what?" Skarre asked with a grin, searching Harry's eyes for a re-action.

"Because of the temperature the wire is perfectly ster-ile," Holm continued. "It doesn't transmit bacteria or poisoned blood from the carcass. And the heat cauterizes the small arteries and restricts the bleeding."

"OK," Harry said. "Do you know for certain that he used a tool like this?"

"No," Holm said. "I could've tested it if I'd got hold of one, but the vet I spoke to said that electric cutting loops haven't been approved by the Norwegian Ministry of Ag-riculture yet." He looked at Harry with an expression of deep and heartfelt regret.

"Well," Harry said, "if it isn't the murder weapon, it would at least explain how he could have cut off her head while standing in the stream. What do the rest of you think?"

"France," Katrine Bratt said. "First the guillotine and now this."

Skarre puckered his lips and shook his head. "Sounds too weird. Anyway, where did he get hold of this loop gizmo? If it isn't approved, I mean?"

"We can start looking there," Harry said. "Would you check that out, Skarre?"

"I said I don't believe all that stuff."

"Sorry, I didn't make myself clear. I meant to say: Check it out, Skarre. Anything else, Holm?"

"No. There must've been masses of blood at the crime scene, but the only blood we found was in the barn after the chickens had been slaughtered. Speaking of the chickens, their body temperatures and the room temperature showed that they were killed at approximately half past six. Bit unsure, though, 'cause one chicken was warmer than the other two."

"Must've been feverish." Skarre laughed.

"And the snowman?" Harry asked.

"You don't find fingerprints on piles of snow crystals changing form from one hour to the next, but you ought to be able to find scraps of skin, since the crystals are sharp. Possibly fibers from gloves or mittens, if he wore them. But we didn't find either."

"Rubber gloves," Katrine said.

"Otherwise not a sniff," Holm said.

"OK. At least we have a head. Have you checked the teeth—?"

Harry was interrupted by Holm, who had straightened up with an offended expression on his face. "For traces left on her teeth? Her hair? Fingerprints on her neck? Other things forensic officers don't think about?"

Harry nodded a "Sorry" and checked his watch. "Skarre, even if you don't think Rolf Ottersen is the type, find out where he was and what he was doing at the time Birte Becker disappeared. I'll have a chat with Filip Becker. Katrine, you hunker down with all the missing-persons cases, including these two, and look for matches."

"OK," she said.

"Compare everything," Harry said. "Time of death, phase of moon, what was on TV, hair color of victims, whether any of them borrowed the same book from the library or attended the same seminar, the sum of their telephone numbers. We have to know how he selects them."

"Hang on a moment," Skarre said. "Have we already decided that there is a connection? Shouldn't we be open to all possibilities?"

"You can be as open as you fucking like," Harry said, getting up and making sure his car keys were in his pocket. "As long as you do what your boss says. Last person turns off the light."

Harry was waiting for the elevator when he heard someone coming. The footsteps stopped right behind him.

"I spoke to one of the twins during the school recess this morning."

"Oh, yes?" Harry turned to Katrine Bratt.

"I asked what they'd been doing on Tuesday."

"Tuesday?"

"The day Birte Becker disappeared."

"Exactly."

"She, her sister and her mother were in town. She remembered that because they were at the Kon-Tiki Museum looking for a toy after a visit to the doctor. And they spent the night at an aunt's while their mother was visiting a girlfriend. The father was at home keeping an eye on the house. Alone."

She was standing so close that Harry could smell her perfume. It wasn't like anything he had ever known a woman to wear. Very spicy, nothing sweet about it.

"Mm. Which twin did you speak to?"

Katrine Bratt held his gaze. "No idea. Does it matter?"

A *pling* told Harry that the elevator had reached their floor.

*   *   *

Jonas was drawing a snowman. The idea was to make it smile and sing, to make it a happy snowman. But he couldn't get it right; it just stared back at him blankly from the enormous white sheet. Around him in the large auditorium, there was hardly a sound, just the scratch of his father's chalk, now and then a bang on the board in front of him and the whisper of students' ballpoint pens on paper. He didn't like pens. If you used a pen you couldn't rub it out, you couldn't change anything, what you drew was there forever. He had woken up today thinking that his mother was back, that everything was fine again, and he'd run into her bedroom. But his father had been in there getting dressed and he told Jonas to get dressed as well because he was going to the university today. Pens.

The room sloped down to where his father stood and was like a theater auditorium. His father had not said a word to the students, not even when he and Jonas entered. Just nodded to them, pointed to the seat where Jonas was to sit and went straight to the board and began to write. And the students were clearly used to that, for they had been sitting ready and started taking notes at once. The boards were covered with numbers and small letters and a few strange doodles that Jonas did not recognize. His father had once explained to him that physics had its own language, one that he used to tell stories. When Jonas asked if they were adventure stories, his father had laughed and said that physics could be used only to explain things that were true, that it was a language that couldn't lie if it tried.

Some of the doodles were funny. And very elegant.

Chalk dust floated down onto his father's shoulders. A fine white layer settled like snow on his jacket. Jonas looked at his father's back and tried to draw him. But this didn't turn out to be a happy snowman, either. And suddenly the lecture room went absolutely still. All the pens stopped writing. Because the piece of chalk had stopped. It stood motionless at the top of the board, so high up that his father had to stretch his arm over his head to reach. And now it looked as if the chalk was stuck and his father was hanging from the board, like when Wile E. Coyote was hanging from a tiny branch on a cliff face and it was a very, very long way down. Then his father's shoulders began to shake, and Jonas thought he was trying to free the chalk, get it to move again, but it wouldn't. A ripple ran through the auditorium as if all the students were opening their mouths and sucking in breath at the same moment. Then his father freed the chalk at last, walked to the exit without turning and was gone. He's going to get some more chalk, Jonas thought. The buzz of students' voices around him grew gradually louder. He caught two words: "wife" and "missing." He looked at the board, which was almost completely covered. His father had been trying to write that she was dead, but the chalk could say only what was true, so it had got stuck. Jonas tried to rub out his snowman. Around him people were packing up their things, and the seats banged as they got up and left.

A shadow fell over the failed snowman on the paper, and Jonas looked up.

It was the policeman, the tall one with the ugly face and the kind eyes.

"Would you like to come with me, and we'll see if we can find your father?" he asked.

Harry knocked gently on the office door with the sign saying PROF. FILIP BECKER.

As there was no answer, he opened it.

The man behind the desk raised his head from his hands. "Did I say you could come in . . . "

He paused when he saw Harry. And shifted his gaze down to the boy standing next to him.

"Jonas!" Filip Becker said, the tone somewhere between bewilderment and a reprimand. His eyes were red-rimmed. "Didn't I say you should sit quietly?"

"I brought him with me," Harry said.

"Oh?" Becker looked at his watch and stood up.

"Your students have left," Harry said.

"Have they?" Becker dropped back into his chair. "I . . . I only meant to give them a break."

"I was there," Harry said.

"Were you? Why . . . "

"We all need a break once in a while. Can we have a chat?"

"I didn't want him to go to school," Becker explained after sending Jonas into the coffee room with instructions to wait there. "All the questions, speculation; I quite simply didn't want it. Well, I'm sure you understand."

"Yes." Harry took out a pack of cigarettes, shot Becker a questioning look and put it back when the professor firmly shook his head. "That, at any rate, is much easier to understand than what was on the board."

"It's quantum physics."

"Sounds weird."

"The world of atoms is weird."

"In what way?"

"They break our most fundamental physical laws. Like the one about an object not being able to be in two places at the same time. Niels Bohr once said that if you aren't profoundly shocked by quantum physics, then you haven't understood it."

"But you understand it?"

"No—are you crazy? It's pure chaos. But I prefer that chaos to this chaos."

"Which one?"

Becker sighed. "Our generation has turned itself into servants and secretaries of our children. That applies to Birte as well, I'm afraid. There are so many appointments and birthdays and favorite foods and soccer practices that it drives me insane. Today someone rang from a doctor's office in Bygdøy because Jonas hadn't turned up for an appointment. And this afternoon he has training God knows where, and his generation has never heard of the possibility of catching a bus."

"What's wrong with Jonas?" Harry took out the notepad he never wrote in; in his experience it seemed to focus people's minds.

"Nothing. Standard checkup, I assume." Becker dismissed it with an irritated flick of the hand. "And I assume you're here for a different reason?"

"Yes," Harry said. "I want to know where you were yesterday afternoon and evening."

"What?"

"Just routine, Becker."

"Has this anything to do with . . . with . . . " Becker nodded toward the *Dagbladet* newspaper lying on top of a pile of papers.

"We don't know," Harry said. "Just answer me, please."

"Tell me, are you all out of your minds?"

Harry looked at his watch without answering.

Becker groaned. "All right, I do want to help you. Last night I sat here working on an article about wavelengths of hydrogen, which I hope to have published."

"Any colleagues who can vouch for you?"

"The reason that Norwegian research contributes so little to the world is that the self-satisfaction of Norwegian academics is surpassed only by their indolence. I was, as usual, utterly on my own."

"And Jonas?"

"He made himself some food and sat watching TV until I got home."

"Which was when?"

"Just past nine, I think."

"Mm." Harry pretended to take notes. "Have you been through Birte's things?"

"Yes."

"Found anything?"

Filip Becker stroked the corner of his mouth with one finger and shook his head. Harry held his gaze, using the silence as leverage. But Becker had shut up shop.

"Thank you for your help," Harry said, stuffing his notepad into his jacket pocket and getting up. "I'll tell Jonas he can come in."

"Give me a moment, please."

Harry found the coffee room where Jonas was sitting and drawing, the tip of his tongue poking out from his mouth. He stood beside the boy, peering down at the paper on which, for the moment, were two uneven circles.

"A snowman."

"Yes," Jonas said, glancing up. "How could you see that?"

"Why was your mother taking you to the doctor's, Jonas?"

"Don't know." Jonas drew a head on the snowman.

"What's the name of the doctor?"

"Don't know."

"Where was it?"

"I'm not allowed to tell anyone. Not even Dad." Jonas leaned over the paper and drew hair on the snowman's head. Long hair.

"I'm a policeman, Jonas. I'm trying to find your mother."

The pencil scratched harder and harder, and the hair became blacker and blacker.

"I don't know what the place's called."

"Do you remember anything nearby?"

"The king's cows."

"The king's cows?"

Jonas nodded. "The woman sitting behind the window is called Borghild. I got a lollipop because I let her take blood with one of those needles."

"Are you drawing anything in particular?" Harry asked.

"No," Jonas said, concentrating on the eyelashes.

Filip Becker stood by the window watching Harry Hole cross the parking lot. Lost in thought, he slapped the small black notebook against the palm of his hand. He was wondering whether Hole had believed him when he pretended not to know that the policeman had attended his lecture. Or when he said he had been working on an article the previous evening. Or that he hadn't found anything among Birte's things. The black notebook had been in her desk drawer; she hadn't even made an attempt to conceal it. And what was written there . . .

He almost had to laugh. The simpleton had believed she could trick him.

Death Mask

Katrine Bratt was bent over her computer when Harry poked his head in.

"Find any matches?"

"Nothing much," Katrine said. "All the women had blue eyes. Apart from that they're all quite different in appearance. They all had husbands and children."

"I have somewhere we can begin," Harry said. "Birte Becker took Jonas to a doctor close to the 'king's cows.' That has to be the royal Kongsgården estate in Bygdøy. And you said the twins were at the Kon-Tiki Museum after a visit to the doctor's. Also Bygdøy. Filip Becker didn't know anything about the doctor, but Rolf Ottersen might."

"I'll call him."

"Then come and see me."

In his office Harry picked up the handcuffs, put one around his wrist and smacked the other against the table leg while listening to his voice mail. Rakel said Oleg was bringing a pal along to the skating rink Valle Hovin. The message was unnecessary. He knew it was a reminder in disguise, in case Harry had forgotten the whole thing. To date, Harry had never forgotten an arrangement with Oleg, but he accepted these little nudges that others might have taken as a declaration of mistrust. Indeed, what was more, he *liked* them. Because it said something about what kind of mother she was. And because she disguised the reminder so as not to offend him.

Katrine walked in without knocking.

"Kinky," she said, nodding toward the table leg Harry was cuffed to. "But I like it."

"Single-handed speed-cuffing." Harry smiled. "Some crap I picked up in the States."

"You should try the new Hiatt speed cuffs. You don't even need to think whether you're going to approach from the left or the right—the cuff arm will close around your wrist or whatever, so long as you get a clean hit. And then you practice with two sets of cuffs, one around each wrist, so that you have two attempts at hitting."

"Mm." Harry unlocked the handcuffs. "What's on your mind?"

"Rolf Ottersen hasn't heard of any doctor's appointment or any doctor in Bygdøy. In fact, they have their own doctor in Bærum. I can ask the twins if either of them remembers the doctor, or we can call the doctors in Bygdøy and check ourselves. There are only four of them. Here."

She put a yellow Post-it on his desk.

"They aren't allowed to disclose names of patients," he said.

"I'll talk to the twins when they're back from school."

"Wait," Harry said, lifting the telephone and dialing the first number.

A nasal voice answered with the name of the practice.

"Is Borghild there?" Harry asked.

No Borghild.

At the second number an equally nasal answering machine said that the office received calls only during a restricted two-hour period, and this had passed some time ago.

Finally, at the fourth attempt, a chirpy, almost laughing voice gave him what he had been hoping for.

"Yes, that's me."

"Hello, Borghild, this is Inspector Harry Hole, Oslo Police."

"Date of birth?"

"Sometime in spring. I'm calling about a murder case. I assume you've read the papers today. What I want to know is whether you saw Sylvia Ottersen last week?"

There was silence at the other end of the line.

"One moment," she said.

Harry heard her getting up, and waited. Then she was back. "I'm sorry, Herr Hole. Information about patients is confidential. And I think the police know that."

"We do. But if I'm not mistaken, it's the daughters who are patients, not Sylvia."

"Nevertheless. You're asking for information that indirectly might reveal the identities of our patients."

"I would remind you that this is a murder investigation."

"I would remind you that you can come back to us with a search warrant. We might perhaps be more guarded with patient information than most, but that's the nature of our work."

"Nature of your work?"

"Our areas of expertise."

"Which are?"

"Plastic surgery and specialist operations. See our Web site—www.kirklinikk.no."

"Thank you, but I think I've learned enough for the time being."

"If you say so."

She put down the phone.

"Well?" Katrine asked.

"Jonas and the twins have been to the same doctor," Harry said, leaning back in the chair. "And that means we're in business."

Harry could feel the adrenaline rush, the trembling that always came when he got the first scent of the brute. And after the rush came the Great Obsession. Which was everything at once: love and intoxication, blindness and clear-sightedness, meaning and madness. Colleagues spoke now and then about excitement, but this was something else, something special. He had never told anyone about the Obsession or made any attempt to analyze it. He hadn't dared. All he knew was that it helped him, drove him, fueled the job he was appointed to perform. He didn't want to know any more. He really didn't.

"And now?" Katrine asked.

Harry opened his eyes and leapt off his seat. "Now we're going shopping."

The shop Taste of Africa was situated close to the busiest street in Majorstuen, Bogstadveien. But unfortunately its location fifty feet down a side street meant that it was still on the periphery.

A bell rang as Harry and Katrine entered. In the muted lighting—or, to be more precise, the lack of lighting—Harry saw brightly colored coarse-weave rugs, sarong-like materials, large cushions with West African patterns, small coffee tables that looked as if they had been carved straight out of the rainforest and tall, thin wooden figures representing Masai tribesmen and a selection of the savannah's best-known animals. Everything seemed carefully planned and executed: There were no visible price tags, the colors complemented one another and the products were placed in pairs as if in Noah's ark.

In short, it looked more like an exhibition than a shop. A somewhat dusty exhibition. This impression was reinforced by the almost unnatural stillness after the door closed behind them and the bell stopped ringing.

"Hello?" called a voice from inside the shop.

Harry followed the sound. In the darkness at the back of the room, behind an enormous wooden giraffe and illuminated only by a single spotlight, he saw the back of a woman who was standing on a chair. She was hanging up a grinning wooden black mask on the wall.

"What is it?" she said without turning.

She gave the impression she was conditioned to expect the unexpected, but not customers.

"We're from the police."

"Oh, yes." The woman turned and the spotlight fell on her face. Harry felt his heart stop, and he automatically took a step back. It was Sylvia Ottersen.

"Something wrong?" she asked with a frown between the lenses of her glasses.

"Who . . . are you?"

"Ane Pedersen," she said, instantly understanding the reason for Harry's perplexed expression. "I'm Sylvia's sister. We're twins."

Harry began to cough.

"This is Inspector Harry Hole," he heard Katrine say behind him. "And I'm Katrine Bratt. We were hoping to find Rolf here."

"He's at the funeral parlor." Ane Pedersen paused, and at that moment all three of them knew what the others were thinking: How do you actually bury a head?

"And you've stepped into the breach?" Katrine said, rallying.

Ane Pedersen smiled briefly. "Yes." She stepped down from the chair with care, still holding the wooden mask.

"Ceremonial or spiritual mask?" Katrine asked.

"Ceremonial," she said. "Hutu. Eastern Congo."

Harry looked at his watch. "When will he be back?"

"I don't know."

"Any guesses?"

"As I said, I don't—"

"That really is a beautiful mask," Katrine interrupted. "You've been to the Congo, and you bought it yourself, didn't you?"

Ane gave her a look of amazement. "How did you know?"

"I can see by the way you're holding it, not covering the eyes or mouth. You respect the spirits."

"Are you interested in masks?"

"Sort of," Katrine said, pointing to a black mask with small arms at the side and legs hanging underneath. The face was half human, half animal. "That's a Kpelie mask, isn't it?"

"Yes, from the Ivory Coast. Senufo."

"A power mask?" Katrine ran a hand over the stiff, greasy animal hair hanging off the coconut shell at the top of the mask.

"Wow, you do know a lot," Ane said.

"What's a power mask?" Harry asked.

"What it says," Ane answered. "In Africa masks like these are not just empty symbols. A person wearing this type of mask in the Lo community automatically has all executive and judicial power bestowed upon him. No one questions the authority of the wearer; the mask confers power."

"I saw two death masks hanging by the door," Katrine said. "Very beautiful."

Ane smiled in response. "I have several of them. They're from Lesotho."

"Can I have a look?"

"Of course. Wait here a moment."

She was gone, and Harry looked at Katrine.

"I just thought it might be useful to have a chat with her," she said, to answer his unspoken question. "To check if there were any family secrets, you understand?"

"I understand. And you'd do that best on your own."

"You've got something to do?"

"I'll be in my office. If Rolf Ottersen turns up, remember to get a written statement waiving patient confidentiality."

By the door, as he left, Harry cast a glance at the human faces, leathery, shrunken and frozen in a scream. He assumed they were imitations.

Eli Kvale trundled her shopping cart between the shelves of the ICA supermarket at Ullevål Stadium. It was huge. A bit more expensive than other supermarkets, but with a much better selection. She didn't come here every day, only when she wanted to make something nice. And tonight her son, Trygve, was coming home from the States. He was in his third year of economics at a university in Montana, but didn't have any exams this autumn and was going to study at home until January. Andreas would drive straight from the church office to pick him up at Gardermoen Airport. And she knew that by the time they were home they would be deep in conversation about fly-fishing and canoe trips.

She leaned over the freezer and felt the cold rise as a shadow passed her. And without looking up she knew it was the same one. The same shadow that had passed her when she was standing by the fresh-food counter, and in the parking lot when she was locking the car. It meant nothing. It was just the old stuff surfacing. She had come to terms with the fact that her fears would never quite let go, even though it was half a human lifetime away now.

At the checkout she chose the longest line; her experience was that this was generally the quickest. Or at least she thought it was her experience. Andreas believed she was mistaken. Someone joined the line behind her. So there were more mistaken people, she noted. She didn't turn around, just thought the person must have been carrying a load of frozen goods: She could feel the cold on her back.

But when she did turn around, there was no longer anyone there. Her eyes wanted to scour the other lines. Don't start, she thought. Don't start this again.

Once outside, she forced herself to walk slowly to the car, not to look around, to unlock the car, put in the groceries, sit down and drive off. And as the Toyota slowly crawled up the long hills to the duplex apartment in Nordberg, her mind was on Trygve and the dinner that had to be ready the moment he and Andreas came in through the door.

Harry was listening to Espen Lepsvik on the telephone and gazing up at the photographs of his dead colleagues. Lepsvik already had his group assembled and was asking Harry for access to all the relevant information.

"You'll get a password from our IT boss," Harry said. "Then you go into the folder labeled 'The Snowman' on the Crime Squad network."

"The Snowman?"

"Got to be called something."

"OK. Thanks, Hole. How often do you want reports from me?"

"Just when you've got something. And, Lepsvik?"

"Yes?"

"Keep off our turf."

"And what exactly is your turf?"

"You concentrate on tips, witnesses and ex-cons who might be possible serial killers. That's where the brunt of the work lies."

Harry knew what the experienced Kripos detective was thinking: the shit jobs.

Lepsvik cleared his throat. "So we agree there is a connection between the disappearances?"

"We don't have to agree. You follow your instincts."

"Fine."

Harry hung up and looked at the screen in front of him. He had gone onto the Web site Borghild had recommended and seen pictures of female beauties and male-model types with dotted lines on their faces and bodies suggesting where their perfect appearance could still—if desired—be adjusted. The doctor, Idar Vetlesen, himself was smiling at Harry from a photograph, indistinguishable from his male models.

Under the picture of Vetlesen there was a résumé listing diplomas and courses with long names in French and English that, for all Harry knew, could have been completed in two months, but still gave you the right to add new Latin abbreviations to your doctorate. He had Googled Idar Vetlesen and come up with a list of results from what he thought were curling competitions, as well as an old Web site from one of his previous employers, the Marienlyst Clinic. It was when he saw the name beside Idar Vetlesen's that he thought it was probably true what people said: Norway is such a small country that everyone is, at most, two acquaintances from knowing everyone else.

Katrine Bratt came in and plumped down onto the chair across from Harry with a deep sigh. She crossed her legs.

"Do you think it's true that beautiful people are more preoccupied with beauty than ugly people?" Harry asked.

"I don't know," Katrine said. "But there's a kind of logic to it, I suppose. People with high IQs are so fixated on IQs that they have founded their own club, haven't they? I suppose you focus on what you have. I would guess you're fairly proud of your investigative talent."

"You mean the rat-catching gene? The innate ability to lock up people with mental illnesses, addiction problems, well-under-average intellects and well-above-average childhood deprivations?"

"So we're just rat-catchers, then?"

"Yep. And that's why we're so happy when once in a blue moon a case like this lands on our table. A chance to go big-game hunting, to shoot a lion, an elephant, a fucking dinosaur."

Katrine didn't laugh. On the contrary, she nodded her head gravely.

"What did Sylvia's twin sister have to say?"

"I was in danger of becoming her best friend." Katrine sighed, folding her hands over a stockinged knee.

"Tell me."

"Well," she began, and Harry noticed his "well" in her mouth, "Ane told me that both Sylvia and Rolf thought that Rolf had been the lucky one when they got together. While everyone else thought the opposite. Rolf had just finished qualifying as an engineer at the Technical University in Bergen and had moved to Oslo and a job with Kværner Engineering. Sylvia was apparently the type who wakes up every morning with a new idea about what she's going to do with her life. She had half a dozen different majors at the university and had never been in the same job for more than six months. She was stubborn, hotheaded, spoiled, a declared socialist and attracted by ideologies that preached the obliteration of the ego. The few girlfriends she had she manipulated, and the men she was involved with left her after a short while because they couldn't take it. Her sister thought that Rolf was so deeply in love with her because she represented his absolute opposite. You see, he had followed in his father's footsteps and become an engineer. He came from a family that believed in the unseen charitable hand of capitalism and middle-class happiness. Sylvia thought that we in the Western world were materialistic and corrupt as human beings, that we had lost touch with our real identity and the source of happiness. And that some king in Ethiopia was the reincarnated Messiah."

"Haile Selassie," Harry said. "Rastafarian beliefs."

"No flies on you."

"Bob Marley records. Well, that may explain the link with Africa."

"Maybe." Katrine shifted position in her chair, her left leg crossing her right now, and Harry directed his gaze elsewhere. "Anyway, Rolf and Sylvia took a year off and traveled around West Africa. It turned out to be a road to Damascus for them both. Rolf discovered that his vocation was to help Africa get back on its feet. Sylvia, who had a big Ethiopian flag tattooed on her back, discovered that everyone looked out for himself, even in Africa. So they started up Taste of Africa. Rolf to help a poor continent, Sylvia because the combination of cheap imports and government support seemed like easy money. She had the same motive when she was caught with a backpack full of marijuana at customs, returning from Lagos."

"There you go."

"Sylvia was given a short conditional sentence because she was able to sow seeds of doubt. She said she didn't know what was in the backpack, she had brought it with her as a favor for a Nigerian living in Norway."

"Mm. What else?"

"Ane likes Rolf. He's kind and thoughtful and has

boundless love for the children. But apparently he's quite blind in all things Sylvia. Twice she fell in love with other men and left Rolf and the children. But the men left her and both times Rolf happily took her back."

"What was her hold over him, do you think?"

Katrine Bratt mounted a smile tinged with sadness and gazed into the air as her hand stroked the hem of her skirt. "The usual, I would guess. No one can leave someone they have good sex with. They can try, but they always go back. We're simple souls like that, aren't we?"

Harry nodded slowly. "And what about the men who left her and didn't come back?"

"It's different with men. Over the course of time some of them suffer from performance issues."

Harry eyed her. And decided not to pursue that subject.

"Did you see Rolf Ottersen?"

"Yes, he arrived ten minutes after you left," Katrine said. "And he looked better than last time. He'd never heard of the plastic surgery clinic in Bygdøy, but he signed the declaration of consent to waive doctor-patient confidentiality." She left the folded sheet on his desk.

An ice-cold wind blew over the low stands at Valle Hovin, where Harry sat watching the ice skaters gliding around the circuit. Oleg's technique had become more supple and effective in the last year. Every time his friend accelerated to pass him, Oleg sank lower, dug in harder and calmly sailed off.

Harry called Espen Lepsvik and they caught up on each other's news. Harry found out that a dark sedan had been seen entering Hoffsveien late on the night Birte disappeared. And it had returned the same way not long afterward.

"Dark sedan," Harry repeated with a grim shiver. "Sometime late that night."

"Yes, I know it's not a lot to go on." Lepsvik sighed.

Harry was stuffing the phone in his jacket pocket when he sensed that something was obscuring one of the floodlights.

"Sorry I'm a bit late."

He looked up into the jovial, smiling face of Mathias Lund-Helgesen.

Rakel's envoy took a seat. "Are you a winter sportsman, Harry?"

Harry noticed that Mathias had this direct way of looking at you, with an expression that was so intense it gave you the feeling he was listening even when he was talking.

"Not really. Bit of skating. And you?"

Mathias shook his head. "But I've decided that the day my life's work is done and I'm so ill I no longer want to live, I'll take the lift up to the top of the ski-jump tower on that hill there."

He jerked his thumb over his shoulder and Harry did not need to turn. Holmenkollen, Oslo's dearest monument and worst ski jump, could be seen from everywhere in town.

"And then I'll jump. Not on skis but from the tower."

"Dramatic," Harry said.

Mathias smiled. "A hundred-and-thirty-foot free fall. Over in seconds."

"Not imminent, I trust."

"With the level of anti-Scl-70 in my blood, you never know." Mathias laughed grimly.

"Anti-Scl-70?"

"Yes, antibodies are a good thing, but you should always be suspicious when they appear. They're there for a reason."

"Mm. I thought suicide was a heretical notion for a doctor."

"No one knows better than doctors what diseases involve. I agree with the stoic Zeno, who considered suicide a worthy action when death was more attractive than life. When he was ninety-eight years old he dislocated his big toe. This upset him so much that he went home and hanged himself."

"So why not hang yourself instead of going to all the trouble of climbing to the top of the Holmenkollen ski jump?"

"Well, death should be a sort of homage to life. Anyway, I have to confess that I like the idea of the publicity that would come in its wake. My research attracts very little attention, I'm afraid." Mathias's jolly laughter was slashed to pieces by the sound of swift-moving skate blades. "By the way, I'm sorry I bought new speed skates for Oleg. Rakel didn't tell me that you had planned to buy a pair for his birthday until afterward."

"No problem."

"He would have preferred to have them from you, you know."

Harry didn't answer.

"I envy you, Harry. You can sit here and read the paper, make a call on your phone, talk to other people; for him it's good enough that you're just *here*. When I cheer and shout and encourage him and do everything the manual says a good father should do, he just gets irritated. Did you know that he polishes his skates every day because he knows that you used to do that? And until Rakel demanded that skates had to be kept indoors, he insisted on leaving them outside on the steps because you once said that skate steel should always be kept cold. You're his role model, Harry."

Harry shuddered at the thought. But somewhere deep

inside—no, not even that far—he was pleased to hear this. Because he was a jealous bastard who would have liked to imprecate a mild curse on Mathias's attempts to win over Oleg.

Mathias fidgeted with a coat button. "It's strange in these divorce-ridden times, with children and their deep awareness of their origins. The way a new father can never replace the real one."

"Oleg's real father lives in Russia," Harry said.

"On paper, yes," Mathias said with a crooked smile. "But not in reality, Harry."

Oleg sped past and waved to the two of them. Mathias waved back.

"You've worked with a doctor called Idar Vetlesen," Harry said.

Mathias eyed him with surprise. "Idar, yes. At Marienlyst Clinic. Goodness, do you know Idar?"

"No, I was Googling his name and found an old Web site listing doctors employed at the clinic. And your name was there."

"That's a few years ago now, but we had a lot of fun at Marienlyst. The clinic was started at a time when everyone believed that private health enterprises were bound to make a lot of money. And closed down when we saw things were not like that, of course."

"You went bust?"

"I think *downsized* was the term used. Are you a patient of Idar's?"

"No, his name came up in connection with a case. Can you tell me what kind of person he is?"

"Idar Vetlesen?" Mathias laughed. "Yes, I can say quite a bit about him. We studied together and hung around in the same crowd for many years."

"Does that mean you no longer have any contact?"

Mathias shrugged. "I suppose we were quite different, Idar and I. Most people in our crowd saw medicine as . . . well, as a calling. Apart from Idar. He made no bones about it. He was studying medicine because it was the profession that commanded the most respect. At any rate, I admire his honesty."

"So Idar Vetlesen was preoccupied with earning respect?"

"There was money, too, of course. No one was surprised when Idar took up plastic surgery. Or that he ended up at a clinic for a select clientele comprising the rich and famous. He had always been attracted by that sort of person. He wants to be like them, to move in their circles. The problem is that Idar tries a bit too hard. I can imagine that these celebrities smile to his face, but behind his back they call him a clinging, pretentious jackass."

"Are you saying he's the kind who would go to great lengths to achieve his goals?"

Mathias mulled this over. "Idar has always searched for something that could bring him fame. Idar's problem is not that he isn't energetic, but that he's never found his mission in life. The last time I spoke to him he sounded frustrated, depressed, even."

"Can you imagine him finding a mission that would bring him fame? Something outside medicine, perhaps?"

"I haven't thought about it, but maybe. He's not exactly a born doctor."

"In what way?"

"In the same way that Idar admires the successful and despises the weak and infirm. He's not the only doctor to do so, but he's the only one to say so outright." Mathias laughed. "In our circle, we all started as out-and-out idealists who at some point or other became more preoccupied with consultant positions, paying off the new garage and overtime rates. At least Idar didn't betray any ideals; he was the same from the get-go."

Idar Vetlesen laughed. "Did Mathias really say that? That I haven't betrayed any ideals?"

He had a pleasant, almost feminine face, with eyebrows so narrow that one might have suspected him of plucking them, and teeth so white and regular that one might have suspected they were not his own. His complexion looked soft and touched up; his hair was thick and rippled with vitality. In short, he looked several years younger than his thirty-seven.

"I don't know what he meant by that," Harry lied.

They were each ensconced in a deep armchair in the library of a spacious white house, built according to the old, august Bygdøy style. His childhood home, Idar Vetlesen had explained as he guided Harry through the two vast, dark lounges and into a room whose walls were lined with books. Mikkjel Fønhus. Kjell Aukrust. Einar Gerhardsen's *Tillitsmannen*. A broad range of popular literature and political biographies. A whole shelf of yellowing issues of *Reader's Digest*. Harry didn't see a single copy published after 1970.

"Oh, I know what he meant." Idar chuckled.

Harry had an inkling what Mathias had implied by the two of them having a lot of fun at the Marienlyst Clinic: They probably competed to see who could laugh the most.

"Mathias, the saintly bastard. Lucky bastard, more like. No, by Christ, I mean both." Idar Vetlesen's laughter pealed out. "They say they don't believe in God, but my God-fearing colleagues are terrified moral strivers accumulating good deeds because deep down they're petrified of burning in hell."

"And aren't you?" Harry asked.

Idar elevated one of his elegantly formed brows and eyed Harry with interest. Idar was wearing soft light-blue moccasins with loose laces, jeans and a white tennis shirt with a polo player over the left breast. Harry couldn't remember which brand it was, only that for some reason he connected it with bores.

"I come from a practical family, Inspector. My father was a taxi driver. We believe what we can see."

"Mm. Nice house for a taxi driver."

"He owned a taxi company, had three licenses. But here in Bygdøy a taxi driver is, and always will be, a plebeian."

Harry looked at the doctor and tried to determine whether he was on speed or anything else. Vetlesen was sitting back in his chair in an exaggeratedly casual fashion, as though anxious to hide a restless or excited state. The same thought had gone through Harry's mind when he had called to explain that the police wanted answers to a few questions and Vetlesen had extended an almost effusive invitation to his home.

"But you didn't want to drive a taxi," Harry said. "You wanted . . . to make people look better?"

Vetlesen smiled. "You could say that I offer my services in the vanity market. Or that I repair people's exteriors to soothe the pain inside. Take your pick. Actually, I don't give a damn." Anticipating a shocked reaction from Harry, Vetlesen laughed. When Harry did not take the bait, Vetlesen's expression became more serious. "I see myself as a sculptor. I don't have a vocation. I like to change appearances, to shape faces. I've always liked that. I'm good at it, and people pay me for it. That's all."

"Mm."

"But that doesn't mean that I'm without principles. And patient confidentiality is one of them."

Harry didn't answer.

"I was talking to Borghild," he said. "I know what you're after, Inspector. And I understand that this is a grave matter. But I can't help you. I'm bound by my oath."

"Not any longer." Harry took the folded sheet of paper out of an inside pocket and placed it on the table between them. "This statement, signed by the father of the twins, exempts you."

Idar shook his head. "That won't make any difference."

Harry frowned in surprise. "Oh?"

"I can't say who has been to see me or what they've said, but I can say in general that those who come to a doctor with their children are protected by the oath of client confidentiality, even with respect to their spouse, if they so wish."

"Why would Sylvia Ottersen hide from her husband the fact that she'd been to see you with her twins?"

"Our behavior may seem rigid, but do remember that many of our clients are famous people who are exposed to idle gossip and unwanted press attention. Go to Kunstnernes Hus on a Friday evening and take a look around. You have no idea how many of them have had parts trimmed here and there at my clinic. They would swoon at the very idea that their visits here might become public knowledge. Our reputation is based on discretion. If it should ever come out that we are sloppy with client information, the consequences for the clinic would be catastrophic. I'm sure you understand."

"We have two murder victims and one single coincidence," Harry said. "They've both been to your clinic."

"That I neither will nor can confirm. But let us suppose for the sake of argument that they have." Vetlesen twirled a hand through the air. "So what? Norway is a country of few people and even fewer doctors. Do you know how few handshakes we all are from having met one another? The coincidence that they have been to the same doctor is no more dramatic than that they might have been on the same tram at some point. Ever met friends on a tram?"

Harry couldn't think of a single occasion. First off, he didn't take the tram that often.

"It was a long trip to be told that you won't tell me anything," Harry said.

"My apologies. I invited you here because I assumed that the alternative was the police station. Where, right now, the press is scrutinizing the comings and goings day and night. Yes, indeed, I know those people . . ."

"You are aware that I can get a search warrant, which would render your oath of confidentiality null and void?"

"Fine by me," Vetlesen said. "In that case the clinic will be on the side of the angels. But until then . . ." He closed an imaginary zipper across his mouth.

Harry shifted in his seat. They both knew that to get the courts to waive the oath of confidentiality, even for a murder case, the police would need clear evidence that the doctor's information would be of significance. And what did they have? As Vetlesen himself put it, a chance meeting on a tram. Harry felt a strong need to do something. To drink. Or to pump iron. With a vengeance. He breathed in.

"I'm still obliged to ask you where you were on the nights of the second and the fourth of November."

"I was counting on that." Vetlesen smiled. "So I had a think. I was here with . . . yes, and here she is."

An elderly woman with mousy hair hanging like a curtain around her head entered the room with mousy steps and a silver tray bearing two cups of coffee, which rattled ominously. The expression on her face suggested she was carrying a cross and a crown of thorns. She cast a glance at her son, who jumped up in a flash and took the tray.

"Thanks, Mother."

"Tie your shoelaces." She half turned to Harry. "Is anyone going to inform me who comes and goes in my house?"

"This is Inspector Hole, Mother. He'd like to know where I was yesterday and three days ago."

Harry stood up and stretched out his hand.

"I remember, of course," she said, giving Harry a resigned look and a hand covered in liver spots. "We watched that talk show featuring your curling friend. And I didn't like what he said about the royal family. What's his name again?"

"Arve Støp." Idar sighed.

The old lady leaned over toward Harry. "He said we should get rid of the royals. Can you imagine anything so dreadful? Where would we have been without the royal family during the war?"

"Right where we are now," Idar said. "Seldom has a head of state done so little during a war. And he also said that broad support for the monarchy was the final proof that most people believe in trolls and fairies."

"Isn't that dreadful?"

"Veritably, Mother." Idar smiled, placing a hand on her shoulder and simultaneously catching sight of his watch, a Breitling, which seemed large and unwieldy on his thin wrist. "My goodness! I have to go now, Hole. We'll have to hurry this coffee along."

Harry shook his head and smiled at Fru Vetlesen. "I'm sure it's delicious but I'll have to save it for another day."

She heaved a deep sigh, mumbled something inaudible, took the tray and shuffled out again.

When Idar and Harry were in the hall, Harry turned. "What did you mean by *lucky*?"

"Sorry?"

"You said Mathias Lund-Helgesen wasn't just a saintly bastard, he was lucky, too."

"Oh that! It's this woman he's fixed himself up with. Mathias is generally pretty helpless in this area, but she must have been with a couple of losers in her life. Must have needed a God-fearer like him. Well, don't tell Mathias I said that. Or actually even mention it."

"By the way, do you know what anti-Scl-70 is?"

"It's an antibody in the blood. May suggest the presence of scleroderma. Do you know someone who's got it?"

"I don't even know what scleroderma is." Harry realized he should let it go. He *wanted* to let it go. But he couldn't. "So Mathias said she had been with some losers?"

"My interpretation. Saint Mathias doesn't use expressions like *loser* about people. In his eyes, every human has the potential to become a better person." Idar Vetlesen's laughter echoed through the dark rooms.

After Harry had said his thank-yous, put on his boots and was standing on the step outside, he turned and watched—as the door slid closed—Idar sitting bent over, tying his shoelaces.

On the way back, Harry called Skarre and asked him to print out the picture of Vetlesen from the clinic Web site and go over to the Narcotics Unit to see if any of the undercover guys had seen him buying speed.

"In the street?" Skarre asked. "Don't all doctors have that kind of thing in their medicine cabinets?"

"Yes, but the rules governing the declaration of drug supplies are now so strict that a doctor would rather buy his amphetamines off a dealer in Skippergata."

They hung up, and Harry called Katrine in the office.

"Nothing for the moment," she said. "I'm leaving now. You on your way home?"

"Yes." Harry hesitated. "What do you think the chances are of the court ruling that Vetlesen can waive his Hippocratic oath?"

"With what we've got? Of course, I could put on an extra-short skirt, pop over to the courthouse and find a judge of the right age. But, to be frank, I think we can forget it."

"Agreed."

Harry headed for Bislett. Thinking about his apartment, stripped bare. He looked at his watch. Changed his mind and turned down Pilestredet toward the Police HQ.

It was two o'clock in the morning as, once again, Harry had Katrine, drowsy with sleep, on the phone.

"What's up now?" she said.

"I'm in the office and have had a look at what you've found. You said all the missing women were married with children. I think there could be something in that."

"What?"

"I have no idea. I just needed to hear myself say that to someone. So that I could decide if it sounded idiotic."

"And how does it sound?"

"Idiotic. Good night."

Eli Kvale lay with her eyes wide open. Beside her, Andreas was breathing heavily, without a care in the world. A stripe of moonlight fell between the curtains across the wall, on the crucifix she had bought during her honeymoon in Rome. What had woken her? Was it Trygve? Was he up? The dinner and the evening had gone just as she had hoped. She had seen happy, shiny faces in the candlelight, and they had all talked at the same time, they had so much to tell! Mostly Trygve. And when he talked about Montana, about his studies and friends there, she had stayed quiet just looking at this boy, this young man who was maturing into an adult, becoming whatever he would become, making his own life. That was what made her happiest: that he could choose. Openly and freely. Not like her. Not on the sly, in secret.

She heard the house creaking, heard the walls talking to one another.

But there had been a different sound, an alien sound. A sound from outside.

She got out of bed, went over to the window and opened the curtains a crack. It had snowed. The apple trees had woolen branches and the moonlight was reflected on the thin white ground covering, emphasizing every detail in the garden. Her gaze swept from the gate to the garage, unsure what it was she was looking for. Then it stopped. She gave a gasp of surprise and terror. Don't start this again, she told herself. It must have been Trygve. He's got jet lag, hasn't been able to sleep and has gone out. The footprints went from the gate to right under the window where she was standing. Like a line of black dots in the thin coating of snow. A dramatic pause in the text.

There were no footprints leading back.

12

The Conversation

"One of the Narc guys recognized him," Skarre said. "When I showed him the picture of Vetlesen, the detective said he'd seen him several times at the intersection of Skippergata and Tollbugata."

"What's at the intersection?" asked Gunnar Hagen, who had insisted on joining the Monday-morning meeting in Harry's office.

Skarre looked at Hagen uncertainly to check if the POB was joking.

"Dealers, whores, bookies," he said. "It's the new *in* place after we chased them out of Plata."

"Only there?" Hagen asked, jutting out his chin. "I was told it was more widespread now."

"It's like the center," Skarre said. "But of course you'll find them down toward the Stock Exchange and up toward Norges Bank. Around the Astrup Fearnley Museum of Modern Art, Gamle Logen concert hall and the Church Mission café . . . " He stopped when Harry yawned out loud.

"Sorry," Harry apologized. "It was a hard weekend. Go on."

"The detective couldn't remember seeing him buy dope. He thought Vetlesen was frequenting Hotel Leon."

At that moment Katrine Bratt came through the door. She was unkempt and pale, and her eyes were slits, but she sang out a cheery Bergensian greeting as she searched the room for a chair. Bjørn Holm leapt up from his, flourished a hand and went to look for another.

"Leon in Skippergata?" Hagen queried. "Is that a place they sell drugs?"

"Could well be," Skarre said. "But I've seen loads of black hookers going in there, so I suppose it must be a so-called massage place."

"Hardly," Katrine Bratt said, standing with her back to them as she hung her coat on the coatrack. "Massage parlors are part of the indoor market, and the Vietnamese have that now. They stay in the suburbs, in discreet residential areas, use Asian women and keep away from the territory of the African outdoor market."

"I think I've seen a poster for cheap rooms hanging outside," Harry said. "Four hundred kroner a night."

"That's right," Katrine said. "They have small rooms that are officially hired out by the day, but in practice on an hourly basis. Black money. Customers don't exactly ask for a receipt. But the hotel owner, who earns the most, is white."

"Lady's spot on." Skarre grinned at Hagen. "Strange that the Bergen Sexual Offenses Unit should suddenly be so well up on Oslo brothels."

"They're the same everywhere," Katrine said. "Want to bet on anything I said?"

"The owner's a Pakistani," Skarre said. "Two hundred kronerooneys."

"Done."

"OK," Harry said, clapping his hands. "What are we sitting here for?"

*　　*　　*

The owner of the Leon Hotel was Børre Hansen, from Solør, in the east; his skin was as grayish white as the slush the so-called guests brought in on their shoes and left on the worn parquet floor underneath the sign saying RE-SEPTION in black letters. As neither the clientele nor Børre was particularly interested in spelling, the sign had remained there, uncontested, for as long as Børre had had it: four years. Before that, he had traveled up and down Sweden selling Bibles, trying his hand at border trade with discarded porno films in Svinesund and acquiring an accent, sounding like a cross between a jazz musician and a preacher. It was in Svinesund that he had met Natasha, a Russian erotic dancer, and they had escaped from her Russian manager only by the skin of their teeth. Natasha had been given a new name and now she lived with Børre in Oslo. He had taken over the Leon from three Serbians who, for a variety of reasons, were no longer able to stay in the country, and he continued where they left off, since there had been no reason to alter the business model: hiring out the rooms on a short-term—often extremely short-term—basis. The revenue generally came in the form of cash, and the guests were undemanding with regard to standards and maintenance. It was a good business. A business he did not want to lose. Consequently he disliked everything about the two people standing in front of him, most of all their ID cards.

The tall man with the cropped hair placed a picture on the counter. "Seen this man?"

Børre Hansen shook his head, relieved in spite of everything that it was not him they were after.

"Sure?" said the man, resting his elbows on the counter and leaning forward.

Børre looked at the picture again, thinking he should

have scrutinized the ID card more closely; this guy seemed more like one of the dopeheads hanging around the streets than a policeman. And the girl behind him didn't look like a policewoman, either. True, she had that hard look, the whore look, but the rest of her was lady, all lady. If she got herself a pimp who didn't rob her, she could earn five times her wage, at least.

"We know you're running a brothel here," the policeman said.

"I'm running a legit hotel, I've got a license and all my papers are in order. Do you want to see?" Børre pointed to the little office directly behind the reception area.

The policeman shook his head. "You hire out rooms to prostitutes and their clients. It's against the law."

"Listen here," Børre said, swallowing. The conversation had taken the course he had feared. "I'm not interested in what my guests are up to so long as they pay their bills."

"But I am," said the policeman in a low voice. "Have a closer look at the picture."

Børre looked. The photo must have been taken some years before because he seemed so young. Young and carefree, without a trace of despair or anguish.

"Last time I checked, prostitution in Norway was not illegal," Børre Hansen said.

"No," the policewoman said. "But running a brothel is."

Børre Hansen did his best to assume an indignant expression.

"As you know, at regular intervals the police are obliged to check that hotel regulations are being complied with," the policeman said. "Such as emergency exits from all rooms in case of fire."

"Submission of foreign guests' registration forms," added the policewoman.

"Fax machine for incoming police inquiries about guests."

"VAT account."

He was teetering. The policeman delivered the knockout blow.

"We're considering bringing in the Fraud Squad to check the accounts you hold for certain customers whom undercover police have observed coming and going in recent weeks."

Børre Hansen could feel the nausea coming. Natasha. The mortgage. And incipient panic at the thought of freezing cold, pitch-black winter evenings on unfamiliar steps with Bibles under his arms.

"Or we might not," the policeman said. "It's a question of priorities. A question of how to use the police's limited resources. Isn't it, Bratt?"

The policewoman nodded.

"He rents a room twice a week," Børre Hansen said. "Always the same room. He's there all evening."

"All evening?"

"He has several visitors."

"Black or white?" the woman asked.

"Black. Only black."

"How many?"

"I don't know. It varies. Eight. Twelve."

"At the same time?" the policewoman exclaimed.

"No, they change. Some come in pairs. They're often in pairs on the street as well, of course."

"Jesus," the policeman said.

Børre Hansen nodded.

"What name does he sign in under?"

"Don't remember."

"But we'll find it in the guest book, won't we? And in the accounts?"

The back of Børre Hansen's shirt was soaked with

sweat under his shiny suit jacket. "They call him Dr. White. The women who ask for him, that is."

"Doctor?"

"Nothing to do with me. He . . . " Børre Hansen hesitated. He didn't want to say any more than he had to. On the other hand, he wanted to show a willingness to cooperate. And this was already a lost customer. "He carries one of those big doctor's bags with him. And always asks for . . . extra towels."

"Oooh," said the woman. "Doesn't sound good. Have you seen any blood when you clean the room?"

Børre didn't answer.

"*If* you clean the room," the policeman corrected. "Well?"

Børre sighed. "Not much, not more than . . . " He paused.

"Than usual?" the woman asked sarcastically.

"I don't think he hurts them," Børre Hansen hastened to say, and regretted it instantly.

"Why not?" the policeman snapped.

Børre shrugged. "They wouldn't come back, I suppose."

"And it's just women?"

Børre nodded. But the policeman must have noticed something. A nervous tautening of his neck muscles, a little twitch in the bloodshot membrane of his eye.

"Men?" he asked.

Børre shook his head.

"Boys?" asked the policewoman, who clearly scented the same thing as her colleague.

Børre Hansen shook his head again, but with that little, almost imperceptible delay that arises when the brain has to choose between alternatives.

"Children," said the policeman, lowering his forehead as if about to charge. "Has he had children here?"

"No!" Børre shouted, feeling the sweat break out over his whole body. "Never! I draw the line at that. There have only been the two times . . . And they didn't come in. I threw them back out on the street!"

"African?" the man asked.

"Yes."

"Boys or girls?"

"Both."

"Did they come alone?" the woman asked.

"No, with women. The mothers, I believe. But, as I said, I didn't let them go up to his room."

"You said he comes here twice a week. Does he have fixed times?"

"Monday and Thursday. From eight to midnight. And he's always on time."

"Tonight, too?" the man said, looking at his colleague. "OK, thanks for your assistance."

Børre released the air from his lungs and discovered that his legs were aching—he had been standing on his toes the whole time. "Glad to help," he said.

The police officers walked toward the door. Børre knew he should keep his mouth shut, but he wouldn't be able to sleep if he didn't receive an assurance.

"But," he said as they were leaving, "but then, we have a deal, don't we?"

The policeman turned, with one eyebrow raised in surprise. "About what?"

Børre swallowed. "About these . . . inspections?"

The policeman rubbed his chin. "Are you implying that you have something to hide?"

Børre blinked twice. Then he heard his own high-pitched nervous laughter as he gushed: "No, no, of course not! Ha-ha! Everything here's in order."

"Excellent, so you have nothing to fear when they come. Inspections are not my responsibility."

They left with Børre opening his mouth, about to protest, to say something, he just didn't know what.

The telephone welcomed Harry on his return to the office.

It was Rakel wanting to give him back the DVD she had borrowed from him.

"*The Rules of Attraction*?" Harry repeated, taken aback. "Have you got it?"

"You said it was on your list of most underrated modern films."

"Yes, but you never like those films."

"That's not true."

"You didn't like *Starship Troopers*."

"That's because it's a crap macho film."

"It's satire," Harry said.

"Of what?"

"American society's inherent fascism. The Hardy Boys meet Hitler Youth."

"Come on, Harry. War on giant insects on a remote planet?"

"Fear of foreigners."

"Anyway, I liked that seventies film of yours, the one about bugging . . ."

"*The Conversation*," Harry said. "Coppola's best."

"That's the one. I agree *that* is underrated."

"It's not underrated," Harry sighed. "Just forgotten. It was nominated for an Oscar for Best Film."

"I'm having dinner with some friends this evening. I can drop the film off on my way home. Will you be up at around midnight?"

"Might be. Why not drop by on your way to the meal instead?"

"Bit more stressful, but I can do it, of course."

Her answer had come fast. But not fast enough for Harry not to hear it.

"Mm," he said. "I can't sleep anyway. I'm inhaling fungus and I can't catch my breath."

"You know what? I'll pop it in the mailbox downstairs so you don't have to get up. OK?"

"OK."

They hung up. Harry saw that his hand was trembling. Concluded it had to be due to lack of nicotine and headed for the elevator.

Katrine came out of her office door as if she knew it was him stomping along. "I spoke to Espen Lepsvik. We can have one of his guys for the job tonight."

"Great."

"Good news?"

"What?"

"You're smiling."

"Am I? Must be happy, then."

"About what?"

He patted his pocket. "Cigarette."

Eli Kvale was sitting at the kitchen table with a cup of tea, looking out at the yard and listening to the comforting rumble of the dishwasher. The black telephone was on the countertop. The receiver had grown hot in her hands, from squeezing it so tight, but it had been a wrong number. Trygve had enjoyed the fish au gratin—it was his favorite, he had said. But he said that about most things. He was a good boy. Outside, the grass was brown and lifeless; there were no signs of the snow that had fallen. And who knows? Perhaps she had just dreamed the whole thing.

She flipped aimlessly through a magazine. She had

taken off the first few days that Trygve was at home so they could have some time together. Have a good talk, just the two of them. But now he was sitting with Andreas in the living room and they were doing what she had made space for. That was fine—they had more to talk about. They were so similar, after all. And in fact she had always liked the idea of a good talk more than the reality. Because the conversation always had to stop somewhere. At the huge, insurmountable wall.

Of course, she had agreed to name the boy after Andreas's father. At least let the boy take a name from Andreas's side. She had been close to spilling the beans before she was due to give birth. About the empty parking lot, about the darkness, about the black prints in the snow. About the knife to her neck and the faceless breath against her cheek. On the way home, with his seed running into her underwear, she had prayed to God that it would continue to run until it was all gone. But her prayers had not been answered.

Later she had often wondered how things would have been if Andreas had not been a priest and his view of abortion so uncompromising, and if she had not been such a coward. If Trygve had not been born. But by then the wall had already been built, an unshakable wall of silence.

That Trygve and Andreas were so similar was a silver lining. It had even sparked a little hope, so she had gone to a doctor's office where no one knew her, given them two strands of hair that she had taken from their pillows and that she had read were enough to find a code of something called DNA, a kind of genetic fingerprint. The doctor had sent the hairs to the Institute of Forensic Medicine at Riks-hospitalet, which was employing this new method in paternity cases. And after two months, all doubt was gone. It had not been a dream: the parking lot, the black prints, the panting, the pain.

She looked at the telephone again. Of course it had been a wrong number. The breathing she had heard at the other end was the perplexed reaction to hearing an unexpected voice, indecision as to whether to put the receiver down or not. That was all.

Harry went into the hall and picked up the entry phone.

"Hello?" he shouted over Franz Ferdinand on the sitting-room stereo.

No answer, just a car whizzing past on Sofies Gate.

"Hello?"

"Hi! It's Rakel. Were you in bed?"

He could hear from her voice that she had been drinking. Not much but enough for her pitch to be half a tone higher, and her laughter, that beautifully deep laughter, rippled over her words.

"No," he said. "Nice evening?"

"Quite."

"It's only eleven o'clock."

"The girls wanted an early night. It's a workday and so on."

"Mm."

Harry visualized her. The teasing look, the alcohol sheen in her eyes.

"I've got the film," she said. "If I'm going to drop it in the mailbox, I think you might have to open up."

"Right."

He raised his finger to press the bell to let her in. Waited. Knowing that this was a window of time. They had two seconds at their disposal. For the moment they had all the fall-back positions. He liked fall-back positions. And he knew very well that he didn't want this to happen—it was too complicated, too painful to go through again. So why was his chest heaving as if he had two hearts? Why hadn't he immediately pressed the button, so that she would have been in and out of the building and out of his head? *Now*, he thought, placing the tip of his finger against the hard plastic of the button.

"Or," she said, "I could come up with it."

Harry already knew before speaking that his voice was going to sound strange.

"You don't need to," he said. "My mailbox is the one without a name. Good night."

"Good night."

He pressed the button. Went into the sitting room, turned up Franz Ferdinand, loud, tried to blast out his thoughts, forget the idiotic jangling of nerves, just absorb the sound, the jagged attack of guitars. Angry, frail and not especially well played. Scottish. But the feverish series of chords was joined by another sound.

Harry turned down the music. Listened. He was going to turn up the volume again when he heard a sound. Like sandpaper on wood. Or shoes shuffling on the floor. He went into the hall and saw a figure behind the door's wavy glass.

He opened up.

"I rang the bell," Rakel said, looking up at him apologetically.

"Oh?"

She waved a DVD box. "It wouldn't go in the slot."

He was going to say something, wanted to say something. But he had already thrust out his arm, caught her, pulled her to him, heard her gasp as he held her tight, saw her mouth opening and her tongue moving toward his, taunting and red. And basically there was nothing to say.

*   *   *

She snuggled up to him, soft and warm.

"Goodness," she whispered.

He kissed her on the forehead.

The sweat was a thin layer that both separated them and glued them together.

It had been exactly as he knew it would be. It had been like the first time, though without the nerves, the fumbling and the unspoken questions. It had been like the last time, without the sadness, without her sobbing afterward. You can leave someone with whom you have good sex. But Katrine was right; you always go back. But Harry knew this was different, too. For Rakel this was an essential, final visit to old pastures, a good-bye to what they had both called the great love of their lives. Before she entered a new era. To a lesser love? Maybe, but to an endurable love.

She was making purring sounds as she stroked his stomach. He could still feel the tension in her body. He could make it difficult or easy for her. He decided on the latter.

"Bad conscience?" he asked and felt her flinch.

"I don't want to talk about it," she said.

He didn't want to talk about it, either. He wanted to lie quite still, listen to her breathing and feel her hand on his stomach. But he knew what she had to do, and he didn't want any more postponements. "He's waiting for you, Rakel."

"No," she said. "He and the technician are preparing a body for an Anatomy Department lecture early tomorrow morning. And I told him he wasn't coming near me after touching a corpse. He'll sleep at his place."

"What about me?" Harry smiled in the dark, thinking that she had planned this, known it would happen. "How do you know I haven't touched a corpse?"

"Have you?"

"No," Harry said, thinking about the pack of cigarettes in the bedside-table drawer. "We don't have any corpses."

They fell silent. Her hand described ever larger circles on his stomach.

"I have a feeling I've been infiltrated," he said out of the blue.

"What do you mean?"

"I don't quite know. I just have the feeling someone is watching me the whole time, that someone is watching me now. I'm part of someone's plan. Do you understand?"

"No." She snuggled up closer to him.

"It's this case I'm working on. It's as though my person is involved in—"

"Shh." She bit his ear. "You're always involved, Harry. That's your problem. Relax."

Her hand placed itself on his flaccid member and he closed his eyes, listened to her whispers and felt his erection come.

At three o'clock she got out of bed. He saw her back in the light from the streetlamps through the window. The arched back and the shadow of her spine. And he fell to thinking about something Katrine had said, that Sylvia Ottersen had had the Ethiopian flag tattooed on her back; he would have to remember to mention that in the briefing. And Rakel was right: He never stopped thinking about cases; he was always involved.

He accompanied her to the door. She kissed him quickly on the mouth and dashed down the stairs. There was nothing to say. He was going to close the door when he saw wet boot prints outside the door. He followed them to where they disappeared down into the darkness of the stairwell. They must have been left by Rakel. And he thought about the Berhaus seals, about the female who finished mating with the male in the breeding period and never went back to him in the next breeding period. Because it wasn't biologically rational. The Berhaus seals must be clever creatures.

13

DAY 8

Paper

It was nine-thirty and the sun was shining on a solitary car negotiating the roundabout on the Sjølyst overpass above the highway. It turned up Bygdøyveien, which led to the idyllic rural peninsula located a mere five minutes' drive from the City Hall Square. It was quiet, there was almost no traffic, no cows or horses in the Kongsgården estate, and the narrow sidewalks where people made pilgrimages to the beaches in summer were deserted.

Harry steered the car around the bends in the rolling terrain and listened to Katrine.

"Snow," Katrine said.

"Snow?"

"I did as you said. I concentrated on the married women with children who had disappeared. And then I began to look at the dates. Most were in November and December. I isolated them and considered the geographical spread. Most were in Oslo; there were some in other parts of the country. Then it struck me, because of the letter you received. The part about the snowman reappearing with the first snow. And the day we were in Hoffsveien was the first snow in Oslo."

"Really?"

"I had the Meteorological Institute check the relevant dates and places. And do you know what?"

Harry knew what. And he should have known it long ago.

"The first snow," he said. "He kills them the day the first snow falls."

"Exactly."

Harry smacked the wheel. "Christ, we had it spelled out for us. How many missing women are we talking about?"

"Eleven. One a year."

"And two this year. He's broken the pattern."

"There was a murder and two disappearances when the first snow fell in Bergen in 1992. I think we should start there."

"Why's that?"

"Because the victim was a married woman with a child. And the woman who disappeared was her best friend. Thus we have one body, one crime scene and case files. As well as a suspect who vanished and has never been seen since."

"Who's that?"

"A policeman. Gert Rafto."

Harry glanced over quickly. "Oh, that case, yes. Wasn't he the one who stole stuff from crime scenes?"

"So it was rumored. Witnesses saw Rafto going into the apartment of one of the women, Onny Hetland, a few hours before she disappeared. And extensive searches turned up nothing. He disappeared without a trace."

Harry stared at the road, at the leafless trees along Huk Aveny leading down to the sea and the museums for what Norwegians regarded as the nation's greatest achievements: a voyage in a raft across the Pacific Ocean and a failed attempt to reach the North Pole.

"And now you think it's conceivable that he didn't disappear after all?" he said. "That he might reappear every year at the first sign of snow?"

Katrine hunched her shoulders. "I think it's worth investing the time to find out what happened there."

"Mm. We'll have to start by asking Bergen for assistance."

"I wouldn't do that," she said quickly.

"Oh?"

"The Rafto case is still an extremely sensitive issue for the police in Bergen. The resources they put into that case were largely spent burying rather than investigating it. They were terrified of what they might unearth. And since the guy had disappeared all by himself . . ." She drew a big *X* in the air.

"I see. What do you suggest?"

"That you and I go on a little trip to Bergen and do a bit of investigating on our own. After all, it's part of an Oslo murder case now."

Harry parked in front of the address, a four-story brick building right by the water, surrounded by a mooring quay. He switched off the engine, but remained in his seat looking across Frognerkilen Bay to Filipstad Harbor.

"How did the Rafto case get onto your list?" he asked. "First of all, it's further back than I asked you to check. Second, I believe it's not a missing-persons case but murder."

He turned to look at Katrine. She met his gaze without blinking.

"The Rafto case was pretty famous in Bergen," she said. "And there was a photo."

"A photo?"

"Yes. All new trainees at Bergen Police Station are shown it. It was of the crime scene at the top of Ulriken Mountain and a kind of baptism of fire. I think most were so terrorized by the details in the foreground that they never looked at the background. Or maybe they had never been to the top of Ulriken. At any rate there was something there that didn't make sense, a mound farther back. When you magnify it, you can see quite clearly what it is."

"Oh?"

"A snowman."

Harry nodded slowly.

"Speaking of photos," Katrine said, taking a padded envelope from her bag and throwing it into Harry's lap.

The clinic was on the second floor, and the waiting room had been immaculately designed at horrendous expense with Italian furniture, a coffee table as low off the ground as a Ferrari, glass sculptures by Nico Widerberg and an original Roy Lichtenstein print showing a smoking gun.

Instead of the obligatory reception area with glass partition, a woman sat behind a beautiful old desk in the middle of the room. She was wearing an open white coat over a blue business suit and a welcoming smile. A smile that did not stiffen appreciably when Harry introduced himself and stated the purpose of their visit and his assumption that she was Borghild.

"Would you mind waiting for a moment?" she said, pointing to the sofas with the practiced elegance of a stewardess gesturing toward the emergency exits. Harry refused the offer of espresso, tea or water, and he and Katrine took a seat.

Harry noticed that the magazines laid out were up to date; he opened a copy of *Liberal* and his attention was caught by the headline in which Arve Støp claimed that politicians' willingness to appear on entertainment shows to "flaunt themselves" and assume the role of clown was the ultimate victory for government by the people—with the populace on the throne and the politician as the court jester.

Then the door marked DR. IDAR VETLESEN opened and a woman strode quickly through the waiting room, said a brief "Bye" to Borghild and was gone without so much as a glance left or right.

Katrine stared after her. "Wasn't that the woman from TV2 News?"

At that moment Borghild announced that Vetlesen was ready to receive them, went to the door and held it open for them.

Idar Vetlesen's office was CEO-size, with a view of the Oslo Fjord. Framed diplomas hung on the wall behind the desk.

"Just a moment," Vetlesen said, without looking up from the computer screen. Then, with a triumphant expression, he pressed a final key, swiveled around in his chair and removed his glasses.

"Face-lift, Hole? Penis enlargement? Liposuction?"

"Thank you for the offer," Harry said. "This is Police Officer Bratt. We've come once again to request your help with information about Ottersen and Becker."

Idar Vetlesen sighed and began to clean his glasses with a handkerchief.

"How can I explain this to you in a way that you can understand, Hole? Even for someone like me, who has a genuine burning desire to help the police and basically couldn't care less about principles, there are some things that are sacrosanct." He raised an index finger. "In all the years I've worked as a doctor I have never, ever"—the finger wagged in time with his words—"broken my Hippocratic oath. And I do not intend to start now."

A long silence ensued in which Vetlesen just looked at them, clearly satisfied with the effect he had created.

Harry cleared his throat.

"Perhaps we can still fulfill your burning desire to help, Vetlesen. We're investigating possible child prostitution at a so-called hotel in Oslo, known as the Leon. Last night two of our officers were outside in a car taking photographs of people going in and out."

Harry opened the brown padded envelope he had been given by Katrine, leaned forward and placed the photographs before the doctor.

"That's you there, isn't it?"

Vetlesen looked as though something had become lodged in his gullet; his eyes bulged and the veins in his neck stuck out.

"I . . . ," he stuttered. "I . . . haven't done anything wrong or illegal."

"No, not at all," Harry said. "We're just considering summoning you as a witness. A witness who can say what's going on there. It's common knowledge that Hotel Leon is a center for prostitutes and their clients; what's new is that children have been seen there. And unlike other prostitution, child prostitution is, as you know, illegal. Thought we should inform you before we go to the press with the whole business."

Vetlesen stared at the photograph, rubbing his face hard.

"By the way, we just saw the TV2 News lady coming out," Harry said. "What's her name again?"

Vetlesen didn't answer. It was as if all the smooth youthfulness had been sucked out of him before their very eyes, as if his face had aged in the space of a second.

"Call us if you can find a loophole in the Hippocratic oath," Harry said.

Harry and Katrine were halfway to the door before Vetlesen stopped them.

"They were here for an examination," he said. "That's all."

"What kind of examination?" Harry asked.

"A disease."

"The same disease? Which one?"

"It's of no importance."

"OK," Harry said, walking to the door. "When you're summoned as a witness you can take that view. It's of no importance, either. After all, we haven't found anything illegal."

"Wait!"

Harry turned. Vetlesen was supporting himself on his elbows with his face in his hands.

"Fahr's Syndrome."

"Father Syndrome?"

"Fahr's. F-a-h-r. A rare hereditary disease, a bit like Alzheimer's. Motor skills deteriorate, especially in cognitive areas, and there is some spasticity of movement. Most develop the syndrome after the age of thirty, but it is possible to have it in childhood."

"Mm. And so Birte and Sylvia knew their children had this disease?"

"They suspected it when they came here. Fahr's Syndrome is hard to diagnose, and Birte Becker and Sylvia Ottersen had been to several doctors, although nothing conclusive was found in their children. I seem to remember that both of them had searched the Internet, typed in the symptoms and discovered Fahr, which matched alarmingly well."

"And so they contacted you? A plastic surgeon?"

"I happen to be a Fahr specialist."

"Happen to be?"

"There are around eighteen thousand doctors in Norway. Do you know how many known diseases there are in the world?" Vetlesen motioned with his head to the wall of diplomas. "Fahr's Syndrome happened to be part of a course I took in Switzerland about nerve channels.

The little I learned was enough to make me a specialist in Norway."

"What can you tell us about Birte Becker and Sylvia Ottersen?"

Vetlesen hunched his shoulders. "They came here with their children once a year. I examined them and was unable to determine any deterioration of their conditions, and, apart from that, I know nothing of their lives. Or for that matter"—he tossed back his hair—"their deaths."

"Do you believe him?" Harry asked as they drove past the deserted fields.

"Not entirely," Katrine said.

"Nor I," Harry said. "I think we should concentrate on this and drop Bergen for the time being."

"No," said Katrine.

"No?"

"There's a link here somewhere."

"Which is?"

"I don't know. It sounds wild, but perhaps there's a link between Rafto and Vetlesen. Perhaps that's how Rafto's managed to hide all these years."

"What do you mean?"

"That he quite simply got himself a mask. An authentic mask. A face-lift."

"From Vetlesen?"

"It could explain the coincidence of having two victims with the same doctor. Rafto could have seen Birte and Sylvia at the clinic and decided they would be his victims."

"You're jumping the gun," Harry said.

"Jumping the gun?"

"This kind of murder investigation is like doing a jigsaw puzzle. In the opening phase you collect the pieces, play with them, are patient. What you're doing is trying to force the pieces into position. It's too early."

"I'm just saying things out loud to someone. To see if they sound idiotic."

"They sound idiotic."

"This isn't the way to the Police HQ," she said.

Harry could hear a curious quiver in her voice and glanced across at her, but her face gave nothing away.

"I'd like to check out some of the things Vetlesen told us with someone I know," he said. "And who knows Vetlesen."

Mathias was wearing a white coat and regulation yellow cleaning gloves when he received Harry and Katrine in the garage beneath Preclinical, the usual name for the brown building in the part of Gaustad Hospital that faces the Ring 3 highway.

He directed their car into what turned out to be his own unused parking space.

"I try to cycle as often as I can," Mathias explained, using his swipe card to open the door leading from the garage into a basement corridor in the Anatomy Department. "This kind of access is practical for transporting bodies in and out. Would have liked to offer you coffee, but I've just finished with one group of students and the next will be here shortly."

"Sorry for the hassle. You must be tired today."

Mathias sent him a quizzical look.

"Rakel and I were talking on the phone. She said you had to work late last night," Harry added, cursing himself inside and hoping his face gave nothing away.

"Rakel, yes." Mathias shook his head. "She was out

late herself. Out with the girls and has had to take the day off work. But when I called her she was in the midst of a big cleanup at home. Women, eh! What can you say?"

Harry put on a stiff smile and wondered if there was a standard response to that question.

A man in green hospital gear trundled a metal table toward the garage door.

"Another delivery for the University of Tromsø?" Mathias asked.

"Say bye-bye to Kjeldsen," said the man in green with a smile. He had a cluster of small rings in one ear, a bit like a Masai woman's neck rings, except that these rings gave his face an irritating asymmetry.

"Kjeldsen?" Mathias exclaimed, and stopped. "Is that true?"

"Thirty years of service. Now it's Tromsø's turn to dissect him."

Mathias lifted the blanket. Harry caught sight of the body. The skin over the cranium was taut, smoothing out the old man's wrinkles into a genderless face, as white as a plaster mask. Harry knew that this was because the body had been preserved—that is, the arteries had been pumped full of a mixture of formalin, glycerin and alcohol to ensure that it did not decompose from inside. A metal tag with an engraved three-digit number had been attached to one ear. Mathias watched the assistant roll Kjeldsen toward the garage door. Then he seemed to wake up again.

"Sorry. It's just that Kjeldsen has been with us for so long. He was a professor at the Anatomy Department when it was down in the center of town. A brilliant anatomist. With well-defined muscles. We're going to miss him."

"We won't hold you up for long," Harry said. "We were wondering if you could tell us something about

Idar's relationships with women patients. And their children."

Mathias raised his head and looked with surprise at Harry, then Katrine, and back again.

"Are you asking me what I think you're asking me?"

Harry nodded.

Mathias led them through another locked door. They entered a room with eight metal tables and a blackboard at one end. The tables were equipped with lamps and sinks. On each of the tables lay something oblong wrapped in white hand towels. Judging by the shape and the size, Harry guessed that today's theme was situated somewhere between hip and foot. There was a faint smell of bleach, but not nearly as pronounced as Harry was used to from the autopsy room at the Institute of Forensic Medicine. Mathias sank down onto one of the chairs and Harry sat on the edge of the lecturer's desk. Katrine walked over to a table and scrutinized three brains; it was impossible to say whether they were models or real.

Mathias thought a long time before answering. "Personally, I've never noticed or heard anyone suggest there was anything between Idar and any of his patients."

Something about the stress placed on *patients* brought Harry up short. "What about nonpatients?"

"I don't know Idar well enough to comment. But I know him well enough to prefer not to comment." He flashed a tentative smile. "If that's OK?"

"Of course. There was something else I was wondering about. Fahr's Syndrome—do you know what it is?"

"Superficially. A terrible disease. And unfortunately very much a hereditary—"

"Do you know of any Norwegian specialists in the disease?"

Mathias reflected. "None that I can think of, off the top of my head."

Harry scratched his neck. "OK, thanks for your help, Mathias."

"Not at all, a pleasure. If you want to know more about Fahr's Syndrome, you can call me tonight, when I have a few books around me."

Harry stood up. Walked over to Katrine, who had lifted the lid off one of the four large metal boxes by the wall, and peered over her shoulder. His tongue prickled and his whole body reacted. Not at the body parts immersed in the clear alcohol, looking like lumps of meat at the butcher's. But at the smell of alcohol. Forty percent.

"They start off more or less whole," Mathias said. "Then we cut them up as and when we need individual body parts."

Harry observed Katrine's face. She seemed totally unaffected. The door opened behind them. The first students came in and began to put on blue coats and white latex gloves.

Mathias followed them back to the garage. At the door, Mathias caught Harry's arm and held him back.

"Just a tiny thing I should mention, Harry. Or shouldn't mention. I'm not sure."

"Out with it," Harry said, thinking that this was it—Mathias knew about him and Rakel.

"I have a slight moral dilemma here. It's about Idar."

"Oh, yes?" Harry said, feeling disappointment rather than relief, to his surprise.

"I'm sure it doesn't mean anything, but it occurred to me that maybe it's not up to me to decide. And that you can't let loyalty take priority in such a terrible case. No matter what. Last year, when I was still working in the emergency room, a colleague who also knows Idar and I popped by Postcafeen to have breakfast after a night shift. It's a café that opens at the crack of dawn and serves beer, so a lot of thirsty early birds gather there. And other poor souls."

"I know the place," Harry said.

"To our surprise we found Idar there. He was sitting at a table with a filthy young boy slurping soup. On seeing us, Idar jumped up from the table in shock and came up with some excuse or other. I didn't think any more about it. That is, I believed I hadn't thought any more about it. Until what you just said. And I remembered what I'd been thinking at the time. That maybe . . . well, you understand."

"I understand," Harry said. And, seeing his interlocutor's tormented expression, added: "You did the right thing."

"Thank you." Mathias forced a smile. "But I feel like a Judas."

Harry tried to find something sensible to say, but all he could do was proffer his hand and mumble a "thanks." And shiver as he pressed Mathias's cold cleaning glove.

Judas. The Judas kiss. As they drove down Slemdalsveien, Harry thought about Rakel's hungry tongue in his mouth, her gentle sigh and loud groan, the pains in his pelvis as it banged against Rakel's, her cries of frustration when he stopped because he wanted it to last longer. For she wasn't there to make it last longer. She was there to exorcise demons, to purify her body so that she could go home and purify her soul. And wash every floor in the house. The sooner the better.

"Call the clinic," Harry said.

He heard Katrine's quick fingers and tiny beeps. Then she passed him the mobile phone.

Borghild answered with a studied mixture of gentleness and efficiency.

"This is Harry Hole speaking. Tell me, who should I see if I have Fahr's Syndrome?"

Silence.

"It depends," answered Borghild hesitantly.

"On what?"

"On the syndrome your father has, I suppose."

"Right. Is Dr. Vetlesen in?"

"He's gone for today."

"Already?"

"They've got a curling match. Try again tomorrow."

She radiated impatience. Harry assumed she was in the process of leaving for the day.

"Bygdøy Curling Club?"

"No, the private one. The one down from Gimle."

"Thanks. Have a good evening."

Harry gave Katrine the phone back.

"We'll bring him in," he said.

"Who?"

"The specialist who has an assistant who's never heard of the disease he specializes in."

After asking the way, they found Villa Grande, a luxurious property that, during the Second World War, had belonged to a Norwegian whose name, unlike those of the raft sailor and the Arctic explorer, was also widely known outside Norway: Quisling, the traitor.

At the bottom of the slope to the south of the building there was a rectangular wooden house resembling an old military barracks. As soon as you entered the building you could feel the cold hit you. And inside the next door the temperature fell further.

There were four men on the ice. Their shouts bounced off the wooden walls, and none of them noticed Harry and Katrine come in. They were shouting at a shiny stone gliding down the rink. The fifty pounds of granite, the type known as ailsite, from the Scottish island of Ailsa Craig, stopped against the guard of three other stones on the front edge of two circles painted into the ice. The men slid around the rink, balancing on one foot and kicking off with the other, discussing, supporting themselves on their brooms and preparing for the next stone.

"Snob sport," Katrine whispered. "Look at them."

Harry didn't answer. He liked curling. The meditative element as you watched the stone's slow passage, rotating in an apparently friction-free universe, like one of the spaceships in Kubrick's odyssey, accompanied not by Strauss but by the stone's quiet rumble and the furious sweeping of brooms.

The men had seen them now. And Harry recognized two of the faces from media circles. One was Arve Støp's.

Idar Vetlesen skated toward him.

"Joining us for a game, Hole?"

He shouted that from far away, as if it was meant for the other men, not Harry. And it was followed by seemingly jovial laughter. But the muscles outlined against the skin of his jaw betrayed the game he was playing. He stopped in front of them, and the breath coming from his mouth was white.

"The game's over," Harry said.

"I don't think so." Idar smiled.

Harry could already feel the cold from the ice creeping through the soles of his shoes and advancing up his legs.

"We'd like you to come with us to the Police HQ," Harry said. "Now."

Idar Vetlesen's smile evaporated. "Why?"

"Because you're lying to us. Among other things, you're not a Fahr's Syndrome specialist."

"Says who?" Idar asked, glancing at the other curling

players to confirm that they were standing too far away to hear them.

"Says your assistant. Since she's clearly never even heard of the disease."

"Listen here," Idar said, and a new sound, that of despair, had crept into his voice. "You can't just come here and take me away. Not here, not in front of . . . "

"Your clients?" Harry asked and peered over Idar's shoulder. He could see Arve Støp sweeping ice off the bottom of a stone while studying Katrine.

"I don't know what you're after," he heard Idar say. "I'm happy to cooperate with you, but not if you're consciously setting out to humiliate and ruin me. These are my best friends."

"We'll keep going, Vetlesen . . . ," resounded a deep baritone voice. It was Arve Støp's.

Harry eyed the unhappy surgeon. Wondered what he understood by "best" friends. And thought that if there was the tiniest chance of gaining anything by fulfilling Vetlesen's wish, then it was worth their while.

"OK," Harry said. "We're off. But you have to be at the Police HQ in Grønland in exactly one hour. If not, we'll come looking for you with sirens and trumpet fanfares. And they're easy to hear in Bygdøy, aren't they?"

Vetlesen nodded and for a moment looked as though he would laugh from force of habit.

Oleg shut the door with a bang, kicked off his boots and ran upstairs. There was a fresh aroma of lemon and soap throughout the house. He stormed into his room, and the mobile hanging from the ceiling chimed in alarm as he pulled off his jeans and put on his sweatsuit bottoms. He ran out again, but as he grabbed the banister to take

the stairs in two long strides, he heard his name from behind the open door of his mother's bedroom.

He went in and found Rakel on her knees in front of
the bed with a long-handled scrubbing brush.

"I thought you did the cleaning over the weekend."

"Yes, but not well enough," his mother said, getting
up and wiping a hand across her forehead. "Where are
you going?"

"To the stadium. I'm going skating. Karsten's waiting
outside. Be back home for dinner." He pushed off from
the door and slid across the floor on stockinged feet,
gravity low, the way Erik V, one of the skating veterans at
Valle Hovin, had taught him.

"Wait a minute, young man. Speaking of skates . . . "

Oleg stopped. Oh, no, he thought. She's found the
skates.

She stood in the doorway, tilted her head and scrutinized him. "What about homework?"

"Haven't got much," he said with a relieved smile. "I'll
do it after dinner."

He saw her hesitate and added quickly: "You look so
nice in that dress, Mom."

She lowered her eyes at the old sky-blue dress with
the white flowers. And even though she gave him an admonitory look, a smile was playing at the corners of her
mouth. "Watch it, Oleg. Now you're sounding like your
father."

"Oh? I thought he only spoke Russian."

He hadn't meant anything with that comment, but
something happened to his mother—a shock seemed to
run through her.

He tiptoed. "Can I go now?"

*   *   *

"Yes, you can go?" Katrine Bratt's voice lashed the fitness-room walls in the basement at the Police HQ. "Did you really say that? That Idar Vetlesen could just go?"

Harry stared up at her face, which was bent over the bench he was lying on. The dome-shaped ceiling light formed a shining yellow halo around her head. He was breathing heavily because an iron bar was lying across his chest. He had been about to perform a bench press of two hundred pounds and had just lifted the bar off the stand when Katrine had marched in and ruined his attempt.

"I had to," Harry said, managing to push the bar a bit higher so that it was on his breastbone. "He had his lawyer with him. Johan Krohn."

"So what?"

"Well, Krohn started by asking what sort of methods we employed to blackmail his client. Then he said the buying and selling of sexual services in Norway is legal, and that our methods for forcing a respected doctor to break his Hippocratic oath would also be worth a headline."

"But damn it!" Katrine shouted in a voice that was shaking with fury. "This is a murder case!"

Harry hadn't seen her lose control before and answered in his gentlest voice.

"Listen, we can't link the murders to the illness or even make the connection seem a possibility. And Krohn knows that. And so I can't hold him."

"No, but you can't just . . . lie there . . . and do nothing!"

Harry could feel his breastbone aching, and it struck him that she was absolutely right.

She put both hands to her face. "I . . . I . . . I'm sorry. I just thought . . . It's been a strange day."

"Fine." Harry groaned. "Could you help me with this bar? I'm almost—"

"The other end!" she exclaimed, removing her hands from her face. "We'll have to begin at the other end. In Bergen!"

"No," Harry whispered with the last air he had left in his lungs. "Bergen's not an end. Could you . . . "

He looked up at her. Saw her dark eyes fill with tears.

"It's my period," she whispered. Then she smiled. It happened so fast that it was like another person was standing above him, a person with an odd sheen to her eyes and a voice under complete control. "And you can just die."

In amazement, he heard the sound of her footsteps fading away, heard his own skeleton crack and red dots begin to dance in front of his eyes. He cursed, wrapped his hands around the iron bar and, with a roar, pushed. The bar wouldn't budge.

She was right; he could in fact die like that. He could choose. Funny, but true.

He wriggled, tipped the bar to one side until he heard the weights slide off and hit the floor with a deafening clang. Then the bar hit the floor on the other side. He sat up and watched the weights careering around the room.

Harry showered, dressed and went upstairs to the sixth floor. Fell into the swivel chair, already feeling the sweet ache of his muscles, which told him that he was going to be stiff in the morning.

There was a message on his voice mail from Bjørn Holm telling him to call back ASAP.

Holm picked up and there was the sound of heart rending sobs accompanied by the slide tones of a pedal steel guitar.

"What is it?" Harry asked.

"Dwight Yoakam," Holm said, turning down the music. "Sexy bastard, ain't he?"

"I mean, what's the call about?"

"We've got the results for the Snowman letter."

"And?"

"Nothing special as far as the writing's concerned. Standard laser printer."

Harry waited. He knew Holm had something.

"What's special is the paper he used. No one at the lab here has seen this type before—that's why it's taken a bit of time. It's made with mitsumata, Japanese papyrus-like bast fibers. You can probably tell mitsumata by the smell. They use the bark to make the paper by hand, and this particular sheet is extremely exclusive. It's called Kono."

"Kono?"

"You have to go to a specialty shop to buy it, the sort of place that sells fountain pens for ten thousand kroner, fine inks and leather-bound notebooks. You know . . . "

"I don't, in fact."

"Me neither," Holm conceded. "But anyway, there is one shop on Gamle Drammensveien that sells Kono writing paper. I spoke to the owner and was told they rarely sold such things now, so it was unlikely they would reorder. People don't have a sense of quality the way they used to, he reckoned."

"Does that mean . . . "

"Yes, I'm afraid that means he couldn't remember when he last sold any Kono paper."

"Mm. And this is the only dealer?"

"Yes," Holm said. "There was one in Bergen, but they stopped selling it a few years ago."

Holm waited for an answer—or, to be more precise, questions—as Dwight Yoakam, at low volume, yodeled the love of his life into her grave. But none came.

"Harry?"

"Yes. I'm thinking."

"Excellent!" said Holm.

It was this slow inland humor that could make Harry

chuckle long afterward, and even then without knowing why. But not at this moment. Harry cleared his throat.

"I think it's very odd that paper like this would be put into the hands of a murder investigator if you didn't want it to be traced back to you. You don't need to have seen many crime shows to know that we would check."

"Perhaps he didn't know it was rare?" Holm suggested. "Perhaps he hadn't bought it?"

"Of course that's a possibility, but something tells me that the Snowman wouldn't slip up like that."

"But he has."

"I mean I don't think it's a slip," Harry said.

"You mean . . . "

"Yes, I think he wants us to trace him."

"Why?"

"It's classic. The narcissistic serial killer staging a game, with himself in the principal role as the invincible, the all-powerful conqueror who triumphs in the end."

"Triumphs over what?"

"Well," Harry replied, saying it for the first time aloud, "at the risk of sounding narcissistic myself, me."

"You? Why?"

"I have no idea. Perhaps because he knows I'm the only policeman in Norway who has caught a serial killer, he sees me as a challenge. The letter would suggest that—he refers to Toowoomba. I don't know, Holm. By the way, have you got the name of the shop in Bergen?"

"Flab speaking!"

Or so it sounded. The word—*flæsk*—was articulated with Bergensian tones and gravity. That is, with a soft *l*, a long *æ* with a dip in the middle and a faint *s*. Peter Flesch, who voluntarily pronounced his name like the word for *flab*, was out of breath, loud and obliging. He was happy to talk; yes, he sold all types of antiques so long as they were small, but he specialized in pipes, lighters, pens, leather briefcases and stationery. Some used, some new. Most of his customers were regulars with an average age in line with his own.

To Harry's questions about Kono writing paper he answered, with regret in his voice, that he no longer had any such paper. Indeed, it had been several years since he had stocked it.

"This might be asking a bit too much," Harry said. "But since you have regular customers for the most part, is it possible that you might remember some of the ones who bought Kono paper?"

"Some maybe. Møller. And old Kikkusæn from Møllaren. We don't keep records, but my wife's got a good memory."

"Perhaps you could write down the full names, rough age and the address of those you can remember and e-mail them—"

Harry was interrupted by tut-tutting. "We don't have e-mail, son. Not going to get it, either. You'd better give me a fax number."

Harry gave the Police HQ number. He hesitated. It was a sudden inspiration. But inspiration never came without a reason.

"You wouldn't by any chance have had a customer a few years back," Harry said, "by the name of Gert Rafto, would you?"

"Iron Rafto?" Peter Flesch laughed.

"You've heard of him?"

"The whole town knew who Rafto was. No, he wasn't a customer here."

POB Møller always used to say that in order to isolate what was possible, you had to eliminate everything that was impossible. And that was why a detective should not despair, but be glad whenever he could discount a clue that did not lead to the solution. Besides, it had just been an idea.

"Well, thank you anyway," Harry said. "Have a good day."

"*He* wasn't a customer," Flesch said. "*I* was."

"Oh?"

"Yes. He brought me bits and bobs. Silver lighters, gold pens. That sort of thing. Sometimes I bought them off him. That was before I realized where they came from . . . "

"And where did they come from?"

"Don't you know? He stole them from crime scenes he worked on."

"But he never bought anything?"

"Rafto didn't have any need for the sort of thing that we had."

"But paper? Everyone needs paper, don't they?"

"Hm. Just a moment and I'll have a word with my wife."

A hand was placed over the receiver, but Harry could hear shouting, then a slightly lower conversation. Afterward the hand was removed and Flesch trumpeted in elated Bergensian: "She thinks Rafto took the rest of the paper when we stopped selling it. For a broken silver penholder, she thinks. Helluva memory the wife has, you know."

Harry put down the telephone knowing he was on his way to Bergen.

At nine o'clock that evening night lights were still burning on the first floor of Brynsalléen 6 in Oslo. From the outside, the six-story building looked like any commercial complex, with its modern red brick and gray steel façade. And for that matter inside, too, as most of the more than four hundred employees had jobs as engineers, IT specialists, social scientists, lab technicians, photographers and so on. But this was nevertheless "the national unit for the combating of organized and other serious crime," generally referred to by its old name of Kriminalpolitisentralen, or in its abbreviated form, Kripos.

Espen Lepsvik had just dismissed his men after reviewing their progress on the murder investigation. Only two people were left in the bare, harshly illuminated meeting room.

"That was a bit thin," Harry Hole said.

"Nice way of saying *zilch*," Espen Lepsvik said, massaging his eyelids with thumb and first finger. "Shall we go and have a beer while you tell me what you've unearthed?"

Harry told him while Espen Lepsvik drove them to the center and Kafé Justisen, which was on the way home for both men. They sat at the table at the back of the busy café, frequented by everyone from beer-thirsty students to even thirstier lawyers and policemen.

"I'm considering taking Katrine Bratt instead of Skarre to Bergen," Harry said, sipping from a bottle of carbonated water. "I checked her employment record before coming here. She's pretty green, but her file says that she worked on two murder cases in Bergen that I seem to remember you were sent over to lead."

"Bratt, yes, I remember her." Espen Lepsvik grinned and raised his index finger for another beer.

"Happy with her?"

"Extremely happy. She's . . . extremely . . . competent." Lepsvik winked at Harry, who saw that the other man already had that glassy look of a tired detective with three beers inside him. "And if both of us hadn't been married, I think I'd have had a chance with her."

He drained his glass.

"I was wondering more if you thought she was stable," Harry said.

"Stable?"

"Yes, there's something about her . . . I don't know quite how to explain it. Something intense."

"I know what you mean." Espen Lepsvik nodded slowly as his eyes tried to focus on Harry's face. "Her record's unblemished. But between you and me I heard one of the guys over there say something about her and her husband."

Lepsvik searched for some encouragement in Harry's face, found none, but continued anyway.

"Something . . . you know . . . that she likes leather and rubber. S and M. Apparently went to that kind of club."

"That's not my concern," Harry said.

"No, no, no, mine neither!" Lepsvik exclaimed, raising his hands in defense. "It's just a rumor. And do you know what?" Lepsvik sniggered, leaning forward across the table, so that Harry could smell his beery breath. "She can dominate me any day."

Harry realized that there must have been something in his eyes because Lepsvik immediately seemed to regret his openness and beat a quick retreat to his side of the table. And went on in a more businesslike tone.

"She's a professional. Clever. Intense and committed. Insisted with a bit too much vehemence that I should help her with a couple of cold cases, I remember. But not at all unstable—more the opposite. She's more the closed, sullen type. But there are lots like that. Yes, in fact I think you two could be a perfect team."

Harry smiled at the sarcasm and stood up. "Thanks for the tip, Lepsvik."

"What about a tip for me? Have you and she . . . got something going?"

"My tip," Harry said, throwing a hundred-krone note on the table, "is that you leave your car here."

14

Bergen

At precisely 8:26, the wheels of Flight DY 604 touched down on the wet tarmac at Flesland Airport, Bergen. So hard that Harry was suddenly wide awake.

"Sleep well?" Katrine asked.

Harry nodded, rubbed his eyes and stared out at the rain-heavy dawn.

"You were talking in your sleep," she said with a smile.

"Mm." Harry didn't want to ask about what. Instead he quickly went back over what he had been dreaming. Not about Rakel. He hadn't dreamed about her for nights. He had banished her. Between them they had banished her. But he had dreamed about Bjarne Møller, his old boss and mentor, who had walked onto the Bergensian plateaus and been found in Lake Revurtjern two weeks later. It was a decision Møller had made because he—just like Zenon, with the sore big toe— didn't think life was worth living any longer. Had Gert Rafto come to the same conclusion? Or was he really still out there somewhere?

"I called Rafto's ex-wife," Katrine said as they were walking through the arrivals hall. "Neither she nor the daughter wants to talk to the police again—they don't want to reopen old wounds. And that's fine. The reports from that time are more than adequate."

They got into a taxi outside the terminal.

"Lovely to be home?" Harry asked in a loud voice over the drumming of the rain and the rhythmic swish of the windshield wipers.

Katrine shrugged indifferently. "I always hated the rain. And I hated Bergensians who maintained it didn't rain here as much as eastern Norwegians made out."

They passed Danmarksplass, and Harry looked up at the top of Ulriken. It was covered with snow, and he could see the cable cars in motion. Then they drove through the viper's nest of service roads by Store Lungegårdsvann Bay and reached the center, which for visitors was always a welcome surprise after the drab approach.

They entered the SAS hotel by Bryggen on the harbor front. Harry had inquired whether she would stay with her parents, but Katrine had answered that for one night it would be too much stress—they would go to too much trouble, and in fact she hadn't even told them she was coming.

They were given key cards for their rooms, and in the elevator they were silent. Katrine looked at Harry and smiled as though silence in elevators were an implicit joke. Harry looked down, hoping his body wasn't sending false signals. Or real ones.

The doors finally slid open, and her hips sashayed down the corridor.

"Lobby in five," Harry said.

"What's the timetable?" he asked when they were sitting in the lobby six minutes later.

Katrine leaned forward from the deep armchair

and flipped through her leather-bound diary. She had changed into an elegant gray suit, which meant she immediately blended in with the hotel's business clientele.

"You meet Knut Müller-Nilsen, the head of the Missing Persons and Violent Crime Unit."

"You're not coming with me?"

"I'd have to say hello and talk to everyone, and the whole day would be wasted. In fact, it would be good if you didn't mention my name at all. They'd just be pissed off that I hadn't dropped by. I'm heading for Øyjordsveien to have a word with the last witness to see Rafto."

"Mm. And where was that?"

"By the docks. The witness saw him leave his car and walk into Nordnes Park. No one returned for the car, and the area was gone over with a fine-toothed comb without yielding a thing."

"Then what do we do?" Harry ran his thumb and middle finger along his jaw, thinking he should have shaved before making a trip out of town.

"You review the old reports with the detectives who were on the case and are still at the station. Get up to speed. Try to see it from a different angle."

"No," Harry said.

Katrine looked up from her diary.

"The detectives at the time drew their own conclusions and will just defend them," Harry explained. "I prefer to read the reports in peace and quiet in Oslo. And to spend my time here getting to know Gert Rafto a bit better. Can we see his possessions anywhere?"

Katrine shook her head. "His family gave everything he owned to the Salvation Army. It wasn't a great deal, apparently. Some furniture and clothes."

"What about where he lived or stayed?"

"He lived alone in an apartment in Sandviken after his divorce, but it was sold ages ago."

"Mm. And there's no childhood home, country cottage or cabin that's still in the family?"

Katrine hesitated. "The reports mentioned a little cabin in the police summerhouse quarter, on the island of Finnøy in Fedje. The cabins stay in the family in such cases, so maybe we can see it. I've got Rafto's wife's telephone number. I'll give her a call."

"I thought she wasn't talking to the police."

Katrine winked at him with a sly grin.

From the hotel reception Harry managed to borrow an umbrella, which turned inside out in the gusts before he got to Fisketorget—the harbor fish market—and looked like a tangled bat by the time he had jogged, head down, to the entrance of the Police HQ.

While Harry was standing in reception, waiting for POB Knut Müller-Nilsen, Katrine called him to say that the cabin on Finnøy was still in the Rafto family's hands.

"But his wife hasn't set foot there since the case. Nor her daughter, she thought."

"We'll go there," Harry said. "I'll be done here by one o'clock."

"OK, I'll get us a boat. Meet me at Zacharias wharf."

Knut Müller-Nilsen was a chuckling teddy bear with smiling eyes and hands the size of tennis rackets. The tall stacks of paper made him look as if he were snowed in at his desk, with his rackets folded behind his head.

"Rafto, hmm," Müller-Nilsen said, after explaining that it didn't rain in Bergen as much as eastern Norwegians made out.

"Seems like policemen have a tendency to slip through your fingers," Harry said, holding up the photo of Gert Rafto that came with the reports in his lap.

"Oh, yes?" Müller-Nilsen queried, looking at Harry,

who had found a spindle-back chair in the one paper-free corner of the office.

"Bjarne Møller," Harry said.

"Right," said Müller-Nilsen, but the tentative delivery gave him away.

"The officer who disappeared from Fløyen," Harry said.

"Of course!" Müller-Nilsen slapped his forehead. "Tragic business. He had only been here a short time so I didn't manage to . . . The assumption was that he got lost, wasn't it?"

"That was what happened," Harry said, peering out the window and thinking about Bjarne Møller's path from idealism to corruption. About his good intentions. About the tragic errors. Which others would never know about. "What can you tell me about Gert Rafto?"

My spiritual doppelgänger in Bergen, Harry thought, after receiving Müller-Nilsen's description: unhealthy attitude toward alcohol, difficult temperament, lone wolf, unreliable, doubtful morality and very blemished record.

"But he had exceptional powers of analysis and intuition," Müller-Nilsen said. "And an iron will. He seemed to be driven by . . . something. I don't know quite how to express it. Rafto was extreme. Well, that goes without saying now that we know what happened."

"And what did happen?" Harry asked, catching sight of an ashtray amid the piles of paper.

"Rafto was violent. And we know he was in Onny Hetland's apartment just before she disappeared, and that Hetland might have had information that would have revealed the identity of Laila Aasen's killer. Furthermore, he disappeared immediately afterward. It's not improbable that he drowned himself. Anyway, we saw no reason to implement a large-scale investigation."

"He couldn't have fled abroad?"

Müller-Nilsen smiled and shook his head.

"Why not?"

"Let me say that in this case we had the advantage of knowing the suspect very well. Even though, in theory, he could well have left Bergen, he was not the type. Simple as that."

"And no relatives or friends have reported any signs of life?"

Müller-Nilsen shook his head. "His parents are no longer with us, and he didn't have many friends, Rafto. He had a strained relationship with his ex-wife, so he would hardly have contacted her anyway."

"What about his daughter?"

"They were close. Nice girl, clever. Turned out well, considering the upbringing she had, of course."

Harry noticed the implied common knowledge. "Turned out well, of course," a phrase typical of small police stations where you were expected to know most things about most things.

"Rafto had a cabin on Finnøy, didn't he?" Harry asked.

"Yes, and that could of course be a natural place to take refuge. To mull things over and then . . . " Müller-Nilsen made a gesture with one of his huge hands across his larynx. "We went through the cabin, searched the island with dogs and dragged the waters. Nothing."

"Thought I would take a look out there."

"Not a lot to see. We have a cabin just opposite Iron Rafto's, and unfortunately it's in total disrepair. It's a disgrace his wife doesn't give it up. She's never there." Müller-Nilsen cast an eye at the clock. "I have a meeting, but one of the senior officers on the case will go through the reports with you."

"No need," Harry said, looking at the photo on his lap. All of a sudden the face seemed strangely familiar, as if he had seen it not long ago. Someone in disguise?

Someone he had passed in the street? Someone in a minor role he wouldn't have noticed, one of the traffic wardens sneaking around on Sofies Gate or an assistant at the Vinmonopol? Harry gave up.

"Not 'Gert,' then?"

"I beg your pardon?" Müller-Nilsen said.

"You said 'Iron Rafto.' You didn't call him just 'Gert,' then?"

Müller-Nilsen sent Harry a dubious look, ventured a chuckle, but then gave him only a wry smile. "No, I don't think that would ever have occurred to us."

"OK. Thanks for your help."

On his way out Harry heard Müller-Nilsen call, and he turned. The POB was standing in his office doorway at the end of the corridor and the words cast a brief vibrating echo between the walls.

"I don't think Rafto would have liked it, either."

Outside the Police HQ, Harry stood looking at the people bent double as they forced their way through the wind and rain. The sensation would not leave him. The sensation that something or someone was there, nearby, on the inside, visible, if he could only see things the right way, in the right light.

Katrine picked Harry up at the wharf, as arranged.

"I borrowed this from a friend," she said as she steered the twenty-one-foot so-called skerry jeep out of the narrow harbor mouth. As they rounded the Nordnes peninsula, a noise made Harry spin, and he caught sight of a totem pole. The wooden faces were screaming hoarsely at him with open mouths. A cold gust of wind swept across the boat.

"Those are the seals in the aquarium," Katrine said.

Harry pulled his coat tighter around him.

Finnøy was a tiny island. Apart from heather, there was no vegetation on the rain-lashed chunk of land, but it did have a quay, where Katrine expertly moored the boat. The residential area consisted of sixty wooden cabins in all, of doll's-house proportions, and reminded Harry of the miners' shacks he had seen in Soweto.

Katrine led Harry down the gravel path between the cabins and then walked up to one of them. It stood out because the paint was peeling. One of the windows was cracked. Katrine stretched up on tiptoes, grabbed the bulkhead light over the door and unscrewed it. A scraping sound came from inside as she rotated the dome and dead insects fluttered out. Plus a key, which she caught in midair.

"The ex-wife liked me," Katrine said, inserting the key in the door.

There was a smell of mold and damp wood inside. Harry stared into the semidarkness and heard the flick of a switch, and the light came on.

"She's got electricity, then, even if she doesn't use the cabin," he said.

"Communal," Katrine said, taking a slow look around. "The police pay."

The cabin was three hundred square feet and consisted of a sitting room–cum–kitchen–cum–bedroom. Empty beer bottles covered the countertop and sitting-room table. There was nothing hanging on the walls and there were no ornaments on the windowsills or books on the shelves.

"There's a cellar, too," Katrine said, pointing to a trapdoor in the floor. "This is your area. What do we do now?"

"We search," Harry said.

"What for?"

"That's the last of our thoughts."

"Why?"

"Because it's easy to miss something important if you're searching for something else. Clear your mind. You'll know what you're searching for when you see it."

"OK," Katrine said with exaggerated slowness.

"You start up here," Harry said, going to the trapdoor and pulling at the inset iron ring. A narrow staircase led down into the gloom. He hoped she didn't see his hesitation.

Dry cobwebs from long-dead spiders stuck to his face as he descended into the damp murk, which smelled of soil and rotten boards. The whole of the cellar was underground. He found a switch by the bottom of the staircase and pressed it, but nothing happened. The only light was the red eye at the top of a freezer by the side wall. He flicked on his flashlight, and the cone of light fell on a storeroom door.

The hinges screamed as he opened it. It was a carpenter's cubbyhole, full of tools. For a man with ambitions to do something meaningful, Harry thought. Besides catching murderers.

But the tools didn't look as if they had been used much, so maybe Rafto had realized that in the end he was no good at anything else; he wasn't the kind to make things, he was the kind to clear up afterward. A sudden noise made Harry whirl around. And he breathed out with relief when he saw that the freezer thermostat had activated the fan. Harry went into a second storeroom. A blanket had been spread over everything. He pulled it off, and the smell of damp and mildew hit him. The flashlight beam revealed a rotting parasol, a plastic table, a pile of freezer drawers, discolored plastic chairs and a croquet set. There was nothing else in the cellar. He heard Katrine rummaging around upstairs and was on the verge of closing the storeroom door. But one of the freezer drawers had slipped down into the doorway when he removed the blanket. He was about to nudge it back with his foot when he stopped and looked at it. In the light he could see the raised lettering on the side. ELECTROLUX. He walked over to the wall, where the fan on the freezer was still humming. It was an Electrolux. He grabbed the handle and pulled, but the door didn't budge. Beneath the handle he noticed a lock and realized that the freezer was simply locked. He went into the tool room to fetch a crowbar. As he returned, Katrine came down the stairs.

"Nothing up top," she said. "I think we should just go. What are you doing?"

"Breaking and entering," Harry said, with the tip of the crowbar inserted in the freezer door just above the lock. He put all his weight against the other end. It didn't give. He readjusted his grip, put one foot against the staircase and pushed.

"Goddamn—"

With a dry snap the door swung open and Harry fell headlong. He heard the flashlight hit the brick floor and felt the cold hit him, like the breath of a glacier. He was fumbling for the light behind him when he heard Katrine. It was a sound that chilled to the marrow, a deep-throated scream that passed into hysterical sobs, sounding like laughter. Then it went quiet for a couple of seconds as she drew breath, before it started again, the same scream, long and drawn out, like the methodical, ritual song of pain of a woman giving birth. But by then Harry had seen everything and knew why. She was screaming because after twelve years the freezer was still functioning perfectly and its internal light revealed something crammed inside, its arms to the fore, its knees bent and the head forced against one side. The body was covered with white ice crystals, as if a layer of white fungus had been feeding on it; and the distorted form was the visual representation of Katrine's screams. But that was not what had made Harry's stomach turn. Moments after the freezer broke open the body fell forward and the forehead hit the edge of the door, causing ice crystals to fall from the face and shower the cellar floor. That was how Harry could tell it was Gert Rafto grinning at them. However, the grin was not formed by the mouth, which was sewn up with coarse, hemplike thread zigzagging in and out of the lips. The grin traversed the chin and arced up to the cheeks and was drawn with a line of black nails that could only have been hammered in. What caught Harry's attention was the nose. He forced down the rising bile out of sheer defiance. The nasal bone and cartilage would have been removed first. The cold had sucked all the color from the carrot. The snowman was complete.

Part Three

15

Number Eight

It was eight o'clock in the evening, yet people walking down Grønlandsleiret could see that lights were burning on the whole of the sixth floor of the Police HQ.

In K1, Holm, Skarre, Espen Lepsvik, Gunnar Hagen and the chief superintendent sat in front of Harry. Six and a half hours had passed since they had found Gert Rafto on Finnøy, and four since Harry had called from Bergen to arrange a meeting for when he returned.

Harry had reported back on the discovery of the body, and even the chief superintendent had quailed in his chair when Harry showed the crime scene photos that the Bergen Police had e-mailed over.

"The autopsy report isn't ready yet," Harry said. "But the cause of death is fairly obvious. A firearm in the mouth and a bullet through the palate and out the back of the head. That happened at the crime scene; the Bergen guys found the bullet in the storeroom wall."

"Blood and cerebral matter?" Skarre asked.

"No," Harry said.

"Not after so many years," Lepsvik said. "Rats, insects . . ."

"There might have been residual traces," Harry said.

"But I spoke to the pathologist and we agreed: Rafto probably helped so that it wouldn't be so messy."

"Eh?" Skarre said.

"Ugh," Lepsvik said with feeling.

Reality seemed to dawn on Skarre and his face crumpled in horror. "Oh, hell . . . "

"Sorry," Hagen said. "Can anyone explain to me what you're talking about?"

"This is something we occasionally experience with suicides," Harry said. "The poor soul sucks the air out of the barrel before shooting himself. The vacuum causes there to be less"—he searched for the word—"soiling. What happened here is probably that Rafto was ordered to suck out the air."

Lepsvik shook his head. "And a policeman like Rafto must have known exactly why."

Hagen paled. "But how . . . how on earth do you make a man suck . . . "

"Perhaps he was given a choice," Harry suggested. "There are worse ways of dying than shooting yourself through the mouth." A stunned silence fell over them. And Harry let it fill the void for a few seconds before going on.

"So far we've never found the bodies. Rafto was also hidden, but he would have been found quickly enough, had it not been for relatives shunning the cabin. This leads me to believe that Rafto was not part of the killer's project."

"And you believe this is a serial killer?" There was no defiance in the chief superintendent's tone, just a wish to have this confirmed.

Harry nodded.

"If Rafto is not part of this so-called project, what could the motive be?"

"We don't know, but when a detective is killed it's natural to think that he's come to represent a threat for the killer."

Espen Lepsvik coughed. "Sometimes the way bodies are treated can tell us something about the motive. In this case, for example, the nose has been replaced with a carrot. In other words, he's thumbing his nose at us."

"Making fun of us?" Hagen asked.

"Perhaps he's telling us not to stick our noses in?" Holm suggested tentatively.

"Exactly!" Hagen exclaimed. "A warning to others to keep their distance."

The chief superintendent lowered his head and looked at Harry from the corner of his eye. "What about the stitched-up mouth?"

"A message: Keep your mouth shut," Skarre crowed.

"Right!" Hagen exclaimed. "If Rafto was a rotten apple he and the killer were probably in cahoots in some way, and Rafto was threatening to expose him."

They all looked at Harry, who had not responded to any of the suggestions.

"Well?" growled the chief superintendent.

"You may well be right, of course," Harry said. "But I believe the only message he wanted to send was that the Snowman had been there. And he likes making snowmen. Period."

The detectives exchanged quick glances, but no one objected.

"We have another problem," Harry said. "The Bergen Police have released a statement saying that a person has been found dead on Finnøy, that's all. And I've asked them to withhold further details for the time being so that we have a couple of days to hunt for clues without the Snowman knowing the body has been found. Unfortunately two days is not so realistic. No police station is *that* watertight."

"The press have Rafto's name for release early tomorrow," said Espen Lepsvik. "I know the people on *Bergens Tidende* and *Bergensavisen.*"

"Wrong," they heard behind them. "It'll be on the TV2 late news tonight. Not just the name but details of the crime scene and the link with the Snowman."

They turned around. In the doorway stood Katrine Bratt. She was still pale, though not as ashen as when Harry had watched her drive the boat from Finnøy, leaving him to wait for the police.

"So you know the TV2 people, do you?" asked Espen Lepsvik with a crooked grin.

"No," Katrine said, sitting down. "I know the Bergen Police Station."

"Where have you been, Bratt?" Hagen was asking. "You've been gone for several hours."

Katrine glanced at Harry, who sent her an imperceptible nod and cleared his throat. "Katrine's been doing a couple of jobs I gave her."

"Must have been important. Let's hear, Bratt."

"We don't need to go into it now," Harry said.

"I'm just curious," Hagen teased.

Mr. goddamn Armchair General, Harry thought. Mr. Punctuality, Mr. Debrief, can't you leave her alone, can't you see the girl's still in shock? You blanched yourself when you saw the pictures. She ran home, ducked everything. So what? She's back now. Give her a pat on the back rather than humiliate her in front of her colleagues. This went through Harry's mind, in loud, clear tones, as he tried to catch Hagen's eye and make him understand.

"Well, Bratt?" Hagen said.

"I've been checking a few things," Katrine said, raising her chin.

"I see. Such as . . . :"

"Such as Idar Vetlesen being a medical student when

Laila Aasen was murdered and Onny Hetland and Rafto disappeared."

"Is that relevant?" asked the chief superintendent.

"It's relevant," Katrine said. "Because he studied at the University of Bergen."

K1 went quiet.

"A medical student?" The chief looked at Harry.

"Why not?" Harry said. "He took up plastic surgery later, and he says he likes shaping faces."

"I checked the places where he trained as an intern and later worked," Katrine said. "They don't coincide with the disappearances of the women we believe the Snowman has killed. But as a young doctor you quite often travel. Conferences, short, temporary posts."

"Damn shame Krohn won't let us talk to the guy," Skarre said.

"Forget it," Harry said. "We'll arrest Vetlesen."

"What for?" Hagen said. "Studying in Bergen?"

"For trying to buy sex from minors."

"On what basis?" asked the chief superintendent.

"We have a witness. The owner of the Leon. And we have photos connecting Vetlesen with the place."

"I hate to say this," said Espen Lepsvik, "but I know the Leon guy, and he will never testify. The case won't stick; you'll have to release Vetlesen within twenty-four hours, no question."

"I know," Harry said, looking at his watch. He was working out how long it would take to drive to Bygdøy. "And it's incredible what people can find to say in that space of time."

Harry pressed the doorbell once more, thinking it was like summer vacation when he was small and everyone had gone and he was the only boy left in Oppsal. When he had stood there ringing the bell at Øystein's place or one of the others', hoping by some miracle that someone would be at home and not with Grandma in Halden or in a cabin in Son or camping in Denmark. He had pressed the bells again and again until he knew that only one possibility remained. Tresko. Tresko, with whom Øystein and he never wanted to play, but who still hung around like a shadow waiting for them to change their minds, to bring him in from the cold, temporarily. He must have chosen Harry and Øystein because they weren't the most popular, either, so he reckoned if he was going to be accepted into a club this was where his greatest hope lay. And now this was his opportunity because he was the only one left, and Harry knew that Tresko was always at home because his family could never afford to go anywhere and he had no other friends to play with.

Harry heard slippers shuffling inside, and the door opened a crack. The woman's face lit up. Just like Tresko's mother's face had lit up when she saw Harry. She never invited him in, just called Tresko, went to get him, gave him an earful, shoved him into his ugly parka and pushed him out onto the step, where he stood looking sulkily at Harry. And Harry knew Tresko knew. And felt his mute hatred as they walked down to the kiosk. But that was fine. It helped time pass.

"I'm afraid Idar's not here," Fru Vetlesen said. "But won't you come in and wait? He was just going out for a little drive, he said."

Harry shook his head, wondering if she could see the blue lights piercing the evening darkness of Bygdøy on the street behind him. He bet it was Skarre who had put them on, the numbskull.

"When did he leave?"

"Just before five."

"But that's several hours ago," Harry said. "Did he say where he was going?"

She shook her head. "Never tells me anything. What do you think about that? Doesn't even want to let his own mother know what he's doing."

Harry thanked her and said he would be back later. Then he walked down the gravel path and the steps to the wicket gate. They hadn't found Idar Vetlesen at his office or at Hotel Leon, and the curling club had been shut up and dark. Harry closed the gate behind him and walked over to the car. The uniformed officer rolled down the window.

"Switch off the blue lights," Harry said, turning to Skarre in the backseat. "She says he's not at home, and she's probably telling the truth. You'll have to wait to see if he returns. Call the duty officer and tell him to mount a manhunt. Nothing over the police radio, OK?"

On the way back to town Harry called the Telenor switchboard, where he was informed that his contact Torkildsen had gone home for the day and that inquiries regarding the location of Idar Vetlesen's mobile phone would have to go through formal channels early the following morning. He hung up and turned up the volume of Slipknot's "Vermilion," but he wasn't in the mood and pressed the EJECT button to change to a Gil Evans CD he had rediscovered at the back of the glove compartment. The NRK twenty-four-hour news was jabbering away on the radio as he fidgeted with the CD cover.

"The police are searching for a male doctor in his thirties, a resident of Bygdøy. He is thought to be connected to the Snowman murders."

"Fuck!" Harry yelled, throwing Gil Evans at the windshield and showering the car with bits of plastic. The disc rolled into the foot well. In sheer frustration Harry stamped on the accelerator and passed a tanker, which was in the left lane. Twenty minutes. It had taken them twenty minutes. Why didn't they just give the Police HQ a microphone and live airtime?

The police cafeteria was closed and deserted for the evening, but that was where Harry found her, her and sandwiches at a table for two. Harry sat in the other chair.

"Thank you for not telling anyone I lost it on Finnøy," she said softly.

Harry nodded. "What did you do?"

"I checked out and caught the three o'clock flight. I just had to get away." She looked down into her cup of tea. "I'm . . . sorry."

"It's fine," Harry said, regarding her slim, bent neck, pinned-up hair and the petite hand placed on the table. He saw her differently now. "When the tough nuts crack, they crack in style."

"Why?"

"Perhaps because they haven't had enough practice at losing control."

Katrine nodded, still staring at the teacup with the police sports team logo.

"You're a control freak, too, Harry. Don't you ever lose it?"

She raised her eyes, and Harry thought it must have been the intense light in her irises that lent her whites a bluish shimmer. He groped for his cigarettes. "I've had masses of practice at it. I've hardly trained at anything else except freaking out. I've got a black belt in losing control."

She gave a faint smile by way of response.

"They've measured the brain activity of experienced boxers," he said. "Did you know that they lose consciousness several times in the course of a fight? A fraction of a second here, a fraction of a second there. But somehow they still manage to stay on their feet. As if the body knows it's temporary, assumes control and holds them up for as long as it takes them to regain consciousness." Harry tapped out a cigarette. "I also lost it at the cabin. The difference is that, after all these years, my body knows that control will return."

"But what do you do," Katrine asked, stroking a wisp of hair from her face, "not to be knocked out by the first blow?"

"Do what boxers do, sway with the punches. Don't resist. If any of what happens at work gets to you, just let it. You won't be able to shut it out in the long term anyway. Take it bit by bit, release it like a dam, don't let it collect until the wall develops cracks."

He poked the unlit cigarette between his lips.

"Yes, I know. The police psychologist told you all this when you were a cadet. My point is this: Even when you release it into real life you have to feel what it's doing to you, feel if it's destroying you."

"OK," Katrine said. "And what do you do if you feel it's destroying you?"

"Then you get yourself another job."

She gave him a long stare.

"And what did you do, Harry? What did you do when you felt it was destroying you?"

Harry bit lightly into the filter, feeling its soft, dry fiber rub against his teeth. Thinking she could have been his sister or daughter—they were made of the same stern stuff. Solid, heavy, ungiving building material with big cracks.

"I forgot to look for another job," he said.

She beamed. "Do you know what?" she whispered.

"What?"

She stretched out her hand, grabbed the cigarette from his mouth and leaned across the table.

"I think—"

The cafeteria door burst open. It was Holm.

"TV2," he said. "It's on the news now. Names and photos of Rafto and Vetlesen."

And with that came the chaos. Even though it was eleven o'clock at night, within half an hour the foyer of the Police HQ was full of journalists and photographers. They were all waiting for the Kripos head, Espen Lepsvik, or Hagen, the head of the Crime Squad, the chief superintendent, the chief constable, or basically anyone, to come down and say something. Mumbling among themselves that the police had to acknowledge their responsibility to keep the general public informed about such a serious, shocking and circulation-increasing matter.

Harry stood by the banister in the atrium looking down at them. They were circling like restless sharks, consulting one another, duping one another, helping one another, bluffing and scenting tidbits. Had anyone heard anything? Would there be a press conference tonight? Or at least an impromptu briefing? Was Vetlesen already on his way to Thailand? The deadline was looming; something had to happen.

Harry had read that the word *deadline* originated from the battlefields of the American Civil War, when, for lack of anything material to lock prisoners behind, the captors gathered together the prisoners and a line was drawn around them in the dirt. Which became known as the "dead line," and anyone who strayed beyond it was shot. And that was precisely what they were, the news warriors down there in the foyer: prisoners of war restrained by a deadline.

Harry was on his way to the meeting room with the others when his mobile phone rang. It was Mathias.

"Have you listened to the voice mail I left you?" he asked.

"Haven't had the chance—things are heating up here," Harry said. "Can we talk about it later?"

"Of course," Mathias said. "But it's about Idar. I saw on the news that he was a wanted man."

Harry shifted the phone to his other hand. "Tell me now, then."

"Idar called me earlier today. He was asking about carnadrioxide. He often calls me to ask about medicines— pharmacy's not Idar's strong suit—so I didn't think too much about it at the time. I'm calling because carnadrioxide is an extremely dangerous medicine. Just thought you would want to know."

"Sure, sure," Harry said, rummaging through his pockets until he found a half-chewed pencil and a tram ticket. "Carna . . . ?"

"Carnadrioxide. It contains venom from the cone snail and is used as a painkiller for cancer and HIV patients. It's a thousand times stronger than morphine and just a tiny overdose will paralyze muscles with immediate effect. The respiratory organs and heart will stop and you will die instantly."

Harry made notes. "OK. What else did he say?"

"Nothing. He sounded stressed. Thanked me and hung up."

"Any idea where he was calling from?"

"No, but there was something odd about the acoustics. He certainly wasn't calling from his consulting room. It sounded as if he were in a church or a cave—do you understand what I mean?"

"I understand. Thank you, Mathias. We'll call you back if we need to know any more."

"Just happy to—"

Harry didn't catch the rest as he pressed the END-CALL button and the line went dead.

Inside K1, the whole of the small investigation team was sitting with cups of coffee—a fresh pot was simmering on the machine—and jackets were hanging from chairs. Skarre had just returned from Bygdøy. He reported back on the conversations he had had with Idar Vetlesen's mother, who had repeated that she didn't know anything and the whole thing must be an enormous misunderstanding.

Katrine had phoned his assistant, Borghild Moen, who had expressed the same sentiments.

"We'll question them tomorrow if need be," Harry said. "Now, I'm afraid, we have a more pressing problem."

The three others looked at Harry as he summarized the conversation with Mathias. Reading from the back of a tram ticket. Carnadrioxide.

"Do you think he murdered them?" Holm asked. "With paralyzing medicine?"

"There we have it," Skarre interrupted. "That's why he has to hide the bodies. So that the medicine isn't discovered at the autopsy and traced back to him."

"The only thing we know," Harry said, "is that Idar Vetlesen is out of control. And if he's the Snowman, he's breaking the pattern."

"The question," Katrine said, "is who he's after now. Someone's definitely going to die from that stuff soon."

Harry rubbed his neck. "Did you get a printout of Vetlesen's phone calls, Katrine?"

"Yes, I was given names for the numbers and went through them with Borghild. Most were patients. And there were two conversations with Krohn, his lawyer, and the one you just summarized with Lund-Helgesen. In addition, there was a number registered under Popper Publishing."

"We haven't got much to work on," Harry said. "We can sit here and drink coffee and scratch our stupid heads. Or we can go home and return with the same stupid, but not quite so exhausted, heads tomorrow."

The others just stared at him.

"I'm not joking," he said. "Get the hell home."

Harry offered to drop Katrine off in the former workers' district of Grünerløkka, where, following her instructions, he stopped outside an old four-story building on Seilduksgata.

"Which apartment?" he asked, leaning forward.

"Second floor, on the right."

He peered up. All the windows were dark. He didn't see any curtains. "Doesn't look like your husband's at home. Or perhaps he's gone to bed."

"Perhaps," she said, not making a move. "Harry?"

He looked at her quizzically.

"When I said the question was who the Snowman was after now, did you know who I meant?"

"Maybe," he said.

"What we found on Finnøy was not the random murder of someone who knew too much. It had been planned long before then."

"What do you mean?"

"I mean that if Rafto had in fact been on his trail, then that was planned, too."

"Katrine . . ."

"Wait. Rafto was the best detective in Bergen. You're the best in Oslo. He could predict that it would be you who would investigate these murders, Harry. That was why you received the letter. I'm merely saying you should be careful."

"Are you trying to frighten me?"

She shrugged. "If you're frightened, do you know what that means?"

"No."

Katrine opened the car door. "That you should find yourself another job."

Harry unlocked his apartment door, took off his boots and stopped at the threshold to the sitting room. The room was completely dismantled now, like a building kit in reverse. The moonlight fell on something white on the bare red wall. He went in. It was a number eight, drawn in chalk. He stretched out his hand and touched it. It must have been done by the mold man, but what did it mean? Perhaps a code to tell him which liquid to apply there.

For the rest of the night wild nightmares racked Harry's body, turning him this way and that. He dreamed that something was forced into his mouth and he had to breathe through some kind of opening so as not to die from suffocation. It tasted of oil, metal and gunpowder, and in the end there was no more air left inside, just a vacuum. Then he spat the thing out and discovered it was not the barrel of a gun, but a figure eight he had been breathing through. An eight with a large circle below, a smaller one above. The big circle at the bottom, the little one at the top. Gradually the figure eight acquired a third, a smaller circle on top. A head. Sylvia Ottersen's head. She tried to scream, tried to tell him what had happened, but she couldn't. Her lips were sewn together.

When he awoke, his eyes were gummed up, he had a headache and there was a coating on his lips that tasted of chalk and bile.

16

Curling

It was a chilly morning in Bygdøy as Asta Johannsen un-locked the curling club at eight, as usual. The soon-to-be seventy-year-old widow cleaned there twice a week, which was more than sufficient, as the private little hall was not used by more than a handful of men and, more-over, it didn't have any showers. She switched on the light. From the cog-jointed timber walls hung trophies, diplomas, pennants adorned with Latin phrases and old black-and-white photographs of men wearing beards, tweeds and worthy expressions. Asta thought they looked comical, like those foxhunters in English TV series about the upper classes. She went through the door to the curl-ing hall and knew from the cold inside that they had for-gotten to turn up the thermostat for the ice, which they usually did to save electricity. Asta Johannsen flicked on the light switch and, as the neon tubes blinked and wres-tled to decide whether they wanted to work, she put on her glasses and saw that the thermostat for the cooling cables was indeed too low, and she turned it up.

The light shone on the gray surface of ice. Through her reading glasses she glimpsed something at the other end of the hall, so she removed them. Slowly things came into focus. A person? She wanted to walk across the ice, but hesitated. Asta Johannsen was not at all the jittery type but she feared that one day she would break her thigh on the ice and have to stay there until the foxhunters found her. She gripped one of the brooms leaning against the walls, used it as a walking stick and, taking tiny steps, teetered across the ice.

The lifeless man lay at the end of the sheet with his head in the center of the rings. The blue-white gleam from the neon tubes fell on the face stiffened in a grimace. There was something familiar about his face. Was he a celebrity? The glazed eyes seemed to be looking for something behind her, beyond what was here. The cramped right hand held an empty plastic syringe containing a residue of red contents.

Asta Johannsen calmly concluded that there was nothing she could do for him and concentrated on making her way back over the ice to the nearest telephone.

After she had called the police and they had come, she went home and drank her morning coffee.

It was only when she picked up the *Aftenposten* newspaper that she realized who it was she had found.

Harry was in a crouch, examining Idar Vetlesen's boots.

"What does our pathologist say about the time of death?" he asked Bjørn Holm, who was standing beside him in a denim jacket lined with white teddy-bear fur. His snakeskin boots made almost no noise as he stamped them on the ice. Barely an hour had passed since Asta Johannsen had made her call, but the reporters were already assembled outside the red police cordon by the curling club.

"He says it's difficult to tell," Holm said. "He can only

guess how fast the temperature of a body lying on ice in a much warmer room might fall."

"But he *has* made a guess?"

"Somewhere between five and seven yesterday evening."

"Mm. Before the TV news announcement about him. You saw the lock, did you?"

Holm nodded. "Standard Yale. It was locked when the cleaning lady arrived. I saw you looking at the boots. I've checked the prints. I'm pretty sure they're identical to the prints we've got from Sollihøgda."

Harry studied the pattern on the sole. "So you think this is our man, do you?"

"I would reckon so, yes."

Harry nodded, deep in thought. "Do you know if Vetlesen was left-handed?"

"Would doubt it. As you can see, he's holding the syringe in his right hand."

Harry nodded. "So he is. Check anyway."

Harry had never really managed to experience a sense of pleasure when, one day, cases he was working on reached a conclusion, were solved, were over. For as long as the case was under investigation this was his aim, but once it was achieved, he knew only that he hadn't arrived at his journey's end. Or that this was not the end he had imagined. Or that it had shifted, he had changed or Christ knows what. The thing was, he felt empty, success did not taste as promised, catching the guilty party always came loaded with the question So what?

It was seven in the evening, witnesses had been questioned, forensic evidence collected, a press conference held and in the Crime Squad corridors there was a burgeoning party atmosphere. Hagen had ordered cakes and beer and summoned Lepsvik's and Harry's teams to some self-congratulation in K1.

Harry sat in a chair eyeing a huge piece of cake someone had placed in his lap. He listened to Hagen speaking, the laughter and the applause. Someone nudged him in the back as he passed, but most left him in peace. There was a buzz of conversation around him.

"The bastard was a real loser. Chickened out when he knew we had him."

"Cheated us."

"Us? Do you mean that you Lepsvik crew—?"

"If we'd caught him alive, the court would have declared him insane and—"

"We should be happy. After all, we didn't have any conclusive evidence, just circumstantial."

Espen Lepsvik's voice boomed from the other side of the room. "OK, folks, shut up! A motion has been put forward, and passed, that we meet at Fenris Bar at eight to get seriously drunk. And that's an order. OK?"

Loud cheering.

Harry put the cake down and was standing up when he felt a light hand on his shoulder. It was Holm.

"I checked. It's as I said—Vetlesen was right-handed."

Carbon dioxide fizzed from a beer being opened, and an already tipsy Skarre put his arm around Holm's shoulder.

"They say that life expectancy is higher for right-handed people than for left-handed. Didn't apply to Vetlesen, though, did it? Ha-ha-ha!"

Skarre left to share his nugget of wisdom with others, and Holm asked Harry: "Are you off?"

"Going for a walk. Might see you at Fenris."

Harry had almost reached the door when Hagen grabbed his arm.

"Nice if no one left quite yet," he said quietly. "The chief constable said he would come down to say a few words."

Harry looked at Hagen, then realized that there must have been something in his eyes because Hagen let go of his arm as though he had been burned.

"Just going to the toilet," Harry said.

Hagen gave a quick smile and nodded.

Harry went to his office, got his jacket and walked slowly downstairs, out of the Police HQ and down to Grønlandsleiret. There were a few flakes of snow in the air, lights twinkled on Ekeberg Ridge, a siren rose and fell like the distant song of a whale. Two Pakistanis were having a good-natured argument outside Harry's local shops as the snow settled on their oranges, and a swaying drunk was singing a sea shanty in Grønlands torg. Harry could sense the creatures of the night sniffing the air, wondering if it was safe to come out. God, how he loved this town.

"You in here?"

Eli Kvale looked in surprise at her son, Trygve, who was sitting at the kitchen table reading a magazine. The radio was droning away in the background.

She was going to ask why he didn't sit in the living room with his father, but it struck her that it should be equally natural for him to want to talk to her. Except that it wasn't. She poured herself a cup of tea, sat down and watched him in silence. He was so good-looking. She had always believed she would find him ugly, but she had been wrong.

The voice on the radio said men were no longer the cause of women's inability to get into Norwegian boardrooms; companies were struggling to reach the legally determined quota of women because the majority seemed to have a chronic aversion to posts where they might be exposed to criticism, find themselves professionally challenged or have no one to hide behind.

"They're like kids who cry and cry to have a pistachio, but spit it out when they finally get it," the voice said. "Damn irritating to see. It's about time women took some responsibility and showed some guts."

Yes, thought Eli. It is about time.

"Someone came up to me in ICA today," Trygve said.

"Oh, yes?" Eli said, her heart in her throat.

"Asked me if I was your son, yours and Dad's."

"Uh-huh," Eli said softly, all too softly, feeling dizzy. "And what did you answer?"

"What did I answer?" Trygve looked up from his magazine. "I answered yes, of course."

"And who was the man who asked?"

"What's the matter, Mom?"

"What do you mean?"

"You're so pale."

"Nothing, my love. Who was he?"

Trygve went back to his magazine. "I didn't say it was a man, did I?"

Eli got to her feet, turned down the radio as a woman's voice was thanking the minister of industry and Arve Støp for the debate. She stared into the dark as a couple of snowflakes swirled hither and thither, aimless, unaffected by gravity and their own will, apparently. They would land wherever chance dictated. And then they would melt and vanish. There was some comfort in that.

She coughed.

"What?" Trygve said.

"Nothing," she said. "I think I'm getting a cold."

*   *   *

Harry drifted aimlessly, without any will of his own, through the streets of Oslo. It was only when he was standing outside the Hotel Leon that he realized that was where he had been heading. The prostitutes and the dope dealers had already taken up their positions in the neighboring streets. It was rush hour. Customers preferred to deal in sex and dope before midnight.

Harry walked into reception and saw from Børre Hansen's horrified expression that he had been recognized.

"We had a deal!" squealed the hotel owner, wiping the sweat from his brow.

Harry wondered why men who lived off others' urges always seemed to wear this glistening film of sweat, like a veneer of false shame at their unscrupulousness.

"Give me the key to the doctor's room," Harry said. "He's not coming tonight."

Three of the hotel-room walls had seventies wallpaper with psychedelic patterns of brown and orange, while the main bathroom wall was painted black and shot through with gray cracks and blotches where the plaster had fallen off. The double bed sagged in the middle. The needlefelt carpet was hard. Water and semen repellent, Harry assumed. He removed a threadbare hand towel from the chair at the foot of the bed and sat down. Listened to the rumbles of expectant excitement in the town and sensed that the dogs were back. They snapped and barked, pulled at the iron chains, shouting: Just one drink, just a shot so that we can leave you in peace and lie at your feet. Harry was not in a laughing mood, but laughed anyway. Demons had to be exorcised, and pain drowned. He lit a cigarette. The smoke curled up to the rice-paper lamp.

What demons had Idar Vetlesen been grappling with? Had he brought them here, or was this the sanctuary, the refuge? Perhaps he had discovered some answers, but not all of them. Never all of them. Like whether madness and evil are two different entities, or whether when we no longer understand the purpose of destruction we simply term it madness. We're capable of understanding that someone has to drop an atomic bomb on a town of innocent civilians, but not that others have to cut up prostitutes who spread disease and moral depravity in the slums of London. Hence we call the former realism and the latter madness.

Christ, how he needed a drink. Just one to take the edge off the pain, off this day, off this night.

There was a knock at the door.

"Yes," Harry yelled and started at the sound of his own anger.

The door opened and a black face came into view. Harry looked her over. Beneath the beautiful, strong head and neck she wore a short jacket, so short that the rolls of fat bulging over the top of her tight trousers could be seen.

"Doctor?" she asked in English. The stress on the second syllable gave the word a French timbre.

He shook his head. She looked at him. Then the door was closed and she was gone.

A couple of seconds passed before Harry got off his chair and went to the door. The woman had reached the end of the corridor.

"Please!" Harry shouted in English. "Please, come back."

She stopped and regarded him warily.

"Two hundred kroner," she said. Stress on the last syllable.

Harry nodded.

She sat on the bed and listened to his questions, perplexed. About Doctor, this evil man. About the orgies with several women. About the children he wanted them to bring. And with every new question she shook her head in incomprehension. In the end, she asked if he was from the police.

Harry nodded.

Her eyebrows puckered. "Why you ask these questions? Where is Doctor?"

"Doctor killed people," Harry said.

She studied him suspiciously. "Not true," she said at length.

"Why not?"

"Because Doctor is a nice man. He helps us."

Harry asked how Doctor helped them. And now he was the one to sit and listen as the black woman told him that every Monday and Thursday Doctor sat in this room with his bag, talked to them, sent them to the bathroom to provide urine samples, took blood samples and tested them for venereal diseases. He gave them pills and treatment if they had any of the usual sexual diseases. And the address of the hospital if they had the other one, the Plague. If there was anything else wrong with them, he gave them pills for that, too. He never took payment, and the only thing they had to do was promise that they wouldn't tell anyone apart from their colleagues on the street. Some of the girls had brought their children when they were ill, but the hotel owner had stopped them.

Harry smoked a cigarette as he listened. Was this Vetlesen's indulgence? The counterpoint to evil, the necessary balance. Or did it just accentuate the evil, set it into relief? Dr. Mengele was said to have been very fond of children.

His tongue kept growing in his mouth; it would suffocate him if he didn't have a drink soon.

The woman had stopped talking. She was fingering the two-hundred-krone note.

"Will Doctor come back?" she asked finally.

Harry opened his mouth to answer her, but his tongue

was in the way. His mobile phone rang and he took the call.

"Hole speaking."

"Harry? This is Oda Paulsen. Do you remember me?"

He didn't remember her; anyway, she sounded too young.

"From NRK," she said. "I invited you to *Bosse* last time."

The researcher. The honey trap.

"We were wondering whether you would like to join us again, tomorrow. We'd like to hear about this Snowman triumph. Yes, we know he's dead, but nevertheless. About what goes through the head of this sort of person. If he can be called that—"

"No," Harry said.

"What?"

"I don't want to join you."

"It's *Bosse*," Oda Paulsen said with genuine bewilderment in her voice. "On NRK TV."

"No."

"But listen, Harry, wouldn't it be interesting to talk—"

Harry threw the mobile phone at the black wall. A chip of plaster fell off.

Harry put his head in his hands, trying to hold it together so that it didn't explode. He had to drink something. Anything. When he looked up again, he was alone in the room.

It might have been avoided if Fenris Bar had not served alcohol. If Jim Beam had not been on the shelf behind the bartender, screaming with its hoarse whiskey-voice about anesthesia and amnesty: "Harry! Come here, let's reminisce about old times. About those awful ghosts we have dispelled, about the nights we could sleep."

On the other hand, perhaps it might not.

Harry hardly registered his colleagues, and they took no notice of him. When he had entered the garish bar with the plush red Danish ferry interior, they were already well on the way. They were hanging off one another's shoulders, shouting and breathing alcohol over one another, singing along with Stevie Wonder, who claimed he had just called to say he loved you. They looked and sounded, in short, like a football team who had won the cup. And as Stevie Wonder finished by stating that his declaration of love came from the bottom of his heart, Harry's third drink was placed in front of him on the bar.

The first drink had numbed everything; he had been unable to breathe and mused that that was how taking carnadrioxide must feel. The second had almost made his stomach turn. But his body had got over the first shock and known that it had received what it had been demanding for so long. And now it was responding with a murmur of well-being. The heat washed through him. This was music for the soul.

"Are you drinking?"

Katrine was standing by his side.

"This is the last," Harry said, his tongue no longer feeling thick, but smooth and supple. Alcohol just improved his articulation. And people hardly noticed that he was drunk, up to a certain point. That was why he still had a job.

"It's not the last," Katrine said. "It's the first."

"That's one of those AA precepts." Harry looked up at her. The intense blue eyes, the thin nostrils, the full lips. God, she looked so wonderful. "Are you an alcoholic, Katrine Bratt?"

"I had a father who was."

"Mm. Was that why you didn't want to visit them in Bergen?"

"You avoid visiting people because they have an illness?"

"I don't know. You may have had an unhappy childhood because of him or something like that."

"He couldn't have made me unhappy. I was born like that."

"Unhappy?"

"Maybe. What about you?"

Harry hunched his shoulders. "Goes without saying."

Katrine sipped her drink, a shiny number. Vodka shiny, not gin gray, he established.

"And what's your unhappiness due to, Harry?"

The words came out before he had time to think. "Loving someone who loves me."

Katrine laughed. "Poor thing. Did you have a harmonious start to life and a cheery disposition that was later destroyed? Or was your path marked out for you?"

Harry stared at the golden-brown liquid in his glass. "Sometimes I wonder. But not often. I try to think about other things."

"Like what?"

"Other things."

"Do you sometimes think about me?"

Someone bumped into her and she stepped closer. Her perfume intermingled with the aroma of Jim Beam.

"Never," he said, grabbing his glass and knocking back the contents. He stared ahead, into the mirror behind the bottles, where he saw Katrine Bratt and Harry Hole standing much too close to each other. She leaned forward.

"Harry, you're lying."

He turned to her. Her eyes seemed to be smoldering, yellow and blurred, like the fog lights on an approaching car. Her nostrils were flared, and she was breathing hard. There was a smell, as if she took lime in her vodka.

"Tell me exactly, in detail, what you feel like doing now, Harry." There was gravel in her voice. "Everything. And don't lie this time."

His mind went back to the rumor Espen Lepsvik had mentioned, about Katrine Bratt and her husband's predilections. Bullshit—his mind didn't go back, the thought had been too far forward in his cerebral cortex the whole time. He breathed in. "OK, Katrine. I'm a simple man with simple needs."

She had tipped back her head, as some animal species do to show submission. He raised his glass. "I feel like drinking."

A colleague unsteady on his legs knocked Katrine from behind and she was sent staggering toward Harry. Harry broke her fall by grasping her left side with his free hand. Her face screwed up with pain.

"Sorry," he said. "An injury?"

She held her ribs. "Fencing. It's nothing. Sorry."

She turned her back on him and plowed a path through her colleagues. He saw several of the guys follow her with their eyes. She went into the bathroom. Harry scanned the room, saw Lepsvik look away as their gazes met. He couldn't stay here. There were other places he and Jim could chat. He paid and was about to leave. There was still a heeltap in his glass. But Lepsvik and two colleagues were watching him from the other side of the bar. It was just a question of some self-control. Harry wanted to move his legs, but they were stuck to the floor like glue. He took the glass, put it to his lips and drained the contents.

The cold night air was wonderful on his burning skin. He could kiss this town.

When Harry got home he tried to masturbate into the

sink, but spewed instead and peered up at the calendar hanging on the nail under the top cupboard. He had been given it by Rakel for Christmas a few years ago. It had photos of all three of them. A photo for every month. November. Rakel and Oleg were laughing at him against a background of yellow autumnal foliage and a pale blue sky. As blue as the dress Rakel was wearing, the one with the small white flowers. The dress she had been wearing the first time. And he decided that tonight he would dream himself into that sky. Then he opened the cupboard under the counter, swept away the empty Coke bottles, which tipped over with a clatter, and—right at the back—there it was. The untouched bottle of Jim Beam. Harry had never risked being without alcohol in the house, not even in his most sober spells. Because he knew what he might do to get hold of the stuff once he had gone on a bender. As if to delay the inevitable, he ran his hand across the label. Then he opened the bottle. How much was enough? The syringe Vetlesen had used was still coated in red after the poison, showing that it had been full. As red as cochineal. My darling, cochineal.

He breathed in and raised the bottle. Put it to his mouth, felt his body tense, steel itself for the shock. And then he drank. Greedily and desperately, as if to get it over and done with. The sound from his throat between swigs sounded like a sob.

17

Good News

Gunnar Hagen strode down the corridor at speed.

It was Monday and four days since the Snowman case had been solved. They should have been four pleasant days. And there had been, it was true, congratulations, smiling bosses, positive comments in the press and even inquiries from foreign newspapers as to whether they could have the whole of the background story and the investigation from start to finish. And that was where the problem had started: The person who could have given Hagen the details of the success story had not been present. Four days had passed and no one had either seen or heard from Harry Hole. And the reason was obvious. Colleagues had seen him drinking at Fenris Bar. Hagen had kept this to himself, but the rumors had reached the ears of the chief superintendent. And Hagen had been summoned to his office that morning.

"Gunnar, this won't do anymore."

Gunnar Hagen had said there might be other explanations. Harry wasn't always that prompt at letting them know he was working away from the office. There was a lot of investigating left to do on the Snowman case even though they had found the killer.

But the chief superintendent had made up his mind. "Gunnar, we've come to the end of the road as far as Hole is concerned."

"He's our best detective, Torleif."

"And the worst representative for our force. Do you want that kind of role model for our young officers, Gunnar? The man's an alcoholic. Everyone in-house knows he was drinking at Fenris, and that he hasn't turned up for work since. If we tolerate that, we're setting a very low standard and the damage will be practically irreparable."

"But dismissal? Can't we—"

"No more warnings. The regulations regarding civil servants and alcohol abuse are abundantly clear."

This conversation was still reverberating in the POB's head as he knocked on the chief superintendent's door once again.

"He's been seen," Hagen said.

"Who?"

"Hole. Li called me to say he'd seen him go into his office and close the door behind him."

"OK," said the chief superintendent, getting to his feet. "Then let's go and have a talk with him right away."

They stomped through the Crime Squad, the red zone on the sixth floor of the Police HQ. And staff, as though scenting something in the air, came to the doors of their offices, poked their heads out and watched the two men walking side by side with stern, closed faces.

When they reached the door labeled 616, they stopped. Hagen took a deep breath.

"Torleif . . . ," he began, but the chief superintendent had already gripped the door handle and thrust it open.

They stood in the doorway, their eyes wide with disbelief.

"Good God," whispered the chief superintendent.

Harry Hole, in a T-shirt, sat behind his desk with an

elastic band tightened around his forearm, his head bent forward. A syringe hung from the skin directly under the elastic band. The contents were transparent, and even from the door they could see several red dots where the needle had punctured the milky-white arm.

"What the hell are you doing, man?" hissed the chief superintendent, pushing Hagen in front of him and slamming the door behind them.

Harry's head bobbed up, and he looked at them from miles away. Hagen observed that Harry was holding a stopwatch. Suddenly Harry snatched out the syringe, looked at the remaining contents, threw aside the syringe and made notes on a piece of paper.

"Th-this makes it easier, in fact, Hole," the chief superintendent stammered. "Because we have bad news."

"*I* have bad news, gentlemen," Harry said, tearing a piece of cotton padding from a bag and dabbing his arm. "Idar Vetlesen can't possibly have committed suicide. And I presume you know what that means?"

Gunnar Hagen felt a sudden urge to laugh. The whole situation appeared so absurd to him that his brain simply could not come up with any other satisfactory reaction. And he could see from the chief superintendent's face that he didn't know what to do, either.

Harry looked at his watch and stood up. "Come to the meeting room in exactly one hour. Then you'll find out why," he said. "Right now I have a couple of other matters that need to be sorted out."

The inspector hurried past his two astonished superiors, opened the door and disappeared down the corridor with long, sinewy strides.

One hour and four minutes later Gunnar Hagen trooped into a hushed K1 with the chief superintendent and the chief constable. The room was filled to the rafters with officers from Lepsvik's and Hole's investigation teams, and Harry Hole's voice was the only thing to be heard. They found standing room at the back. Pictures of Idar Vetlesen were projected onto the screen, showing how he was found in the curling hall.

"As you can see, Vetlesen has the syringe in his right hand," Harry Hole said. "Not unnatural since he was right-handed. But it was his boots that triggered my curiosity. Look here."

Another picture showed a close-up of the boots.

"These boots are the only real forensic evidence we have. But it's enough. Because the print matches those we found in the snow at Sollihøgda. However, look at the laces." Hole indicated with a pointer. "Yesterday I carried out some tests with my own boots. For the knot to lie like that, I would have to do up my laces back to front. As if I were left-handed. The alternative would be to stand in front of the boot as if I were doing it for someone else."

A ripple of unease went through the room.

"I'm right-handed." It was Espen Lepsvik's voice. "And I tie my laces like that."

"Well, this may just be an oddity. However, it's this sort of thing that arouses a certain"—Hole looked as if he were tasting the word before he chose it—"disquiet. A disquiet that forces you to ask other questions. Are they really Vetlesen's boots? These boots are a cheap make. I visited Vetlesen's mother yesterday and got permission to see his collection of shoes. They're expensive, every pair, without exception. And, as I thought, he was no different from the rest of us—he sometimes kicked his shoes off without undoing the laces. That's why I can say"—Hole banged the pointer on the image—"that I know Idar Vetlesen did not tie his shoelaces like this."

Hagen glanced across at the chief superintendent, whose forehead was lined with a deep furrow.

"The question that emerges," Hole said, "is whether someone could have put the boots on Vetlesen. The same ones that the individual in question wore in Sollihøgda. The motive would be to make it seem as if Vetlesen were the Snowman, of course."

"A shoelace and cheap boots?" shouted an inspector from Lepsvik's team. "We have a sicko who wanted to buy the sexual favors of children, who knew both victims here in Oslo and whom we can place at the crime scene. All you have is speculation."

The tall policeman bowed his shorn skull. "That's correct, as far as it goes. But now I'm coming to hard facts. On the face of it, Idar Vetlesen took his own life with carnadrioxide by inserting a syringe with a very fine point into a vein. According to the postmortem, the concentration of carnadrioxide was so great that he must have injected twenty milliliters into his arm. That stacks up with the residue inside the syringe, which showed that it had been full. Carnadrioxide, as we now know, is a paralyzing substance, and even small doses can kill as the heart and respiratory organs are instantly incapacitated. According to the pathologist, it would take at most three seconds for an adult to die if that dose was injected into a vein, as was the case with Idar Vetlesen. And that simply does not make sense."

Hole waved a piece of paper on which Hagen could see he had jotted down some numbers in pencil.

"I've done some tests on myself with the same kind of syringe and needle that Vetlesen used. I injected a saltwater solution that matches carnadrioxide, in that all such solutions are at least ninety-five percent water. And I've kept track of the numbers. However hard I pressed, the narrow needle means that you can't inject twenty milliliters in less than eight seconds. Ergo . . . " The inspector waited for the inescapable conclusion to sink in before continuing. "Vetlesen would have been paralyzed before injecting a third of the contents. In short, he can't have injected everything. Not without help."

Hagen swallowed. This day was going to be even worse than he had anticipated.

When the meeting was over, Hagen saw the chief constable whisper something into the chief superintendent's ear, and the chief superintendent leaned over to Hagen.

"Ask Hole and his team to meet in my office now. And put a muzzle on Lepsvik and his lot. Not *one* word of this must get out. Understand?"

Hagen did understand. Five minutes later they were sitting in the chief superintendent's large, cheerless office.

Katrine Bratt closed the door and was the last person to sit down. Harry Hole had slid into his chair, and his outstretched legs rested directly in front of the chief superintendent's desk.

"Let me be brief," the chief superintendent said, running a hand across his face as if to erase what he saw: an investigation team back at square one. "Have you any good news, Hole? To sweeten the bitter fact that in your mysterious absence we have told the press that the Snowman is dead as a result of our unflagging toil?"

"Well, we can assume that Idar Vetlesen knew something he should not have known, and that the killer discovered we were on his trail and therefore eliminated the possibility that he might be unmasked. If that's correct, it's still true that Vetlesen died as a result of our unflagging toil."

The chief superintendent's cheeks had gone rosy with the stress. "That's not what I mean by good news, Hole."

"No, the good news is that we're getting warmer. If

not, the Snowman wouldn't have gone to such lengths to make it seem as if Vetlesen were the man we were hunting. He wants us to call off the investigation, believing we have solved the case. In short, he's under pressure. And that's when killers like the Snowman begin to make mistakes. In addition, it suggests that he dare not resume the bloodbath."

The chief superintendent sucked at his teeth and ruminated. "So that's what you think, is it, Hole? Or is it just what you hope?"

"Well," said Harry Hole, scratching his knee through the tear in his jeans, "you were the one who asked for good news, boss."

Hagen groaned. He looked out the window. It had clouded over. Snow was forecast.

Filip Becker gazed down at Jonas, who was sitting on the living-room floor with his eyes riveted to the TV screen. Since Birte had been reported missing the boy had sat for hours like this every single afternoon. As though it were a window into a better world. A world in which he could find her if only he looked hard enough.

"Jonas."

The boy glanced up at him obediently, but without interest. His face stiffened with horror when he spotted the knife.

"Are you going to cut me?" the boy asked.

The expression on his face and the reedy voice were so amusing that Filip Becker almost burst into laughter. The light from the lamp over the coffee table glinted on the steel. He had bought the knife from a hardware store in Storo Mall. Right after he had phoned Idar Vetlesen.

"Just a tiny bit, Jonas. Just a tiny bit."

Then he made an incision.

18

View

At two o'clock Camilla Lossius was driving home from the gym. She had, as usual, driven across town, to Oslo West, and the Colosseum Park fitness center. Not because they had different equipment from the gym near their house in Tveita, but because the people at Colosseum were more like her. They were West End types. Moving to Tveita had been part of the marriage deal with Erik. And she had needed to consider it as a whole package. She turned into the street where they lived. Saw the lights in the windows of the neighbors she had greeted, but with whom she had never really spoken. They were Erik's people. She braked. They weren't the only ones to have a two-car garage in this street in Tveita, but it was the only one with electric doors. Erik was obsessed by these things; she couldn't give a damn. She pressed the remote, the door tipped and rose and she depressed the clutch and slid in. As expected, Erik's car was not there; he was at work. She leaned over to the passenger seat, grabbed her gym bag and the groceries from ICA supermarket, snatched a customary glance at herself in the rearview mirror before getting out. She looked good, her friends said.

Not yet thirty and a detached house, second car and country retreat outside Nice, they said. And they asked what it was like living in the East End. And how her parents were after the bankruptcy. Strange how their brains automatically linked the two questions.

Camilla looked in the mirror again. They were right. She did look good. She thought she saw something else, a movement at the edge of the mirror. No, it was just the door tipping back into position. She got out of the car and was searching for her house keys when she realized her mobile phone was still in the hands-free holder in the car.

Camilla turned and uttered a short scream.

The man had been standing behind her. Terrified, she took a step back with a hand over her mouth. She was about to apologize with a smile, not because there was anything to apologize for, but because he looked entirely innocuous. But then she caught sight of the gun in his hand. It was pointed at her. The first thing she thought was that it looked like a toy.

"My name's Filip Becker," he said. "I called. There was no one at home."

"What do you want?" she asked, trying to control the quiver in her voice as her instinct told her she must not show her fear. "What's this about?"

He flashed a quick smirk. "Whoring."

In silence, Harry watched Hagen, who had interrupted the team meeting in Harry's office to repeat the chief superintendent's order that the "theory" of Vetlesen's murder was not to be leaked under any circumstances, not even to partners, marital or otherwise. At length, Hagen caught Harry's eye.

"Well, that was all I wanted to say," he concluded quickly and left the room.

"Go on," Harry said to Bjørn Holm, who had been summarizing their findings at the curling-hall crime scene. Or, to be more accurate, the lack of findings.

"We'd only just got going when it was determined it was a suicide. We didn't find any forensic evidence, and now the crime scene's contaminated. I looked this morning and there's not a lot to see, I'm afraid."

"Mm," Harry said. "Katrine?"

Katrine looked down at her notes. "Yes, well, your theory is that Vetlesen and the killer met at the curling club and this must have been prearranged. The obvious conclusion to draw is that they were in phone contact. You asked me to check the list of calls."

"Yes," said Harry, stifling a yawn.

She flicked through. "I got lists from Telenor for Vetlesen's clinic phone and mobile. I took them to Borghild's house."

"House?" Skarre queried.

"Of course—she doesn't have a job to go to anymore. She told me that Idar Vetlesen didn't have any visitors except for patients during the last two days. Here's a list of them."

She took a piece of paper from a file and placed it on the table between them.

"As I had presumed, Borghild has a good knowledge of Vetlesen's professional and social contacts. She helped me to identify practically all of the people on the call list. We divided them in two: professional contacts and social contacts. Both show phone numbers, the time and date of the call, whether it was incoming or outgoing and how long it lasted."

The other three put their heads together and studied the lists. Katrine's hand touched Harry's. He didn't detect any signs of embarrassment in her. Perhaps he had dreamed it all, the suggestion she had made at Fenris Bar.

The thing was, though, that Harry didn't dream when he was drinking. That was the whole point of drinking. Nevertheless, he had woken up the next day with an idea that must have been conceived somewhere between the systematic emptying of the whiskey bottle and the pitiless moment of awakening. The idea of cochineal and of Vetlesen's full syringe. And that was the idea that had saved him from running straight to the liquor store on Thereses Gate, and instead propelled him back into work. One drug for another.

"Whose number is that?" Harry asked.

"Which one?" Katrine asked, leaning forward.

Harry pointed to a number on the list of social contacts.

"What makes you ask about that number in particular?" Katrine asked, peering up at him with curiosity.

"Because it's the social contact who called him, and not vice versa. We have to believe it's the killer who's stage-managing here, therefore he's the one who called."

Katrine checked the number against the list of names. "Sorry, but that person is on both lists, a patient as well."

"OK, but we have to start somewhere. Who is it? Man or woman?"

Katrine gave a wry grin. "Definitely a man."

"What do you mean?"

"Manly. As in macho. Arve Støp."

"Arve Støp?" Holm burst out. "*The* Arve Støp?"

"Put him at the top of our visiting list," Harry said.

When they had finished, they had a list of seven calls to investigate. They had the names to match all seven numbers except for one: a pay phone in Storo Mall the morning of Idar's murder.

"We've got the exact time," Harry said. "Is there a surveillance camera by the phone?"

"I don't think so," Skarre said. "But I know there's a

camera at each entrance. I can check with the security firms whether they've got a recording."

"Monitor all the faces half an hour before and after," Harry said.

"That's a big job," Skarre said.

"Guess who you need to ask," Harry said.

"Beate Lønn," Holm said.

"Correct. Say hello."

Holm nodded, and Harry felt a pang of bad conscience. Skarre's mobile went off with the La's "There She Goes" as a ringtone.

They watched as Skarre listened. Harry reflected on how he had put off calling Beate for a long time now. Since the one visit in the summer, after the birth, he hadn't seen her. He knew she didn't blame him for Jack Halvorsen's being killed in the line of duty. But it had been a bit too much for him: seeing Beate and Halvorsen's child, the child the young officer never got to see, and knowing deep down that Beate was wrong. He could—he should—have saved Halvorsen.

Skarre hung up.

"A woman up in Tveita's been reported missing by her husband. Camilla Lossius, twenty-nine years old, no children. It came in only a couple of hours ago, but there are a few worrying details. There's a shopping bag on the countertop, nothing has been put in the fridge. The mobile phone was left in the car, and according to the husband she never goes anywhere without it. And one of the neighbors told the husband she saw a man hanging around their property and garage as if waiting for someone. The husband can't say whether anything's missing, not even toiletries or suitcases. These are the types who have a villa outside Nice and so many possessions they don't notice if something's missing. Understand what I mean?"

"Mm," Harry said. "What does the Missing Persons Unit think?"

"That she'll turn up. They just wanted to keep us posted."

"OK," Harry said. "Let's go on, then."

No one commented on the report for the rest of the meeting. However, Harry could feel it was in the air, like the rumble of distant thunder that might—or might not—come closer. After being allocated names off the call list, the group dispersed from Harry's office.

Harry went back to the window and gazed down at the park. The evenings were drawing in earlier and earlier; it was almost tangible as the days passed. He thought about Idar Vetlesen's mother when he had told her about the free medical help he had given to black prostitutes in the evenings. And for the first time she had dropped her mask—not in grief but in fury—and screamed it was lies, her son did not tend Negro whores. Perhaps it was better to lie. Harry thought about what he had told the chief superintendent the day before, that the bloodbath was over for the time being. In the gathering darkness beneath him he could just make it out under his window. The kindergarten classes often played there, especially if snow had fallen, as it had last night. At least that was what he had thought when he saw it on his way to work this morning. It was a big grayish white snowman.

Above the *Liberal* editorial offices in Aker Brygge, on the top floor, with a view of the Oslo Fjord, Akershus Fortress and the village of Nesoddtangen, were situated 2,500 of Oslo's most expensive privately owned square feet. They belonged to the owner and editor of *Liberal*, Arve Støp. Or just Arve, as it said on the door where Harry rang the bell. The stairway and landing had been decorated in a functional, minimalist style, but there was a hand-painted jug on either side of the oak door, and Harry caught himself wondering what the net gain would be if he made off with one of them.

He had rung once, and now at last he could hear voices inside. One was a bright twitter, and one deep and calm. The door opened and a woman's laughter tinkled out. She was wearing a white fur hat—synthetic, Harry assumed—from which cascaded long blond hair.

"I'm looking forward to it!" she said, turning and only then catching sight of Harry.

"Hello," she said in a neutral tone, until recognition caused her to replace it with an enthusiastic "Well, hi!"

"Hi," said Harry.

"How are you?" she asked, and Harry could see she had just recalled their last conversation. The one that ended against the black wall in the Hotel Leon.

"So you and Oda know each other?" Arve Støp stood in the hallway with his arms crossed. He was barefoot and wearing a T-shirt with a barely perceptible Louis Vuitton logo and green linen trousers that would have looked feminine on any other man. For Arve Støp was almost as tall and broad as Harry and had a face an American presidential candidate would have killed for: determined chin, boyish blue eyes edged with laughter lines and thick gray hair.

"We've just exchanged greetings," Harry said. "I was on their talk show once."

"I have to go, guys," Oda said, imparting air-kisses on the run. Her footsteps drummed down the stairs as if her life depended on it.

"Yes, this was about that damn talk show, too," Støp said, beckoning Harry in and grasping his hand. "My exhibitionism is approaching pathetic levels, I'm afraid. This time I didn't even ask what the topic was before agreeing to take part. Oda was here doing her research. Well, you've done this, so you know how they work."

"In my case, they just phoned," Harry said, still feeling the heat from Støp's hand on his skin.

"You sounded very serious on the telephone, Hole. What can a miserable journalist help you with?"

"It's about your doctor and curling colleague, Idar Vetlesen."

"Aha! Vetlesen. Of course. Shall we go in?"

Harry wriggled out of his boots and followed Støp down the corridor to a living room that was two steps lower than the rest of the apartment. One look was enough to tell Harry where Idar had found the inspiration for his waiting room. The moonlight glittered on the fjord outside the window.

"You're running kind of an a priori investigation, I understand?" Støp said, flopping into the smallest item of furniture, a single molded plastic chair.

"I beg your pardon?" Harry said, sitting on the sofa.

"You're starting with the solution and working backward to find out how it happened."

"Is that what 'a priori' means?"

"God knows—I just like the sound of Latin."

"Mm. And what do you think of our solution? Do you believe it?"

"Me?" Støp laughed. "I don't believe anything. But that's my profession, of course. As soon as something begins to resemble an established truth, it's my job to argue against it. That's what liberalism is."

"And in this case?"

"Oof. I can't see that Vetlesen had any rational motive. Or was crazy in a way that would defy standard definitions."

"So you don't think Vetlesen is the murderer?"

"Arguing against the belief that the world is round is

not the same as believing it to be flat. I assume you have evidence. An alcoholic beverage? Coffee?"

"Yes, coffee, please."

"I was teasing." Støp smiled. "I've got only water and wine. No, I tell a lie—I've got some sweet cider from Abbediengen Farm. And you have to taste that whether you want to or not."

Støp scuttled into a kitchen and Harry stood up to inspect his surroundings.

"Quite an apartment you've got here, Støp."

"It was in fact three apartments," Støp shouted from the kitchen. "One belonged to a successful shipowner who hanged himself out of boredom more or less where you're sitting now. The second, where I am, belonged to a stockbroker who was indicted for insider trading. He found deliverance in prison, sold the apartment to me and gave all the money to an Inner Mission preacher. But that's a kind of insider trading, too, if you know what I mean. Still, I've heard the man is a lot happier now, so why not?"

Støp came into the living room carrying two glasses with pale yellow contents. He passed one to Harry.

"The third apartment was owned by a plumber from Østensjø who decided when they were planning the Aker Brygge harbor area that this was where he would live. A kind of class journey, I guess. After scrimping and saving—or working in the black market and overcharging—for ten years, he bought it. But it cost so much he couldn't afford a moving company and did the move himself with a couple of pals. He had a safe weighing eight hundred pounds. I suppose he must have needed it for all his black market money. They had reached the final landing and there were only eighteen steps left when the infernal safe slipped. The plumber was dragged under it, broke his back and was paralyzed. Now he lives in a nursing home

in the area he came from, with a view of Lake Østen-
sjøvannet." Støp stood by the window, drank from his
glass and gazed thoughtfully across the fjord. "True, it's
only a lake, but it's still a view."

"Mm. We were wondering about your connection
with Idar Vetlesen."

Støp spun around theatrically, as nimble in his movements as a twenty-year-old. "Connection? That's a
damned strong word. He was my doctor. And we happened to curl together. That is, *we* curled. What Idar did
can at best be described as pushing a stone and cleaning
the ice." He waved his hand dismissively. "Yeah, yeah, I
know, he's dead, but that's how it was."

Harry put the glass of cider on the table untouched.
"What did you talk about?"

"By and large about my body."

"Huh?"

"He was my doctor, for Christ's sake."

"And you wanted to change parts of your body?"

Arve Støp laughed heartily. "I've never felt a need for
any of that. Of course I know that Idar performed these
ridiculous plastic surgery operations, liposuction and all
that, but I recommend prevention rather than repair. I
play sports, Inspector. Don't you like the cider?"

"It contains alcohol," Harry said.

"Really?" Støp said, contemplating his glass. "That I
can't imagine."

"So which parts of the body did you discuss?"

"The elbow. I have tennis elbow and it bothers me
when we curl. He prescribed the use of painkillers before training, the idiot. Because it also suppresses in-
flammation. And therefore I strained my muscles every
time. Well, I suppose I don't need to issue any medical
warnings since we're talking about a dead doctor here,
but you shouldn't take pills for pain. Pain is a good thing;

we would never survive without it. We should be grateful for pain."

"Should we?"

Støp tapped his index finger on a windowpane so thick that it didn't let in a single sound from the town. "If you ask me, it's not the same as a view of fresh water. Or is it, Hole?"

"I haven't got a view."

"Haven't you? You should. A view gives perspective."

"Speaking of perspectives, Telenor gave us a list of Vetlesen's recent telephone calls. What did you talk about the day before he died?"

Støp fixed an inquisitive eye on Harry while leaning back and finishing off the cider. Then he took a deep, contented breath. "I had almost forgotten we spoke, but I suppose it was about elbows."

Harry's childhood friend Tresko had once explained that the poker player who bases his game on his ability to intuit a bluff is bound to lose. It's true that we all give ourselves away with superficial mannerisms when lying; however, you have no chance of exposing a good bluffer unless you coldly and calculatedly chart all these mannerisms against each individual, in Tresko's opinion. Harry tended to think Tresko was right. And so he didn't base his conviction that Støp was lying on the man's expression, his voice or his body language.

"Where were you between four and eight o'clock the day Vetlesen died?" Harry asked.

"Hey!" Støp raised an eyebrow. "Hey! Is there something about this case I or my readers ought to know?"

"Where were you?"

"That sounds manifestly like you haven't caught the Snowman after all. Is that right?"

"I would appreciate it if you would let me ask the questions, Støp."

"Fine, I was with . . . "

Arve paused. And his face suddenly lit up in a boyish smile.

"No, hang on a moment. You're insinuating that I could have had something to do with Vetlesen's death. If I were to answer I would be conceding the premise of the question."

"I can easily register that you refused to answer the question, Støp."

Støp raised his glass in a toast. "A familiar counter-move, Hole. One that we press people use every single day. Hence the name. Press. People. But please note that I'm not refusing to answer, Hole. I'm just refraining from doing so at this minute. In other words, I'm giving it some thought." He nodded to himself. "I'm not refusing—I just haven't decided whether to answer or indeed what. And in the meantime you'll have to wait."

"I've got plenty of time."

Støp turned. "And I don't mean to waste it, Hole, but I have declared in the past that *Liberal's* only capital and means of production is my personal integrity. I hope you appreciate that I as a pressman have an obligation to ex-ploit this situation."

"Exploit?"

"Hell, I know I'm sitting on a little atomic bomb of a news scoop here. I assume no newspapers have been tipped off that there's something fishy about Vetlesen's death. If I were to give you an answer now that would clear me of suspicion, I would have already played my hand. And then it's too late for me to ask for relevant in-formation before I answer. Am I right, Hole?"

Harry had an inkling where this was leading. And that Støp was a smarter bastard than he had anticipated.

"Information isn't what you need," Harry said. "What you need is to be told that you can be prosecuted for consciously obstructing the police in the course of their duties."

"Touché." Støp laughed, distinctly enthusiastic now. "But as a pressman and a liberalist I have principles to consider. The issue here is whether I, as a declared anti-establishment watchdog, should unconditionally make my services available to the ruling power's forces of law and order." He spat out the words without concealing the sarcasm.

"And what would your preconditions be?"

"Exclusivity on the background information, of course."

"I can give you exclusivity," Harry said. "Together with a ban on passing the information to a single soul."

"Hm, well, that doesn't take us anywhere. Shame." Støp stuffed his hands in the pockets of his linen trousers. "But I already have enough to question whether the police have apprehended the right man."

"I'm warning you."

"Thank you. You've already done that." Støp sighed. "Consider, however, whom you're dealing with, Hole. On Saturday we're having the mother of all parties at the Plaza. Six hundred guests are going to celebrate twenty-five years of *Liberal*. That's not bad for a magazine that has always pushed the boundaries of our freedom of speech, that has navigated in legally polluted waters every day of its existence. Twenty-five years, Hole, and we have yet to lose a single case in the courts. I'll take this up with our lawyer, Johan Krohn. I fancy the police know him, Hole?"

Harry nodded glumly. Støp indicated with a discreet flourish toward the door that he regarded the visit over.

"I promise to assist in any way that I'm able," Støp said as they stood in the hall by the door. "If you in the force assist us."

"You know quite well that it's impossible for us to make such a deal."

"You have no idea what deals we've already made, Hole." Støp smiled, opening the door. "You really don't. I expect to see you again soon."

"I didn't expect to see you again so soon," Harry said, holding the door open.

Rakel trotted up the last steps to his apartment.

"Yes, you did," she said, stealing into his arms. Then she shoved him inside, kicked the door shut with her heel, grabbed his head with both hands and kissed him greedily.

"I hate you," she said while slackening his belt. "You know I didn't need this in my life right now."

"Go, then," Harry said, unbuttoning her coat and then her blouse. Her trousers had a zip at the side. He undid it and slipped his hand in, right to the bottom of her spine, over her cool, silky-smooth panties. It was quiet in the hall, just their breathing and a single click of her heel on the floor as she moved her foot to allow him in.

In bed afterward, sharing a cigarette, Rakel accused him of being a drug dealer.

"Isn't that how they do it?" she said. "The first doses are free. Until they're hooked."

"And then they have to pay," Harry said, blowing one large and one small ring toward the ceiling.

"A lot," Rakel said.

"You're only here for sex," Harry said. "Aren't you? Just so that I know."

Rakel stroked his chest. "You've got so thin, Harry."

He didn't answer. He waited.

"It's not working so well with Mathias," she said. "That is, he works well. He works perfectly. It's me who doesn't work."

"What's the problem?"

"If only I knew. I look at Mathias and I think, There's your dream guy. And I think, He lights my fire, and I try to light his, I almost attack him because I want some pleasure—do you understand? It would be so good, so right. But I can't do it . . . "

"Mm. I have some difficulty imagining that, but I hear what you're saying."

She pulled his earlobe hard. "The fact that we were always hungry for each other wasn't necessarily a hallmark of quality for our relationship, Harry."

Harry watched as the smaller smoke ring caught up with the larger one and formed a figure eight. Yes, it was, he thought.

"I've started looking for pretexts," she said. "Take this amusing physical quirk that Mathias inherited from his father, for example."

"What?"

"It's nothing special, but he's a bit embarrassed about it."

"Come on, tell me."

"No, no, it has absolutely no significance, and to start with I thought his embarrassment was just sweet. Now I've started to think it's annoying. As if I'm trying to make a flaw out of this bagatelle of Mathias's, an excuse for . . . for . . . " She fell silent.

"For being here," Harry completed.

She hugged him tight. Then she got up.

"I'm not coming back," she said with a pout.

It was almost midnight when Rakel left Harry's apartment. Silent, fine drizzle made the pavement shine under the streetlamps. She turned onto Stensberggata, where she had parked the car. She got inside and was about to start the engine when she spotted a handwritten note placed under the windshield wiper. Opening the door a

crack, she grabbed it and tried to read the writing that the
rain had nearly washed away.

We're going to die, whore.

Rakel flinched. Looked around. But she was alone. All
she could see on the street were other parked cars. Were
there notes on them, too? She couldn't see any. It had to
be chance; no one could have known where her car was.
She rolled down the window, held the note between two
fingers and let it go, started the engine and pulled out
onto the road.

Just before the end of Ullevålsveien she suddenly had
a feeling someone was sitting in the backseat staring at
her. She looked and saw a boy's face. Not Oleg, but another boy's unfamiliar face. She slammed on the brakes
and the rubber screamed on the pavement. Then came
the angry sound of a car horn. Three times. She stared
into her mirror as her chest heaved. And saw the face
of the terrified young man in the car right behind her.
Trembling, she put the car back into gear.

Eli Kvale stood in the hallway as if rooted to the floor. In
her hand she was still holding the telephone receiver. She
had not been imagining things, not at all.

Only when Andreas had said her name twice did she
come to.

"Who was it?" he said.

"No one," she said. "Wrong number."

When they were in bed, she wanted to snuggle up to
him. But she couldn't. Couldn't bring herself to do it. She
was impure.

"We're going to die," the voice on the phone had said.
"We're going to die, whore."

19

TV

By the time the investigation team was assembled the following morning they had checked out six of the seven names on Katrine Bratt's list. There was just one remaining.

"Arve Støp?" Bjørn Holm and Magnus Skarre queried in unison.

Katrine Bratt said nothing.

"OK," Harry said. "I've spoken to Krohn on the phone. He made it quite clear that Støp does not wish to answer the question of whether he has an alibi. Or any other questions. We can arrest Støp, but he is perfectly within his rights not to make a statement. The only thing we'll achieve by doing this is to announce to the world that the Snowman is still out there. The point at issue is whether Støp is telling the truth or this is all an act."

"But an A-list celebrity as a murderer," Skarre said with a grimace. "Who's ever heard of that?"

"O. J. Simpson," Holm said. "Phil Spector. Marvin Gaye's father."

"Who the hell's Phil Spector?"

"It'd be better if you all told me what you think," Harry said. "Straight from the hip, spontaneous. Has Støp got anything to hide? Holm?"

Bjørn Holm rubbed his cutlet-shaped sideburns. "It's suspicious that he doesn't wanna answer a question as specific as where he was when Vetlesen died."

"Bratt?"

"I think Støp just finds being under suspicion amusing. And as far as his magazine is concerned, it doesn't mean a thing. The opposite, in fact. It reinforces its outsider image. The great martyr standing firm against the current of opinion, as it were."

"Agreed," Holm said. "I'm changing sides. He wouldn't have taken this risk if he'd been guilty. He'd have gone for a scoop."

"Skarre?" Harry asked.

"He's bluffing. This is just bullshit. Did anyone actually understand the stuff about the press and principles?"

None of the others answered.

"OK," Harry said. "Assuming the majority is right and he's telling the truth, then we should eliminate him as quickly as possible and move on. Is there anyone we can think of who might have been with him at the time of Vetlesen's death?"

"Hardly," Katrine said. "I called a girl I know at *Liberal*. She said that outside working hours Støp isn't particularly sociable. By and large he keeps to himself in his apartment in Aker Brygge. Ladies excepted, that is."

Harry looked at Katrine. She reminded him of the overzealous student who is always a term ahead of the lecturer.

"Ladies in the plural?" Skarre asked.

"To quote my friend, Støp is notorious for buzzing around the honey pot. Right after she had rejected one of his advances, he told her in no uncertain terms that she wasn't living up to his expectations as a journalist and ought to think about grazing in new pastures."

"The two-faced bastard," Skarre said, snorting.

"A conclusion you and she share," Katrine said. "But the fact is she's a crappy journalist."

Holm and Harry burst into laughter.

"Ask your friend if she can name any of the lovers," Harry said, getting up. "And afterward call the rest of the staff at the magazine and ask them the same. I want him to feel us breathing down his neck. So let's get going."

"And what about you?" said Katrine, who had not moved.

"Me?"

"You didn't tell us if you think Støp is bluffing."

"Well." Harry smiled. "He's definitely not telling the whole truth."

The other three looked at him.

"He said he didn't remember what he and Vetlesen had been talking about during their last telephone conversation."

"And?"

"If you found out that a man you'd just been talking to was a wanted serial killer who'd now committed suicide, wouldn't you have instantly remembered the conversation, gone over it in great detail, asking yourself if you should have picked up anything?"

Katrine nodded slowly.

"The other thing I'm wondering," Harry said, "is why the Snowman would contact me to tell me to look for him. And when I get close, as he should have anticipated, why does he become desperate and try to make it look as if Vetlesen were the Snowman?"

"Perhaps that was the idea the whole time," Katrine said. "Perhaps he had a motive for pointing the finger at Vetlesen, some unsettled score between them. He led you that way right from the word go."

"Or perhaps that was how he was going to beat you,"

Holm suggested. "To force you to make mistakes. And then quietly enjoy the victory."

"Come on," Skarre said. "You're making this sound as if it's something personal between the Snowman and Harry Hole."

The other three eyed the detective in silence.

Skarre frowned. "Is it?"

Harry took his jacket from the coatrack. "Katrine, I want you to visit Borghild again. Say that we've got a warrant entitling us to look at patients' medical records. I'll take the rap if it comes. Then see what you can dig up on Arve Støp. Anything else before I go?"

"This woman in Tveita," Holm said. "Camilla Lossius. She's still missing."

"You go take a look, Holm."

"What are you going to do?" Skarre asked.

Harry gave a thin smile. "Learn to play poker."

Standing outside Tresko's door on the sixth floor of the only apartment building in Frogner Plass, Harry had that same feeling he had when he was small and everyone else in Oppsal was on vacation. This was the last resort, his last desperate action, having rung the doorbells at all the other houses. Tresko—or Asbjørn Treschow, which was his real name—opened up and stared sullenly at Harry. Because he knew now, just as he had then. Last resort.

The front door led straight into a three-hundred-square-foot living space one might call, charitably, a lounge with an open-plan kitchen, and uncharitably, an SRO. The stench was breathtaking. It was the smell of bacteria vegetating on damp feet and stale air, hence the vernacular but accurate Norwegian term *tåfis*, or toe-fart. Tresko had inherited his sweaty feet from his father. Just as he had inherited the sobriquet *tresko*, clogs, this dubious footwear he always wore in the belief that the wood absorbed the smell.

The only positive thing you could say about Tresko junior's foot odor was that it masked the smell of the dishes piled up in the sink, the overflowing ashtrays and the sweat-impregnated T-shirts drying over chair backs. It occurred to Harry that in all probability Tresko's sweaty feet had driven his opponents to the edge of sanity on his passage through to the semifinals of the world poker championship in Las Vegas.

"Been a long while," Tresko said.

"Yes. Great that you had some time for me."

Tresko laughed as if Harry had told him a joke. And Harry, who had no desire to spend any longer than necessary in the place, got straight to the point.

"So why is poker just about being able to see when your opponent is lying?"

Tresko didn't seem to mind skipping the social niceties.

"People think poker's about statistics, odds and probability. But if you play at the highest level all the players know the odds by heart, so that's not where the battle takes place. What separates the best from the rest is their ability to read others. Before I went to Vegas I knew I was going to be up against the best. And I could see the best playing on the Gamblers' Channel, which I received on satellite TV. I recorded it and studied every single one of the guys when they were bluffing. Ran it in slow motion, logged what went on in their faces down to the tiniest detail, what they said and did, every repeated action. And after I'd worked at it for long enough there was always something, some recurrent mannerism. One scratched his right nostril; another stroked the back of the cards.

Leaving Norway, I was sure I was going to win. Sadly it turned out I had even more telltale tics."

Tresko's grim laughter sounded more like a kind of sobbing and caused his amorphous frame to shake.

"So if I bring a man in for questioning, you can see whether he's lying or not?"

Tresko shook his head. "It's not that simple. First of all, I need to have a recording. Second, I must have seen the cards so that I know when he's been bluffing. Then I can rewind and analyze what he does differently. It's like when you calibrate a lie detector, isn't it? Before you run the test, you get the guy to say something that is obviously true, such as his name. And then something that is obviously a lie. And afterward you read the printout so that you have points of reference."

"An obvious truth," Harry mumbled. "And an obvious lie. On a film clip."

"But, as I said on the phone, I can't guarantee anything."

Harry found Beate Lønn in the House of Pain, the room where she had spent most of her time when she had been working in the Robberies Unit. The House of Pain was a windowless office packed with equipment for watching and editing closed-circuit TV footage, blowing up images and identifying people in grainy shots or voices on fuzzy telephone recordings. But now she was head of the Forensics Unit, in Brynsalléen, and furthermore just back from maternity leave.

The machines were buzzing, and the dry heat had put roses in her almost transparent, pale cheeks.

"Hi," Harry said, letting the iron door close behind him.

The small, agile woman got up and they hugged, both feeling a bit awkward.

"You're thin," she said.

Harry shrugged. "How's . . . everything going?"

"Tulla sleeps when she has to, eats what she has to and hardly ever cries." She smiled. "And for me that's everything now."

He thought he should say something about Halvorsen. Something to show that he hadn't forgotten. But the right words wouldn't come. And instead, seeming to understand, she asked how he was.

"Fine," he said, dropping into a chair. "Not bad. Absolutely dreadful. Depends on when you ask."

"And today?" She turned to the TV monitor and pressed a button, and people on the screen started running backward into the Storo Mall.

"I'm paranoid," Harry said. "I have the feeling I'm hunting someone who is manipulating me, that everything is chaotic and he is making me do exactly what he wants. Do you know the feeling?"

"Yes," Beate said. "I call her Tulla." She stopped rewinding. "Do you want to see what I've found?"

Harry pushed his chair closer. It was no myth that Beate Lønn had special gifts, that her fusiform gyrus, the part of the brain that stores and identifies human faces, was so highly developed and sensitive that she was a walking index file of criminals.

"I went through the shots you have of those involved in the case," she said. "Husbands, children, witnesses and so on. I know what our old friends look like, of course."

She moved the images frame by frame. "There," she said, stopping.

The image was frozen and jumped on the screen, showing a selection of people in grainy black and white, out of focus.

"Where?" Harry said, feeling as witless as he usually did when he was studying pictures with Beate Lønn.

"There. It's the same person in this picture." She took out one of the photos from her file.

"Could this be the person who is tailing you, Harry?"

Harry stared at the photo in astonishment. Then he nodded slowly and grabbed his phone. Katrine Bratt answered after two seconds.

"Get your coat and meet me down in the garage," Harry said. "We're going for a drive."

Harry drove along Uranienborgveien and Majorstuveien to avoid the traffic lights on Bogstadveien.

"Was she really sure it was him?" Katrine said. "The picture quality on surveillance cameras—"

"Believe me," Harry said. "If Beate Lønn says it's him, it's him. Call directory assistance and get his home number."

"I saved it on my mobile," Katrine said, bringing it up.

"Saved?" Harry glanced at her. "Do you do that with everyone you encounter?"

"Yep. Put them in a group. And then I delete the group when the case is over. You should try it. It's a wonderful feeling when you press delete. Really . . . tangible."

Harry stopped across from the yellow house in Hoff. All the windows were dark.

"Filip Becker," Katrine said. "Fancy that."

"Remember, we're just having a talk with him. He might have had quite understandable reasons for calling Vetlesen."

"From a pay phone in Storo Mall?"

Harry eyed Katrine. The pulse in the thin skin on her neck was visibly throbbing. He looked away and at the living-room window of the house.

"Come on," he said. The moment he seized the car-door handle his mobile rang. "Yes?"

The voice at the other end sounded excited, but still reported in short, concise sentences. Harry interrupted the stream with two *Mms*, a surprised *What?* and a *When?*

Then, at last, the other end went quiet.

"Call the Incident Room," Harry said. "Ask them to send the two nearest patrol cars to Hoffsveien. No sirens and tell them to stop at each end of the residential block . . . What? . . . Because there's a boy inside and we don't want to make Becker any more nervous than we have to. OK?"

Evidently it was OK.

"That was Holm." Harry leaned in front of Katrine, opened the glove compartment, rummaged through it and took out a pair of handcuffs. "His people have found quite a few fingerprints on the car in the Lossiuses' garage. They checked them against the other prints we have in the case."

Harry took the bunch of keys from the ignition, bent forward and produced a metal box from under the seat. Inserted a key in the lock, opened the box and lifted out a black short-barreled Smith & Wesson. "One off the windshield matched."

Katrine shaped her mouth into a mute O and inquired with a nod of her head if it was the yellow house.

"Yup," Harry responded. "Professor Filip Becker."

He saw Katrine Bratt's eyes widen. But her voice was as calm as before. "I have a feeling I'll soon be pressing delete."

"Maybe," Harry said, flipping open the cylinder of the revolver and checking that there were bullets in all the chambers.

"There can't be two men who kidnap women in this way." She tilted her head from side to side as if warming up for a boxing contest.

"A reasonable assumption."

"We should've known the first time we came here."

Harry observed her, wondering why he didn't share her excitement. What had happened to the intoxicating pleasure of making an arrest? Was it because he knew it would soon be replaced by the empty sensation of having arrived too late, of being a fireman sifting through the ruins? Yes, but it wasn't that. It was something else—he could sense it now. He had a nagging doubt. The fingerprints and the recordings from Storo Mall would go a long way in a court case, but it had been too easy. This killer wasn't like that; he didn't make such banal errors. This was not the same person who had placed Sylvia Ottersen's head on top of a snowman, who had frozen a policeman in his own freezer, who had sent Harry a letter saying, *What you should ask yourself is this: "Who made the snowman?"*

"What should we do?" Katrine asked. "Should we arrest him ourselves?"

Harry couldn't hear from the intonation whether this was a question or not.

"For the time being we wait," Harry said. "Until backup is in position. Then we'll ring the bell."

"And if he isn't at home?"

"He's at home."

"Oh? How do—"

"Look at the living-room window. Keep your eyes focused."

She watched. And when the white light changed behind the large panoramic window he could see she understood. The light came from a TV.

They waited in silence. There were no sounds. A crow screeched. Then it was quiet again. Harry's phone rang.

Their backup was in position.

Harry briefed them quickly. He didn't want to see any

uniforms until they were summoned, except perhaps if they heard shots or shouting.

"Put it on vibrate," Katrine said after he had hung up.

He smiled briefly, did as she said and stole a glance at her. Thought about her face when the freezer door fell open. But now her face revealed no fear or tension, just concentration. He put the phone in his jacket pocket and heard it clunk against his revolver.

They got out of the car, crossed the road and opened the gate. The wet gravel sucked greedily at their shoes. Harry kept his eyes on the large window, watching for shadows and any movement toward the white wall.

Then they were standing on the doorstep. Katrine glanced at Harry, who nodded. She rang the bell. A deep, hesitant *ding-dong* sounded from inside.

They waited. No footsteps. No shadows against the wavy glass of the oblong window beside the front door.

Harry moved forward and placed his ear against the glass, a simple and surprisingly effective way of monitoring a house. But he could hear nothing, not even the TV. He took three paces back, grabbed the eaves that protruded over the front steps, held on to the gutter with both hands and pulled himself up until he was high enough to see the whole of the living room through the window. On the floor sat a figure, legs crossed, with its back to him, wearing a gray coat. A pair of enormous headphones encircled the cranium like a black halo. A cable stretched from the headphones to the TV.

"He can't hear us because he's got headphones on," Harry said, dropping down in time to see Katrine grip the door handle. The rubber seal around the frame released the door with a sucking noise.

"Seems we're welcome," Katrine said in a soft voice and entered.

Caught unawares and quietly cursing, Harry strode in

after her. Katrine was already by the living-room door, and opened it. She stood there until Harry came alongside. She stepped back, banged into a pedestal where a vase teetered perilously until it decided to stay upright.

There were at least fifteen feet between them and the person still sitting with his back to them.

On the screen a baby was trying to walk while holding the index fingers of a smiling woman. The blue light of the DVD player button shone under the TV. Harry experienced a moment of déjà vu, a sense that a tragedy was going to repeat itself. Exactly like this: silence, home movie of happy times with the family, the contrast between then and now, the tragedy that has already been played out and just needs a conclusion.

Katrine pointed, but he had already seen it.

The gun was lying behind the figure, between a half-finished puzzle and a Game Boy, and looked like a toy. A Glock 21, Harry guessed, feeling queasy as his body geared up and more adrenaline entered his bloodstream.

They had a choice. Stay by the door, shout Becker's name and risk the consequences of confronting an armed man. Or disarm him before he saw them. Harry placed a hand on Katrine's shoulder and pushed her behind him while visualizing how long it would take for Becker to turn, pick up the gun, aim and fire. Four long strides would be enough, and there was no light behind Harry that would cast a shadow and too much light on the screen for him to be reflected there.

Harry took a deep breath and set off. Placed his foot as gently as possible on the parquet floor. The back did not react. He was in the middle of his second stride when he heard the crash behind him. And knew instinctively it was the vase. He saw the figure spin around, saw Filip Becker's agonized expression. Harry froze and the two of them stared at each other. The TV screen behind Becker went black. Becker's mouth opened as if he wanted to say something. The whites of his eyes contained rivers of red, and his cheeks were puffy, as though he had been crying.

"The gun!"

It was Katrine shouting and Harry automatically lifted his eyes and saw her reflection in the dark screen. She was standing by the door, legs apart with her arms stretched out in front, her hands squeezed around a revolver.

Time seemed to slow, to become a thick, shapeless material in which only his senses continued to function in real time.

A trained policeman like Harry should have instinctively thrown himself to the ground and drawn his gun. But there was something else, something that was tardier than his instincts, but worked with greater power. Harry would later change his opinion, but at first he thought he acted as he did because of another déjà vu experience, the sight of a dead man on a floor struck by a police bullet because he knew he had reached the end of the road, that he didn't have the energy to grapple with any more ghosts.

Harry stepped to the right, into Katrine's line of fire.

He heard a smooth, oiled click behind him. The sound of the revolver hammer being uncocked, of the finger easing the pressure on the trigger.

Becker's hand was pressed against the floor near the pistol. His fingers and the flesh between them were white. Which meant that Becker was supporting his body weight on them. The other hand—his right—was holding the remote control. If Becker went for his gun with his right hand as he was sitting now, he would lose balance.

"Don't move," Harry said loudly.

Becker's only move was to blink twice, as though wishing to erase the sight of Harry and Katrine. Harry moved forward calmly but efficiently. Bent down to pick up the gun, which was surprisingly light. So light that it would have been impossible for there to have been bullets in the magazine, he reflected.

Harry stowed the gun in his jacket pocket, beside his own revolver, and crouched down. On the screen he could see Katrine's gun pointed at them as she nervously shifted her weight from foot to foot. He stretched out a hand to Becker, who retreated like a timid animal, and removed the man's headphones.

"Where's Jonas?" Harry asked.

Becker scrutinized Harry as if he understood neither the situation nor the language.

"Jonas?" Harry repeated. Then he shouted. "Jonas! Jonas, are you here?"

"Shh," Becker said. "He's asleep." His voice was somnambulant, as if he had taken tranquilizers.

Becker pointed to the headphones. "He mustn't wake up."

Harry swallowed. "Where is he?"

"Where?" Becker angled his head and looked at Harry, seeming only then to recognize him. "In bed, of course. All boys have to sleep in their own beds." His voice rose and fell as if he were quoting from a song.

Harry plunged his hand down into his other jacket pocket and took out the handcuffs. "Put out your hands," he said.

Becker blinked again.

"It's for your own safety," Harry said.

It was a well-used line, one they drilled into you back at the police academy, and was primarily intended to relax arrestees. However, when Harry heard himself say it, he knew at once why he had stepped into the firing line. And it was not because of ghosts.

Becker raised his hands to Harry as though in supplication, and the steel snapped shut around his narrow, hairy wrists.

"Stay where you are," Harry said. "She'll take care of you."

Harry straightened up and went toward the doorway where Katrine stood. She had lowered her gun, and she smiled at him with a curious gleam in her eyes. The coals deep inside seemed to be smoldering.

"Are you OK?" Harry asked in an undertone. "Katrine?"

" 'Course." She laughed.

Harry hesitated. Then he continued up the stairs. He remembered where Jonas's room was, but opened the other doors first. Trying to delay the dreaded moment. Although the light was off in Becker's bedroom, he could make out the double bed. The duvet had been removed from one side. As if he already knew that she would never return.

Then Harry was outside Jonas's room. He emptied his mind of thoughts and images before opening the door. An off-key assortment of delicate tinkles rang out in the dark, and even though he couldn't see anything, he knew that the draft from the door had set off a small array of thin metal pipes, because Oleg had the same wind chimes hanging from the ceiling in his room. Harry went in and glimpsed someone or something under the duvet. He listened for breathing. But all he could hear was the tones continuing to vibrate, not wanting to die away. He placed his hand on the duvet. And for a moment he was numb with horror. Even though there was nothing in this room that presented a physical danger, he knew what he was afraid of. Because someone else, his old boss Bjarne Møller, had once formulated it for him. He was afraid of his own humanity.

Carefully, he pulled back the duvet from the body lying there. It was Jonas. In the dark he really did seem to be sleeping. Apart from his eyes, which were open and staring at the ceiling. Harry noticed a bandage on his forearm. He stooped over the boy's half-open mouth and touched his forehead. And gave a start when he felt warm skin and a current of air against his ear. And heard a sleepy voice mumble: "Mommy?"

Harry was completely unprepared for his own reaction. Perhaps it was because he was thinking of Oleg. Or perhaps because he was thinking of himself when once, as a boy, he woke up, thinking she was still alive, and charged into his parents' bedroom in Oppsal and saw the double bed with the duvet removed from one side.

Harry was unable to stem the flow of tears that suddenly welled up in his eyes, filling them until Jonas's face blurred before him, and they ran down his cheeks, leaving hot trails before finding grooves that led them to the corners of his mouth and Harry became aware of his own salty taste.

Part Four

20

The Sunglasses

It was seven o'clock in the morning when Harry unlocked Cell 23 in the custody block. Becker was sitting fully clothed on the prison bed, regarding him with a blank expression. Harry brought in the chair he had found in the duty room, sat astride it and offered Becker a cigarette from his crumpled Camel pack.

"Hardly legal to smoke here," Becker said.

"If I were sitting here awaiting a life sentence," Harry said, "I think I'd take the risk."

Becker just stared.

"Come on," Harry said. "You won't find a better place for a sly puff."

The professor smirked and took the cigarette Harry had flipped out.

"Jonas is fine, under the circumstances," Harry said, taking out his lighter. "I've spoken to the Bendiksens, and they've agreed to have him with them for a few days. I had to argue with social services a bit, but they went for it. And we haven't released news of your arrest to the press yet."

"Why not?" Becker asked, inhaling over the flame from the lighter with care.

"I'll come back to that. But I'm sure you understand that if you don't cooperate I can't continue to sit on the news."

"Aha, you're the good cop. And the one who questioned me yesterday is the bad cop, right?"

"That's right, Becker, I'm the good cop. And I'd like to ask you a few questions off the record. Whatever you tell me will not and cannot be used against you. Are you with me on this?"

Becker shrugged.

"Espen Lepsvik, who interviewed you yesterday, thinks you're lying," Harry said, blowing blue cigarette smoke at the smoke alarm on the ceiling.

"About what?"

"When you said you only spoke to Camilla Lossius in the garage and then you left."

"It's the truth. What does he think?"

"What he told you last night. That you kidnapped, killed and hid her."

"That's just crazy!" Becker erupted. "We were talking, that was all, and that's the truth!"

"Why are you refusing to tell us what you talked about?"

"It's a private matter. I've told you."

"And you admit that you called Idar Vetlesen the day he was found dead, but you regard that conversation as a private matter, too, I take it?"

Becker cast around as if thinking there ought to be an ashtray somewhere. "Listen, I haven't done anything illegal, but I didn't want to answer any more questions without my lawyer being present. And he's not coming until later today."

"Last night we offered you a lawyer who would have been able to come at once."

"I want to have a decent lawyer, not one of those . . .

local government employees. Isn't it time you told me why you think I've done something to this wife of Lossius's?"

Harry was taken aback by the phraseology: "This wife of Lossius's."

"If she's missing, you should arrest Erik Lossius," Becker went on. "Isn't it always the husband who does it?"

"Yes, it is," Harry said. "But he has an alibi; he was working at the time she disappeared. The reason you're sitting here is that we think you're the Snowman."

Becker's jaw half dropped and he blinked as he had done in the living room on Hoffsveien the night before. Harry pointed to the spiraling cigarette smoke from between his fingers. "You'll have to inhale a bit so we don't set off the alarm."

"The Snowman?" Becker blurted. "That was Vetlesen, wasn't it?"

"No," Harry said. "We know it wasn't."

Becker blinked twice before bursting into laughter so dry and bitter that it sounded like coughing. "So that's why you haven't leaked anything to the press. They can't find out that you've screwed up. And in the meantime you're desperate to find the right man. Or a potential right man."

"Correct," Harry said, sucking on his own cigarette. "And at the moment that's you."

" 'At the moment'? I thought your role was to persuade me that you knew everything, so I might as well confess right away."

"But I don't know everything," Harry said.

Becker scrunched up one eye. "Is this a trick?"

Harry shrugged. "It's just a gut instinct. I need you to convince me that you're innocent. The short interview reinforced the impression that you're a man with a lot to hide."

"I had nothing to hide. I mean, I *have* nothing to hide. And I just don't see why I should tell you anything if I've done nothing wrong."

"Listen to me carefully, Becker. I don't think you're the Snowman or that you killed Camilla Lossius. And I think you're a rational, thinking person. The kind who can appreciate that it will damage you less if you reveal private matters to me here and now rather than read in tomorrow's papers that Professor Filip Becker has been arrested on suspicion of being Norway's most notorious killer. Because you know that even if you were cleared and released the day after tomorrow, your name would be forever connected with these headlines. And your son's."

Harry watched Becker's Adam's apple rise and fall in his unshaven neck. Watched his brain drawing the logical conclusions. The simple conclusions. And then it came, in an anguished tone that Harry initially thought was due to the unaccustomed cigarette.

"Birte, my wife, was a whore."

"Eh?" Harry tried to conceal his astonishment.

Becker dropped his cigarette on the floor, leaned forward and pulled a black notebook from his back pocket. "I found this the day after she disappeared. It was in her desk drawer, wasn't even hidden. At first sight it looked quite innocent. Commonplace memoranda to herself and telephone numbers. It was just that when I checked the numbers with directory assistance, they didn't exist. They were codes. But my wife wasn't much good at writing in code, I'm afraid. It took me less than a day to crack them all."

Erik Lossius owned and ran Rydd & Flytt, a moving company that had found a niche in an otherwise less than lucrative market by dint of standardized prices, aggressive marketing, cheap foreign labor and contracts that demanded cash payment as soon as the vehicles were loaded up but before they left for their destination. He had never lost any money on a customer, because, among other things, the small print stated that any complaints regarding damage or theft had to be made within two days, which in practice meant that 90 percent of the fairly numerous complaints came too late and could therefore be dismissed. As far as the final 10 percent were concerned, Erik Lossius had devised routines to make himself inaccessible or to slow the usual procedures, which became so draining that even those who had lost plasma TVs or had had pianos wrecked during the move gave up in the end.

Erik Lossius had started in the industry at a young age with the former owner of Rydd & Flytt. The owner was a friend of Erik's father, and his father had got him a job there.

"The boy's too restless to go to school and too smart to be a crook," the father had said. "Can you take him?"

As a salesman working on commission Erik soon distinguished himself with his charm, efficiency and brutality. He had inherited his mother's brown eyes and his father's thick curly hair and had an athletic build; women in particular decided not to collect quotes from other moving companies and signed on the spot. And he was intelligent and nifty with figures and ploys on the rare occasions the company was asked to bid for bigger jobs. The price was set low and the loss or damage excess set high. After five years the firm enjoyed a substantial profit and Erik had become the owner's right hand in most areas of the business. However, during a relatively easy job just before Christmas—moving a table up to Erik's new office next to the boss's on the first floor—the owner had suffered a heart attack and dropped dead. In the days that followed, Erik comforted the owner's wife as well as he was able—and he was well able—and a week after the funeral they agreed on an almost symbolic transfer sum that reflected what Erik had emphasized was "a little business in a less than lucrative market with high risks and non-existent profit margins." But, he asserted, the most important thing for him was that someone would carry on her husband's life's work. A tear glistened in his brown eyes as he said that, and she laid a trembling hand on his and said that he personally should visit her to keep her informed. With that Lossius became the owner of Rydd & Flytt and the first thing he did was to throw all the letters of complaint into the garbage, rewrite the contracts and send circulars to all the households in Oslo's wealthy West End, where residents moved most frequently and were most price-sensitive.

By the time Erik Lossius was thirty, he had enough money to buy two BMWs, a summer residence to the north of Cannes and a five-thousand-square-foot detached house somewhere in Tveita, where the high-rise flats he had grown up in didn't block the sun. In short, he could afford Camilla Sandén.

Camilla came from bankrupt clothing nobility in the West End, from Blommenholm, an area that was as alien to the workingman's son as the French wine he now had stacked a yard high in his cellar in Tveita. But when he entered the Sandéns' great house to give them a quote and saw all the things that had to be moved, he discovered what he still didn't have and therefore had to have: class, style, former splendor and a natural superiority that politeness and smiles only served to reinforce. And all this was personified in the daughter, Camilla, who sat on the balcony looking across Oslo Fjord through a pair of large sunglasses, which, for all Erik knew, could have been bought at the local gas station, but which on her became Gucci, Dolce & Gabbana or whatever the other brands were called.

Now he knew what all the other brands were called.

He moved all their things, minus a couple of paintings that had to be sold, to a smaller house with a less fashionable address and never received a loss report on the one thing he had pinched off the load. Not even when Camilla Lossius was standing outside the Tveita church as a bride, with the high-rises as silent witnesses, did her parents show with so much as a moue that they disapproved of their daughter's choice. Perhaps because they saw that Erik and Camilla complemented each other in a way; he lacked refinement and she lacked money.

Erik treated Camilla like a princess, and she let him. He gave her what she wanted, left her in peace in the bedroom department whenever she wished and demanded no more than that she should pretty herself up when they went out or invited "couples they were friendly with"— that is, friends from his childhood—to supper. She wondered from time to time whether he really loved her, and she slowly began to develop a deep affection for the ambitious, energetic Oslo East boy.

For his part, Erik was extremely happy. He had known from the start that Camilla was not the hot-blooded type; in fact, that was one of the things that, in his eyes, placed her in a higher sphere than the girls he was used to. He had his physical needs covered by close customer contact anyway. Erik had come to the conclusion that there had to be something in the nature of moving that made people sentimental, distressed and open to new experiences. At any rate, he screwed single women, separated women, cohabiting and married women, on dining tables, on staircase landings, on plastic-wrapped mattresses and freshly washed parquet floors amid taped-up cardboard boxes and echoing bare walls while wondering what he would buy Camilla next.

The genius of the arrangement was that naturally he would never see these women again. They would move out and disappear. And they did. Apart from one.

Birte Olsen was dark-haired and sweet and had a *Penthouse* body. She was younger than he was, and her high-pitched voice and the language it produced made her seem even younger. She was two months into a pregnancy, moving into town from his part of Tveita to Hoffsveien with the child's father-to-be, a West End man she was going to marry. This was a move Erik Lossius could identify with. And—he realized after taking her on a plain spindle-back chair in the middle of the stripped room—sex he could not do without.

In a nutshell, Erik Lossius had met his match.

Yes, indeed, because he thought of her as a man, one who did not pretend she wanted anything different from what he wanted: to fuck the other person's brains out. And in a way they did just that. At any rate they began to meet in bare apartments, being moved out of or into, at least once a month, and always there was a distinct risk of being found out. They were quick and efficient and their rituals were fixed and without variation. Nevertheless, Erik Lossius looked forward to these assignations like a child to Christmas—that is, with unfeigned, uncomplicated joy that was increased only by the certainty that everything would be the same, that their expectations would be fulfilled. They lived parallel lives, had parallel realities, and that seemed to suit him as much as it suited her. And so they continued to meet, interrupted only by the birth—which, fortunately, was accomplished with a Cesarean section—some fairly long holidays and an innocent STD whose source he neither was able to nor attempted to trace. And now ten years had passed, and in front of Erik Lossius, sitting on a cardboard box in a half-emptied apartment in Torshov, a tall man with buzzed hair and a lawn-mower voice was asking if he had known Birte Becker.

Erik Lossius gulped.

The man had introduced himself as Harry Hole, an inspector from the Crime Squad, but he looked more like one of his moving men than an inspector of anything. The police officers Erik had spoken to after he had reported Camilla's disappearance were from the Missing Persons Unit. However, when this one had shown his ID, Erik's first thought had been that he had news of Camilla. And—since the officer in front of him hadn't called but tracked him down here—he feared it was bad news. Accordingly, he had sent his moving crew out and asked the inspector to take a seat while he found a cigarette and tried to prepare himself for what was to come.

"Well?" said the inspector.

"Birte Becker?" Erik Lossius repeated, trying to light his cigarette and think fast. He didn't manage either. Christ, he couldn't even think slowly.

"I appreciate that you have to compose yourself," the inspector said, taking out his own pack of cigarettes. "Take your time."

Erik watched the inspector light up a Camel and leaned over when he held the lighter out to Erik.

"Thanks," Erik mumbled, sucking so hard that the tobacco crackled. The smoke filled his lungs, and it was as if the nicotine were being injected into his bloodstream, clearing all the obstructions. He had always thought this would happen sooner or later, that the police would somehow discover a link between him and Birte and come asking questions. But at that time he had worried only about how he would keep it hidden from Camilla. Now everything was different. From right now, in fact.

Because up until this moment he hadn't realized that the police might think there was a connection between the two disappearances.

"Birte's husband, Filip Becker, found a notebook in which Birte had entered a kind of easy, decipherable code," the policeman said. "There were telephone numbers, dates and tiny messages. Leaving little doubt that Birte had regular contact with other men."

"Men?" Erik let slip.

"If it's any consolation, Becker thought you were the one she met most often. At a huge variety of addresses, I'm led to believe," Harry added.

Erik, adrift in a boat watching a tidal wave growing on the horizon, didn't answer.

"So Becker found your address, took his son's toy gun along with him—a very authentic-looking imitation of a Glock 21—and went to Tveita to wait for you to come home. He wanted to see the fear in your eyes, he said. Threaten you to make you tell whatever you knew so that he could pass your name on to us. He followed the car into the garage, but it turned out your wife was driving."

"And he . . . he . . . "

"Told her everything, yes."

Erik rose from the cardboard box and walked over to the window. The apartment had a view of Torshov Park and an Oslo bathed in wan morning sun. He didn't like the old apartment buildings with views. They meant stairs. The better the view, the more stairs there were and the more exclusive the apartments, which meant heavier, more expensive goods, higher payouts for damage and more days with his men out sick. But that was the way it was when you exposed yourself to the risks of maintaining fixed low rates; you always won the competition for the worst jobs. Over time there is a price to pay with all risks. Erik took a deep breath and heard the policeman scuffing his feet on the wood floor. And he knew. This detective would not be worn down by any delaying tactics. This was one damage report he would not be throwing in the garbage. Birte Olsen, now Becker, was going to be the first customer he would suffer a loss on.

"Then he told me he'd been having an affair with Birte Becker for ten years," Harry said. "And that when they met and had sex for the first time she'd been pregnant with her husband."

"You're pregnant with a girl or a boy," Rakel corrected, patting down the pillow so that she could see him better. "Or by your husband."

"Mm," Harry said, levering himself up on his arm, stretching across her and grabbing the cigarette pack on the bedside table. "Not more than eighty percent of the time."

"What?"

"They said on the radio that somewhere between fifteen and twenty percent of all children in Scandinavia have a different father from the one they think." He shook a cigarette out of the pack and held it up against the afternoon light seeping in under the blind. "Share one?"

Rakel nodded without speaking. She didn't smoke, but this was something they had always done after making love: shared this one cigarette. The first time Rakel had asked to taste his cigarette, she had said it was because she wanted to feel the same as he did, to be as poisoned and stimulated as he was, to get as close to him as she could. And he had thought of all the girl junkies he had met who had had their first fix for the same idiotic reason, and refused. But she had persuaded him and eventually it had become a ritual. After they had made love slowly, lingering over it, the cigarette was like an extension of their lovemaking. At other times it was like smoking a peace pipe after a fight.

"But he had an alibi for the whole evening Birte disappeared," Harry said. "A boys' night in Tveita that started at six and lasted all night. At least ten witnesses, admittedly wasted for the most part, but no one had been allowed to go home before six in the morning."

"Why keep it a secret that Vetlesen wasn't the Snowman?"

"As long as the real Snowman thinks we think we've got the killer he'll lie low, hopefully, and won't commit any more murders. And he won't be so wary if he thinks the hunt has been called off. In the meantime we can quietly work our way closer at our leisure . . . "

"Do I hear irony there?"

"Maybe," Harry said, passing her the cigarette.

"You don't quite believe that, then?"

"I think our superiors have many reasons for concealing the fact that Vetlesen wasn't our man. The chief superintendent and Hagen held the press conference at the time when they were congratulating themselves on solving the case . . . "

Rakel sighed. "And yet still I do occasionally miss the Police HQ."

"Mm."

Rakel studied the cigarette. "Have you ever been unfaithful, Harry?"

"Define unfaithful."

"Having sex with someone other than your partner."

"Yes."

"While you were with me, I mean."

"You know I can't be absolutely certain."

"OK, sober, then."

"No, never."

"So what does that make you think of me? Being here now?"

"Is this a trick question?"

"I mean it seriously, Harry."

"I know. I just don't know if I feel like answering it."

"Then you can't have any more of the cigarette."

"Mm. All right. I think you believe you want me, but you wish you wanted him."

The words hung over them as if imprinted in the darkness.

"You're so damn . . . detached," Rakel erupted, handing Harry the cigarette and crossing her arms.

"Perhaps we shouldn't talk about it?" Harry suggested.

"But I have to talk about it! Don't you see? Otherwise I'll go out of my mind. My God, I'm already out of my mind, being here, now . . . " She pulled the duvet up to her chin.

Harry turned and slid over to her. Already before he had touched her she had closed her eyes and tipped back her head, and from between her parted lips he could hear her breathing accelerate. And he thought: How does she do it? From shame to sexual abandon in a flash? How can she be so . . . detached?

"Do you think . . . ," he said, seeing her open her eyes and stare at the ceiling in surprise and frustration at the caresses that hadn't materialized, "a bad conscience makes us wanton? That we're unfaithful not in spite of the shame but because of it?"

She blinked a couple of times.

"There's something in that," she said at length. "But it's not everything. Not this time."

"This time?"

"Yes."

"I asked you once and at that time you said—"

"I was lying," she said. "I've been unfaithful before."

"Mm."

They lay in silence listening to the distant drone of the afternoon rush hour on Pilestredet. She had come to him straight from work; he knew Rakel and Oleg's routines, and knew she would have to go soon.

"Do you know what I hate about you?" she said finally, giving his ear a tweak. "You're so goddamned proud and stubborn you can't even ask if it was to you."

"Well," Harry said, taking the half-smoked cigarette and admiring her naked body as she jumped out of bed, "why would I want to know?"

"For the same reason Birte's husband did. To reveal the lie. To have the truth out in the open."

"Do you think the truth will make Filip Becker any less unhappy?"

She pulled her sweater over her head, a tight-fitting black one in coarse wool that lay straight over her soft skin. It occurred to Harry that if he was jealous of anything, it was the sweater.

"Do you know what, Herr Hole? For someone whose job it is to uncover unpleasant truths, you certainly enjoy living a lie."

"OK," Harry said, stubbing the cigarette in the ashtray. "Out with it, then."

"It was in Moscow while I was with Fjodor. There was a Norwegian attaché at the embassy I had trained with. We fell head over heels in love."

"And?"

"He was also in a relationship. As we were about to finish with our respective partners, she got in first and told him she was pregnant. And since by and large I have good taste as far as men go"—pulling on her boots, she screwed up her top lip—"I had of course chosen someone who would not desert his responsibilities. He applied for a transfer back to Oslo, and we never saw each other again. And Fjodor and I got married."

"And right afterward you became pregnant?"

"Yes." She buttoned up her coat and looked down at him. "Now and then I've wondered whether it was to get over him. And whether Oleg was a product not of love but of lovesickness. Do you think he was?"

"I've no idea," Harry said. "I just know he's one great product."

She smiled down at him in gratitude and stooped to give him a kiss on the forehead. "We'll never see each other again, Hole."

"Of course not," he said, sitting up in bed and staring at the bare wall until he heard the heavy door to the street close behind her with a dull thud. Then he walked into the kitchen, turned on the tap and took down a glass from the top cupboard. While waiting for the water to run cold his gaze fell on the calendar with the picture of Oleg and Rakel in the sky-blue dress and then onto the floor. There were two wet boot prints on the linoleum. They must have been Rakel's.

He donned his coat and boots, was about to leave, then turned, fetched his Smith & Wesson service revolver from the top of the wardrobe and stuffed it in his coat pocket.

The lovemaking was still in his body like a quiver of well-being, a mild intoxication. He had reached the street door when a sound, a click, made him spin around and peer into the yard, where the darkness was denser than in the street. He was intending to go on his way, and would have, had it not been for the prints. The boot prints on the linoleum. So he went into the yard. The yellow lights from the windows above him bounced off the remnants of snow that still lay where the sun could not quite reach. It stood by the entrance to the cellar storerooms. A crooked figure with its head at an angle, pebbles for eyes and a gravel grin laughing at him. Silent laughter reverberated between the brick walls and blended into a hysterical shriek he recognized as his own as he grabbed the snow shovel beside the cellar steps and swung it in violent fury. The sharp metal edge of the shovel struck below the head, lifting it off the body and sending the wet snow flying against the wall. The next hefty swipe sliced the snowman's torso into two and the third scattered the remains across the black pavement in the middle of the yard. Harry stood there gasping for breath when he heard another click behind him. Like the sound of a revolver being cocked. In one smooth movement he swirled around, dropped the shovel and drew the black revolver.

Muhammad and Salma stood by the wooden fence, underneath the old birch, mutely staring at their neighbor with big, frightened children's eyes. In their hands they were holding dry branches. The branches looked as if they might have been elegant arms for a snowman, had Salma not snapped hers in two, out of sheer terror.

"Our . . . s-snowman," Muhammad stammered.

Harry returned the revolver to his coat pocket and closed his eyes. Cursing himself, he swallowed and instructed his brain to let go of the gun stock. Then he opened his eyes again. Tears were welling under Salma's brown irises.

"I'm sorry," he said softly. "I'll help you make another one."

"I want to go home," Salma whispered in a thick voice.

Muhammad took his little sister by the hand and accompanied her home, giving Harry a wide berth.

Harry felt the revolver grip against his hand. The click. He had thought it was the sound of the hammer being raised. But he was wrong, of course; this phase of the firing procedure is noiseless. What you hear is the sound of the hammer being cocked, the sound of the shot that has not been fired, the sound of being alive. He took out his service revolver again. Pointed it at the ground and pressed the trigger. The hammer still didn't move. Only when he had forced the trigger a third of the way back and he was thinking that the gun could fire at any moment did the hammer begin to rise. He let go of the trigger. The hammer fell back into position with a metallic click. And again he heard the sound. And realized that anyone who pressed the trigger so far back that the hammer rose intended to shoot.

Harry looked up at the windows of his apartment on the second floor. They were dark, and a thought struck him: He had no idea what went on behind them when he wasn't there.

Erik Lossius listlessly stared out the window in his office and mused about how little he had known of what went on behind Birte's brown eyes. About how it felt worse that she had been with other men than that she had disappeared and was perhaps dead. And wishing he had lost Camilla to a murderer than in this way. But mostly Erik Lossius was thinking that he must have loved Camilla. And still did. He had called her parents, but they hadn't heard from her, either. Perhaps she was living with one of those Oslo West girlfriends he knew about only from hearsay.

He gazed at the afternoon gloom slowly descending on Groruddalen as it became thicker and erased the detail. There was nothing more to do today, but he didn't want to go home to the much too large and empty house. Not yet. There was a case of assorted spirits in the cupboard behind him, the so-called slush fund from various liquor cabinets in transit. But no mixers. He poured gin into his coffee cup and managed a little sip before the phone on the desk rang. He recognized the French international code on the display. The number wasn't on the complaints list, so he took it.

He knew it was his wife from her breathing, even before she had spoken a word.

"Where are you?" he asked.

"Where do you think?" Her voice sounded a long way away.

"And where are you calling from?"

"From Casper."

That was the café two miles from their country house.

"Camilla, the police are looking for you."

"Are they?"

She sounded as if she were dozing on a sunbed. Bored, just going through the motions of being interested, with that polite but distant nonchalance he had fallen for all those years ago on the balcony in Blommenholm.

"I . . . ," he began. But stopped. What could he really say?

"I thought it was right to call you before our lawyer did," she said.

"*Our* lawyer?"

"My family's," she said. "One of the best at this kind of thing, I'm afraid. He'll go for a straightforward split down the middle as far as possessions and money are concerned. We'll ask for the house, and we'll get it, even though I'll make no secret of the fact that I intend to sell it."

Goes without saying, he thought.

"I'll be home in five days. By then I assume you'll have moved out."

"That's short notice," he said.

"You can do it. I've heard no one works faster or cheaper than Rydd and Flytt."

She pronounced the latter with such distaste that he shrank. The way he had shrunk ever since the conversation with Inspector Hole. He was a blanket that had been washed on too high a temperature; he had become too small for her, become unusable. And with the same certainty that he knew now, at this moment, that he loved her more than ever before, he knew that he had lost her irrevocably, that there would be no reconciliation. And when she had hung up he saw her squinting into the sunset on the French Riviera through a pair of sunglasses she had bought for twenty euros but on her they looked like three thousand kroners' worth of Gucci or Dolce & Gabbana or . . . he had forgotten what the other brands were called.

Harry had driven to the top of the Holmenkollen Ridge on the west side of town. He had parked his car at the sports center, in the large, deserted parking lot, and walked up Holmenkollen. There he had stood on the viewing promontory beside the ski jump, where he and a couple of out-of-season tourists were peering across at the grandstands grinning emptily on both sides of the landing slope, the pond at the bottom, which was drained in the winter, and the town stretching out to the fjord. A view gives perspective. They had no concrete evidence. The Snowman had been so close, it had felt as if all they had to do was reach out and arrest him. But then he had slipped from their grasp again, like a wily professional boxer. The inspector felt old, heavy and clumsy. One of the tourists was looking at him. The weight of his service revolver pulled his coat down on the right-hand side. And the bodies, where the hell were the bodies? Even buried corpses turned up again. Was he using acid?

Harry sensed the onset of resignation. No, he damn well didn't! At the FBI course they had examined cases where it had taken more than ten years to catch the killer. As a rule, it had been one tiny, random detail, it seemed, that had solved the case. However, what actually cracked it was the fact that they had never given up; they had gone all fifteen rounds, and if the opponent was still standing they screamed for a return fight.

The afternoon darkness stole upward from the town beneath, and the lights around him were slowly being switched on.

They had to start looking where there was light. It was a banal but important procedural rule. Begin wherever you have a clue. On this occasion it meant beginning with the least likely person you could imagine and the worst, the craziest idea he had ever had.

Harry sighed, took out his mobile phone and searched back through the list of calls. There weren't that many, so it was still there, the very short conversation at the Hotel Leon. He pressed OK.

Bosse researcher Oda Paulsen replied at once with the happy, animated voice of someone who views all incoming calls as an exciting new opportunity. And this time, in a sense, she was right.

21

The Waiting Room

It was the heebie-jeebies room. Perhaps that was why some people called it the "waiting room," as if you were at the dentist's. Or the "antechamber," as if the heavy door between the two Studio 1 sofas led to something important or even holy. But on the floor plan for the government-owned NRK's buildings in the Marienlyst district of Oslo, it was simply, and boringly, termed Lounge, Studio 1. Nevertheless, it was the most exciting room Oda Paulsen knew.

Most of the guests taking part in the evening's edition of *Bosse* had arrived. As usual, it was the guests who were least known and who would be appearing for the shortest time who had got there first. Now they were sitting on one of the sofas, made up, their cheeks flushed with tension as they chatted and sipped tea or red wine, their eyes inevitably seeking the monitor that gave a full view of the studio on the other side of the door. There, the audience had been admitted and the TV floor manager was instructing them on how to clap, laugh and cheer. The screen also showed the host's chair and four guests' chairs, empty, waiting for people, content and entertainment.

Oda loved these intense, nervous minutes before they went live. Every Friday, for forty minutes, this was as close to the center of the world as it was possible to get in Norway. Between 20 and 25 percent of the country's population saw the program, an insanely high viewing percentage for a talk show. Those working here were not only *where* it happened, they *were* what happened. This was celebrity's magnetic North Pole, which attracted everything and everyone. And because celebrity is an addictive drug and there is only one compass point from the North Pole—south, downward—everyone clung to his or her job. A freelancer like Oda had to deliver in order to be on the team next season, and that was why she was so happy, on her own behalf, to have received the call late yesterday afternoon, just before the editorial meeting. Bosse Eggen himself had smiled at her and said this was a scoop. Her scoop.

The evening's theme was to be adult games. It was a typical *Bosse* theme, suitably serious without being too weighty. Something about which all the guests could express a semiqualified opinion. Among the guests was a woman psychologist who had written a thesis on the topic, but the main guest was Arve Støp, who would be celebrating *Liberal*'s twenty-fifth anniversary the following day. Støp hadn't objected to the angle of the playful adult, the playboy, when Oda had had a preparatory meeting with him in his apartment. He had just laughed when she had drawn a parallel between him and an aging Hugh Hefner wearing a bathrobe and smoking a pipe at an eternal bachelors' party in his mansion. She had felt his eyes on her, inspecting, curious, right up to the moment she had asked him whether he regretted not having a child, an heir to the kingdom.

"Have *you* got any children?" he had asked.

And when she had replied in the negative, he had,

to her astonishment, suddenly seemed to lose interest in both her and their conversation. She had therefore quickly finished up by giving him the usual information: arrival and makeup times, the request that he not wear striped clothing, the fact that themes and guests could change at short notice since this was a topical show, and so on.

And now here was Arve Støp in Lounge, Studio 1, straight from makeup, with his intense blue eyes and thick gray hair, which was groomed, but just long enough for the tips to bob up and down in suitably rebellious style. He was wearing a plain gray suit, which everyone knew cost an arm and a leg, though no one could say how he or she knew that. A tanned hand was already out to greet the psychologist, who was sitting on a sofa with peanuts and a glass of red wine.

"I didn't know psychologists could be so beautiful," he said to the woman. "Hope people can listen to what you say as well."

Oda watched the psychologist hesitate before beaming. And even though the woman clearly knew that Støp's compliment was a joke, Oda saw from the sparkle in her eyes that it had hit home.

"Hi, everyone—thank you all for coming!" This was Bosse Eggen sweeping into the room. He started with the guests on the left, shook hands, looked them in the eye, declared how happy he was to have them on board, told them that they could interrupt with questions for the other guests or make comments; it would enliven the conversation.

Gubbe, the producer, signaled that Støp and Bosse should withdraw into a side room to have a chat about the structure of the main interview and the introduction to the show. Oda checked her watch. Eight and a half minutes until they were live. She was just beginning to be concerned and wondered whether to phone reception to find out if he was waiting there: the real main guest. The scoop. But as she raised her eyes, there he was in front of her with one of the assistants, and Oda felt her heart skip a beat. He wasn't exactly good-looking, perhaps he was even ugly, but she was not ashamed to confess that she felt a certain attraction. And this had something to do with the fact that he was the guest all TV channels in Scandinavia wanted to get their hands on right now. For he was the man who had caught the Snowman, the biggest crime story in Norway for many years.

"I said I would be late," Harry Hole got in before she could utter a word.

She sniffed his breath. The last time he had been on the show he had been visibly drunk and had annoyed a whole nation. Or at least between 20 and 25 percent of it.

"We're just happy you're here," she chirped. "You'll be on second. Then you sit in for the rest of the show; the others will take their turns."

"Fine," he said.

"Take him to makeup," Oda said to the assistant. "Use Guri."

Guri wasn't just efficient, she knew how to make a worn face presentable for a TV audience with some simple, and some less simple, tricks.

They went off and Oda took a deep breath. She loved, loved the last edgy minutes when everything seemed to be chaos but still fell into place.

Bosse and Støp returned from the side room. She gave Bosse the thumbs-up. She heard the audience clapping as the studio door slid shut. On the monitor she saw Bosse taking his seat and knew that the floor manager had started the countdown. Then the signature tune began, and they were on air.

* * *

Oda realized something was amiss. The show had run like clockwork so far. Arve Støp had been brilliant and Bosse was reveling in it. Støp had said he was perceived as elitist because he was elitist. And that he wouldn't be remembered unless he suffered a real failure or two.

"Good stories are never about a string of successes but about spectacular defeats," Støp had said. "Even though Roald Amundsen won the race to the South Pole, it's Robert Scott the world outside Norway remembers. None of Napoleon's victories is remembered like the defeat at Waterloo. Serbia's national pride is based on the battle against the Turks at Kosovo Polje in 1389, a battle the Serbs lost resoundingly. And look at Jesus! The symbol of the man who is claimed to have triumphed over death ought to be a man standing outside the tomb with his hands in the air. Instead, throughout time Christians have preferred the spectacular defeat: when he was hanging on the cross and close to giving up. Because it's always the story of the defeat that moves us most."

"And you're thinking of doing a Jesus?"

"No," Støp had answered, looking down and smiling as the audience laughed. "I'm a coward. I'm going for forgettable success."

Støp had shown an unexpectedly likable, indeed even humble, side of himself, instead of his notorious arrogance. Bosse asked him whether he, as a single man of many years' standing, didn't long for a woman at his side. And when Støp answered yes, Oda knew there would be an avalanche of marriage proposals heading his way. The audience responded with a long round of warm applause. Then Bosse dramatically announced: "Ever on the hunt, the lone wolf of the Oslo Police, Inspector Harry Hole," and Oda thought she caught an expression of astonishment as the camera rested on Støp for a second.

Bosse had evidently enjoyed the response he had received to the question about a regular woman, because he tried to maintain the thread by asking Harry—since he knew he was also single—if he didn't long for a woman. Harry smirked and shook his head. But Bosse wouldn't let it drop and asked if there was perhaps someone special he was waiting for.

"No," Harry answered, short and sweet.

Usually this kind of rejection spurred Bosse to press further, but he knew he shouldn't spoil the party. The Snowman. So he asked Harry if he could tell them about the case all Norway was talking about, the nation's first real serial killer. Harry wriggled in his chair as if it were too small for his long body, while summarizing the chain of events in short, sculpted sentences. In recent years there had been some missing-persons cases with obvious similarities. All the missing women had been in relationships and had children, and there had never been a trace of the bodies.

Bosse assumed the grave expression that informed all and sundry that this was a flippancy-free zone.

"This year Birte Becker disappeared from her home in Hoff, here in Oslo, under similar circumstances," Harry said. "And soon afterward Silvia Ottersen was found dead in Sollihøgda outside Oslo. That was the first time we had found a body. Or at least part of it."

"Yes, because you found her head, didn't you?" Bosse interjected. Warily informative for those not in the know, and blood and tabloid for those who were. He was so professional that Oda immediately swelled with satisfaction.

"And then we found the body of a missing police officer outside Bergen." Harry plowed on. "He'd been missing for twelve years."

"Iron Rafto," Bosse said.

"Gert Rafto," Harry amended. "A few days ago we found the body of Idar Vetlesen in Bygdøy. Those are the only bodies we have."

"What would you say has been the worst aspect of this case?" Oda could hear the impatience in Bosse's voice, probably because Harry had neither taken the "head" bait nor portrayed the murders in the gory detail Bosse would have hoped for.

"So many years passing before we realized that there was a connection among the disappearances."

Another dull answer. The floor manager signaled to Bosse that he had to start thinking about a link to the next topic.

Bosse pressed his fingertips together. "And now the case is solved and you're a star again, Harry. How does it feel? Do you get fan mail?" The disarming boyish smile. They were out of the flippancy-free zone.

The inspector nodded slowly and moistened his lips with concentration, as if how he phrased the answer was crucial. "Well, I got one letter earlier this autumn, but I'm sure Støp can say more about that."

Close-up of Støp as he looked at Harry with mild curiosity. Two long, silent TV seconds followed. Oda chewed her lower lip. What did Harry mean? Then Bosse swept in and tidied up.

"Yes, Støp does get a lot of fan mail, of course. And groupies. What about you, Hole? Have you got groupies, too? Do the police have their own groupies?"

The audience laughed cautiously.

Harry Hole shook his head.

"Come on," Bosse said. "A female recruit must sometimes come and ask for some extra lessons on body searches."

The studio was really laughing now. With gusto. Bosse grinned with pleasure.

Harry Hole didn't even crack a smile; he just looked resigned and cast a glance toward the exit. For one short, frantic moment Oda had visions of him getting up and leaving. Instead he turned to Støp in the chair beside him.

"What do you do, Støp? When a woman comes to you after a lecture in Trondheim, saying she has only one breast, but she would like to have sex with you. Do you invite her for a bit of extracurricular in your hotel room?"

The audience went deadly quiet, and even Bosse looked perplexed.

Only Arve Støp seemed to think the question was amusing. "No, I don't think I would do that. Not because sex wouldn't be fun with only one breast, but because the hotel beds in Trondheim are so narrow."

The audience laughed, though without conviction, mostly from relief that the exchange had not been more embarrassing. The psychologist was introduced.

They talked about playful adults, and Oda noticed that Bosse was navigating the conversation away from Harry Hole. He must have decided that the unpredictable policeman was not in good form today. And therefore Arve Støp, who definitely was in good form, had even more airtime.

"How do you play, Støp?" Bosse asked with an innocent expression underlining the noninnocent subtext. Oda rejoiced—she had written that question.

But before Støp could answer, Harry Hole leaned forward and asked him in loud, clear tones, "Do you make snowmen?"

And that was when Oda knew that something was amiss. Hole's peremptory, angry tone, the aggressive body language; Støp, who raised an eyebrow in surprise as his face seemed to shrink and tense up. Bosse paused. Oda didn't know what was going on, but counted four seconds, an eternity on live TV. Then she realized that

Bosse knew what he was doing. For even though Bosse saw it as his duty to create a good atmosphere on the panel, he of course knew that the most important thing, his highest duty, was to entertain. And there is no better entertainment than people who are angry, cry, break down or in some other way display their feelings in front of a large audience on the air. Accordingly, he simply let go of the reins and just looked at Støp.

"Of course I make snowmen," Støp said after the four seconds were up. "I make them on the roof terrace beside my swimming pool. I make each one look like a member of the royal family. That way—when spring comes—I can look forward to the unseasonable elements melting and disappearing."

For the first time that evening Støp earned neither laughter nor applause. Oda thought Støp should have known that fundamentally antiroyalist comments never did.

Undaunted, Bosse broke the silence by introducing the pop star, who was to talk about her recent onstage breakdown and then conclude the show by singing the single that would be released on Monday.

"What the hell was that?" asked Gubbe, the producer, who had taken up a position directly behind Oda.

"Perhaps he isn't sober after all," Oda said.

"He's a fucking goddamn policeman!"

At that moment Oda remembered he was hers. Her scoop. "But, Jesus, can he deliver the goods."

The producer didn't answer.

The pop star talked about psychological problems, explaining that they were inherited, and Oda looked at her watch. Forty seconds. This was too serious for a Friday night. Forty-three. Bosse interrupted after forty-six.

"What about you, Arve?" Bosse was usually on first-name terms with the main guest by the end of the broadcast. "Ever experienced madness or a serious hereditary illness?"

Støp smiled. "No, Bosse, I haven't. Unless you count a craving for total freedom as an illness. In fact, it's a family weakness."

Bosse had come to round-up time; now he just had to sign off with the other guests before introducing the song. Final few words from the psychologist about the ludic in life. And then:

"And as the Snowman's no longer with us, I suppose you'll have time to play for a couple of days, Harry?"

"No," Harry said. He had slumped so far down into his chair that his long legs almost reached over to the pop star. "The Snowman hasn't been caught."

Bosse frowned, smiled and waited for him to go on, waited for the punch line. Oda hoped to God it was better than his opening line promised.

"I never said Idar Vetlesen was the Snowman," Harry said. "On the contrary. Everything points to the Snowman still being at large."

Bosse gave a little chuckle. It was the laugh he used to smooth over a guest's hapless attempt to be funny.

"I hope for the sake of my wife's beauty sleep that you're joking now," Bosse said mischievously.

"No," Harry said. "I'm not."

Oda looked at her watch and knew the floor manager was standing behind the camera now, shifting nervously as she ran a finger across her throat to show Bosse that they were running over and he would have to begin the song if they were to manage the first verse before the credits started rolling. But Bosse was the best. He knew that this was more important than all the singles in the world. Thus he ignored the raised baton and leaned forward in his chair to show those who might have been in any doubt about what this was. The scoop. The sensational announcement. Here on his, on their, program. The quaver in his voice was almost genuine.

"Are you telling us here and now that the police have been lying, Hole? That the Snowman is out there and can take more lives?"

"No," Harry said. "We haven't been lying. New details have come to light."

Bosse swiveled around in his chair, and Oda thought she could hear the technical director shouting for camera one, and then Bosse's face was there, the eyes staring straight at them.

"And I would guess we'll hear more about those details on the news tonight. *Bosse* is back next Friday. Thank you for watching."

Oda closed her eyes as the band began to play the single.

"Jesus," she heard the producer wheeze behind her. And then, "Jesus fucking Christ." Oda just felt like howling. Howling with pleasure. Here, she thought. Here at the North Pole. We aren't *where* it happens. We *are* what happens.

22

DAY 18

Match

Gunnar Hagen was standing inside the door at Schrøder's, scanning the room. He had set out from home exactly thirty-two minutes and three telephone conversations after the credits had rolled on *Bosse*. He hadn't found Harry in his apartment, at Kunstnernes Hus or in his office. Bjørn Holm had tipped him off that he might try Harry's local, Schrøder's. The contrast between the young, beautiful and almost-famous clientele at Kunstnernes Hus and Schrøder's somewhat dissipated beer drinkers was striking. At the back, in the corner, by the window, alone at a table, sat Harry. With a large glass.

Hagen made his way to the table.

"I've been trying to call you, Harry. Have you switched off your mobile?"

The inspector looked up, bleary-eyed. "There's been so much hassle. Loads of fucking reporters suddenly after me."

"At NRK they said the *Bosse* crew and guests usually went to Kunstnernes Hus after the show."

"The press was standing outside waiting for me. So I cleared out. What do you want, boss?"

Hagen plumped down onto a chair and watched Harry

raise the glass to his lips and the golden-brown liquid slip down into his mouth.

"I've been talking to the chief super," Hagen said. "This is serious, Harry. Leaking that the Snowman is still at large is a direct breach of his orders."

"That's right," Harry said, taking another swig.

"Right? Is that all you've got to say? But in the name of all that's sacred, Harry, why?"

"The public has a right to know," Harry said. "Our democracy is built on openness, boss."

Hagen banged his fist on the table and received a few encouraging looks from neighboring tables and an admonitory glance from the waitress passing them with an armful of sixteen-ounce glasses.

"Don't mess with me, Harry. We've gone public and said the case was solved. You've put the force in a very bad light—are you aware of that?"

"My job is to catch villains," Harry said. "Not to appear in a good light."

"It's two sides of the same thing, Harry! Our working conditions are dependent on how the public perceives us. The press is crucial!"

Harry shook his head. "The press has never hindered or helped me in solving a single case. The press is crucial only for individuals who want to be in the limelight. The people you report to are just concerned with having concrete results that will give them good press. Or prevent bad press. I want to catch the Snowman, period."

"You're a danger to your colleagues," Hagen said. "Do you know that?"

Harry seemed to be considering the statement, then nodded slowly, drained his glass and signaled to the waitress that he wanted another.

"I've just been talking to the chief superintendent and the chief constable," Hagen said, bracing himself. "I was told to find you instantly to muzzle you. From this very second. Understood?"

"Fine, boss."

Hagen blinked in amazement, but Harry's face revealed nothing.

"As of this moment, I'm going to be very hands-on, all the time," said the POB. "I want regular reports. I know that you won't do that, so I've spoken to Katrine Bratt and given her the job. Any objections?"

"None at all, boss."

Hagen was thinking that Harry must be drunker than he looked.

"Bratt told me you'd asked her to go and see this assistant of Idar Vetlesen's to check Arve Støp's files. Without going through the public prosecutor. What the hell are you two doing? Do you know what we would have been exposed to if Støp had found out?"

Harry's head shot up like a watchful animal's. "What do you mean by if he *had* found out?"

"Fortunately there was no file on Støp. This secretary of Vetlesen's said they never kept one."

"Oh? And why not?"

"How should I know, Harry? I'm just relieved. We don't want any more trouble now. Arve Støp, my God! Be that as it may, from now on Bratt will dog your every step so that she can report to me."

"Mm," Harry said, nodding to the waitress, who set down another glass for him. "Hasn't she already been informed?"

"What do you mean?"

"When she started you told her I would be her—" Harry stopped in his tracks.

"Her what?" Hagen snapped.

Harry shook his head.

"What's up? Something wrong?"

"Nothing," Harry said, sinking half the glass in one big gulp and placing a hundred-krone note on the table. "Have a nice evening, boss."

Hagen sat at the table until Harry had left the restaurant. Only then did he notice that there were no carbon dioxide bubbles rising in the half-empty glass. He stole a few sidelong glances and put the glass cautiously to his lips. It tasted tart. Nonalcoholic cider.

Harry walked home through silent streets. The windows of the old, low buildings shone like cats' eyes in the night. He felt an urge to speak to Tresko to find out how things were going, but decided to let him have the night, as agreed. He rounded the corner to Sofies Gate. Deserted. He was heading for his building when he caught a movement and a tiny glint. Light reflecting off a pair of glasses. Someone standing by the line of vehicles parked along the pavement, apparently struggling to open a car door. Harry knew which cars generally parked at this end of the street. And this car, a blue Volvo C70, was not one of them.

It was too dark for Harry to see the face clearly, but he could tell from the way the person was holding his head that he was keeping an eye out for Harry. A journalist? Harry passed the car. In the side mirror of another, he glimpsed a shadow flit between the cars and approach from behind. Without any undue haste Harry slipped his hand inside his coat. Heard the footsteps coming. And his anger. He counted to three, then turned around. The person behind him froze on the pavement.

"Is it me you're after?" Harry growled, stepping forward with gun raised. He collared the man, dragged him sideways, knocking him off balance, and launched himself at him, sending both of them over the hood of a car.

Harry pressed his forearm against the man's throat and thrust the barrel against one lens of his glasses.

"Is it me you want?" Harry hissed.

The man's answer was drowned out by the car alarm going off. The sound filled the whole street. The man tried to free himself, but Harry had him in a tight grip and he gave up. His head hit the car's hood with a soft thud and the light from the streetlamp fell on the man's face. Then Harry let go. The man doubled up, coughing.

"Come on," Harry shouted over the relentless howl, grabbed the man under the arm and dragged him over the road. He unlocked the front door and shoved the man inside.

"What the hell are you doing here?" Harry said. "And how do you know where I live?"

"I've been trying to call the number you gave me all evening. In the end I called directory assistance and got your address."

Harry observed the man. That is, he observed the ghost of the man. Even in the remand cell there had been more of Professor Filip Becker left.

"I had to switch off my mobile," Harry said.

Harry walked ahead of Becker up to his apartment, opened the door, kicked off his boots, went into the kitchen and switched on the kettle.

"I saw you on *Bosse* this evening," Becker said. He had come into the kitchen, still wearing his coat and shoes. His face was ashen, lifeless. "You were brave. So I thought I should be brave, too. I owe you that."

"Owe me?"

"You believed me when no one else did. You saved me from public humiliation."

"Mm." Harry pulled up a chair for the professor, but he shook his head.

"I'll be off in a minute, but I'll tell you something no

one else must know. I'm not sure if it has anything to do
with the case, but it's about Jonas."

"Uh-huh?"

"I took some blood from him the night I visited Camilla Lossius."

Harry remembered the bandage on Jonas's forearm.

"Plus a mouth swab. Sent it to the paternity section
of the Institute of Forensic Medicine for DNA testing."

"Huh? I thought you had to go through a lawyer."

"You did before. Now anyone can buy the test. Twenty-
eight hundred kroner per person. Bit more if you want a
quick answer. Which I did. And the answer came today.
Jonas"—Becker paused and took a deep breath—"Jonas
is not my son."

Harry nodded slowly.

Becker rocked back on his heels as if about to start a
race.

"I asked them to match him against all the data in the
data bank. They found a perfect match."

"Perfect? So Jonas was in the bank?"

"Yes."

Harry pondered. It was starting to dawn on him what
Becker meant.

"In other words, someone had already sent in a sample
for Jonas's DNA profile," Becker said. "I was informed
that the previous sample was seven years old."

"And they confirmed it was Jonas?"

"No, it was anonymous. But they had the name of the
client who had ordered the test."

"And that was?"

"A medical center that no longer exists." Harry knew
the answer before Becker said it. "Marienlyst Clinic."

"Idar Vetlesen," Harry said, angling his head as though
studying a picture to see if it was hanging straight.

"Right," Becker said, clapping his hands together and

smiling weakly. "That was it. All I wanted to say was that
. . . I have no son."

"I'm sorry."

"Actually, I've had that feeling for a long time."

"Mm. Why the hurry to come here and tell me?"

"I don't know," Becker said.

Harry waited.

"I . . . I had to do something tonight. Like this. If I
hadn't I don't know what I would've done. I . . . " The
professor hesitated before going on. "I'm alone now. My
life no longer has much meaning. If the gun had been
real . . . "

"Don't," Harry said. "Don't even think it. The thought
will only become more tempting the more you dwell on
it. And you're forgetting one thing. Even if your life has
no meaning for you, it has meaning for others. For Jonas,
for example."

"Jonas?" Becker said with a bitter laugh. "The evidence of Birte's infidelity? 'Don't dwell on it'—is that
what they teach you at the police academy?"

"No," Harry said.

They eyed each other.

"Whatever," Becker said. "Now you know."

"Thank you," Harry said.

After Becker had left, Harry was still sitting there, trying to decide if the picture was hanging straight, not noticing that the water had boiled, the kettle had switched
itself off and the little red eye under the ON button was
slowly dying.

23

Mosaic

The thick, fluffy clouds concealed the dawn as Harry entered the corridor on the sixth floor of the high-rise in Frogner. Tresko had left his door ajar, and when Harry entered, Tresko had his feet up on the coffee table, his ass on the sofa and the remote control in his left hand. The images that flicked backward across the screen dissolved into a digital mosaic.

"Don't want a beer, then?" Tresko repeated, lifting his half-empty bottle. "It's Saturday."

Harry thought he could discern bacterial gases in the air. Both ashtrays were full of cigarette butts.

"No thanks," Harry said, taking a seat. "Well?"

"Well, I've just had one night on it," Tresko said, stopping the DVD player. "It usually takes me a couple of days."

"This person's not a pro poker player," Harry said.

"Don't be too sure," Tresko said and took a swig from the bottle. "He bluffs a lot better than most card players. This is the place where you ask him the question you reckoned he would answer with a lie, isn't it?"

Tresko pressed PLAY and Harry saw himself in the TV studio. He was wearing a pinstriped suit jacket, a Swedish brand, slightly too tight. A black T-shirt that was a present from Rakel. Diesel jeans and Doc Martens boots. He was sitting in a strangely uncomfortable position, as if the chair had nails in the back. The question sounded hollow through the TV speakers. "Do you invite her for a bit of extracurricular in your hotel room?"

"No, I don't think I would do that," Støp answered, but froze as Tresko pressed the PAUSE button.

"And there you know he's lying?" Tresko asked.

"Yup," Harry answered. "He fucked a friend of Rakel's. Women don't usually like to boast. What can you see?"

"If I ran this on the computer I could enlarge the eyes, but I don't need to. You can see the pupils have dilated." Tresko pointed an index finger with a chewed nail at the screen. "That's the classic sign of stress. And look at the nostrils. Can you see they've flared a tiny bit? We do that when we're stressed and the brain needs more oxygen. But that doesn't mean he's lying; many people get stressed even when they're telling the truth. Or don't get stressed when lying. You can see, for example, that his hands are still."

Harry noticed that Tresko's voice had undergone a transformation; the jarring sounds were gone and it had become soft, almost pleasant. Harry looked at the screen, at Støp's hands, which lay still in his lap, the left hand over the right.

"I'm afraid there are no immutable signs," Tresko continued. "All poker players are different, so what you have to do is spot the differences. Find out what's different in a person from when he's lying and when he's telling the truth. It's like triangulation—you need two fixed points."

"A lie and an honest answer. Sounds easy."

"*Sounds* is right. If we assume he's telling the truth when he's talking about the founding of his magazine

and why he hates politicians, we have the second point."
Tresko rewound the clip and played it. "Look."

Harry looked. But obviously not where he was supposed to. He shook his head.

"The hands," Tresko said. "Look at his hands."

Harry looked at Støp's tanned hands resting on the
chair arms.

"They're not moving," Harry said.

"Yes, but he isn't hiding them," Tresko said. "A classic
sign of bad poker players with poor cards is all the effort
they make to hide them behind their hands. And when
they bluff they like to place an apparently pensive hand
over their mouth to hide their expression. We call them
hiders. Others exaggerate the bluff by sitting upright in
the chair or leaning back to appear bigger than they are.
They're the bluffers. Støp is a hider."

Harry leaned forward. "Did you . . . "

"Yes, I did," Tresko said. "And it runs all the way
through. He takes his hands off the arms of the chair and
hides the right one—I would guess he's right-handed—
when he's lying."

"What does he do when I ask him if he makes snowmen?" Harry made no attempt to conceal his eagerness.

"He's lying," Tresko said.

"Which bit? The bit about making snowmen or making them on his roof terrace?"

Tresko uttered a short grunt, which Harry realized
was meant to be laughter.

"This is not an exact science," Tresko said. "As I said,
he's not a bad card player. In the first seconds after you
asked the question he has his hands on the arms as if he's
considering telling the truth. At the same time his nostrils
flare as though he's becoming stressed. But then he changes
his mind, hides his right hand and comes up with a lie."

"Exactly," Harry said. "And that means he has something to hide, doesn't it?"

Tresko pressed his lips together to show this was a tricky one. "It may also mean he's choosing to tell a lie he knows will be found out. To hide the fact that he could easily have told the truth."

"What do you mean?"

"When pro card players have good hands, sometimes, instead of trying to bump up the pot, they bid high first time and give tiny signals that they're bluffing. Just enough to hook inexperienced players into believing they've spotted a bluff and to get them to join the bidding. That's basically what this looks like. A bluffed bluff."

Harry nodded slowly. "You mean he wants me to believe that he has something to hide?"

Tresko looked at the empty beer bottle, looked at the fridge, made a halfhearted attempt to lever his huge body off the sofa and sighed.

"As I said, this is not an exact science," he said. "Would you mind . . . "

Harry got up and went over to the fridge. Cursing inside. When he had rung Oda at *Bosse* he had known they would accept his offer to appear. And he had also known that he would be able to ask Støp direct questions unhindered; that was the format of the show. And that the camera would film the person answering, with close-ups or so-called medium shots—that is, the upper half of the body. All of this had been perfect for Tresko's analysis. And yet they had failed. This had been the last ray of hope, the last place to look where there was some light. The rest was darkness. And perhaps ten years of fumbling and praying for luck, serendipity, a slipup.

Harry stared at the neatly stacked rows of Ringnes beer bottles in the fridge, a comical contrast to the chaos reigning in the apartment. He hesitated. Then he took two bottles. They were so cold that they burned his palms. The fridge door was swinging shut.

"The only place where I can say with certainty that Støp is lying," Tresko said from the sofa, "is when he answers that there isn't any madness or hereditary illness in his family."

Harry managed to catch the fridge door with his foot. The light from the crack was reflected in the black, curtainless window.

"Repeat," he said.

Tresko repeated.

Twenty-five seconds later Harry was halfway down the stairs and Tresko halfway down the beer Harry had chucked him.

"Yes, there was one more thing, Harry," Tresko mumbled to himself. "Bosse asked you if there was someone special you were cooling your heels waiting for, and you answered no." He belched. "Don't take up poker, Harry."

Harry called from his car.

There was an answer before he could introduce himself. "Hi, Harry."

The thought that Mathias Lund-Helgesen either recognized his number or had his number listed made Harry shudder. He could hear Rakel's and Oleg's voices in the background. Weekend. Family.

"I have a question about the Marienlyst Clinic. Are there still any patient records from there?"

"I doubt it," Mathias said. "I think the rules say that sort of thing has to be destroyed if no one takes over the practice. But if it's important I'll check, of course."

"Thank you."

Harry drove past the Vinderen tram stop. A glimpse

of a ghost fluttered by. A car chase, a collision, a dead colleague, a rumor that it had been Harry driving and he should have been forced to take a Breathalyzer test. That was a long time ago. Water under the bridge. Scars under the skin. Versicolor on the soul.

Mathias called back after fifteen minutes.

"I spoke to Gregersen—he was the boss of Marienlyst. Everything was deleted or destroyed, I'm afraid. But I think some people, including Idar, took their patient information with them."

"And you?"

"I knew I wouldn't go into private practice, so I didn't take anything."

"Can you remember any of the names of Idar's patients, do you think?"

"Some, maybe. Not many. It's a while ago, Harry."

"I know. Thank you anyway."

Harry hung up and followed the sign to Rikshospitalet. The collection of buildings ahead of him covered the low ridge.

Gerda Nelvik was a gentle, buxom lady in her mid-forties and the only person in the paternity department at the Institute of Forensic Medicine at Rikshospitalet this Saturday. She met Harry in reception and took him through. There was not much to suggest that this was where society's worst criminals were hunted. The bright rooms, decorated in homey fashion, were, rather, testimony to the fact that the staff consisted almost entirely of women.

Harry had been here before and knew the routines for DNA testing. On a weekday, behind the laboratory windows, he would have seen women dressed in white lab coats, caps and disposable gloves, bent over solutions and machines, busy with mysterious processes they called hair-prep, blood-prep and amplification, which would ultimately become a short report with a conclusion in the form of numerical values for fifteen different markers.

They passed a room fitted with shelves, on which lay brown padded envelopes marked with names of police stations around the country. Harry knew they contained articles of clothing, strands of hair, furniture covers, blood and other organic material that had been submitted for analysis. All to extract the numeric code that represented selected points on the mysterious garland that is DNA and identified its owner with a certainty of 99.999 . . . percent.

Gerda Nelvik's office was no larger than it needed to be to accommodate shelves of ring files and a desk with a computer, piles of paper and a large photograph of two smiling boys, each with a snowboard. "Your sons?" Harry asked, sitting down.

"I think so." She smiled.

"What?"

"Insiders' joke. You said something about someone submitting tests?"

"Yes. I'm anxious to know about all the DNA tests submitted by a particular institution. Starting from twelve years back. And who they were for."

"I see. Which institution?"

"The Marienlyst Clinic."

"The Marienlyst Clinic? Are you sure?"

"Why?"

She shrugged. "In paternity cases it's usually a court or a lawyer who submits the request. Or individuals directly."

"These aren't paternity suits but tests to establish possible family links because of the danger of hereditary medical conditions."

"Aha," Gerda said. "Then we've got them in the database."

"Is that something you can check on the spot?"

"Depends on whether you've got the time to wait"—Gerda looked at her watch—"for thirty seconds."

Harry nodded.

Gerda tapped away on the keyboard as she dictated to herself. "M-a-r-i-e-n-l-y-s-t C-l-i-n-i-c."

She leaned back in her chair and let the machine work.

"Terrible autumn weather we're having, isn't it," she said.

"Yes, it is," Harry answered, miles away, listening to the whirring of the hard drive as if that could reveal whether the answer was the one he was hoping for.

"The darkness can get to you," she said. "Hope snow is on its way soon. Then it'll brighten up, at least."

"Mm," Harry said.

The whirring stopped.

"There you go," she said, looking at the screen.

Harry took a deep breath.

"Yes, the Marienlyst Clinic has been a client here. But not for quite some time."

Harry tried to think back. When was it Idar Vetlesen had finished there?

Gerda furrowed her brow. "But before that there were a lot, I can see."

She hesitated. Harry waited for her to say it. And then she said: "An unusually high number for a medical center, I would say."

Harry had a feeling. This was the path they should take; this one led out of the labyrinth. Or to be more precise: into the labyrinth. Into the heart of darkness.

"Have you got any names or personal details of those tested?"

Gerda shook her head. "Usually we do, but in this case the center wanted them to be anonymous, evidently."

Fuck! Harry closed his eyes and deliberated.

"But you still have the test results? About whether individuals are fathers or not, I mean."

"Yes, indeed," Gerda said.

"And what do they tell you?"

"I can't give you an answer off the cuff. I'll have to go into each one, and that'll take more time."

"OK. But have you saved the DNA profiles of those you have tested?"

"Yes."

"And the test is as comprehensive as in criminal cases?"

"More comprehensive. To establish paternity beyond a doubt we require more markers, since half of the genes are from the mother."

"So what you're saying is that I can collect a swab from a specific person, send it here and have you check it for any similarities with those you've checked from the Marienlyst Clinic?"

"The answer is yes," Gerda said with an intonation that suggested she would appreciate an explanation.

"Good," Harry said. "My colleagues will send you some swabs from a number of people who are husbands and children of women who have disappeared in recent years. To check whether they've been submitted before. I'll make sure this is authorized to receive top priority."

A light seemed to be switched on in Gerda's eyes. "Now I know where I've seen you! On *Bosse*. Is this about . . ."

Even though there were only two of them there, she lowered her voice as if the name they had given the monster was a curse, an obscenity, an incantation that was not to be uttered aloud.

*   *   *

Harry called Katrine and asked her to meet him at the Java café in St. Hanshaugen. He parked in front of an old apartment building with a sign on the entrance threatening that parked cars would be towed away, although the entrance was barely the width of a lawn mower. Ullevålsveien was full of people hurrying up and down doing their essential Saturday shopping. An ice-cold northerly wind swept down from St. Hanshaugen, blowing black hats off a bowed funeral procession on its way to the Vår Frelsers cemetery.

Harry paid for a double espresso and a cortado, both in paper cups, and sat on one of the chairs on the pavement. On the pond on the other side of the road a lone white swan drifted around quietly with a neck formed like a question mark. Harry watched it and was reminded of the name of the fox trap. The wind blew goose pimples onto the surface of the water.

"Is the cortado still hot?"

Katrine was standing in front of him with outstretched hand.

Harry passed her the paper cup, and they walked to his car.

"Great that you could work on a Saturday morning," he said.

"Great that you could work on a Saturday morning," she said.

"I'm single," he said. "Saturday morning has no value for people like us. You, on the other hand, should have a life."

An elderly man stood glaring at their car as they arrived.

"I've ordered a tow truck," he said.

"Yes, I hear they're popular," Harry said, unlocking

the door. "The only problem is finding somewhere to
park them."

They got in and a wrinkled knuckle rapped on the
glass. Harry rolled down the window.

"Truck's on its way," the old man said. "You've got to
stay here and wait."

"Do I?" Harry said, holding up his ID.

The man ignored the card and glowered at his watch.

"Your space's too narrow to qualify as an entrance,"
Harry said. "I'm sending over a man from the traffic department to unscrew your illegal sign. I'm afraid there'll
be a big fat fine, too."

"What?"

"We're police."

The old man snatched the ID card, looked suspiciously at Harry, at the card and back at Harry.

"That's fine this time. You can go," the man mumbled
with a sour expression and gave back the card.

"It's not fine," Harry said. "I'm calling the traffic department now."

The old man stared at him with fury.

Harry twisted the key in the ignition, let the engine
roar, then turned to the old man again. "And you are to
stay here."

They could see his openmouthed expression in the
rearview mirror as they drove off.

Katrine laughed. "You are *bad*! That was an old man."

Harry shot her a sidelong glance. Her facial expression was strange, as if it hurt her to laugh. Paradoxically,
the episode at Fenris Bar had made her more relaxed with
him. Perhaps that was a thing about attractive women: A
rejection demanded their respect, made them trust you
more.

Harry smiled. He wondered how she would have reacted if she had known that this morning he had woken

with an erection and fragments of a dream in which he had fucked her while she was sitting on the sink with her legs wide apart in the Fenris Bar bathroom. Screwed her so hard the pipes creaked, water slopped in the toilet bowls and the neon tubes buzzed and flickered as he felt the freezing porcelain on his balls every time he thrust. The mirror behind her had vibrated so much his features had blurred as they banged hips, backs and thighs against taps, hand dryers and soap holders. Only when they had stopped did he see that it wasn't his but someone else's face in the mirror.

"What are you thinking about?" she asked.

"Reproduction," Harry said.

"Oh?"

Harry passed her a packet, which she opened. At the top was a piece of paper with the heading INSTRUCTIONS FOR DNA SWABBING KIT.

"Somehow this is all tied up with paternity," Harry said. "I just don't know how or why yet."

"And we're off to . . . ?" Katrine asked, lifting a small pack of Q-tips.

"Sollihøgda," Harry said. "To get a swab from the twins."

In the fields surrounding the farm the snow was in retreat. Wet and gray, it squatted on the countryside it still occupied.

Rolf Ottersen received them on the doorstep and offered them coffee. As they removed their outer clothing Harry told him what they wanted. Rolf Ottersen didn't ask why, just nodded.

The twins were in the living room knitting.

"What's it going to be?" Katrine asked.

"Scarf," the twins said in unison. "Auntie's teaching us."

They motioned to Ane Pedersen, who was sitting in

the rocking chair knitting and smiling a "Nice to see you again" at Katrine.

"I just want a bit of spit and mucus from them," Katrine said brightly, raising a Q-tip. "Open wide."

The twins giggled and put down their knitting.

Harry followed Rolf Ottersen to the kitchen, where a large kettle had boiled and there was a smell of hot coffee.

"So you were wrong," Rolf said. "About the doctor."

"Maybe," Harry said. "Or maybe he has something to do with the case after all. Is it OK if I take a look at the barn again?"

Rolf Ottersen made a gesture inviting Harry to help himself.

"But Ane has tidied up in there," he said. "There's not a lot to see."

It was indeed tidy. Harry recalled the chicken blood lying on the floor, thick and dark, as Holm took samples, but now it had been scrubbed. The floorboards were pink where the blood had seeped into the wood. Harry stood by the chopping block and looked at the door. Tried to imagine Sylvia standing there and slaughtering chickens as the Snowman came in. Had she been surprised? She had killed two chickens. No, three. Why did he think it was two? Two plus one. Why plus one? He closed his eyes.

Two of the chickens had been lying on the chopping block, their blood pouring out onto the sawdust. That was how chickens should be slaughtered. But the third had been lying some distance away and had soiled the floorboards. Amateur. And the blood had clotted where the third chicken's throat had been cut. Just like on Sylvia's throat. He recalled how Holm had explained this. And knew the thought wasn't new; it had been lying there with all the other half-thought, half-chewed, half-

dreamed ideas. The third chicken had been killed in the
same way as Sylvia, with an electric cutting loop.

He went to the place where the floorboards had absorbed the blood and crouched down.

If the Snowman had killed the last chicken, why had
he used the loop and not the hatchet? Simple. Because
the hatchet had disappeared in the depths of the forest
somewhere. So this must have happened after the murder. He had come all the way back here and slaughtered
a chicken. But why? A kind of voodoo ritual? A sudden
inspiration? Bullshit—this killing machine stuck to the
plan, followed the pattern.

There was a reason.

Why?

"Why?" Katrine asked.

Harry hadn't heard her come in. She stood in the
doorway of the barn, the light from the solitary bulb falling on her face, and she was holding up two plastic bags
containing Q-tips. Harry shuddered to see her standing
like that again, in a doorway with her hands pointing in
his direction. Just like at Becker's. But there was something else, another realization, too.

"As I said," Harry mumbled, studying the pink residue, "I think this is about family relationships. About
covering things up."

"Who?" she asked and moved toward him. The heels
of her boots clicked on the wooden floor. "Who have you
got in mind?"

She crouched down beside him. Her masculine perfume wafted past him, rising from her warm skin into the
cold air.

"I haven't a clue."

"This is not systematic processing; this is an idea
you've had. You've got a theory," she stated simply and
ran her right index finger through the sawdust.

Harry held back. "It's not even a theory."

"Come on, out with it."

Harry took a deep breath. "Arve Støp."

"What about him?"

"According to Arve Støp, he went to Idar Vetlesen for medical help with his tennis elbow. But, according to Borghild, Vetlesen didn't have any records for Støp. I've been asking myself why that might be."

Katrine shrugged. "Perhaps it was more than an elbow. Perhaps Støp was afraid it might be documented that he was having cosmetic surgery."

"If Idar Vetlesen had agreed not to keep records for all the patients who were afraid of that, he wouldn't have had a single name in his files. So I thought it had to be something else, something that really couldn't bear close scrutiny."

"Like what?"

"Støp was lying on *Bosse*. He said there was no madness or hereditary illness in his family."

"And there is?"

"Let's assume there is, as a theory."

"The theory that's not even a theory?"

Harry nodded. "Idar Vetlesen was Norway's most secret expert on Fahr's Syndrome. Not even Borghild, his own assistant, knew about it. So how on earth did Sylvia Ottersen and Birte Becker find their way to him?"

"How?"

"Let's assume Vetlesen's specialty was not hereditary illness but discretion. After all, he said himself that's what his business was founded on. And that was why a patient and friend went to him and said he had Fahr's Syndrome, a diagnosis that he had been given somewhere else, by a real specialist. But this specialist did not have Vetlesen's expertise in discretion, and this was something that had to be kept secret. The patient insisted, perhaps paid extra for it. Because this person could really pay."

"Arve Støp?"

"Yes."

"But he's already been diagnosed by someone and that might leak out."

"This is not what Støp is primarily afraid of. He's afraid that it could come to light that he goes there with his offspring. Whom he wants checked to see if they have the inherited illness. And this has to be treated with the utmost confidentiality because no one knows they're his children. In fact there are some people who believe them to be their own. As indeed Filip Becker thought he was Jonas's father. And . . . " Harry nodded toward the farmhouse.

"Rolf Ottersen?" Katrine whispered, breathless. "The twins? Do you think"—she lifted the plastic bags—"that they have Arve Støp's genes?"

"Possibly."

Katrine looked at him. "The missing women . . . the other children . . . "

"If the DNA test shows that Støp is the father of Jonas and the twins, we'll do tests on the children of the other missing women on Monday."

"You mean . . . that Arve Støp has been bonking his way around Norway? Impregnating a variety of women and then killing them years after they've given birth?"

Harry rolled his shoulders.

"Why?" she asked.

"If I'm right, we're talking about madness, of course, and this is pure speculation. There's often a pretty clear logic behind madness. Have you heard about Berhaus seals?"

Katrine shook her head.

"The father of the species is cold and rational," Harry said. "After the female has given birth to their young and it has survived the first critical phase, the father tries to kill the mother. Because he knows she won't want to breed with him again. And he doesn't want other young seals to compete with his own offspring."

Katrine seemed to be having trouble absorbing this.

"It's madness, yes," she said. "But I don't know what's more insane: thinking like a seal or thinking that someone's thinking like a seal."

"As I said"—Harry stood up with an audible creak of his knees—"it's not even a theory."

"You're lying," she said, peering up at him. "You're already certain that Arve Støp's the father."

Harry responded with a crooked smile.

"You're as crazy as I am," she said.

Harry subjected her to a searching gaze. "Let's get going. The institute is waiting for your Q-tips."

"On a Saturday?" Katrine ran her hand over the sawdust, smoothing over her doodles, and stood up. "Haven't they got a life?"

After delivering the plastic bags to the institute and receiving a promise that they would get back to him that evening or early the following morning, Harry drove Katrine home to Seilduksgata.

"No lights on in the windows," Harry said. "On your own?"

"Good-looking girl like me?" She smiled, grasping the door handle. "Never on my own."

"Mm. Why didn't you want me to tell your colleagues at the Bergen Police Station that you were there?"

"What?"

"Thought they would be amused to hear you were working on a big murder case in the capital."

She shrugged and opened the door. "Bergensians don't think of Oslo as a capital. Good night."

"Good night."

Harry drove to Sannergata.

He wasn't certain, but he thought he had seen Katrine stiffen. But what could you be certain of? Not even a click, which you took to be a gun being cocked but turned out to be a girl cracking a dry twig out of sheer fright. He couldn't pretend any longer, though, couldn't pretend he didn't know. Katrine had pointed her service revolver at Filip Becker's back that evening. And when Harry had stepped into her firing line he had heard the sound, the sound he had thought he heard when Salma cracked a twig in the yard. It was the lubricated click of a revolver hammer being released. Which meant that it had been raised, that Katrine had squeezed the trigger more than two-thirds of the way and that the gun could have gone off at any time. She had meant to shoot Becker.

No, he couldn't pretend. Because the light had fallen on her face in the doorway to the barn. And he had recognized her. And, as he had said to her, this was all about family relationships.

POB Knut Müller-Nilsen loved Julie Christie. So much that he had never dared to tell his wife the whole truth. However, since he suspected her of having an extramarital affair with Omar Sharif, he didn't feel too guilty as he sat beside her, devouring Julie Christie with his eyes. The only fly in the ointment was that his Julie at this moment was in a passionate embrace with said Sharif. And when the telephone on the living-room table rang and he answered, his wife pressed the PAUSE button, causing the frame of this wonderful yet unbearable moment of their favorite movie, *Doctor Zhivago*, to freeze in front of them.

"Well, good evening, Hole," said Müller-Nilsen after the inspector had introduced himself. "Yes, I imagine you've got enough to keep you busy for the time being."

"Have you got a minute?" asked the hoarse but soft voice at the other end.

Müller-Nilsen gazed at Julie's quivering red lips and raised misty eyes. "We'll take the time we need, Hole."

"You showed me a photo of Gert Rafto when I was in your office. There was something about it I recognized."

"Oh, yes?"

"And then you said something about his daughter. She had turned out very well, of course, you said. It was this understood 'of course.' As if this were information I already knew."

"Yes, but she did turn out well, didn't she?" said Müller-Nilsen.

"Depends on how you look at it," Harry said.

24

Toowoomba

There was an expectant buzz under the chandeliers in the Sonja Henie Ballroom at the Plaza Hotel. Arve Støp stood in the doorway where he had received the guests. His jaw was aching from all the smiling, and the glad-handing had given him back the sensation of tennis elbow. A young woman from the publicity firm who was responsible for logistics slid alongside him and told him that the guests were now seated around the table. Her neutral black suit and headset with its almost invisible microphone made him think of a female agent in *Mission Impossible*.

"We're going in," she said, adjusting his bow tie with a friendly, quasi-tender movement.

She wore a wedding ring. Her hips swayed in front of him toward the room. Had those hips given birth to a child? Her black trousers were tight against her well-exercised bottom, and Arve Støp visualized the same bottom, without trousers, in front of him on the bed in his Aker Brygge apartment. But she seemed too professional. It would be too much hassle. Too much heavy persuasion. He met her eyes in the big mirror beside the door, knew he had been caught and beamed an apology. She laughed at the same time as a slightly unprofessional flush shot up into her cheeks. Mission impossible? Hardly. But not tonight.

Everyone at his table of eight rose as he entered. His dinner partner was his own assistant editor. A dull but necessary choice. She was married and had children and the ravaged face of a woman who worked twelve to fourteen hours every day. Poor kids. And poor him the day she found out that life consisted of more than *Liberal*. The table reacted with a *skål* for him as Støp's gaze swept across the room. The sequins, jewels and smiling eyes sparkled under the chandeliers. And the dresses. Strapless, shoulderless, backless, shameless.

Then the music erupted. The vast tones of "Also Sprach Zarathustra" boomed out of the loudspeakers. At the meeting with the publicists Arve Støp had pointed out that it wasn't exactly an original introduction—it was pompous and made him think of the creation of man. And was told that was the idea.

Onto the large stage, wreathed in smoke and light, stepped a TV celebrity who had demanded—and been given—a six-figure sum to be the master of ceremonies.

"Ladies and gentlemen!" he shouted into a large cordless microphone that reminded Støp of a large, erect penis. "Welcome!" The celeb's famous lips were almost touching the black dick. "Welcome to what I promise you is going to be a very special evening!"

Arve Støp was already looking forward to it being over.

Harry stared at the photographs on the bookshelf in his office, the Dead Policemen's Society. He tried to think, but his mind was spinning, unable to find a foothold, an entire image. He had felt the whole time that there was someone on the inside; someone had known what he would do at all times. But he hadn't expected it to be like this. It was so unimaginably easy. And at the same time so incomprehensibly complicated.

Knut Müller-Nilsen had told him that Katrine had been regarded as one of the most promising Crime Squad detectives at the Bergen HQ, a rising star. Never any problem. Yes, there was of course the incident that led to her application for a transfer to the Sexual Offenses Unit. A witness from a shelved case had called to complain that Katrine Bratt was still bothering him with new questions. She wouldn't stop, even though he had made it plain that he had already made a statement to the police. It came to light that Katrine had been independently investigating this case for months without notifying her superiors. As she had been doing it in her own free time, this would not normally have been a problem, but this particular case was not one they wanted her raking up. She had been made aware of this, and her reaction had been to point out several flaws in the original investigation, but she didn't gain a sympathetic ear, and in her frustration she had applied for a transfer.

"This case must have been an obsession for her," was the last Müller-Nilsen had said. "As far as I remember, that was the time her husband left her."

Harry got up, went into the corridor and over to Katrine's office door. It was, as office regulations stipulated, locked. He continued down the corridor to the photocopy room. On the lowest shelf beside the packs of paper he pulled out the guillotine, a large, heavy iron base with a mounted blade. It had never been used as far as he could recall, but now he carried it with both hands into the corridor and back to Katrine Bratt's door.

He raised the paper cutter over his head and took aim. Then he brought his arms down hard.

The guillotine hit the handle, knocking the lock into the frame, which split with a loud crack.

Harry just managed to shift his feet before the machine landed on the floor with a muffled groan. The door spat splinters of wood and swung open at the first kick. He picked up the guillotine and carried it inside.

Katrine Bratt's office was identical to the one he had shared with Jack Halvorsen in times gone by. Tidy, bare, no pictures or any other personal possessions. The desk had a simple lock at the top controlling all the drawers. After two doses of the guillotine, the top drawer and the lock were smashed. Harry rifled through, pushing papers to the side and rummaging through plastic folders, hole punches and other office equipment until he found a knife. He removed the sheath. The top edge was serrated. Definitely not a scout's knife. Harry pressed the blade into the pile of papers it was lying on and the knife sank without resistance into the wad.

In the drawer beneath there were two unopened boxes of bullets for her service revolver. The only personal belongings Harry found were two rings. One was studded with gems that glinted angrily in the light of the desk lamp. He had seen it before. Harry closed his eyes trying to visualize where. A large, gaudy ring. Las Vegas–style. Katrine would never have worn such a ring. And then he knew where he had seen it. He felt his pulse throbbing: hard, but steady. He had seen it in a bedroom. In Birte Becker's bedroom.

In the Sonja Henie Ballroom dinner was over and the tables were cleared away. Arve Støp leaned against the rear wall while staring toward the stage. The guests had huddled together next to it and were gazing in rapture at the band. It was a big sound. It was an expensive sound. It was the sound of megalomania. Arve Støp had had his doubts, but in the end the publicists had convinced him that investing in an experience was a way to buy his employees' loyalty, pride and enthusiasm for their workplace. And by buying a bit of international success he was underscoring the magazine's own success and building the *Liberal* brand, a product with which advertisers would want to be associated.

The vocalist held a finger against his earpiece as he attacked the highest note of their song, which had been an international hit in the eighties.

"No one hits a bum note as beautifully as Morten Harket," said a voice next to Støp.

He turned. And knew at once that he had seen her before, because he never forgot a beautiful woman. What he was beginning to forget more and more was who, where and when. She was slim and wearing a plain black dress with a slit that reminded him of someone. Of Birte. Birte had had a dress like that.

"It's scandalous," he said.

"It's a difficult note to hit," she said, without taking her eyes off the vocalist.

"It's scandalous I can't remember your name. I only know we've met before."

"We haven't met," she said. "You just gave me the once-over." She brushed her black hair off her face. She was attractive in a stern, classical way. Kate Moss–attractive. Birte had been Pamela Anderson–attractive.

"That, I think, can definitely be excused," he said, with a feeling that he was waking up, that his blood was beginning to surge through his body, bringing Champagne to parts of his brain that relaxed him rather than making him drowsy.

"Who are you?"

"I'm Katrine Bratt," she said.

"Oh, yes. Are you one of our advertisers, Katrine? A bank connection? A lessor? A freelance photographer?"

To every question Katrine shook her head with a smile.

"I'm a gate-crasher," she said. "One of your female journalists is a friend of mine. She told me who was playing after dinner, and said I could just put on a dress and slip in. Feel like throwing me out?"

She raised her Champagne glass to her lips. They weren't as full as he usually liked, but nevertheless deep red and moist. She was still looking at the stage, so he could study her profile at his leisure. The whole of her profile. The hollow back, the perfect arch of her breasts. No need for any silicone, maybe just a good bra. But could they have suckled a child?

"I'm considering the option," he said. "Any arguments you would like to put forward?"

"Will a threat do?"

"Perhaps."

"I saw the paparazzi outside waiting for your celebrity guests to emerge with the evening's catch. What if I told them about my journalist friend? That she was given to understand her prospects at *Liberal* were poor after she had rejected your advances?"

Arve Støp laughed aloud and from his heart. He saw that they had already been attracting inquisitive looks from other guests. Leaning toward her, he noticed that the aroma of her perfume was not unlike the cologne he used.

"First, I'm not frightened of a bad reputation, least of all among my colleagues in the gossip rags. Second, your friend is a useless journalist and third, she's lying. I've fucked her three times. And you can tell the paparazzi *that*. Are you married?"

"Yes," said the unknown woman, turning to the stage

and shifting her weight so that the slit of her dress allowed a glimpse of a lacy garter. Arve Støp felt his mouth go dry and took a sip of Champagne. Watched the flock of tiptoeing women at the front of the stage. Breathed through his nose. He could smell pussy from where he was standing.

"Have you got any children, Katrine?"

"Do you want me to have children?"

"Yes."

"Why?"

"Because through creating life women have learned to subject themselves to nature, and that gives them a more profound insight into life than other women. And men."

"Bullshit."

"No, it makes you women less desperate to hunt for a potential father. You just want to enjoy the game."

"OK." She laughed. "Then I've got children. What games do you like to play?"

"Whoa," Støp said, looking at his watch. "We're moving too fast."

"What games do you like to play?"

"All of them."

"Great."

The singer closed his eyes, grabbed the microphone with both hands and attacked the song's crescendo.

"This is a boring party, and I'm going home." Støp put his empty glass on a tray whistling past. "I live in Aker Brygge. Same entrance as *Liberal*, top floor. Top bell."

She gave a thin smile. "I know where it is. How much of a head start do you want?"

"Give me twenty minutes. And a promise that you won't talk to anyone before you leave. Not even your girlfriend. Is that a deal, Katrine Bratt?"

He looked at her, hoping he had said the right name.

"Trust me," she said, and he noticed a strange gleam

in her eyes, like that of a forest fire in the sky. "I'm just as keen as you that this stay between us." She raised her glass. "And, by the way, you fucked her four times, not three."

Støp enjoyed a last glance before making his way to the exit. Behind him the vocalist's falsetto was still quivering, almost inaudibly, under the chandeliers.

A door slammed and loud, enthusiastic voices reverberated down Seilduksgata. Four youths on their way from a party to one of the bars in Grünerløkka. They passed the car parked at the edge of the pavement without noticing the man inside. Then they rounded the corner, and the street was quiet again. Harry leaned toward the windshield and looked up at the windows of Katrine Bratt's apartment.

He could have called Hagen, could have sounded the alarm, taken Skarre along and a patrol car. But he might be wrong. And he had to be certain first; there was too much to lose, both for him and for her.

He got out of the car and went to the door and the unmarked second-floor bell. Waited. Rang once more. Then he went back to his car, fetched the crowbar from the trunk, returned to the door and rang the first-floor bell. A man answered with a sleepy *ja*, the TV droning in the background. Fifteen seconds later the man came down and opened up. Harry showed him his police ID.

"I didn't hear a domestic dispute," the man said. "Who called you?"

"I'll find my own way out," Harry said. "Thanks for your help."

The door on the second floor didn't have a nameplate, either. Harry knocked, rested his ear against the cold wood and listened. Then he inserted the tip of the crowbar between the door and the frame immediately above the lock. Since the blocks of apartment buildings in Grünerløkka had been built for workers in the factories along the Akerselva River with the cheapest possible materials, Harry's second forced entry in under an hour was easy.

He listened for a few seconds in the dark of the corridor before he switched on the light. Looked down at the shoe rack in front of him. Six pairs of shoes. None of them big enough to belong to a man. He lifted one pair, the boots Katrine had worn earlier today. The soles were still wet.

He went into the living room. Switched on the flashlight instead of the ceiling light so that she wouldn't see from the street that she had a visitor.

The cone of light swept over the worn pine floor with large nails between the boards, a plain white sofa, low bookshelves and an exclusive Linn loudspeaker. There was an alcove in the wall, with a tidy, narrow bed, and a kitchenette with a stove and a fridge. The impression was austere, spartan and neat. Like his own place. The light had caught a face staring stiffly at him. And then another. And one more. Black wooden masks with carvings and painted patterns.

He looked at his watch. Eleven. He let the flashlight wander farther afield.

There were newspaper clippings pinned up above the only table in the room. They covered the wall from floor to ceiling. He went closer. His eyes skimmed them as he felt his pulse begin to tick like a Geiger counter.

These were murder cases.

Many murder cases, ten or twelve, some so old the newspaper had yellowed. But Harry could remember them all quite clearly. He remembered them because they had one thing in common: He had led the investigation.

On the table, beside a computer and a printer, lay a heap of folders. Case reports. He opened one of them. There weren't any reports of his cases, but Laila Aasen's murder on Ulriken Mountain was there. Another folder was of Onny Hetland's disappearance in Fjellsiden. A third was about a case of police violence in Bergen, about complaints against Gert Rafto. Harry flicked through. Found the same photograph of Rafto that he had seen in Müller-Nilsen's office. Looking at it now, he thought it was obvious.

Beside the printer was a pile of paper. Something was drawn on the top sheet. A quick, amateur penciled sketch, but the motif was clear enough. A snowman. The face was long, as if it had leaked, melted; the coal eyes had died and the carrot was long and thin and pointed downward. Harry leafed through the sheets. There were several drawings. All of snowmen, most just of the face. Masks, Harry thought. Death masks. One of the faces had a beak, small human arms at the side and bird feet at the bottom. Another had a pig's snout and a top hat.

Harry started to search the other end of the room. And told himself the same thing he had said to Katrine on the island of Finnøy: Empty your mind of expectations and look, don't search. He went through all the cupboards and drawers, rummaged through kitchen utensils and washing paraphernalia, clothes, exotic shampoos and bizarre creams in the bathroom, where the smell of her perfume hung heavily in the air. The floor of the shower was wet and on the sink there was a Q-tip stained with mascara. He came out again. He didn't know what he was after, just that it wasn't here. He straightened up and looked around.

Wrong.

It was here. He just hadn't found it yet.

He took the books off the shelves, opened the toilet

cistern, checked whether there were any loose boards
in the floor or the walls and turned the mattress in the
alcove. Then he was finished. He had searched everywhere. Without any success, except for the most important premise of any search: What you *don't* find is just
as important as what you do. And he knew now what he
hadn't found. Harry looked at his watch. Then he began
to tidy up.

It was only when he was putting the drawings in order that it occurred to him that he hadn't checked the
printer. He pulled out the tray. The top sheet was yellow-
ish and thicker than normal printer paper. He lifted it up.
It had a particular aroma, as if it had been impregnated
with a spice or burned. He turned on the desk lamp and
held the sheet up to it as he hunted for the mark. And
found it. Down in the bottom right-hand corner, a kind
of watermark in between the fine paper fibers, visible if
held against the lightbulb. The blood vessels in his throat
seemed to widen; the blood was suddenly in a hurry, his
brain screaming for more oxygen.

Harry switched on the computer. Checked his watch
again and listened while it took an eternity for the operating system and programs to boot up. He went straight
to the search function and typed in a single word. Clicked
the mouse on SEARCH. An animated dog, in both senses,
appeared, jumping up and down and barking soundlessly
in an attempt to shorten the waiting time. Harry stared
at the text flashing by as the documents were scanned.
Shifted his gaze to the rubric where it said for the moment, *No items matched your search*. He examined the
spelling of the search word. *Toowoomba*. He closed his
eyes. Heard the deep purr of the machine, like an affec-
tionate cat. Then it stopped. Harry opened his eyes. *One
item matched your search*.

He placed the cursor over the Word icon. A yellow

rectangular box popped up. *Date modified: September 9.* He felt his finger tremble as he double-clicked. The white background of the short text shone into the room. There was no doubt. The words were identical to those in the letter from the Snowman.

25

Deadline

Arve Støp was lying in a bed that had been sewn and weighed to customer specifications in the Misuku factory in Osaka and shipped already assembled to a tannery in Chennai, India, because the laws in the state of Tamil Nadu did not permit the direct exportation of this type of leather. It had taken six months from order to receipt of the goods, but it had been worth the wait. Like a geisha, it adapted perfectly to his body, supported him where necessary and allowed him to adjust it to every conceivable level or direction.

He watched the teak blades of the ceiling fan slowly rotate.

She was in the elevator on her way up to him. He had explained on the intercom that he was waiting for her in the bedroom, and had left the door ajar. He could feel the cool silk of his boxer shorts against his alcohol-warmed body. The music from a Café del Mar CD streamed out of the Bose audio system, with its small, compact speakers hidden in every room of the apartment.

He heard her heels clacking on the parquet floor of the living room. Slow but resolute footsteps. Just the sound made him go hard. If only she knew what was awaiting her . . .

His hand foraged under the bed; his fingers found what they were groping for.

And then she was in the doorway, silhouetted against the moonlight over the fjord, looking at him with a half-smile. She loosened the belt of her long black leather coat and let it fall. He gasped, but she was still wearing her dress beneath. She went over to the bed and passed him something rubbery. It was a mask. A pink animal mask.

"Put this on," she said in a neutral, businesslike voice.

"Well, well," he said. "A pig's face."

"Do as I say." Again this strange yellow gleam in her eyes.

"Mais oui, madame."

Arve Støp put it on. It covered his whole face and smelled like rubber gloves, and he could only just see her through the small slits for eyes.

"And I want you to—" he began and heard his own voice, encased and alien. That was as far as he got before he felt a stinging pain over his left eye.

"You shut your mouth!" she shouted.

Slowly it reached his consciousness that she had hit him. He knew he shouldn't—it would ruin her role play—but he could not help himself. It was too comical. A pig mask! A clammy, pink rubbery thing with pig ears, snout and overbite. He let out a guffaw. The next blow hit him in the stomach with shocking power, and he doubled up, groaned and fell back on the bed. He was unaware that he wasn't breathing until everything went black. Desperately he fought for air inside the tight-fitting mask as he felt her wrench his arms behind his back. Then, finally, oxygen reached his brain and the pain came at the same time. And the fury. Fucking cow, what did she think she was doing? He wriggled free and would have grabbed her, but couldn't move his hands; they were held tight behind his back. He jerked and felt something sharp cut into his wrists. Handcuffs? The perverted bitch.

She pushed him into a sitting position.

"Can you see what this is?" he heard her whisper.

But his mask had slipped sideways; he couldn't see anything.

"I don't need to," he said. "I can smell it's your cunt."

The blow hit him over the temple. It was like a CD skipping, and when he had the sound back he was still sitting upright in bed. He could feel something running down between his cheek and the inside of his mask.

"What the hell are you hitting me with?" he shouted. "I'm bleeding, you madwoman!"

"This."

Arve Støp felt something hard pressed against his nose and mouth.

"Smell," she said. "Isn't it good? It's steel and gun oil. Smith and Wesson. Smells like nothing else, doesn't it? The smell of powder and cordite is even better. If you ever get to smell it, that is."

Just a violent game, Arve Støp told himself. A role play. But there was something else, something in her voice, something about the whole situation. Something that put all that had happened in a new light. And for the first time in ages—so long ago he had to think back to his childhood, so long that initially he didn't recognize the feeling—Arve Støp noticed: he was frightened.

"Sure we shouldn't fire her up?" said Bjørn Holm, shivering and pulling the leather jacket around him more tightly. "When the Amazon came out she was well known for having a helluva heater."

Harry shook his head and looked at his watch. One-thirty. They had been sitting in Holm's car outside Katrine's apartment building for more than an hour. The night was blue-gray, the streets empty.

"She was actually California white," Holm continued. "Volvo color number forty-two. Previous owner sprayed it black. Qualifies as a veteran car and all that now. Mere three hundred and sixty-five kroner road tax a year. A krone a day . . . "

Bjørn Holm paused when he saw Harry's warning look and instead turned up David Rawlings and Gillian Welch, which was the only new music he could tolerate. He had recorded it from a CD onto a cassette, not just so that it could play on the newly installed cassette player in the car, but because he belonged to that extremely small yet unbending faction of music lovers who opined that the CD had never managed to reproduce the cassette's uniquely warm sound quality.

Bjørn Holm knew he was talking too much because he was nervous. Harry hadn't told him any more than that Katrine had to be eliminated from some inquiries. And that Holm's daily grind for the next few weeks would be eased if he didn't know the details. And being the peaceful, laid-back, intelligent person he was, Holm didn't try to cause any trouble. That didn't mean he liked the situation, though. He checked his watch.

"She's gone back to some guy's place."

Harry reacted. "What makes you think that?"

"She's not married, after all. Wasn't that what you said? Single women are like us single guys nowadays."

"And by that you mean . . . "

"Four steps. Go out, observe the herd, select the weakest prey, attack."

"Mm, you need four steps?"

"The first three," said Bjørn Holm, adjusting the mirror and his red hair, "just cock-teasers in this town." Holm had considered hair oil, but concluded it was too radical. On the other hand, perhaps that was just what was needed. Go the whole hog.

"Fuck," Harry burst out. "Fuck, fuck, fuck."

"Eh?"

"Wet shower. Perfume. Mascara. You're right." The inspector had taken out his mobile, maniacally punched the numbers in and got an almost immediate answer.

"Gerda Nelvik? This is Harry Hole. Are you still doing the tests? . . . OK. Any preliminary results?"

Bjørn Holm watched as Harry mumbled two *mm*s and three *right*s.

"Thank you," Harry said. "And I was wondering if any other officers had called earlier this evening and asked you the same . . . What? . . . I see. Yes, just call me when the tests are finished."

Harry hung up. "You can start the engine now," he said.

Bjørn Holm twisted the key in the ignition. "What's the deal?"

"We're going to the Plaza Hotel. Katrine Bratt called the institute earlier this evening to ask about paternity."

"This evening?" Holm put his foot down and turned right, toward Schous Plass.

"They're running preliminary tests to establish paternity to ninety-five percent probability. Then they'll try to increase the certainty to ninety-nine point nine."

"And?"

"It's ninety-five percent certain that the father of the Ottersen twins and Jonas Becker is Arve Støp."

"Holy moly."

"And I think Katrine's followed your recommendations for a Saturday evening. And the prey is Arve Støp."

Harry called the Incident Room and asked for assistance as the old reconditioned engine roared through the night-still streets of Grünerløkka. And as they passed the Akerselva emergency room and skidded on the tram tracks on Storgata, the heater was indeed blowing red-hot air on them.

Odin Nakken, a newspaper reporter at *Verdens Gang*, stood freezing on the pavement outside the Plaza Hotel cursing the world, people in general and his job in particular. As far as he could judge, the last guests were leaving the *Liberal* celebration. And the last, as a rule, were the most interesting, the ones who could create the next day's headlines. But the deadline was approaching; in five minutes he would have to go. Go to the office in Akersgata a few hundred yards away and write. Write to the editor that he was a grown-up now, that he was fed up with standing outside a party like a teenager, with his nose pressed against the windowpane staring in and hoping someone would come out and tell him who had danced with whom, who had bought drinks for whom, who had been in a clinch with whom. Write that he was handing in his notice.

A couple of rumors had been floating about that had been too fantastic to be true, but naturally they couldn't print those. There was a limit, and there were unwritten rules. Rules to which, at least in his generation, journalists adhered. For what that was worth.

Odin Nakken took stock. There were only a couple of reporters and photographers still holding out. Or who had the same deadlines for celebrity gossip as his newspaper. A Volvo Amazon came hurtling toward them and pulled up to the curb with a squeal of brakes.

Out jumped a man from the passenger seat, and Odin Nakken immediately recognized him. He signaled to the photographer, and they ran after the police officer, who was sprinting for the door.

"Harry Hole," panted Nakken when he had caught up. "What are the police doing here?"

The red-eyed policeman turned to him. "Going to a party, Nakken. Where is it?"

"Sonja Henie Room on the first. But I reckon it's finished now."

"Mm. Seen anything of Arve Støp?"

"Støp went home early. What do you want with him?"

"Nothing. Was he alone?"

"To all outward appearances."

The inspector pulled up sharply and turned to him. "What do you mean?"

Odin Nakken angled his head. He had no idea what this was about, but he was in no doubt that there was something.

"A rumor was going around that he was negotiating with a pretty foxy lady. With fuck-me eyes. Nothing we can print, more's the pity."

"So?" growled the inspector.

"A woman answering the description left the party twenty minutes after Støp. She got into a taxi."

Hole was soon walking back the same way he had come. Odin hung onto his coattails.

"And you didn't follow her, Nakken?"

Odin Nakken ignored the sarcasm. It was water off a duck's back. Now.

"She wasn't a celebrity, Hole. A celeb screwing a non-celeb is non-news, if I can put it like that. Unless the lady decides to talk, of course. And this one's long gone."

"What did she look like?"

"Slim, dark. Good-looking."

"Clothes?"

"Long black leather coat."

"Thanks." Hole jumped into the Amazon.

"Hey," Nakken shouted. "What do I get in return?"

"A good night's sleep," Harry said. "The knowledge that you've helped to make our town a safer place."

Grimacing, Odin Nakken watched the old boat of a car embellished with rally stripes accelerate away with a throaty roar of laughter. It was time to get out of this. Time to hand in his notice. It was time to grow up.

"Deadline," the photographer said. "We'll have to go and write this shit up."

Odin Nakken heaved a sigh of resignation.

Arve Støp stared into the darkness of the mask wondering what she was doing. She had dragged him into the bathroom by the handcuffs, pressed what she claimed was a revolver against his ribs and ordered him into the bathtub. Where was she? He held his breath and heard his heart and a crackling electric hum. Was one of the neon tubes in the bathroom on its way out? The blood from his temple had reached the corner of his mouth; he could taste the sweet metallic tang with the tip of his tongue.

"Where were you the night Birte Becker disappeared?" Her voice came from over by the sink.

"Here in my apartment," Støp answered, trying to think. She had said she was from the police and then he remembered where he had seen her before: in the curling hall.

"Alone?"

"Yes."

"And the night Sylvia Ottersen was killed?"

"The same."

"Alone all evening, without talking to anyone?"

"Yes."

"So no alibi?"

"I'm telling you I was here."

"Good."

Good? thought Arve Støp. Why was it good that he didn't have an alibi? What was it she wanted? To force a confession out of him? And why did it sound as if the electric hum was getting louder as she came closer?"

"Lie down," she said.

He did as instructed and felt the cold bath enamel sting the skin of his back and thighs. His breath had condensed on the inside of the mask, made it wet, made it even more difficult to breathe. Then the voice was there again, close by now.

"How do you want to die?"

Die? She was out of her mind. Insane. Stark raving mad. Or was she? He told himself to keep a clear head; she was just trying to frighten him. Could Harry Hole be behind this? Could it be that he had underestimated the drunken asshole? But his whole body was shaking now, shaking so much that he could hear his TAG Heuer watch clink against the enamel, as if his body had accepted what his brain still had not. He rubbed the back of his head against the bottom of the tub, trying to straighten the pig mask so that he could see through the small holes. He was going to die.

That was why she had put him in the bathtub. So that there wouldn't be so much mess, so all the traces could be quickly removed. Bullshit! You're Arve Støp and she's with the police. They know nothing.

"OK," she said. "Lift up your head."

The mask. At last. He did as she said, felt her hands touch his forehead and at the back, but she didn't loosen the mask. Something thin and strong tightened around his neck. What the fuck? A noose!

"Don't . . . ," he began, but his voice died as the noose pressed against his windpipe. The handcuffs rattled and scraped against the bottom of the tub.

"You killed them all," she said, and the noose was tightened a notch. "You're the Snowman, Arve Støp."

There. She had said it out loud. The lack of blood to his brain was already making him dizzy. He shook his head frantically.

"Yes, you are," she said, and as she jerked the noose he felt as if his head were being severed. "You've just been appointed."

The darkness came all of a sudden. He raised a leg and let it fall again, the heel of his foot banging impotently against the bathtub. A hollow boom reverberated around.

"Do you know that rushing sensation, Støp? It's the brain not getting sufficient oxygen. Quite wonderful, isn't it? My ex-husband used to jerk himself off while I had him in a stranglehold."

He tried to scream, tried to force the little air that was left in his body past the iron grip of the noose, but it was impossible. Jesus, didn't she even want a confession? Then he felt it. A slight swishing sound in his brain, like the hiss of Champagne bubbles. Was that how it would happen? So easy. He didn't want it to be easy.

"I'm going to hang you in the living room," said the voice by his ear as a hand affectionately patted his head. "Facing the fjord. So that you have a view."

Then came a thin peeping sound, like the alarm on one of those heart monitors you see in films, he thought. When the curve flattens out and the heart no longer beats.

The Silence

Harry pressed Arve Støp's doorbell again.

A night owl was walking over the canal bridge and peering down at the black Amazon parked in the middle of the car-free square in Aker Brygge.

"Not gonna open up if he's got a dame there, I s'pose," Bjørn Holm said, looking up at the ten-foot-high glass door.

Harry pressed the other doorbells.

"Those are just offices," Holm said. "Støp lives alone at the top. I've read that."

Harry looked around.

"No," said Holm, who had guessed what he was thinking. "It won't work with the crowbar. And the steel glass is unbreakable. We'll have to wait until the care—"

Harry was on his way back to the car. And this time Holm was unable to follow the inspector's train of thought. Not until Harry got into the driver's seat and Bjørn remembered that the key was still in the ignition.

"No, Harry! No! Don't . . . "

The remainder was drowned in the roar of the engine. The wheels spun on the rain-slippery surface before gaining purchase. Bjørn Holm stood waving in the road, but caught a glimpse of the inspector's eyes behind the wheel and leaped out of the way. The Amazon's bumper hit the door with a muffled crash. The glass in the door turned to white crystals, as for one noiseless second it hovered in the air before tinkling to the ground. And before Bjørn could gauge the extent of the damage, Harry was out of the car and striding through the now-glassless entrance.

Bjørn ran desperately after him, cursing. Harry had grabbed a pot containing a six-foot-high palm tree, dragged it over to the elevator and pressed the button. As the shiny aluminum doors slid apart, he jammed the pot between them and pointed to a white door with a green exit sign.

"If you take the fire escape and I take the main stairs we have all the escape routes covered. Meet you on the sixth, Holm."

Bjørn Holm was drenched with sweat before he reached the second floor on the narrow iron staircase. Neither his body nor his head was prepared for this. He was a forensics officer, for Christ's sake! His bag was *re*-constructing dramas, not constructing them.

He stopped for a moment. But all he could hear was the fading echo of his own footsteps and his own panting. What would he do if he met someone? Harry had told him to bring his service revolver along to Seilduksgata, but had Harry meant that he would have to use it? Bjørn took hold of the railing and started running again. What would Hank Williams have done? Buried his head in a drink. Sid Vicious? Shown him a finger and legged it. And Elvis? Elvis. Elvis Presley. Right. Bjørn Holm wrapped his fingers around his revolver.

The steps finished. He opened the door and there, at the end of the corridor, was Harry, leaning back against the wall beside a brown door. He had his revolver in one hand and was holding the other to his mouth. Forefinger over his lips as he watched Bjørn and pointed to the door. It was ajar.

"We'll do it room by room," Harry whispered when Bjørn was alongside. "You take the ones on the left, I'll take the ones on the right. Same rhythm, back to back. And don't forget to breathe."

"Wait!" Bjørn whispered. "What if Katrine's there?"

Harry studied him and waited.

"I mean . . . ," Bjørn Holm went on, trying to artic-ulate what he meant. "In a worst-case scenario would I shoot . . . a colleague?"

"In the *worst*-case scenario," Harry said, "a colleague would shoot *you*. Ready?"

The young forensics officer from Skreia nodded and promised himself that if this went well he would wear goddamned hair oil.

Harry silently prodded the door open with his foot and went in. He felt the current of air at once. The draft. He reached the first door to the right and grabbed the handle with his left hand as he pointed the revolver. Pushed the door open and went in. It was a study. Empty. Over the desk hung a large map of Norway with pins stuck in it.

Harry walked back into the hall, where Holm was waiting for him. Harry motioned to Holm to keep his revolver raised the whole time.

They moved through the apartment with stealth.

Kitchen, library, fitness room, conservatory, guest room. All empty.

Harry felt the temperature drop. And as they came into the living room he saw why. The sliding door to the terrace and pool was wide open; white curtains flapped nervously in the wind. On either side of the room ran narrow pathways, each leading to a door. Harry pointed to Holm to take the door on the right while he took up position in front of the other.

Harry breathed in, huddled up to make the target as small as possible and opened.

In the darkness he could make out a bed, white linen and something that might have been a body. His left hand groped for a switch inside the door.

"Harry!"

It was Holm.

"Over here, Harry!"

Holm's voice was excited, but Harry turned a deaf ear and concentrated on the darkness in front of him. His hand found the switch, and the next moment the room was bathed in light from overhead spots. It was empty. Harry checked the closets, then left. Holm stood outside the other door with his gun pointing into the room.

"He's not moving," Holm whispered. "He's dead. He . . ."

"Then you needn't have called me so urgently," Harry said, walking to the bathtub, bending over the naked man and removing the pig mask. A thin red stripe ran around his neck, his face was pale and swollen and his eyes were bulging out from beneath the eyelids. Arve Støp was barely recognizable.

"I'll call the Crime Scene people," Holm said.

"Hang on." Harry held a hand in front of Støp's mouth. Then he took the editor's shoulder and shook him.

"What are you doing?"

Harry shook harder.

Bjørn laid a hand on Harry's shoulder. "But, Harry, can't you see . . ."

Holm recoiled. Støp had opened his eyes. And now he was drawing breath—like a skin diver breaking the surface—deep, painful and with a rattle in his throat.

"Where is she?" Harry said.

Støp was unable to focus his eyes, and short gasps were all that emerged from his mouth.

"Wait here, Holm."

Holm nodded and watched his colleague leave the bathroom.

Harry stood on the edge of Arve Støp's roof terrace. Twenty-five yards below glittered the black water of the canal. In the moonlight he could discern the sculpture of the woman on stilts in the water and the deserted bridge. And there . . . something shiny bobbing on the surface of the water, like the belly of a dead fish. The back of a black leather coat. She had jumped. From the sixth floor.

Harry stepped up to the edge of the terrace, between the empty flower boxes. An image from the past flashed through his brain. Østmarka, and Øystein, who had dived from the mountain into Lake Hauktjern. Harry and Tresko dragging him to the shore. Øystein in bed at Rikshospitalet with what looked like scaffolding around his neck. What Harry had learned from this was that you should jump from great heights, not dive. And remember to keep your arms against your body so that you don't break your collarbone. But above all you have to make up your mind before you look down, and jump before terror has engaged your common sense. And that was why Harry's jacket slid to the terrace floor with a soft smack while Harry was already in the air, listening to the roar in his ears. The black water accelerated toward him. As black as pavement.

He put his heels together, and the next moment it was as if the air had been knocked out of him and a large hand were trying to tear off his clothes, and all sound was gone. Then came the numbing cold. He kicked and rose to the surface. Got his bearings, located the coat and began to swim. He had already started losing sensation in his feet and knew he only had a few minutes before his body would stop functioning in this temperature. But he also knew that if Katrine's laryngeal reflex was working and closed itself when it came into contact with water it would be the sudden cooling down that could save her; it would stop the metabolism, send the body's cells and organs into hibernation mode and allow the vital functions to survive on a minimum of oxygen.

Harry lunged and glided through the thick, heavy water toward the glistening leather.

Then he was there and he grabbed her.

His first unconscious thought was that she was already heaven-bound, consumed by demons. For only her coat was there.

Harry cursed, spun around in the water and stared up at the terrace. Followed the edge up to the eaves, the metal pipework and the sloping roofs that led down the other side of the building, to other buildings. Other terraces and the multitude of fire escapes and routes through the labyrinth of façades in Aker Brygge. He treaded water with legs that could no longer feel while confirming to himself that Katrine had not even underestimated him; he had fallen for one of the oldest tricks in the book. And for a moment of madness he considered death by drowning; it was supposed to be pleasant.

It was four o'clock in the morning, and on the bed in front of Harry, wearing a bathrobe, was a trembling Arve Støp. The tan seemed to have been sucked from his complexion, and he had shrunk into an old man. But his pupils had regained their normal size.

Harry had taken a boiling hot shower and seated himself in a chair, wearing a sweater from Holm and sweatpants he had borrowed from Støp. In the living room they could hear Bjørn Holm trying to organize the hunt for Katrine Bratt via a mobile phone. Harry had told him to contact the Incident Room to put out a general alert; the police at Gardermoen Airport in case she attempted to take one of the early-morning flights; and the Special Forces Unit, Delta, to raid her apartment, even though Harry was fairly sure that they wouldn't find her there.

"So you think this was not just a sex game but Katrine trying to kill you?" Harry asked.

"Think?" Støp said with chattering teeth. "She was trying to strangle me!"

"Mm. And she asked you if you had an alibi for the times of the murders?"

"For the third time, yes!" Støp groaned.

"So she thinks you're the Snowman?"

"Christ knows what she thinks. The woman's obviously out of her mind."

"Maybe," Harry said. "But that doesn't prevent her from having a point."

"And what sort of point would that be?" Støp looked at his watch.

Harry knew that Krohn was on his way and that the lawyer would muzzle his client as soon as he got there.

He made up his mind and leaned forward. "We know that you're the father of Jonas Becker and Sylvia Ottersen's twins."

Støp's head shot up. Harry had to take a risk.

"Idar Vetlesen was the only person who knew. You're the one who sent him to Switzerland and paid for the Fahr's Syndrome course he enrolled in, aren't you? The disease you yourself inherited."

Harry could see he wasn't far off the mark by the way Arve Støp's pupils dilated.

"It's my guess Vetlesen told you we were putting the squeeze on him," Harry persisted. "Perhaps you were frightened he would crack. Or perhaps he was exploiting the situation to extort favors? Money, for example."

The editor stared at Harry in disbelief and shook his head.

"Nevertheless, Støp, you would obviously have had a lot to lose if the truth about these paternities had come out. Enough to give you a motive for killing those who could expose you: the mothers and Idar Vetlesen. Isn't that correct?"

"I . . . " Støp's gaze began to roam.

"You?"

"I have . . . nothing else to say." Støp fell forward and lowered his head into his hands. "Talk to Krohn."

"Fine," Harry said. He didn't have much time. Though he did have one last card. A good one. "I'll tell them you said that."

Harry waited. Støp was still bent forward, motionless. Then at last he raised his head.

"Who's *them*?"

"The press, of course," Harry said. "There is reason to believe they will give us quite a grilling, don't you think? This is what you people would call a scoop, wouldn't you?"

Something clicked behind Støp's eyes.

"How do you mean?" he asked, but with intonation that suggested he already knew the answer.

"A well-known figure thinks he's luring a young woman home, whereas in fact the opposite is the case," Harry said, studying the painting on the wall behind Støp. It seemed to represent a naked woman balancing on a tightrope. "He's persuaded to wear a pig mask in the belief that this is a sex game and this is how he's found by the police, naked and crying in his bathtub."

"You can't tell them that!" Støp exploded. "That . . . that's breaking the principle of client confidentiality."

"Well," Harry said, "it might be breaking the image you've built up around yourself, Støp. However, it doesn't break any obligation to remain silent. More the opposite."

"The opposite?" Støp almost yelled. The chattering of teeth was gone now and the color was back in his cheeks.

Harry coughed. "My only capital and means of production is my personal integrity." Harry waited until he saw that Støp was savoring his own words. "And as a policeman that means, among other things, keeping the public informed to the extent that it is possible without damaging the investigation. In this case, it is possible."

"You can't do that," Støp said.

"I can, and I will."

"That . . . that would crush me."

"More or less the way *Liberal* crushes someone every week on its front page?"

Støp opened and closed his mouth like a fish in an aquarium.

"But of course, even for men with personal integrity there are compromises," Harry pointed out.

Støp studied him hard.

"I hope you appreciate," Harry said, smacking his lips as if to memorize the precise wording, "that as a policeman I have a duty to exploit this situation."

Støp nodded slowly.

"Let's start with Birte Becker," Harry said. "How did you meet her?"

"I think we should stop there," a voice said.

They turned to the door. Appearances suggested that Johan Krohn had found time to shower, shave and iron his shirt.

"OK," Harry said with a shrug. "Holm!"

Bjørn Holm's freckled face appeared in the doorway behind Krohn.

"Call Odin Nakken of *Verdens Gang*," Harry said, facing Arve Støp. "Is it all right if I return your clothes later today?"

"Wait," said Støp.

The room went silent as Arve Støp raised both hands and rubbed the backs of his hands against his forehead as though to start his blood circulating.

"Johan," he said at length, "you'll have to go. I can manage this on my own."

"Arve," the lawyer said, "I don't think you should—"

"Go home and sleep, Johan. I'll call you later."

"As your lawyer I have to—"

"As my lawyer you have to keep your mouth shut and go, Johan. Got that?"

Johan Krohn straightened up, mobilized the remainder of his wounded lawyer dignity, then changed his mind on seeing Støp's expression. Nodded quickly, turned and left.

"Where were we?" Støp asked.

"At the beginning," said Harry.

27

DAY 20

The Beginning

Arve Støp saw Birte Becker for the first time one cold winter's day in Oslo, during a lecture he was giving for a publicity firm at Sentrum Auditorium. It was a motivational seminar where companies sent their jaded employees for a so-called refresher course, that is, lectures intended to make them work even harder. In Arve Støp's experience most lecturers at this seminar were businessmen who had enjoyed a bit of success with not very original ideas, gold medalists from major championships in minor sports, or mountaineers who had made a career out of climbing up mountains and coming down them again to tell others about the experience. What they had in common was that they claimed that their success was a result of their very special willpower and morale. They were motivated. This was what was supposed to be motivating.

Arve Støp was last on the program—he always stipulated that as a prerequisite for his appearances. So that he could start by slating the other lecturers as greedy narcissists, divide them into the three above-mentioned categories and place himself in the first—success with a not very original business idea. The money that was spent on this motivational day was wasted; most people in the room would never advance that far because they were lucky enough not to have the abnormal drive for recognition that tormented those standing on the platform. Including himself. A condition that he said was caused by his father's lack of affection. So he had been obliged to seek love and admiration from others and he should therefore have become an actor or a musician, only he had no talent in those areas.

At this point in the lecture the audience's amazement had turned into laughter. And sympathy. And Støp knew this would culminate in admiration. For he stood there and shone. Shone because he and everyone else knew that whatever he said, he was a success, and you can't argue with success, not even your own. He stressed that luck was the most important factor in success, he played down his own talent and he emphasized that general incompetence and idleness in the Norwegian business sector ensured that even mediocrity can succeed.

At the end they gave him a standing ovation.

And he smiled as he eyed the dark-haired beauty in the first row who would prove to be Birte. He had noticed her the minute he had entered. He was aware that the combination of slim legs and large breasts was often synonymous with silicone implants, but Støp was no opponent of cosmetic surgery for women. Nail polish, silicone: In principle, what was the difference? With the applause pounding in his ears he simply stepped down from the stage, walked along the first row and began to shake hands with the audience. It was a fatuous gesture, something an American president could permit himself to do, but he didn't give a damn; if he could annoy someone he was happy. He stopped in front of the dark-haired woman, who glowed back at him with elated red cheeks. As he passed her, she curtsied as if for a royal, and he felt the sharp corners of his business card stick in his palm as he pressed it against hers. She looked for a wedding ring.

Her ring was lusterless. And her right hand narrow and pale, but it held his in an astonishingly firm grip.

"Sylvia Ottersen," she said with a foolish smile. "I'm a great admirer so I just had to shake hands."

That was how he had met Sylvia Ottersen for the first time, in her shop Taste of Africa one hot summer's day in Oslo. Her looks were run-of-the-mill. Married, though.

Arve Støp looked up at the African masks and asked about something so as not to make the situation any more awkward than it already was. Not that it was awkward for him, but he noticed that the woman at his side had stiffened when Sylvia Ottersen had shaken his hand. Her name was Marita. No, it was Marite. She had insisted on bringing him here to show him some zebra-skin cushions that Marite—or was it Marita?—thought he just *had* to have for the bed that they had left not long before and that now sported strands of long blond hair, which, he made a mental note, would have to be removed.

"We don't have any left in zebra," Sylvia Ottersen said. "But what about these?"

She walked over to a shelf by the window; the daylight fell on her curves, which, he reflected, were not bad at all. Her commonplace brown hair, however, was straggly and dead.

"What is it?" asked the woman whose name began with *M.*

"Imitation gnu skin."

"Imitation?" M. snorted, tossing her blond hair over her shoulder. "We'll wait until you get in more zebra."

"The zebra skin's imitation, too," Sylvia said, smiling

the way you do at children when you have to explain that the moon isn't made of cheese after all.

"I see," M. said, breaking her red lips into a sour smile and hooking her arm under Arve's. "Thank you for letting us browse."

He hadn't liked M.'s idea of going out and parading around in public, and even less the grip she now had on his arm. She may have noticed his distaste when they were outside. At any rate, she let go. He glanced at his watch.

"Ooh," he said. "I've got a meeting."

"No lunch?" She regarded him with a surprised expression, quite able to hide how hurt she was.

"I'll call you, maybe," he said.

She called him. Only thirty minutes had passed since he had been standing on the Sentrum stage, and now he was sitting in a taxi behind a snowplow churning filthy snow onto the roadside.

"I was sitting right in front of you," she said. "I'd like to thank you for the lecture."

"Hope my staring wasn't too obvious!" he shouted exultantly over the scraping of iron on pavement.

She chuckled.

"Any plans for the evening?" he asked.

"Well," she said, "none that can't be changed . . . " Beautiful voice. Beautiful words.

The rest of the afternoon he went around thinking about her, fantasizing about screwing her on the chest of drawers in the hallway, her head banging against the Gerhard Richter painting he had bought in Berlin. And thinking this was always the best bit: the wait.

At eight she rang the bell downstairs. He was in the

hall. Heard the echo of the elevator's mechanical clicking, like a weapon being loaded. A humming tone that rose. The blood was throbbing in his dick.

And then there she stood. He felt as if he had been slapped.

"Who are you?" he said.

"Stine," she said, and a mild expression of surprise spread across the smiling fleshy face. "I phoned . . . "

He scanned her from top to toe and for a moment considered the possibility regardless; every so often he was turned on by the ordinary and fairly unattractive type. However, he could feel his erection dwindling and rejected the idea.

"I'm sorry, but I was unable to get hold of you," he said. "I've just been summoned to a meeting."

"A meeting?" she said, quite unable to hide how hurt she was.

"An emergency meeting. I'll call you, perhaps."

He stood in the hallway and heard the elevator doors outside opening and closing. Then he began to laugh. He laughed until he realized he might never see the dark-haired beauty in the first row again.

He saw Sylvia again an hour later. After he had eaten lunch alone in the aptly named Bar&Restaurant, bought a suit at Kamikaze that he put on right away and twice walked past Taste of Africa, which was a refuge from the boiling hot sun. The third time he went in.

"Back already?" Sylvia Ottersen smiled.

Just as an hour before, she was alone in the cool, dark shop.

"I liked the cushions," he said.

"Yes, they're elegant," she said, stroking the imitation gnu skin.

"Do you have anything else you could show me?" he asked.

She put a hand on her hip. Tilted her head. She knows, he thought. She can smell.

"Depends what you want to see," she said.

He heard the quaver in his voice as he answered. "I'd like to see your pussy."

She let him fuck her in the back room and didn't even bother to lock the shop door.

Arve Støp came almost at once. Now and then the ordinary, fairly unattractive type made him so damned horny.

"My husband's in the shop on Tuesdays and Wednesdays," she said as he was leaving. "Thursday?"

"Maybe," he said and saw that his suit from Kamikaze was already stained.

The snow was swirling in flurries between the office buildings in Aker Brygge when Birte called.

She said she assumed he had given her his business card for her to contact him.

Sometimes Arve Støp asked himself why he had to have these women, these kicks, these sexual relations that were actually no more than ceremonial rituals of surrender. Hadn't he had enough conquests in his life? Was it the fear of getting old? Did he believe that by penetrating these women he could steal some of their youth? And why the hurry, the frenetic tempo? Perhaps it came from the certainty of the disease he was carrying; that before long he would not be the man he once was. He didn't have the answers, and what would he do with them anyway? That same night he listened to Birte's groans, as deep as a man's, her head banging against the Gerhard Richter painting he had bought in Berlin.

* * *

Arve Støp ejaculated his infected seed as the bell over the front door angrily warned them that someone was on his way into Taste of Africa. He tried to free himself, but Sylvia Ottersen grinned and tightened her grip around his buttocks. He tore himself free and pulled up his trousers. Sylvia slid down off the counter, adjusted her summer skirt and went around the corner to serve the customer. With his back to the room Arve Støp hurried over to the shelves of ornaments and buttoned up his fly. Behind him he heard a man's voice apologizing for being late; it had been difficult to find somewhere to park. And Sylvia had said in a sharp voice that he should have known; after all, the summer holidays were over now. She was meeting her sister and she was already late and he would have to take over with the customer.

Arve Støp heard the man's voice at his back. "May I help you?"

He turned and saw a skeleton of a man with unnaturally large eyes behind round glasses, a flannel shirt and a neck that reminded him of a stork.

He looked over his shoulder at the man, caught Sylvia going out the door, the hem of her skirt ridden up, a wet line running down the back of her bare knee. And it struck him that she had known this scarecrow, presumably her husband, would be coming now. She had *wanted* him to catch them at it.

"I'm fine, thank you. I got what I came for," he said, heading for the door.

Every once in a while Arve Støp imagined how he would react if he were told he had made someone pregnant. Whether he would insist on an abortion or that the child should be born. The only thing he was absolutely sure of was that he would insist on one or the other; leaving decisions to others was not in his nature.

Birte Becker had told him they didn't need to use contraception since she couldn't have children. When, three months and six acts of sexual intercourse later, she informed him with a rapturous smile that she could after all, he knew at once that she would have the baby. He reacted by panicking and insisting on the alternative option.

"I have the best contacts," he said. "In Switzerland. No one will ever know."

"This is my opportunity to become a mother, Arve. The doctor says it's a miracle that may never be repeated."

"Then I want to see neither you nor any children you may have again. Do you hear me?"

"The child needs a father, Arve. And a secure home."

"And you won't find either here. I'm the carrier of an awful inherited disease. Do you understand?"

Birte Becker understood. And since she was a straightforward but quick-witted girl with a drunkard of a father and a nervous wreck of a mother, accustomed from early years to coping on her own, she did what she had to do. She found her child a father and a secure home.

Filip Becker could not believe it when this beautiful woman he had wooed with such determination, yet to no avail, suddenly surrendered and set her heart on becoming his. And since he could not believe it, the seeds of suspicion were already sown. At the moment she announced that he had made her pregnant—only a week after she had given herself to him—the seeds were still well entrenched.

When Birte rang Arve to say that Jonas had been born and was the spitting image of him, Arve stood with his ear against the receiver staring into the air. Then he asked her for a photograph. It arrived in the mail, and two weeks later she was sitting, as arranged, in a coffee bar with Jonas on her lap and a wedding ring on her finger while Arve sat at another table pretending to read a paper.

That night he tossed and turned between the sheets, restlessly brooding over the disease.

It had to be handled with discretion, by a doctor he could trust to keep his mouth shut. In short, it would have to be the feeble, obsequious fool of a surgeon at the curling club: Idar Vetlesen.

He contacted Vetlesen, who was working at the Marienlyst Clinic. The idiot said yes to the job and yes to the money, and at Støp's expense traveled to Geneva, where the foremost Fahr's Syndrome experts in Europe gathered every year to hold a conference and present the latest discouraging findings from their research.

The first tests Jonas underwent revealed nothing wrong, but even though Vetlesen repeated that the symptoms usually came to light in adulthood—Arve Støp had himself been symptom-free until he was forty—Støp insisted that the boy be examined once a year.

Two years had passed since he had seen his seed running down Sylvia Ottersen's leg as she walked out of the shop and out of Arve Støp's life. He had quite simply never contacted her again, nor she him. Until now. When she called he said immediately that he was on his way to an emergency meeting, but she kept the message brief. In four sentences she told him that obviously not all his seed had dribbled out, she now had twins, her husband thought they were his and they needed a kindly disposed investor to keep Taste of Africa afloat.

"I think I've injected enough into that shop," said Arve Støp, who often reacted to bad news with witticisms.

"I could, on the other hand, raise the money by going to *Se og Hør*. They love these the-father-of-my-child's-a-celeb stories, don't they?"

"Bad bluff," he said. "You've got too much to lose by doing that."

"Things have changed," she said. "I'm going to leave Rolf if I can scrape together enough cash to buy him out of the shop. The problem with the shop is its location, so I will make it a condition that *Se og Hør* publishes pictures of the place to get it some decent publicity. Do you know how many people read the rag?"

Arve Støp knew. Every sixth Norwegian adult. He had never objected to a nice glitzy scandal every once in a while, but to be made to look like a slippery Lothario exploiting his celebrity status with an innocent married woman in such a craven way? The public image of Arve Støp as upright and fearless would be smashed, and *Liberal*'s morally indignant outbursts would be cast in a hypocritical light. And she wasn't even attractive. This was not good. Not good at all.

"What sort of money are we talking?" he asked.

Upon reaching an agreement, he called Idar Vetlesen at the Marienlyst Clinic and explained that he had two new patients. They arranged to do the same as with Jonas, first make the twins take DNA tests and send them to the Institute of Forensic Medicine to confirm paternity, then start checking for symptoms of the unmentionable disease.

After hanging up, Arve Støp leaned back in the high leather chair and saw the sun shining on the treetops in Bygdøy and on the Snarøya peninsula, knowing he should feel deeply depressed. But he didn't. He felt excited. Yes, almost happy.

* * *

The distant memory of this happiness was the first thing that went through Arve Støp's mind when Idar Vetlesen phoned to tell him that the newspapers were alleging that the decapitated woman in Sollihøgda was Sylvia Ottersen.

"First Jonas Becker's mother disappears," Vetlesen said. "And then they find the mother of the twins killed. I'm no whiz at the calculus of probability, but we have to go to the police, Arve. They're anxious to find connections."

In recent years Vetlesen had made a lucrative career out of embellishing the appearances of celebrities, but in Arve Støp's eyes he was nevertheless—or perhaps as a consequence—a fool.

"No, we're not going to the police," Arve said.

"Oh? Then you'll have to give me a good reason."

"Fine. What sort of money are we talking about?"

"My God, Arve, I'm not trying to blackmail you. I just can't—"

"How much?"

"Stop it. Do you have an alibi or not?"

"I don't have an alibi, but I do have an awful lot of money. Tell me how many zeros and I'll think about it."

"Arve, if you have nothing to hide—"

"Of course I've got something to hide, you twat! Do you think I want to be publicly exposed as a home wrecker and murder suspect? We'll have to meet and talk this through."

"And did you meet?" Harry Hole asked.

Arve Støp shook his head. Outside the bedroom window he could see the heralding of dawn, but the fjord was still black.

"We didn't get that far before he died."

"Why didn't you tell me any of this when I came here the first time?"

"Isn't it obvious? I don't know anything that may be of value to the police, so why should I interfere? Don't forget, I have a brand to attend to, and that is my name. This label is in fact *Liberal*'s only capital."

"I seem to remember you said the only capital was your personal integrity."

Støp shrugged his shoulders with displeasure. "Integrity. Label. It's the same thing."

"So if something looks like integrity, then it's integrity?"

Støp stared at Harry. "That's what sells *Liberal*. If people feel they're given the truth, they're satisfied."

"Mm." Harry glanced at his watch. "And do you think I'm satisfied now?"

Arve Støp didn't answer.

28

Disease

Bjørn Holm drove Harry from Aker Brygge to the Police HQ. The inspector had put on his wet clothes, and the artificial leather squelched as he shifted position.

"Delta raided her apartment twenty minutes ago," Bjørn said. "She wasn't there. They've left three guards on the door."

"She won't be back," Harry said.

In his office on the sixth floor Harry changed into the police uniform hanging on the coatrack; he hadn't worn it since Jack Halvorsen's funeral. He scrutinized himself in the mirror. The jacket hung off him.

Gunnar Hagen had been alerted and had come to the office on short notice. He sat behind his desk as Harry debriefed him. The story was so dramatic that he forgot to be irritated by the inspector's creased uniform.

"The Snowman's Katrine Bratt," Hagen repeated slowly, as if saying it aloud made it more comprehensible.

Harry nodded.

"And do you believe Støp?"

"Yes," Harry said.

"Can anyone corroborate his story?"

"They're all dead. Birte, Sylvia, Idar Vetlesen. He

could have been the Snowman. That was what Katrine Bratt wanted to find out."

"Katrine? But you're saying she's the Snowman. Why would she . . . ?"

"I'm saying that she wanted to find out if he *could* be the Snowman. She wanted to set up a scapegoat. Støp says that when he said he had no alibi for the times of the murders she said, 'Good,' and told him he had just been appointed the Snowman. Then she started to strangle him. Until she heard the car crash into the front door, realized we were on the way and fled. The plan was probably that we would find Støp dead in the apartment and that it would look as if he had hanged himself. And we would relax in the belief that we had found the guilty party. Just as she killed Idar Vetlesen. And when she tried to shoot Filip Becker during his arrest."

"What? She tried . . . ?"

"She had her revolver pointed at him with the hammer cocked. I heard her release the hammer as I positioned myself in the firing line."

Gunnar Hagen closed his eyes and massaged his temples with the tips of his fingers. "I hear you. But for the moment all this is just speculation, Harry."

"And then there's the letter," Harry said.

"The letter?"

"From the Snowman. I found the document on her computer at home, dated before any of us knew anything about the Snowman. And the paper in the printer."

"Christ!" Hagen banged his elbows down hard on the desk and buried his face in his hands. "We employed the woman here! Do you know what that means, Harry?"

"Well, an almighty scandal. Lack of confidence in the whole police force. Heads will roll in the upper echelons."

A crack opened between Hagen's fingers and he squinted at Harry. "Thank you for being so explicit."

"My pleasure."

"I'll summon the chief superintendent and the chief constable. In the meantime I want you and Bjørn Holm to keep this under your hats. What about Arve Støp? Will he blab?"

"Hardly, boss." Harry smirked. "He's run out."

"Run out of what?"

"Integrity."

It was ten o'clock and from his office window Harry watched the pale, almost hesitant daylight settle on the rooftops and a Sunday-still Grønland. Several hours had passed since Katrine Bratt had vanished from Støp's apartment, and so far the search had borne no fruit. Of course she could still be in Oslo, but if she had been prepared for a strategic withdrawal she could well be over the hills and far away. Harry had no doubt that she had made preparations.

Just as he had no doubt now that she was the Snowman.

First of all, there was the evidence: the letter and the murder attempts. And all his instincts were confirmed: the feeling that he was being observed from close range, the feeling that someone had infiltrated his life. The newspaper clippings on the wall, the reports. Katrine had got to know him so well that she could predict his next moves, could use him in her game. And now she was a virus in his bloodstream, a spy inside his head.

He heard someone come in, but didn't turn around.

"We've traced her mobile phone," Skarre's voice said. "She's in Sweden."

"Huh?"

"Telenor says that the signals are moving south. The location and speed match the Copenhagen train that departed from Oslo Central Station at seven oh five. I've spoken to the police in Helsingborg; they need a formal application to make an arrest. The train's due to arrive in half an hour. What should we do?"

Harry nodded slowly, as though to himself. A seagull sailed past on stiff wings before suddenly changing direction and swooping down to the trees in the park. Perhaps it had spotted something. Or just changed its mind. The way humans do. Oslo Station at seven o'clock in the morning.

"Harry? She might make it to Denmark unless we—"

"Ask Hagen to talk to Helsingborg," Harry said, swiveling and grabbing his jacket from the coatrack in one quick movement.

Skarre watched in amazement as the inspector hurried down the corridor with long, purposeful strides.

Officer Orø at the equipment counter at the Police HQ looked at the tall inspector with undisguised astonishment and repeated: "CS? Gas, that is?"

"Two canisters," Harry said. "And a box of ammo for the revolver."

The officer limped to the supplies, mouthing imprecations. This Hole guy was a complete fruitcake—everyone knew that—but tear gas? If it had been anyone else at the station, he would have guessed that it was for a stag night with the pals. But from what he heard, Hole had no pals, at least not on the force.

The inspector coughed as Orø returned. "Has Katrine Bratt in Crime Squad requested any weapons here?"

"The woman from the Bergen Police Station? Only the one stipulated in the rule book."

"And what does the rule book say?"

"Return all weapons and unused ammo to the old police station upon departure and request a new revolver and two boxes of bullets from the new station."

"So she has nothing heavier than a revolver?"

Orø shook his head, mystified.

"Thank you," Hole said, putting the boxes of ammunition in a black bag beside the green cylindrical gas canisters.

The officer didn't answer, not until he had received Hole's signature for the delivery, then he mumbled, "Have a peaceful Sunday."

Harry was sitting in the waiting room at Ullevål University Hospital with the black bag beside him. There was a smell of alcohol, old people and slow death. A female patient had taken a seat opposite him and was staring at him as though trying to locate someone who was not there: a person she had known, a lover who had never materialized, a son she thought she recognized.

Harry sighed, glanced at his watch and visualized the police storming the train in Helsingborg. The engineer who was instructed by the stationmaster to stop the train half a mile before the station. The armed police dispersed along both sides of the track, standing by with dogs. The efficient inspection of the carriages, the compartments, the bathrooms. The terrified passengers reacting to the sight of armed police, still an unusual sight here in Scandinavian dreamland. The trembling, groping hands of women requested to present ID. The hunched shoulders of the police, the nervousness, but also the anticipation. Their impatience, doubt, irritation and ultimately their disappointment and despair that they didn't find what they were looking for. And, at the end, if they were lucky and competent, the loud curses when they found the source of the signals the base stations had picked up: Katrine Bratt's mobile phone in a bathroom garbage bin.

A smiling face appeared before him. "You can see him now."

Harry followed the clatter of clogs and broad, energetic hips in white trousers. She pushed open the door. "But don't stay too long. He needs rest."

Ståle Aune lay on the bed in a private room. His round, red-veined face was sunken and so pale it almost blended in with the pillowcase. Thin hair, like a child's, lay on the chubby sixty-year-old's forehead. Had it not been for the same sharp-eyed, jovial eyes, Harry would have believed he was looking at the corpse of the Crime Squad's resident psychologist and Harry's personal spiritual adviser.

"Goodness me, Harry," Ståle Aune said. "You look like a skeleton. Aren't you well?"

Harry had to smile. Aune sat up with a grimace.

"Sorry not to have visited you before," Harry said, dragging and scraping a chair along the floor to the bed. "It's just that the hospital . . . it . . . I don't know."

"The hospital reminds you of your mother when you were a boy. That's fine."

Harry nodded and dropped his gaze to his hands. "Are they treating you well?"

"That's what you ask when you're visiting people in prison, Harry, not in a hospital."

Harry nodded again.

Ståle Aune sighed. "I know you're concerned about me, Harry. But I know you too well, so I know this is not a courtesy visit. Come on, spit it out."

"It can wait. They said you weren't well."

"Being well is a relative thing. And, relatively speaking, I'm tremendously well. You should have seen me yesterday. By which I mean, you should *not* have seen me yesterday."

Harry smiled at his hands.

"Is it the Snowman?" Aune asked.

Harry nodded.

"At long last," Aune said. "I've been bored to death in here. Out with it."

Harry breathed in. Then he recited all that had happened in the case. Trying to trim the tedious, irrelevant information without losing the essential details. Aune interrupted him only a few times with pithy questions; otherwise he listened in silence with a concentrated, quasi-entranced expression on his face. And when Harry had finished, the sick man appeared to have perked up; there was color in his cheeks and he was sitting up straighter in bed.

"Interesting," he said. "But you already know who the guilty person is, so why come to me?"

"This woman is insane, isn't she?"

"People who commit such crimes are without exception insane. Though not necessarily in a criminal sense."

"Nevertheless, there are one or two things I don't understand about her," Harry said.

"Goodness me—there are only one or two things I *do* understand about people, so in that case you're a better psychologist than I."

"She was just nineteen years old when she killed the two women in Bergen and Gert Rafto. How can a person who is that crazy get through the psychological tests for the police academy and function in a job for all these years with no one being any the wiser?"

"Good question. Perhaps she's a cocktail case."

"Cocktail case?"

"Someone with a bit of everything. Schizophrenic enough to hear voices, but capable of concealing her illness from those around her. Obsessive-compulsive personality disorder mixed with a dash of paranoia, which creates delusions about the situation she is in and what she has to do to escape, but which to the outside world is simply perceived as a certain reticence. The bestial fury that emerges during the murders you describe tallies with a borderline personality, though one that can control its fury."

"Mm. In other words, you haven't a clue?"

Aune laughed. The laughter degenerated into a coughing fit.

"I'm sorry, Harry," he growled. "Most cases are like this. In psychology we have set up a number of corrals that our cattle refuse to be herded into. They're nothing less than impudent, ungrateful, muddle-headed creatures. Think of all the research we've done for them!"

"There's something else. When we stumbled on the body of Gert Rafto she was genuinely frightened. I mean, she wasn't acting. I could see the shock; her pupils were still enlarged and black even though I was shining the flashlight straight into her face."

"Aha! This is interesting." Aune levered himself up higher. "Why did you shine the flashlight in her face? Did you suspect something even then?"

Harry didn't answer.

"You may be right," Aune said. "She may have repressed the murders; that is by no means untypical. You've told me that in fact she has been a great help in the investigation and hasn't sabotaged it. That may suggest she has a suspicion about herself and a genuine desire to uncover the truth. How much do you know about noctambulism—in other words, sleepwalking?"

"I know that people can walk in their sleep. Talk in their sleep. Eat, get dressed and even go out and drive a car in their sleep."

"Correct. The conductor Harry Rosenthal conducted and sang the parts of instruments for entire symphonies in his sleep. And there have been at least five murder cases in which the murderer has been acquitted because the court determined that he or she was a parasomniac, that is, a sufferer of sleep disorders. There was a man in Canada who, some years ago, got up, drove more than ten miles, parked, killed his mother-in-law, with whom he generally had an excellent relationship, almost strangled his father-in-law, drove home and went back to bed. He was acquitted."

"You mean she might have killed in her sleep? That she's one of these parasomniacs?"

"It's a controversial diagnosis. But imagine a person who regularly goes into a hibernation-like state and is subsequently unable to remember with any clarity what she has done. Someone who has a blurred, fragmented image of events, like a dream."

"Mm."

"And suppose that this woman in the course of the investigation has begun to realize what she has done."

Harry nodded slowly. "And realizes that to get away she needs a scapegoat."

"It's conceivable." Ståle Aune made a face. "However, most things are conceivable as far as the human psyche is concerned. The problem is that we cannot see the disorders we're talking about; we have to assume they exist based on the symptoms."

"Like mold."

"What?"

"What makes a person like this woman so psychologically sick?"

Aune groaned. "Everything in existence! And nothing! Nature and nurture."

"A violent, alcoholic father?"

"Yes, yes, yes. Ninety points for that. Add a mother with a psychiatric history, a traumatic experience or two in her childhood and you have the round hundred."

"Does it seem likely that if she had become stronger than her violent, alcoholic father she would try to hurt him? Kill him?"

"By no means impossible. I remember a ca—" Ståle Aune stopped midword. Stared at Harry. Then leaned forward and whispered with a gleam dancing wildly in his eyes. "Are you saying what I think you're saying?"

Harry Hole studied his fingernails. "I was given a photo of a man at the Bergen Police Station. It struck me there was something strangely familiar about him, as if I had met him before. I've only just figured out why. It was the family likeness. Before Katrine Bratt got married her name was Rafto. Gert Rafto was her father."

On his way to the airport express train Harry received a call from Skarre. He had been mistaken. They hadn't found her mobile phone in the bathroom; it had been on the luggage rack in one of the coaches.

Eighty minutes later he was enshrouded in gray. The captain announced that there were low-lying clouds and rain in Bergen. Zero visibility, Harry thought. They were flying on instruments alone now.

The front door was torn open seconds after Thomas Helle, from the Missing Persons Unit, had pressed the doorbell over the sign reading ANDREAS, ELI AND TRYGVE KVALE.

"Thank the Lord you came so quickly." The man standing in front of Helle looked over his shoulder. "Where are the others?"

"There's just me. You still haven't heard anything from your wife?"

The man, who Helle presumed was the Andreas Kvale who had called the HQ, stared at him in amazement. "She's gone, I told you."

"We know, but they usually come back."

"Who's *they*?"

Thomas Helle sighed. "May I come in, Herr Kvale? This rain . . . "

"Oh, sorry! Please . . . " The man in his fifties stepped aside, and in the gloom behind him Helle caught sight of a dark-haired man in his early twenties.

Thomas Helle decided to do the business standing in the hallway. They barely had enough staff to man the phones today; it was a Sunday and those who were on duty were out searching for Katrine Bratt. One of their own. It was all hush-hush, but the rumors going around suggested she might be involved in the Snowman case.

"How did you discover she was missing?" Helle asked, getting ready to take notes.

"Trygve and I just returned from a camping trip in Nord-marka today. We'd been away for two days. No mobile phone, just fishing rods. She wasn't here, no messages, and, as I said on the phone, the door was unlocked. It's always locked, even when she's at home. My wife is a very anxious woman. And none of her coats is missing. Nor her shoes. Only her slippers. In this weather . . . "

"Have you called everyone she knows? Including the neighbors?"

"Of course. No one has heard from her."

Thomas Helle took notes. A familiar feeling had already surfaced. Missing wife and mother.

"You said your wife was an anxious woman," he said. "So who might she have opened the door to? And who might she have let in?"

He saw father and son exchange glances.

"Not too many people," the father said with conviction. "It must have been someone she knew."

"Or someone she didn't feel threatened by, maybe," Helle said. "Like a child or a woman?"

Andreas Kvale nodded.

"Or someone with a plausible reason for coming in. Someone from the electric company to read the meter, for example."

The husband hesitated. "Perhaps."

"Have you seen anything unusual around the house?"

"Unusual? What do you mean?"

Helle bit his lower lip. Braced himself. "Something that may resemble a . . . snowman?"

Andreas Kvale looked at his son, who energetically shook his head, petrified.

"Just so that we can eliminate that from our investigation," Helle said conversationally.

The son said something. In a low mumble.

"What?" Helle asked.

"He said there isn't any more snow."

"No, of course not." Helle stuffed his notepad in his jacket pocket. "I'll radio the patrol cars. If she hasn't turned up by this evening we'll intensify the search. In ninety-nine percent of cases the person will have found her way home by then. So this is my card . . . "

Helle felt Andreas Kvale's hand on his upper arm.

"There's something I want to show you, Officer."

Thomas Helle followed Kvale through a door at the end of the hall and down a staircase into the cellar. He opened a door to a room that smelled of soap and clothes hanging out to dry. In the corner stood an old-fashioned clothes mangle beside an Electrolux washing machine of older vintage. The brick floor sloped down to a drain in the middle. The floor was wet and there was water on the wall, as though the floor had recently been sluiced with the green hose lying there. But that was not primarily what attracted Thomas Helle's attention. It was the garment hanging on the wash line, attached with a clothespin at each shoulder. Or, to be precise, what was left of it. It had been cut off under the chest. The edge was crooked and black with burned, shriveled threads of cotton.

29

Tear Gas

The rain leaked through the heavens down onto Bergen, which lay bathed in the blue afternoon dusk. The boat Harry had reserved was ready at the quayside by the foot of Puddefjord Bridge when his taxi stopped there.

The boat was a well-used twenty-seven-foot Finnish cabin cruiser.

"I'm going fishing," Harry said, pointing to the nautical chart. "Any submerged rocks or anything I ought to know about if I go here?"

"Finnøy island?" said the boat-rental man. "Take a rod with a sinker and a spinner, but the fishing's bad out there."

"Soon find out, won't I. How do you start this thing?"

As Harry chugged past the Nordnes headland in the gathering gloom, he could make out the totem pole among the bare trees in the park. The sea lay flat under the rain, which whipped up the surface and made it foam. Harry thrust the lever next to the wheel forward, the bow lifted—he had to take a step back for balance—and the boat powered away.

Fifteen minutes later Harry pulled the lever back and swung in toward a quay on the far side of Finnøy, hidden from Rafto's cabin. He moored the boat, took out the fishing rod and listened to the rain. Fishing was not his thing. The spinner was heavy, the hook got snagged at the bottom and Harry pulled up seaweed that swirled around the rod as he tugged. He freed the hook and cleaned it. Then he tried to drop the spinner in the water again, but something in the reel had locked and the spinner hung ten inches under the tip of the rod and would go neither up nor down. Harry looked at his watch. If someone had been alerted by the throb of the boat engine he or she would have relaxed by now, and he had to get this done before dark. He placed the rod on the seat, opened his bag, removed the revolver and opened the box of bullets and eased them into the chamber. He then stuffed the thermos-like CS canisters in his pockets and went ashore.

It took him five minutes to reach the top of the deserted island and descend to the cabins boarded up for the winter on the other side. Rafto's cabin stood before him, dark and uninviting. He found a place on a rock twenty yards away, from which he had a full view of all the doors and windows. The rain had seeped through the shoulders of his green military jacket a long time ago. He took out one of the CS canisters and removed the safety pin. In five seconds the spring-loaded valve would discharge and the gas would begin to hiss out. He ran toward the cabin with the canister held in his outstretched arm and hurled it at the window. The glass smashed, making a thin tinkling sound. Harry retreated to the rock and raised his revolver. Above the rain he could hear the canister hissing and he could see the inside of the window turning gray.

If she was there she wouldn't be able to stand more than a few seconds.

He took aim. Waited, with the cabin in his sights.

After two minutes still nothing had happened.

Harry waited for two more.

Then he prepared the second canister, walked toward the cabin with gun raised and tried the door. Locked. Flimsy, though. He stepped back four paces and then ran forward.

The door split off along the hinges, and he plunged into the smoke-filled room, right shoulder first. The gas immediately assailed his eyes. Harry held his breath as he groped his way to the cellar trapdoor, flipped it up, pulled out the safety pin of the second canister and let it fall. Then he ran out again. Found a pool of water and sank to his knees with streaming nose and eyes, put his head in with both eyes open, as deep as he could, until his nose scraped the stones. Twice he repeated the shallow dip. His nose and palate still smarted like hell, but his eyes had cleared. He pointed the revolver toward the hut again. Waited. And waited.

"Come on! Come on, you bitch!"

But no one came out.

After fifteen minutes the smoke had stopped issuing from the hole in the pane. Harry went back down to the cabin and kicked open the door. Coughed and cast a final glance inside. Wasteland wreathed in mist. Flying on instruments. Fuck, fuck, fuck!

As he walked back to the boat it had become so dark that he knew he was going to have visibility problems. He untied the moorings, went on board and grasped the starter lever. A thought went through his mind: He hadn't slept for nearly thirty-six hours, hadn't eaten since early morning, was drenched to the skin and had flown to fucking Bergen for absolutely nothing. If this engine didn't start immediately he would pepper the hull with lead and swim ashore. The engine started with a roar. Harry almost thought it was a shame. He was just about to push the lever forward when he saw her.

She was standing right in front of him on the steps leading down below deck. Nonchalantly leaning against the door frame, in a gray sweater over a black dress.

"Hands up," she ordered.

It sounded so childish it seemed almost a joke. The black revolver pointing at him was not. Nor was the threat that followed. "If you don't do as I say I'll shoot you in the stomach, Harry. Which will smash the nerves in your back and paralyze you. Then one in the head. But let's start with the stomach . . . "

The gun barrel was lowered.

Harry let go of the wheel and the lever and put up his hands.

"Back off, if you would be so kind," she said.

She came up the stairs, and it was only now that Harry could see the gleam in her eyes, the very same he had seen when they arrested Becker, the very same he had seen in Fenris Bar. But sparks were flying from the quivering irises. Harry retreated until he felt the seat at the stern against his legs.

"Sit down," Katrine said, switching off the motor.

Harry slumped back, sat on the fishing rod and felt the water on the plastic seat soak through his trousers.

"How did you find me?" she asked.

Harry shrugged.

"Come on," she said, raising the gun. "Satisfy my curiosity, Harry."

"Well," Harry replied, trying to read her pale, drawn face. But this was unknown territory; the face of this woman did not belong to the Katrine Bratt he knew. Thought he knew.

"Everyone has a pattern of behavior," he heard himself say. "A game plan."

"I see. And what's mine?"

"Pointing one way and running the other."

"Oh?"

Harry sensed the weight of the revolver in his right jacket pocket. He raised his backside and moved the fishing rod, leaving his right hand on the seat.

"You write a letter from 'the Snowman,' send it to me and several weeks later stroll into the Police HQ. The first thing you do is to tell me Hagen has said I should take care of you. Hagen never said that."

"All correct so far. Anything else?"

"You threw your coat into the canal in front of Støp's apartment and fled in the opposite direction, over the roof. The pattern, therefore, is that when you plant your mobile phone on an eastbound train, you flee west."

"Bravo. And how did I flee?"

"Not by plane, of course. You knew that Gardermoen would be under surveillance. My guess is that you planted the phone in Oslo Central Station well before the train was due to depart, crossed over to the bus terminal and caught an early bus west. I would guess you split the journey into various legs. Kept changing buses."

"The Notodden express," Katrine said. "The Bergen bus from there. Got off in Voss and bought clothes. Bus to Ytre Arna. Local bus from there to Bergen. Paid a fisherman at Zacharias wharf to bring me here. Not bad guesswork, Harry."

"It wasn't so difficult. We're pretty similar, you and I."

Katrine tilted her head. "If you were so sure, why did you come alone?"

"I'm not alone. Müller-Nilsen and his people are on their way by boat now."

Katrine laughed. Harry shifted his hand closer to his jacket pocket.

"I agree we're similar, Harry. But when it comes to lying, I'm better than you."

Harry swallowed. His hand was cold. Fingers had to

obey. "Yes, I'm sure that comes easier to you," Harry said. "Like murder."

"Oh? You look as if you could murder me now. Your hand is getting alarmingly close to your jacket pocket. Stand up and remove your jacket. Slowly. And throw it here."

Harry swore inwardly, but did as she said. His coat landed on the deck in front of Katrine with a thud. Without taking her eyes off Harry, she grabbed it and slung it overboard.

"It was time you got yourself a new one anyway," she said.

"Mm," Harry said. "You mean one to match the carrot in the middle of my face?"

Katrine blinked twice and Harry saw what appeared to be confusion in her eyes.

"Listen, Katrine. I've come here to help you. You need help. You're sick, Katrine. It was the illness that made you kill them."

Katrine had started to shake her head slowly. She pointed to land.

"I've been sitting in the boathouse for two hours waiting for you, Harry. Because I knew you would come. I've studied you, Harry. You always find what you're looking for. That was why I chose you."

"Chose me?"

"Chose you. To find the Snowman for me. That was why I sent you the letter."

"Why couldn't you find the Snowman yourself? You didn't exactly have to go far."

She shook her head. "I've tried, Harry. I've tried for many years. I knew I wouldn't be able to do it on my own. It had to be you. You're the only person who's succeeded in catching a serial killer. I needed Harry Hole." She gave a sad smile. "A last question, Harry. How did you figure out that I had deceived you?"

Harry was wondering how this would end. A bullet to the forehead? The electric cutting loop? A trip out to sea and then death by drowning? He swallowed. He ought to be afraid. So frightened that he would be unable to think, so frightened that he would fall sobbing to the deck and implore her to let him live. Why wasn't he? It couldn't be pride; he had swallowed that with whiskey and spat it out again several times. It could of course be his rational brain working, knowing that being frightened wouldn't help; on the contrary, it would only shorten his life further. He concluded, however, it was the tiredness that did it. A profound, all-encompassing exhaustion that made him feel as if he just wanted to get it over and done with.

"Deep down I've always known that this all started a long time ago," Harry said, noting that he no longer felt the cold. "It was planned and the person behind it had managed to get into my head. There are not so many people to choose from, Katrine. And when I saw the newspaper clippings in your apartment, I knew it was you."

Harry saw her blinking, disoriented. And he felt a wedge of doubt being driven into his line of thought, into the logic he had seen so clearly. Or had he? Hadn't the doubt always been there? The steady drizzle gave way to a deluge; the water hammered down on the deck. He saw her mouth open and her finger curl around the trigger. He grabbed the fishing rod beside him and stared down the gun barrel. This was how it would end, in a boat on the western coast, without witnesses, without evidence. An image sprang into his mind. Of Oleg. Alone.

He swung the rod in front of him, at Katrine. It was a last desperate lunge, a pathetic attempt to turn the tables, to divert fate. The soft tip hit Katrine's cheek, not hard— she could hardly have felt it—and the blow neither hurt nor unbalanced her. In retrospect, Harry couldn't re- member if what happened was intentional, half thought through or sheer unadulterated luck: The accelerated movement of the spinner caused the eight-inch-long stretch of line to wrap itself around her head in such a way that the spinner continued around and struck the front teeth in her open mouth. And when Harry pulled hard at the rod, the tip of the hook did what it was de- signed to do: it found flesh. It dug into the right-hand corner of Katrine Bratt's mouth. And Harry's despairing pull was so violent that, in consequence, Katrine Bratt's head was wrenched back and around to the right with such power that for a moment he had the impression that he was screwing the head off her body. After an infini- tesimal lag, her body followed the head's rotation, first to the right, then propelled toward Harry. Her body was still spinning when she fell onto the deck in front of him.

Harry dropped onto her, knees first. They hit her on either side of the collarbone, and he knew he had ren- dered her arms immobile.

He twisted the revolver out of the paralyzed hand and pushed the barrel against one of her dilated eyes. The weapon felt light and he could see the iron press- ing against her soft eyeball, but she didn't blink. Quite the opposite. She was grinning. A broad grin. From the ripped corner of her mouth and bloodstained teeth, which the rain was trying to wash clean.

30

Scapegoat

Knut Müller-Nilsen had appeared on the quay under Puddefjord Bridge in person as Harry arrived in the cabin cruiser. He, two police officers and the duty psychiatrist joined him below deck, where Katrine Bratt lay handcuffed to the bed. She was given a shot of an antipsychotic tranquilizer and transported to a waiting vehicle.

Müller-Nilsen thanked Harry for agreeing to handle the matter with discretion.

"Let's try to keep this to ourselves," Harry said, looking up at the leaking heavens. "Oslo will want to take control if this is made public."

" 'Course." Müller-Nilsen nodded.

"Kjersti Rødsmoen," said a voice that made them turn around. "The psychiatrist."

The woman peering up at Harry was in her forties, with light, tousled hair and a big bright red down jacket. She was holding a cigarette in her hand and didn't appear to be bothered that the rain was drenching both her and the cigarette.

"Was it dramatic?" she asked.

"No," Harry said, feeling Katrine's revolver pressing

against his skin under his waistband. "She surrendered without resistance."

"What did she say?"

"Nothing."

"Nothing?"

"Not a word. What's your diagnosis?"

"Obviously a psychosis," Rødsmoen said without hesitation. "Which does not imply in any way that she's mad. It's just the mind's way of managing the unmanageable. Much the same as the brain choosing to faint when the pain is too great. I would conjecture that she's been under extreme stress for a lengthy period. Could that be correct?"

Harry nodded. "Will she be able to speak again?"

"Yes," Kjersti Rødsmoen said, gazing with disapproval at the wet, extinguished cigarette. "But I don't know when. Right now she needs rest."

"Rest?" Müller-Nilsen snorted. "She's a serial killer."

"And I'm a psychiatrist," Rødsmoen said, dispensing with the cigarette and departing in the direction of a small red Honda that even in the pouring rain looked dusty.

"What are you going to do?" Müller-Nilsen asked.

"Catch the last plane home," Harry said.

"No way. You look like a skeleton. The station's got a deal with the Rica travel hotel. We can drive you there and send on some dry clothes. They've got a restaurant, too."

Once Harry had checked in and was standing in front of the bathroom mirror in the cramped single room, he thought about what Müller-Nilsen had said about looking like a skeleton. And about how close he had been to death. Or had he? After taking a shower and eating in the empty restaurant he went back to his room and tried to sleep. He couldn't and switched on the TV. Crap on all the channels except NRK2, which was showing *Memento*. He had seen the film before. The story was told from the point of view of a man with brain damage and the short-term memory of a goldfish. A woman had been killed. The protagonist had written the name of the killer on a Polaroid, as he knew he would forget. The question was whether he could trust what he had written. Harry kicked off the duvet. The minibar under the TV had a brown door and no lock.

He should have caught the plane home.

He was on his way out of bed when his mobile phone rang somewhere in the room. He put his hand in the pocket of the wet trousers hanging over a chair by the radiator. It was Rakel. She asked where he was. And said they had to talk. And not in his apartment, but somewhere public.

Harry fell back on the bed with closed eyes.

"You're going to tell me we can't keep meeting?" he asked.

"I'm going to tell you we can't keep meeting," she said. "I can't take it."

"It's enough if you tell me on the phone, Rakel."

"No, it's not. It won't hurt enough."

Harry groaned. She was right.

They agreed on eleven o'clock the next morning by Bygdøy's Fram Museum, a tourist attraction where you could disappear in crowds of Germans and Japanese. She asked him what he was doing in Bergen. He told her and said she was to keep it to herself until she read about it in the papers after a couple of days.

They hung up, and Harry lay staring at the minibar as *Memento* continued its course in reverse chronological order. He had almost been killed, the love of his life didn't want to see him anymore and he had concluded the worst case in his experience. Or had he? He hadn't

answered when Müller-Nilsen asked why he had chosen
to hunt for Bratt on his own, but now he knew. It was the
doubt. Or the hope. This desperate hope that it would
not end up the way it seemed to be going. Hope that was
still there. But now it had to be extinguished, drowned.
Come on, he had three good reasons and a pack of dogs
in the pit of his stomach all barking as though possessed.
So why not just open the minibar anyhow?

Harry got to his feet, went to the bathroom, turned
on the tap and drank, letting the jet of water gush over
his face. He straightened up and looked into the mirror.
Like a skeleton. Why won't the skeleton drink? Aloud,
he spat out the answer to his face: "Because then it won't
hurt enough."

Gunnar Hagen was tired. Tired down to his soul. He
looked around. It was almost midnight and he was in a
conference room at the top of one of Oslo's central buildings. Everything here was shiny brown: the wood floor,
the ceiling with the spotlights, the walls with painted
portraits of former club chairmen who had owned the
premises, the thirty-square-foot mahogany table and the
leather blotting pad in front of each of the twelve men
around it. Hagen had been phoned by the chief super
intendent an hour earlier and summoned to this address. Some of the people in the room—such as the chief
constable—he knew, others he had seen in newspaper
photographs, but he had no idea who most of them were.
The chief superintendent brought them up to date. The
Snowman was a policewoman from Bergen who had been
operating for a while from her post in the Crime Squad
in Grønland. She had pulled the wool over their eyes,
and now that she was caught, they would soon have to go
public with the scandal.

When he had finished, the silence lay as thick as the cigar smoke.

The smoke was filtering upward from the end of the table, where a white-haired man leaned back in his chair, his face hidden in shadow. For the first time, he made a sound. Just a tiny sigh. And Gunnar Hagen realized that everyone who had spoken so far had turned to this man.

"Damned tedious, Torleif," said the white-haired man in a surprisingly high-pitched, effeminate voice. "Extremely damaging. Confidence in the system. We are at the top. And that means"—the whole room seemed to be holding its breath as the man puffed on his cigar—"heads will have to roll. The question is whose."

The chief constable cleared his throat. "Do you have any suggestions?"

"Not yet," said the white-hair. "But I believe you and Torleif do. Go ahead."

"In our view, specific mistakes have been made in the appointment and follow-up phases. Human blunders and not systemic flaws. Hence this is not directly a management problem. Therefore we propose that we make a distinction between responsibility and guilt. Management takes the responsibility, is humble and—"

"Skip the basics," said the white-hair. "Who's your scapegoat?"

The chief superintendent adjusted his collar. Gunnar Hagen could see that he was extremely ill at ease.

"Inspector Harry Hole," said the chief superintendent.

Again there was silence as the white-haired man lit his cigar anew. The lighter clicked and clicked. Then sucking noises issued from the shadows and the smoke rose again.

"Not a bad idea," said the high-pitched voice. "Had it been anyone other than Hole I'd have said you would have to find your scapegoat higher up in the system. An inspector is not fat enough as a sacrificial lamb. Indeed, I might have asked you to consider yourself, Torleif. But Hole is an officer with a profile; he's been on that talk show. A popular figure with a certain reputation as a detective. Yes, that would be perceived as fair game. But would he be cooperative?"

"Leave that to us," said the chief superintendent. "Eh, Gunnar?"

Gunnar Hagen gulped. His mind turned—of all things—to his wife. To the sacrifices she had made so that he could have a career. When they'd got married she had broken off her studies and moved with him to wherever the Special Forces, and later the police force, had sent him. She was a wise, intelligent woman, an equal to him in most areas, his superior in some. It was to her he went with both career and moral issues. And she always imparted good advice. Nevertheless, he had perhaps not succeeded in achieving the illustrious career for which they had both hoped. But now things were looking rosier. It was in the cards that his position as Crime Squad supremo would lead onward and upward. It was just a question of not putting a foot wrong. That needn't be so difficult.

"Eh, Gunnar?" repeated the chief superintendent.

It was just that he was so tired. So tired down to the soul. This is for you, he thought. This is what you would have done, darling.

31

The South Pole

Harry and Rakel stood at the bow of the wooden ship *Fram* in the museum, observing a group of Japanese tourists taking pictures of the ropes and masts as, with smiles and nods, they ignored the guide, who was explaining that this simple vessel had transported both Fridtjof Nansen on his failed attempt to be the first to the North Pole in 1893 and Roald Amundsen, when he beat Scott to the South Pole in 1911.

"I left my watch on your table," Rakel said.

"That's an old trick," Harry said. "It means you'll have to come back for it."

She laid a hand over his on the railing and shook her head. "Mathias gave it to me for my birthday."

Which I forgot, Harry thought.

"We're going out and he's going to ask, if I'm not wearing it. And you know what I'm like about lying. Could you . . . ?"

"I'll drop it off before four," he said.

"Thanks. I'll be working, but just put it in the birdhouse on the wall by the door. That's . . . "

She didn't need to say any more. That was where she had always put the house key when he got there after she had gone to bed. Harry slapped the railing with his hand. "According to Arve Støp, Roald Amundsen's problem was that he won. He thinks all the best stories are about losers."

Rakel didn't answer.

"I suppose it's a kind of consolation," Harry said. "Shall we go?"

Outside it was snowing.

"So it's over now?" she said. "Until next time?"

He shot her a quick glance to assure himself she was talking about the Snowman and not them.

"We don't know where the bodies are," he said. "I was with her in her cell this morning before going to the airport, but she won't say anything. Just stares into the air as if there's someone there."

"Did you tell anyone you were going to Bergen alone?" she asked out of the blue.

Harry shook his head.

"Why not?"

"Well," Harry said, "I might have been wrong. Then I could have returned quietly without losing face."

"That wasn't why," she said.

Harry glanced at her again. She looked more fed up than he did.

"To be frank, I have no idea," he said. "I suppose I hoped it wouldn't be her after all."

"Because she's like you? Because it could have been you?"

Harry couldn't even remember telling her they were similar.

"She looked so alone and frightened," Harry said as the snowflakes stung his eyes. "Like someone who'd got lost in the twilight."

Fuck, fuck, fuck! He blinked and felt the tears, like a clenched fist, trying to force their way up his windpipe.

Was he having a breakdown? He froze as Rakel's warm hand caressed his neck.

"You're not her, Harry. You're different."

"Am I?" He smiled thinly, removing her hand.

"You don't kill innocent people, Harry."

Harry turned down Rakel's offer of a lift and caught the bus. He stared at the flakes falling and the fjord beyond the window, thinking how Rakel had inserted the word *innocent* only at the last minute.

Harry was about to open his front door on Sofies Gate when he remembered he didn't have any instant coffee, and walked the fifty yards to Niazi, the corner shop.

"Unusual to see you at this time of day," Ali said, taking the money.

"Day off," Harry said.

"What weather, eh? They say there's going to be a foot and a half of snow over the next twenty-four hours."

Harry fidgeted with the coffee jar. "I happened to frighten Salma and Muhammad in the yard the other day."

"Yes, I heard."

"I'm sorry. I was a bit stressed, that's all."

"That's OK. I was just afraid you'd started drinking again."

Harry shook his head and gave a weak smile. He liked the Pakistani's direct approach.

"Good," said Ali, counting out the change. "How's the redecorating going?"

"Redecorating?" Harry took his change. "Do you mean the mold man?"

"The mold man?"

"Yes, the guy who's checking the cellar for fungus. Stormann or something like that."

"Fungus in the *cellar*?" Ali looked horrified.

"Didn't you know?" Harry said. "You're the chairman of the residents' committee. I'd have thought he would have spoken to you."

Ali shook his head slowly. "Perhaps he spoke to Bjørn."

"Who's Bjørn?"

"Bjørn Asbjørnsen, who's lived on the ground floor for thirteen years," Ali said, giving Harry a reproving look. "And has been the vice chair for just as long."

"Oh, right, Bjørn," Harry said, pretending to note the name.

"I'll check that out," Ali said.

Upstairs in his apartment, Harry pulled off his boots, headed straight for the bedroom and fell asleep. He had hardly slept at the hotel in Bergen. When he awoke his mouth was dry and he had stomach pains. He got up to drink some water and came to a sudden halt when he entered the hall.

He hadn't noticed when he got in, but the walls were back.

He walked from room to room. Magic. It had been done to such perfection that he could swear they hadn't been touched. No old nail holes visible, no lines askew. He touched the sitting-room wall as if to assure himself that this was not a hallucination.

On the sitting-room table, in front of the wing chair, there was a yellow piece of paper. A handwritten message. The letters were neat and strangely attractive.

It's gone. You won't see me anymore. Stormann.

P.S. Had to turn one of the boards in the wall since I cut myself and blood got onto it. When blood gets into untreated wood it's impossible to wash off. The alternative would have been to paint the wall red.

Harry fell into the wing chair and studied the smooth walls.

It was only when he went into the kitchen that he discovered the miracle was not complete. The calendar with Rakel and Oleg was gone. The sky-blue dress. He swore aloud and feverishly ransacked the wastepaper baskets and even the plastic garbage can in the yard before concluding that the happiest time of his life had been eradicated along with the fungus.

It was definitely a different workday for psychiatrist Kjersti Rødsmoen. And not just because the sun had made a rare appearance in the Bergen sky and was at this moment shining through the windows as she hurried along a corridor in Haukeland University Hospital's psychiatric department, in Sandviken. The department had changed its name so many times that very few Bergensians knew that the current official name was Sandviken Hospital. However, a closed ward was, until further notice, a closed ward, while Bergen waited for someone to claim that the terminology was misleading or at any rate stigmatizing.

She was both dreading and looking forward to the imminent session with the patient who was confined under the strictest security measures she could ever remember. They had reached agreement on the ethical boundaries and procedures with Espen Lepsvik from Kripos and Knut Müller-Nilsen from the Bergen Police. The patient was psychotic and could therefore not undergo a police interview. Kjersti was a psychiatrist and entitled to talk to the patient, but with the patient's best interests at heart, not in a way that might be construed as police questioning. And ultimately there was the issue of client confidentiality. Kjersti Rødsmoen would have to assess for herself whether any information that emerged from the conversation could have such great significance for the police that she should take it further. And this information would have no validity in a court of law anyway, since it came from a psychotic person. In short, they were moving in a legal and ethical minefield where even the slightest slip might have catastrophic consequences, since everything she did would be scrutinized by the judicial system and the media.

A nurse and a uniformed policeman stood outside the door of the consulting room. Kjersti pointed to the ID card pinned to her white medical coat, and the officer opened the door.

The agreement was that the nurse would keep an eye on what was happening in the room and sound the alarm if necessary.

Kjersti Rødsmoen sat down on the chair and observed the patient. It was hard to imagine that she represented any danger, this small woman with hair hanging over her face, black stitches where her torn mouth had been sewn up and wide-open eyes that seemed to be staring with unfathomable horror at something Kjersti Rødsmoen could not see. Quite the contrary. The woman appeared so incapable of any action that you had the feeling she would be blown over if you so much as breathed on her. The fact that this woman had killed people in cold blood was quite simply inconceivable. But it always was.

"Hello," said the psychiatrist. "I'm Kjersti."

No response.

"What do you think your problem is?" she asked.

The question came straight from the manual governing conversations with psychotics. The alternative was: *How do you think I can help you?*

Still no response.

"You're quite safe in this room. No one will harm you. I won't hurt you. You're absolutely safe."

According to the manual, this solid statement was supposed to reassure the psychotic patient, because a psychosis is primarily about boundless fear. Kjersti Rødsmoen felt like a flight attendant running through the safety procedures before takeoff. Mechanical, routine. Even on routes crossing over the driest of deserts you demonstrate the use of the life jacket. Because the statement proclaims what passengers want to hear: You're allowed to be frightened, but we'll take care of you.

It was time to check her perception of reality.

"Do you know what day it is today?"

Silence.

"Look at the clock on the wall over there. Can you tell me what time it is?"

She received a hunted stare by way of an answer.

Kjersti Rødsmoen waited. And waited. The minute hand of the clock shifted with a quivering goose step.

It was hopeless.

"I'm going now," Kjersti said. "Someone will come fetch you. You're quite safe."

She went to the door.

"I have to talk to Harry." Her voice was deep, almost masculine.

Kjersti stopped and turned. "Who's Harry?"

"Harry Hole. It's urgent."

Kjersti tried to establish eye contact, but the woman was still staring into her own distant world.

"I'm afraid you'll have to tell me who Harry Hole is, Katrine."

"Crime Squad inspector in Oslo. And if you have to say my name, use my surname, Kjersti."

"Bratt?"

"Rafto."

"I see. But can't you tell me what you want to talk to Harry Hole about, so that I can pass it on—"

"You don't understand. They're all going to die."

Kjersti sank slowly back into the chair. "I do understand. And why do you think they're going to die, Katrine?"

And finally there was eye contact. And what Kjersti Rødsmoen saw made her think of one of those orange cards in the game of Monopoly she had in her vacation house: Your houses and hotels have all burned down.

"None of you understands anything," answered the low, masculine voice. "It's not me."

At two o'clock Harry pulled up to the curb in front of Rakel's timber house on Holmenkollveien. It had stopped snowing and he thought it wouldn't be wise to leave telltale tire prints on the driveway. The snow emitted soft, drawn-out screeches under his boots and the sharp daylight flashed against the sunglass-black windows as he approached.

He went up the steps by the front door, opened the hatch of the birdhouse, put Rakel's watch inside and closed it again. He had turned around to leave as the door behind him was wrenched open.

"Harry!"

Harry spun around, swallowed and essayed a smile. Before him stood a man naked but for a towel around his waist.

"Mathias," he said, bewildered, staring at the other man's chest. "You gave me a shock. Thought you'd be working at this time of day."

"Sorry." Mathias laughed, quickly crossing his arms. "I was working late last night. Day off today. I was on my way to the shower when I heard some noise at the door. I assumed it would be Oleg; his key sticks a bit, you see."

Sticks, Harry mused. That must mean Oleg has the key he used to have. And that Mathias has Oleg's. A woman's mind.

"Can I help you, Harry?" Harry noticed that his crossed arms were unnaturally high up on his chest, as though he was trying to hide something.

"Nope," Harry said casually. "I was just driving by and had something for Oleg."

"Why didn't you knock?"

Harry swallowed. "I suddenly realized he wasn't back from school yet."

"Oh? How did you know that?"

Harry nodded to Mathias, as though bestowing approval for an apposite question. There wasn't a shred of suspicion in Mathias's friendly, open face, only a genuine desire to have something clarified that he couldn't grasp.

"The snow," Harry said.

"The snow?"

"Yes. It stopped snowing two hours ago, and there are no prints on the steps."

"Well, I'll be damned, Harry," Mathias burst out enthusiastically. "Now that's what I call applying deductive reasoning to your everyday life. You're a detective, all right, no question about that."

Harry's laughter was strained. Mathias's crossed arms had sunk a little, and now Harry could see what Rakel must have meant by Mathias's physical quirk. Where you expected to see two nipples, the skin just continued, white and unbroken.

"It's hereditary," said Mathias, who had clearly been following Harry's eyes. "My father didn't have any, either. It's rare but quite harmless. And what are we men supposed to do with them anyway?"

"Indeed," Harry said, feeling his earlobes go warm.

"Would you like me to give the something to Oleg?"

Harry shifted his gaze. It settled instinctively on the birdhouse, then moved on.

"I'll drop it off another time," Harry said, grimacing in a way he hoped inspired trust. "You have a shower."

"OK."

"See you."

The first thing Harry did when he got back into the car was to smack both hands on the wheel and curse aloud. He had behaved like a twelve-year-old pilferer caught red-handed. He had lied to Mathias's face. Lied and crawled and been a shit.

He gunned the engine and let the clutch go with a jerk to punish the car. He didn't have the energy to think about it now. Had to focus on other things. But he couldn't, and his mind was racing in a chaotic chain of associations as he tore down to Oslo city center. He thought of blemishes, of flat, red nipples that looked like bloodstains on bare skin. Of bloodstains on untreated wood. And for some reason the mold man's words came into his head: "The alternative would have been to paint the wall red."

The mold man had bled. Harry half closed his eyes and visualized the cut. It must have been a deep cut to have made such a mess that . . . that the alternative would have been to paint the wall red.

Harry jumped on the brakes. He heard a horn, looked in the mirror and saw a Hiace sliding on new snow until the tires got a grip and it skidded alongside him and past.

Harry kicked open the car door, leaped out and saw that he was by the stadium at the bottom of Holmenkollveien. He took a deep breath and broke his tower of thoughts into pieces, dismantled it to see if he could reassemble it. Rebuilt it quickly, without forcing any of the parts. For they slotted in by themselves. His pulse was accelerating. If this made credible sense, everything was turned upside down. And it all fit, it fit that the Snowman had planned how to infiltrate Harry and had just walked in off the street and made himself comfortable. And the bodies—that would explain what had happened to the bodies. Trembling, Harry lit a cigarette and started to try to reconstruct what he had seen in a flash. The chicken feathers with blackened edges.

Harry didn't believe in inspiration, divine insights or telepathy. But he did believe in luck. Not the luck you were born with, but the systematic luck you earned through hard work and spinning yourself such a fine-meshed net that at some point chance would play into your hands. But this was not that kind of luck. This was just a fluke. An atypical fluke. If he was right, of course. Harry looked down and discovered that he was wading through snow. That in fact—quite literally—he had his feet on the ground.

He walked back to the car, took out his mobile phone and rang Bjørn Holm's number.

"Yes, Harry?" answered a sleepy, almost unrecognizable nasal voice.

"You sound hungover."

"I wish." Holm sniffled. "Goddamn cold. Freezing under two duvets. Ache all over—"

"Listen," Harry interrupted. "Do you remember when I asked you to take the temperature of the chickens to find out how long it had been since Sylvia had been in the barn slaughtering them?"

"Yes?"

"And you said afterward that one was warmer than the other two."

Bjørn Holm sniffled. "Yes. Skarre suggested it had a temperature. A theory that's perfectly plausible."

"I think it was warmer because it was killed after Sylvia was killed, in other words, at least an hour later."

"Oh? Who by?"

"By the Snowman."

Harry heard a long, loud snort as snot traveled backward before Holm answered. "You mean she took Sylvia's hatchet, went back and—"

"No, the hatchet was in the forest. I should have reacted when I saw it, but of course I'd never heard of this cutting loop when we were there looking at the chicken carcasses."

"And what did you see?"

"A sliced feather with a blackened edge. You see, I think the Snowman was using the cutting loop."

"Right," said Holm. "But why on earth would she kill a chicken?"

"To paint the whole wall red."

"Eh?"

"I've got an idea," Harry said.

"Shit," mumbled Bjørn Holm. "I suppose this idea means I have to get out of bed."

"Well . . . ," Harry began.

The snowy weather must have just been taking a breather, for at three it started again, and thick, furry flakes began to sweep down over Østland. A gray glazed coat of slush lay on Route E16, winding upward from Bærum.

At the highest point on the road, Sollihøgda, Harry and Holm turned and skidded their way along the forest road.

Five minutes later Rolf Ottersen was standing in front of them in the doorway. Behind him, in the sitting room, Harry could see Ane Pedersen sitting on the sofa.

"We just wanted to have another look at the barn floor," Harry said.

Rolf Ottersen pushed his glasses back up his nose. Bjørn Holm let out a rasping chesty cough.

"Help yourselves," Ottersen said.

As Holm and Harry walked toward the barn Harry could feel that the thin man was still standing by the door watching them.

The chopping block was in the same place, but there was no sign of any chickens, living or dead. Leaning against the wall there was a spade with a pointed blade. To dig in the ground, not to shovel snow. Harry headed for the tool board. The outline of the hatchet that should have been hanging there reminded Harry of the chalk outlines after bodies have been removed from crime scenes.

"It's my belief the Snowman came here and slaughtered the third chicken to spray blood over the floorboards. The Snowman couldn't turn the boards and the alternative was to paint them red."

"You told me that in the car as well, but I'm still lost."

"If you want to hide red stains you can either remove them or paint everything red. I think the Snowman was trying to hide something. A clue."

"What kind of clue?"

"Something red that's impossible to remove because untreated wood soaks it up."

"Blood? She was trying to hide blood with more blood? Is that your idea?"

Harry snatched a broom and swept away the sawdust around the chopping block. He crouched down and felt Katrine's revolver pressing into him under his belt. Studied the floor. There was still a pink glow.

"Did you bring the photos we took?" Harry asked.

"Start checking the places where there was the most blood. It was some way from the chopping block, around here."

Holm took the photos from his bag.

"We know that it was chicken blood on top," Harry said. "But imagine that the first blood that was spilled here had time to saturate the wood and be absorbed into it and therefore didn't mix with the new blood that was poured on top a good while later. What I'm wondering is whether you can still get samples of the first blood—in other words, the blood that soaked into the wood."

Bjørn Holm blinked in dismay. "What the fuck am I supposed to answer to that?"

"Well," Harry said, "the only answer I will accept is yes."

Holm responded with a prolonged fit of coughing.

Harry strolled over to the farmhouse. He knocked, and Rolf Ottersen came out.

"My colleague will be here for a while," Harry said. "Would you mind if he popped in now and again to get warm?"

"Fine," Ottersen said with reluctance. "What are you digging for now?"

"I was going to ask you the same thing," Harry said. "I saw there was soil on the spade over there."

"Oh, that. Fence posts."

Harry scoured the snow-covered ground that stretched into the dense, dark forest. Wondering what it was Ottersen wanted to fence in. Or out. For he had seen it: the fear in Rolf Ottersen's eyes.

Harry motioned toward the sitting room. "You've got a visitor . . . " He was interrupted by a call on his mobile phone.

It was Skarre.

"We've found another one," he said.

Harry stared into the forest and felt the large snow-flakes melting on his cheeks and forehead.

"Another what?" he mumbled in response, even though he had already heard the answer in Skarre's tone.

"Another snowman."

The psychiatrist Kjersti Rødsmoen contacted POB Knut Müller-Nilsen as he and Espen Lepsvik from Kripos were leaving the police station.

"Katrine Bratt has talked," she said. "And I think you should come to the hospital to hear what she has to say."

32

The Tanks

Skarre trod in the tracks in the snow leading to the trees, ahead of Harry. Early-afternoon darkness presaged that winter was on its way. Above them flashed the Tryvann communications tower, and below them twinkled Oslo. Harry had driven straight from Sollihøgda and parked in the large empty parking lot where new graduates collected like lemmings every spring for the obligatory enactment of adult rituals of the species: cavorting around a fire, stupefying themselves with alcohol and indulging in sex with wild abandon. Harry's graduation celebrations were different. He had had just two companions, Bruce Springsteen and "Independence Day," which shrieked from his boom box on top of the German bunker on Nordstrand beach.

"A hiker found it," Skarre said.

"And considered it necessary to report a snowman in the forest to the police?"

"He had a dog with him. It . . . well . . . you'll see for yourself."

They emerged into open terrain. A young man straightened up on catching sight of Skarre and Harry and came toward them.

"Thomas Helle, Missing Persons Unit," he said. "We're glad you're here, Hole."

Harry sent the young officer a look of surprise, but saw that he really meant it.

On a hill in front of him Harry watched the Crime Scene Unit at work. Skarre crawled under the red police cordon and Harry stepped over. A path marked out where they were to walk so as not to destroy any forensic evidence that had not already been destroyed. The Crime Scene officers became aware of Harry and Skarre's presence and silently moved aside to observe the newcomers. As if they had been waiting for this: a chance to display. To collate reactions.

"Oh, shit," Skarre said, recoiling a step.

Harry felt his head go cold, as if all the blood had drained from his brain, leaving a numb, dead sensation of nothing.

It was not the details, because at first glance the naked woman did not seem to have been brutally mutilated. Not like Sylvia Ottersen or Gert Rafto. What scared the living daylights out of him was the construction, the studied, cold-blooded nature of the arrangement. The body sat on top of two large balls of snow that had been rolled up against a tree trunk, one on top of the other like an incomplete snowman. The body leaned against the tree but any sideways movement would have been prevented by a steel wire attached to the thick branch over her head. The wire ended in a rigid noose around her neck, bent in such a way that it touched neither her shoulders nor her neck, like a lasso frozen in motion as it falls perfectly over the victim. Her arms were tied behind her back. The woman's eyes and mouth were closed, affording the face a peaceful expression; she could have been asleep.

It was almost possible to believe the body had been arranged with loving attention. Until the stitches on the naked, pale skin became evident. The edges of the skin under the nearly invisible thread were separated only by a fine, even join of black blood. One welt of stitches ran across her torso, just under her breasts. The other around her neck. Immaculate workmanship, Harry mused. Not a stitch hole visible, not a line askew.

"Looks like that abstract-art shit," Skarre said. "What's it called?"

"Installation art," said a voice behind him.

Harry cocked his head. They were right. But there was something that conflicted with the impression of perfect surgery.

"He chopped her up into chunks," he said in a voice that sounded as if someone had him in a stranglehold. "And reassembled her."

"He?" queried Skarre.

"Maybe to ease transportation," Helle said. "I think I know who she is. She was reported missing by her husband yesterday. He's on his way here now."

"Why do you think it's her?"

"Her husband found a dress with scorch marks." Helle pointed to the body. "Roughly where the stitches are."

Harry concentrated on his breathing. He could see the imperfection now. This was the unfinished snowman. And the knots and angles of the twisted wire were jagged. They seemed rough, arbitrary, tentative. As though this was a mock-up, a rehearsal. The first draft of an unfinished work. And why had he tied her hands behind her back? She must have been dead long before she came here. Was that part of the mock-up? He cleared his throat.

"Why wasn't I told about this before?"

"I reported it to my boss, who reported it to the chief superintendent," said Helle. "All we were told was that we should keep it under our hats until further notice. I assume that had something to do with"—he shot a quick glance at the Crime Scene officers—"this anonymous fugitive."

"Katrine Bratt?" Skarre suggested.

"I didn't hear that name," a voice behind them said.

They turned. The chief superintendent was standing with his hands in trench-coat pockets, legs apart. His cold blue eyes were examining the body. "That should have been in the autumn art exhibition."

The younger officers stared wide-eyed at the chief superintendent, who, unmoved, turned to Harry.

"A couple of words in your ear, Inspector."

They walked over to the police cordon.

"One hell of a mess," the chief superintendent said. He was facing Harry but his eyes wandered down to the carpet of lights below. "We've had a meeting. That's why I had to talk to you in private."

"Who's had a meeting?"

"That doesn't matter, Harry. The crux is that we've made a decision."

"Uh-huh?"

The chief superintendent stamped his feet in the snow, and Harry wondered for a moment if he should point out that he was contaminating a crime scene.

"I'd been thinking of discussing this with you tonight, Harry. In quieter, calmer surroundings. But the matter has become urgent with the discovery of this new body. The press will be on it within a couple of hours. And as we don't have the time we hoped for, we'll have to go live with naming the Snowman. And explain how Katrine Bratt managed to get her post and operate without our knowing. Top management has to take responsibility, of course. That's what management is for, goes without saying."

"What's this really about, boss?"

"The credibility of the Oslo Police. Shit is subject to gravity, Harry. The higher up it starts, the greater the soiling of the force as a whole. Individuals at a lower level can commit blunders and be forgiven. But if we lose people's confidence that the police are being governed with a modicum of competence, that we have some control, then we're lost. I assume you realize what's at stake, Harry."

"Time's pressing, boss."

The chief superintendent's gaze returned from its urban perambulations and locked on to the inspector. "Do you know what *kamikaze* means?"

Harry shifted his weight from one foot to the other. "Being Japanese, brainwashed and crashing your plane into an American aircraft carrier?"

"That's what I thought, too. But Gunnar Hagen says the Japanese never used the word themselves; the American code breakers misinterpreted it. *Kamikaze* is the name of a typhoon that rescued the Japanese in a battle against the Mongolians sometime in the thirteenth century. Literally translated, it means 'divine wind.' Quite picturesque, isn't it?"

Harry didn't answer.

"We need a wind like that now," said the chief superintendent.

Harry nodded slowly. He understood. "You want someone to take the blame for Katrine Bratt's appointment? For not checking her out? For the whole shitty mess, in short?"

"Asking someone to sacrifice himself in this way doesn't feel good. Especially when said sacrifice means your own skin is saved. Then you have to remember that this is all about something greater than the individual." The chief superintendent's gaze veered out over the town again. "The anthill, Harry. The hard work, the loyalty, the at times senseless self-denial. It's the anthill that makes it all worthwhile."

Harry ran a hand over his face. Treachery. Stabbed in the back. Cowardliness. He tried to swallow his fury. Told himself the chief superintendent was right. Someone had to be sacrificed and the blame had to be placed as low down in the hierarchy as possible. Fair enough. He should in fact have checked Katrine out before.

Harry straightened up. In a strange way it felt like a relief. For a very long time he had sensed it would end like this for him, so long that basically he had come to accept it. The way his colleagues in the Dead Policemen's Society had made their exit: without any fanfares and badges of honor, without anything except self-respect and the respect of those who knew them, the few who knew what it was all about. The anthill.

"I understand," Harry said. "And I accept. You'll have to instruct me on the manner in which you would like it to happen. However, I still believe we'll have to postpone the press conference for a few hours until we know a little more."

The chief superintendent shook his head. "You don't understand, Harry."

"There may be new factors in the case."

"You're not the one who will be taking the short straw."

"We're checking to see—" Harry paused. "What did you just say, boss?"

"That was the original suggestion, but Gunnar Hagen refused to go along with it. So he will accept the blame. He's in his office now, writing his letter of resignation. I just wanted to inform you so that you know when the press conference takes place."

"Hagen?" said Harry.

"A good soldier," said the chief superintendent, patting Harry on the shoulder. "I'm off now. The press conference is at eight in the Great Hall, OK?"

Harry watched the chief superintendent's back fade into the distance and felt his mobile phone vibrate in his jacket pocket. He read the display before deciding to answer.

"*Love me tender*," Bjørn Holm said in English. "I'm at the institute."

"What have you got?"

"It was human blood in the floorboards. The lab lady here says that unfortunately blood is pretty overrated as a source of DNA, so she doubts we'll find any cell material for a DNA profile. But she checked the blood type and guess what we found."

Bjørn Holm paused before realizing that Harry had no intention of playing *Who Wants to Be a Millionaire*, and went on.

"There's one blood type that eliminates most people, let's put it like that. Two out of every hundred have it, and in the whole of the archives there are only a hundred and twenty-three criminals with it. If Katrine Bratt has this blood type it's an excellent indicator that she bled in Ottersen's barn."

"Check with the Incident Room. They've got a list of the blood types of every officer at the HQ."

"They do? Jeez, then I'll check them out right away."

"But don't be disappointed if you find out she's not B negative."

Harry enjoyed his colleague's speechless amazement and waited.

"How in Christ's name did you know it was B negative?"

"How quickly can you meet me at the Anatomy Department?"

It was six o'clock and employees not on flextime at Sandviken Hospital had gone home some time ago. But the light in Kjersti Rødsmoen's office was still burning. The psychiatrist saw that Knut Müller-Nilsen and Espen Lepsvik had their notebooks at the ready, then glanced at her own and started off.

"Katrine Rafto tells me she loved her father above all else." She peered up at the two men. "She was just a girl when he was hung out to dry in the newspapers as a man of violence. Katrine was hurt, frightened and very confused. At school she was bullied because of what was written in the press. Shortly afterward her parents split up. When Katrine was nineteen her father disappeared at the same time as one woman was killed in Bergen and another vanished. The investigation was dropped, but inside the police force and out it was thought her father had murdered the women and taken his own life, knowing that he couldn't get away with it. Katrine decided then and there that she would join the police, clear up the murders and avenge her father."

Kjersti Rødsmoen looked up. Neither of the two was taking notes; they were just watching her.

"So after her law degree she applied to the police academy," Rødsmoen continued. "And after finishing her training she was employed by the Crime Squad in Bergen. Where she soon started going through her father's case in her free time. Until this was discovered and stopped, and Katrine applied for a transfer to the Sexual Offenses Unit. Is that correct?"

"Affirmative," said Müller-Nilsen.

"It was seen to that she did not go anywhere near the investigation into her father, so instead she started to examine related cases. While she was going through the national missing-persons reports she made an interesting discovery. Namely, that in the years after her father's disappearance women were being reported missing under conditions that bore several points of similarity with the disappearance of Onny Hetland." Kjersti Rødsmoen flicked over the page. "However, to make any progress Katrine needed help, and she knew she wouldn't get this help in Bergen. Accordingly, she resolved to put someone on the case who had experience with serial killers. Though this had to happen without anyone knowing that she, Rafto's daughter, was behind it."

The Kripos officer, Espen Lepsvik, slowly shook his head as Kjersti continued.

"After thorough groundwork she decided on Inspector Harry Hole at the Crime Squad in Oslo. She wrote a letter to him under the mysterious-sounding sobriquet the Snowman, in order to awaken his curiosity, and because a snowman had been mentioned in several of the witnesses' statements connected with the disappearances. A snowman had also been mentioned in her father's notes on the Ulriken Mountain killing. When the Oslo Crime Squad advertised for a detective, stating a preference for a woman, she applied and was invited to an interview. She said they offered her the job more or less before she had even sat down."

Rødsmoen paused, but as the two men said nothing, she went on. "From the very first day, Katrine made sure that she came into contact with Harry Hole and was put onto the investigation. With all that she already knew about Hole and the case, it was relatively easy for her to manipulate him and steer him toward Bergen and her father's disappearance. And, with Hole's help, she also found her father. In a freezer on Finnøy."

Kjersti removed her glasses.

"You don't need much imagination to understand that an experience of this nature forms the basis of a psychological reaction. The stress became even worse when three times she thought the killer had been unmasked. First Idar Vetlesen, then a"—she squinted at her notes—"Filip Becker. And finally Arve Støp. Only to discover that it was the wrong person each time. She tried to force a confession out of Støp herself, but gave up when she realized that he was not the man she was hunting. She fled the place when she heard her colleagues approaching. She says she didn't want to be stopped until she had completed her mission. Which was to identify the perpetrator. At this point I think we can safely say that she was well into the psychosis. She returned to Finnøy, where she was convinced Hole would track her down. And, in fact, she turned out to be correct. When he appeared, she disarmed him to make him listen while she instructed him on what he had to do next in the investigation."

"Disarmed?" said Müller-Nilsen. "It's our understanding that she surrendered without any fuss."

"She says the injury to her mouth was caused by Harry Hole catching her off guard," said Kjersti Rødsmoen.

"Should we believe a psychotic?" Lepsvik asked.

"She's no longer psychotic," Rødsmoen stated with emphasis. "We ought to keep her under observation for a couple more days, but after that you should be prepared to take her back. If you still consider her a suspect, that is."

The last remark was left hanging in the air until Espen Lepsvik leaned across the table.

"Does that mean you think that Katrine Bratt is telling the truth?"

"That doesn't fall within my special field and I cannot comment," Rødsmoen said, closing her notebook.

"And if I were to ask you as a non-specialist?"

A brief smile played on Rødsmoen's lips. "I think you should continue to believe what you already believe, Inspector."

Bjørn Holm had walked the short distance from the Institute of Forensic Medicine to its neighbor, the Anatomy Department, and was waiting in the garage when Harry arrived by car from Tryvann. Beside Holm was the green-overalled technician with earrings, the one who had been trundling a body away the last time Harry had been here.

"Lund-Helgesen's not here today," Holm informed him.

"Perhaps you can show us around, then," Harry said to the technician.

"We aren't allowed to show—," Green Overalls began, but was interrupted by Harry.

"What's your name?"

"Kai Robøle."

"OK, Robøle," Harry said, presenting his police ID. "I give you permission."

Robøle shrugged and unlocked the door. "You were lucky to find anyone in. It's always empty after five o'clock."

"I had the impression you people did a lot of overtime," Harry said.

Robøle shook his head. "Not in the cellar with all the stiffs, man. Here we like to work in daylight." He smiled, although he didn't seem to be amused. "What is it you'd like to see?"

"The most recent bodies," Harry said.

The technician unlocked and led them through two doors to a tiled room with eight sunken tanks, four on each side with a narrow aisle between. Each tank was covered with a metal lid.

"They're under there," Robøle said. "Four in each tank. The tanks are filled with alcohol."

"Neat," said Holm under his breath.

It was impossible to say whether the technician misunderstood on purpose, but he answered: "Forty percent, no mixers."

"Thirty-two bodies, then," Harry said. "Is that all?"

"We have around forty bodies, but these are the latest. They usually have them lying here for a year before we start to use them."

"How are they brought in?"

"By car from the funeral parlor. Some we collect ourselves."

"And you bring them in via the garage?"

"Yes."

"And what happens then?"

"What happens? Well, we preserve them, make an incision at the top of the thigh and inject a fixative. They keep well like that. Then we make metal tags and stamp the number that's in the paperwork."

"Which paperwork?"

"The paperwork that comes with the body. It's filed up in the office. We attach one tag to the toe, one to a finger and one to an ear. We try to keep the body parts registered, even when they've been split up, so that as much of the body can be cremated together as possible when the time comes."

"Do you regularly check the bodies against the paperwork?"

"Check?" He scratched his head. "Only if we have to transport bodies. Most bodies are bequeathed here in Oslo, so we supply universities in Tromsø, Trondheim and Bergen when they don't have enough."

"So it's conceivable that someone might be lying here who shouldn't be?"

"Oh, no. Everyone here has donated his body to the institute in a will."

"That's what I was wondering," Harry said, squatting down by one of the tanks.

"What?"

"Listen now, Robøle. I'm going to ask you a hypothetical question. And I want you to think carefully before you answer. OK?"

The technician gave a hurried nod.

Harry stood up to his full height. "Is it conceivable that anyone with access to these rooms could bring bodies here through the garage at night, put on a metal tag with a fictitious number, place the body in one of these tanks and assume with a relatively high degree of probability that it will never be discovered?"

Kai Robøle hesitated. Scratched his head a bit more. Ran a finger down the row of earrings.

Harry shifted his weight. Holm's mouth had slipped half open.

"In a sense," Robøle said. "There's nothing to stop it happening."

"Nothing to stop it happening?"

Robøle shook his head and gave a quick laugh. "No, not at all. It's perfectly feasible."

"In that case I'd like to see these bodies now."

Robøle looked up at the tall policeman. "Here? Now?"

"You can start at the back on the left."

"I think I'll have to call someone to give me authorization."

"If you want to delay our murder investigation, then be my guest."

"Murder?" Robøle screwed up one eye.

"Heard of the Snowman?"

Robøle blinked twice. Then he turned, walked over to the chains hanging from a motorized pulley in the ceiling, pulled them down to the tank with a loud rattle and attached the two hooks to the metal lid on the tank, grabbed the remote control and pressed. The pulley hummed and the chains began to coil. From the tank the lid slowly rose as Harry and Holm followed it with their eyes. Fixed to the underside of the lid were two horizontal sheets of metal, one beneath the other, separated by one vertical sheet. On each side of the central partition lay a naked white body. They resembled pale dolls, and this impression was reinforced by the rectangular black incisions on their thighs. When the bodies were at hip height the technician pressed the STOP button. In the ensuing silence they could hear the deep sigh of dripping alcohol echoing around the white-tiled room.

"Well?" said Robøle.

"No," Harry said. "Next."

The technician repeated the procedure. Four new bodies rose from the neighboring tank.

Harry shook his head.

As the third quartet came into view Harry flinched. Kai Robøle, who misinterpreted Harry's reaction as horror, smiled with satisfaction.

"What's that?" Harry asked, pointing to the headless woman.

"Probably a return from one of the other universities," Robøle said. "Ours tend to be whole."

Harry bent down and touched the body. It was cold, and the consistency unnaturally firm because of the fixative. He ran a finger along the severed edge. It was smooth and the flesh pallid.

"We use a scalpel on the exterior and then a fine saw," the technician explained.

"Mm." Harry leaned across the body, grabbed the woman's right arm and pulled her over so that she was facing him.

"What are you doing?" screamed Robøle.

"Can you see anything on her back?" Harry asked Holm, who was standing on the other side of the body.

Holm nodded. "A tattoo. Looks like a flag."

"Which one?"

"Haven't a clue. Green, yellow and red. With a pentagram in the middle."

"Ethiopia," Harry said, letting go of the woman, who fell back into position. "This woman did not donate her body, but she has been donated, if I can put it like that. This is Sylvia Ottersen."

Kai Robøle kept blinking as though hoping something would go away if he blinked enough times.

Harry placed a hand on his shoulder. "Get hold of someone who has access to the paperwork for the bodies and go through all of them. Now. I have to be on my way."

"What's going on?" Holm asked. "I honestly can't get my head around this."

"Try," Harry said. "Forget everything you thought you knew and try."

"Right, but what's going on?"

"There are two answers to that," Harry said. "One is that we're closing in on the Snowman."

"And the other?"

"I don't know."

Part Five

33

The Snowman

It was the day the snow came. At eleven o'clock in the morning, large flakes had appeared from a colorless sky and invaded the fields, gardens and lawns of Romerike like an armada from outer space.

Mathias was sitting alone in his mother's Toyota Corolla in front of a house on Kolloveien. He had no idea what his mother was doing inside the house. She had said it wouldn't take long. But it had already taken a long time. She had left the key in the ignition and the car radio was playing "Under Snø," by the new girl group Dollie. He kicked open the car door and went out. Because of the snow an almost unnatural silence had settled over the houses. He bent down, picked up a handful of the sticky white stuff and cupped it into a snowball.

Today they had thrown snowballs at him in the school playground and called him "Mathias No-Nips," his so-called classmates in 7A. He hated secondary school, hated being thirteen years old. It had begun after the first gym class, when they found out he didn't have any nipples. According to the doctor, it could have been hereditary, and he had been tested for a number of illnesses. Mom had told him and Dad that her father, who died when Mom was small, didn't have any nipples, either. But looking through one of his grandmother's photo albums Mathias had found a picture of his grandfather during the mowing season in trousers and suspenders with a bare chest. And he definitely had nipples then.

Mathias packed the snowball harder between his hands. He wanted to throw it at someone. Hard. So hard that it hurt. But there was no one to launch it at. He could make someone to throw it at. He placed the packed snowball in the snow beside the garage. Started rolling it. The snow crystals hooked into one another. After he had done a circuit of the lawn, it already reached his stomach and had left a trail of brown grass. He continued to roll it. When he couldn't push it any farther, he started a new one. It was big, too. He just managed to lift it up onto the first one. Then he made a head, climbed up and placed it on top. The snowman stood by one of the windows in the house. Sounds were coming out. He broke a couple of twigs off the apple tree and stuck them in the snowman's sides. Dug up some gravel by the front steps, shinnied up again and made two eyes and a line of pebbles for a smile. Then he placed his thighs around the snowman's head, and, sitting on the shoulders, looked through the window.

In the illuminated room stood a man with a bare chest thrusting his hips backward and forward with his eyes closed, as if he were dancing. From the bed in front of him protruded a pair of spread legs. Mathias couldn't see, but he knew that it was Sara. That it was his mother. That they were fucking.

Mathias tightened his thighs around the snow head, felt the cold in his crotch. He was unable to breathe; a steel wire seemed to tauten around his throat.

Again and again the man's hips banged against his mother. Mathias stared inside at the man's chest as the cold numbness spread from his crotch to his stomach and up until it reached his head. The man was thrusting his willy inside her. As they did in the magazines. Soon the man would be spraying sperm inside his mother. And the man didn't have any nipples.

Suddenly the man stopped. His eyes were open now. And they were looking at Mathias.

Mathias loosened his grip, slid down the back of the snowman, curled up and sat as quiet as a mouse, waiting. His mind was reeling. He was a smart boy, he'd always been told that. Strange, but with excellent mental faculties, the teachers had said. Thus all his thoughts were falling into place now, like pieces of a jigsaw he had been doing for a long time. But the picture that emerged was still incomprehensible, intolerable. It couldn't be right. It had to be right.

Mathias listened to his own breathless gasps.

It was right. He just knew it. Everything fit. His mother's coldness to his father. The conversations they thought he couldn't hear; his father's desperate threats and pleas for her to stay, not just for his sake but for Mathias's sake. Good God, they had a child together, didn't they? And his mother's bitter laugh. Grandfather in the photo album and Mom's lies. Of course, Mathias hadn't believed it when Stian from his class had said that Mathias No-Nips's mom had a lover living on the plateau—he said his aunt had told him. For Stian was just as stupid as the others and didn't understand anything. Not even when, two days later, Stian found his cat hanging from the top of the school flagpole.

Dad didn't know. Mathias could feel it in his whole body that Dad thought Mathias was . . . was his. And he must never know that he wasn't. Never. It would kill him. Mathias would rather die himself. Yes, that was exactly what he wanted. He wanted to die, wanted to go, to go away from his mother and the school and Stian and . . . everything. He got up, kicked the snowman and ran to the car.

He would take her with him. She would die, too.

When his mother came out and he unlocked the door, almost forty minutes had passed since she had gone into the house.

"Is there anything wrong?" she asked.

"Yes," Mathias said, moving on the backseat so that she could see him in the mirror. "I saw him."

"What do you mean?" she said, putting the key in the ignition and turning.

"The snowman . . . "

"And what did the snowman look like?" The engine started with a roar and she let the clutch go with such a jerk that he almost dropped the car jack he was clinging to.

"Dad's waiting for us," she said. "We'll have to get a move on."

She switched on the radio. Just an announcer droning on about the American elections and Ronald Reagan. Nonetheless she turned up the volume. They drove over the crest of the hill, down toward the main road and the river. In the field ahead of them stiff yellow straw poked through the snow.

"We're going to die," Mathias said.

"What did you say?"

"We're going to die."

She turned down the voice on the radio. He steeled himself. Leaned forward between the seats and raised his arm.

"We're going to die," he whispered.

Then he struck.

The jack hit the back of her head with a crunch. And his mother didn't seem to react, just sort of stiffened in her seat, so he hit her again. And again. The car jumped as her foot slid off the clutch pedal, but still no sound came from her. Perhaps the talking thing in her brain had been smashed, Mathias thought. At the fourth blow he could feel her head give; it seemed to have gone soft. The car rolled forward and picked up speed, but he knew she was no longer conscious. His mother's Toyota Corolla crossed the main road and continued across the field on the other side. The snow slowed the car but not enough for it to stop. Then it hit the water and glided out into the broad black river. It tilted and was motionless for a moment before the current caught it and spun it around. The water seeped in through the doors and the body-work, through the handles and at the side of the windows as they gently floated downstream. Mathias looked out the window, waved to a car on the main road, but the driver didn't appear to have seen him. The water was rising in the Toyota. And suddenly he heard his mother mumble something. He watched her, saw the deep gashes under her bloodstained hair at the back of her head. She was moving under the seat belt. The water was rising quickly now; it was already up to Mathias's knees. He felt his panic mounting. He didn't want to die. Not now, not like this. He smashed the jack into the side window. The glass shattered and the water poured in. He jumped up onto the seat and squeezed his way through the gap between the top of the window and the mass of water flooding in. One of his boots got snagged on the frame; he twisted his foot and felt the boot float away. Then he was free and began to swim ashore. He saw that a car had stopped on the main road and two people had got out and were on their way through the snow to the river.

Mathias was a good swimmer. He was good at a lot of things. So why didn't they like him? A man waded out and dragged him ashore as he approached the riverbank.

Mathias slumped into the snow. Not because he couldn't stand but because instinctively he knew it was the smartest thing to do. He closed his eyes and heard an agitated voice by his ear ask whether there was anyone else in the car. If there was they might still be able to save them. Mathias slowly shook his head. The voice asked whether he was sure.

The police would later ascribe the accident to the slippery road conditions and the drowned woman's head injuries to the impact from driving off the road and hitting the water. In fact the car was barely damaged, but in the end it was the only plausible explanation. Just as shock was the only possible explanation for the boy's answer when those first on the scene asked him several times whether there was anyone else in the car and he said at length: "No, only me. I'm alone."

"No, only me," Mathias repeated six years later. "I'm alone."

"Thanks," said the boy standing in front of him and putting down his tray on the cafeteria table that until then Mathias had had to himself. Outside, the rain was drumming its welcome march on the medical students in Bergen, a rhythmical march that would last until spring.

"You new to medicine as well?" the boy asked, and Mathias watched his knife cut the thick Wiener schnitzel.

He nodded.

"You've got an Østland accent," the boy said. "Didn't get into Oslo?"

"Didn't want to go to Oslo," Mathias said.

"Why not?"

"Don't know anyone there."

"Who do you know here, then?"

"No one."

"I don't know anyone here, either. What's your name?"

"Mathias. Lund-Helgesen. And you?"

"Idar Vetlesen. Have you been up Ulriken Mountain?"

"No."

But Mathias had been up Ulriken. And up Fløyen and Sandviksfjellet. He had been in the narrow alleyways, to Fisketorget, to Torgalmenningen—the main square, seen the penguins and the sea lions at the aquarium, drunk beer in Wesselstuen, listened to an overrated new band in Garage and seen SK Brann lose a football match at Brann Stadium. Mathias had found time to do all these things that you should do with student friends. Alone.

He did the circuit with Idar again and pretended it was the first time.

Mathias soon discovered that Idar was a social sucker-fish, and by fastening on to him, Mathias found himself at the heart of all the action.

"Why did you choose to study medicine?" Idar asked Mathias at a party in an apartment belonging to a student with a traditional Bergensian name. It was the evening of the medical students' annual autumn ball, and Idar had invited two nice Bergen girls in black dresses and with pinned-up hair, who were leaning forward to hear what the two of them were saying.

"To make the world a better place," Mathias said, drinking up his lukewarm Hansa beer. "What about you?"

"To earn money, of course," Idar said, winking at the girls.

One of them sat down beside Mathias.

"You've got a blood-donor badge," she said. "What blood type are you?"

"B negative. And what do you do?"

"Let's not talk about that. B negative? Isn't that extremely rare?"

"Yes. How did you know?"

"I'm training as a nurse."

"Oh," Mathias said. "Which year?"

"Third."

"Have you thought about what you're going to speciali—"

"Let's not talk about that," she said and placed a hot little hand on his thigh.

She repeated the same sentence five hours later while lying naked beneath him in his bed.

"That's never happened to me before," he said.

She smiled up at him and stroked his cheek. "So there's nothing wrong with me, then?"

"What?" he stammered. "No."

She laughed. "I think you're sweet. You're nice and thoughtful. What happened to these, by the way?"

She pinched his chest.

Mathias felt something black descend. Something nasty and black and wonderful.

"I was born like that," he said.

"Is it a disease?"

"It comes with Raynaud's phenomenon and scleroderma."

"What?"

"A hereditary disease causing connective tissue in the body to thicken."

"Is it dangerous?" She carefully stroked his chest with her fingers.

Mathias smiled and sensed an incipient erection. "Raynaud's phenomenon just means that your toes and fingers go cold and white. Scleroderma is worse . . . "

"Oh?"

"The thickened connective tissue makes the skin

tighten. Everything is smoothed out and wrinkles disappear."

"Isn't that good?"

He was aware of her hand groping southward. "The tightened skin begins to hinder facial expressions—you have fewer of them. It's like your face is stiffening into a mask."

The hot little hand closed around his dick.

"Your hands and, in time, your arms are bent and you can't straighten them. In the end you're left standing there, quite unable to move, as if you're suffocated by your own skin."

She whispered breathlessly: "Sounds like a gruesome death."

"The best advice is to commit suicide before the pain drives you insane. Would you mind lying at the end of the bed? I'd like to stand and do it."

"That's why you study medicine, isn't it?" she said. "To find out more. To find a way of living with it."

"All I want," he said, getting up and standing at the end of the bed with his erect penis swaying in the air, "is to find out when it's time to die."

The newly qualified Dr. Mathias Lund-Helgesen was a popular man in the Neurology Department of Bergen's Haukeland University Hospital. Both colleagues and patients described him as a competent, thoughtful person and, not least, a good listener. The latter was a great help, as he often received patients with a variety of syndromes, generally inherited and often without much prospect of a cure, only some relief. And when on rare occasions patients were diagnosed with the dreadful condition of scleroderma they were always referred to the friendly young doctor who was beginning to consider specializing in immunology. It was early autumn when Laila Aasen and her husband came to him with their daughter. The daughter's joints had stiffened and she was in pain; Mathias's first thought was that it could be Bekhterev's disease. Both Laila Aasen and her husband confirmed that there had been rheumatic illnesses on their side of the family, so Mathias took blood samples from them as well as from the daughter.

When the results came back Mathias was sitting at his desk and had to read them three times. And the same nasty and black and wonderful feeling surged to the surface again. The tests were negative. Both in the medical sense—Bekhterev's disease could be eliminated as a cause of the afflictions—and in the more familiar sense, Herr Aasen could be eliminated as the girl's father. And Mathias knew he didn't know. But she knew; Laila Aasen knew. He had seen her face twitch when he asked for blood samples from all three of them. Was she still screwing the other man? What did he look like? Did he live in a detached house with a big front lawn? What secret flaws did he have? And how and when would the daughter find out that all her life she had been deceived by this lying whore?

Mathias looked down and realized he had knocked over his glass of water. A large wet stain was spreading across his crotch, and he felt the cold spread to his stomach and up toward his head.

He phoned Laila Aasen and informed her of the result. The medical result. She thanked him, audibly relieved, and they hung up. Mathias stared at the telephone for a long time. God, how he hated her. That night he lay unable to sleep on the narrow mattress in his apartment. He tried to read, but the letters danced in front of his eyes. He tried masturbating, which as a rule made him tired enough to sleep afterward, but he couldn't concentrate.

He stuck a needle in the big toe that had gone completely white again, just to see if he had any sensation. In the end he huddled up under the duvet and cried until daybreak painted the night sky gray.

Mathias was also responsible for more general neurological cases, and one of them was an officer from the Bergen Police Station. After the examination, the middle-aged policeman stood up and dressed. The combination of body odor and boozy breath was numbing.

"Well?" growled the policeman, as if Mathias were one of his subordinates.

"First stages of neuropathy," Mathias replied. "The nerves under your feet are damaged. There is reduced sensation."

"Do you think that's why I've started walking like a goddamned drunk?"

"Are you a drunk, Rafto?"

The policeman stopped buttoning up his shirt and a flush rose up his neck, like mercury up a thermometer. "What did you say, you snot-nosed bastard?"

"As a rule too much alcohol is the cause of polyneuropathy. If you continue to drink, you risk permanent brain damage. Have you heard of Korsakoff, Rafto? You haven't? Let's hope you never do because if you hear his name it's generally in connection with an extremely unpleasant syndrome named after him. When you look in the mirror and ask yourself if you're a drunk, I don't know what you answer, but I suggest that next time you ask an additional question: Do I want to die now or do I want some more time?"

Gert Rafto scrutinized the young man in the doctor's coat. Then he swore under his breath, marched out and slammed the door behind him.

Four weeks later Rafto called. He asked if Mathias could come to see him.

"Drop in tomorrow," Mathias said.

"I can't. It's urgent."

"Then get yourself to the emergency room."

"Listen to me, Lund-Helgesen. I've been in bed for three days without being able to move. You're the only one who's asked me straight out if I'm a drunk. Yes, I am a drunk. And no, I don't want to die. Not yet."

Gert Rafto's apartment stank of garbage, empty beer bottles and him. But not of leftovers, for there was no food in the house.

"This is a B-one vitamin supplement," Mathias said, holding the syringe to the light. "It will get you back on your feet."

"Thank you," Gert Rafto said. Five minutes later he was asleep.

Mathias walked around the apartment. On the desk there was a photograph of Rafto with a dark-haired girl on his shoulders. Above the desk on the wall hung photographs of what must have been murder scenes. Many photographs. Mathias stared at them. Took a couple of them down and studied the details. Goodness, how sloppy they had been, the murderers. Their inefficiency was especially noticeable on the bodies with wounds from both sharp and blunt instruments. He opened drawers and looked for more photographs. He found reports, notes, a few valuables: rings, ladies' watches, necklaces. And newspaper clippings. He read them. Gert Rafto's name ran right through them, often with quotes from press conferences at which he talked about the murderers' stupidity and how he had caught them. Because it was clear he had caught them, every single one.

Six hours later, when Gert Rafto awoke, Mathias was

still there. He was sitting by the bed with two murder reports in his lap.

"Tell me," Mathias said. "How would you commit a murder if you didn't want to get caught?"

"Avoid my beat," Rafto said, looking around for something to drink. "If the detective's good, you haven't got a hope in hell anyway."

"And if I still wanted to do it on the beat of a good detective?"

"Then I would cozy up to the detective before committing the murder," Gert Rafto said. "And then, after the murder, I would kill him, too."

"Funny," Mathias said. "That's just what I was thinking."

In the weeks that followed, Mathias made quite a few house calls to Gert Rafto. He recovered quickly and they talked often and at length about illness, lifestyle and death, and about the only two things Gert Rafto loved on this earth: his daughter, Katrine, who, incomprehensibly, returned his love, and the little cabin on Finnøy, which was the one place he could be sure of finding peace. Mostly, though, they talked about the murder cases Gert Rafto had solved. About the triumphs. And Mathias encouraged him, told him the fight against alcohol could be won, he could celebrate new triumphs so long as he kept off the bottle.

And by the time late autumn came to Bergen, with even shorter days and even longer showers, Mathias had his plan ready.

One morning he called Laila Aasen at home.

He gave his name, and she listened in silence as he explained the reason for his call. The daughter's blood sample had revealed new information and he now knew that Bastian Aasen was not the child's biological father. It was important that he be given the real father's blood sample. This would of necessity mean that the daughter and Bastian would be apprised of the relationship. Would she give her consent?

Mathias waited, allowing this to sink in.

Then he said that if she considered it important that the matter remain behind closed doors, he would still like to help, but it would have to be done "off the record."

"Off the record?" she repeated with the apathy of someone in shock.

"As a doctor I'm bound to observe ethical rules regarding candor to the patient, here, your daughter. But I'm researching syndromes and am therefore particularly interested in following up her case. If, with the utmost discretion, you could meet me this afternoon . . . "

"Yes," she whispered in a tremulous voice. "Yes, please."

"Good. Catch the last cable car of the day to the top of Ulriken. There we will be undisturbed and can walk back down. I hope you appreciate what I'm risking, and please don't mention this meeting to a living soul."

"Of course not! Trust me."

He was still holding the receiver to his ear after she had hung up. With his lips to the gray plastic, he whispered: "And why should anyone trust you, you little whore?"

It was only when she was lying in the snow with a scalpel to her throat that Laila Aasen admitted she had told a friend she was going to meet him. Because in fact they had originally had a dinner date. But she'd mentioned only his Christian name and not why they were meeting.

"Why did you say anything at all?"

"To tease her," Laila howled. "She's so nosy."

He pressed the thin steel harder against her skin and Laila sobbed her friend's name and address. After which she said no more.

When, two days later, Mathias was reading about the murder of Laila Aasen and the disappearances of Onny Hetland and Gert Rafto in the newspaper, he had mixed feelings. First of all, he was displeased with the murder of Laila Aasen. It had not gone as he had planned; he had lost control in a frenzy of fury and panic. Hence there had been too much mess, too much to clean up, too much that reminded him of the photographs in Rafto's apartment. And too little time to enjoy the revenge, the justice of it.

The murder of Onny Hetland had been even worse, nearly a catastrophe. Twice his courage had failed him as he was about to ring her doorbell, and he had walked away. The third time he had realized he was too late. Someone was already there ringing the bell. Gert Rafto. After Rafto had left he had rung and introduced himself as Rafto's assistant and had been let in. But Onny had said she wouldn't tell him what she had told Rafto; she had given a promise that the matter would stay strictly between them. Only when he had made an incision in her hand with the scalpel did she talk.

Mathias gleaned from what she said that Gert Rafto had decided to solve the case under his own steam. He wanted to rebuild his reputation, the fool!

There had been nothing to criticize about the disposal of Onny Hetland, however. Very little noise, very little blood. And the carving up of her body in the shower had been efficient and quick. He had packed all the parts in plastic and placed them in the large backpack and bag he had brought along for the purpose. On his visits to Rafto, Mathias had been told that one of the first things the police check in murder cases is cars observed in the vicinity and registered taxi rides. So he walked the whole way back to his apartment.

All that remained now was the last part of Gert Rafto's instructions for the perfect murder: Kill the detective.

Strangely enough this was the best of the three murders. Strange because Mathias had no feelings for Rafto, none of the hatred that he had felt for Laila Aasen. It was more about him getting close, for the first time, to the aesthetics he had envisaged, to the idea he had of how the murder should be executed. His experience of the very act itself was above all as gruesome and heart-rending as he had hoped it would be. He could still hear Rafto's screams echoing around the deserted island. And the strangest thing of all: On the way back he discovered that his toes were no longer white and numb; it was as if the gradual freezing process of his extremities had been halted for a moment, as if he had thawed.

Four years later, after Mathias had killed another four women, and he could see that all the murders were an attempt to reconstruct the murder of his mother, he concluded that he was mad.

Or, to be more precise, that he was suffering from a serious personality disorder. All the specialist literature he had read certainly pointed to that. The ritual nature of the murders, their having to take place on the day the first snow of the year came, his having to build a snowman. And, not least, his growing sadism.

But this insight in no way prevented him from continuing. For time was short; Raynaud's phenomenon was already appearing with increasing frequency, and he thought he could detect the first symptoms of scleroderma: a stiffness in the face that would eventually give him the revolting pointed nose and the pursed carp mouth with which the worst afflicted were ultimately burdened.

He had moved to Oslo to continue his work on immunology and water channels in the brain, as the research center for this was the Anatomy Department in Gaustad. In addition he was working at the Marienlyst Clinic, where Idar was employed and had recommended him. Mathias also did night shifts at the emergency room since he couldn't sleep anyway.

It was not difficult to find victims. Initially it was the patients' blood samples that in many cases ruled out paternity, and then there were the DNA tests by the Paternity Unit at the Institute of Forensic Medicine. Idar, who had fairly limited competence even for a general practitioner, covertly took advice on all cases concerning hereditary illness and syndromes. And, if the patients were young people, Mathias's advice was invariably the same.

"Get both parents to appear at the first consultation, take mouth swabs from everyone, say it's just to check the bacterial flora and send the samples to the Paternity Unit so that we at least know we're working from an accurate starting point."

And Idar, the idiot, did as he was told. Which meant that Mathias soon had a little file on women with children who were sailing under a false flag, so to speak. And best of all was that there was no link between him and these women, since the mouth swabs were submitted under Idar's name.

The method for luring the women into the trap was the same as the one applied with such success to Laila Aasen. A telephone call and an agreement to meet at a secret location unknown to anyone. Only once had it happened that the appointed victim broke down on the phone and went to her husband to tell all. And that had

ended with the family splitting up, so she had received
her just deserts anyway.

For a long time Mathias had pondered how he could dis-
pose of the bodies with increased efficiency. At any rate,
it was obvious that the method he had used with Onny
Hetland was not viable for the long term. He had done
it piecemeal with hydrochloric acid in the bathtub in his
apartment. It was a risky, laborious process and injurious
to his health, and it had taken almost three weeks. So he
was greatly pleased when he chanced upon the solution.
The body storage tanks at the Anatomy Department. It
was as brilliant as it was simple. Just like the cutting loop.

He had read about the loop in an anatomy journal; a
French anatomist recommended it for use on bodies that
had started to decompose, because the loop cut through
soft, rotting tissue with the same precise efficiency as
through bone, and because it could be used on several
bodies at the same time without any danger of transmitting bacteria. He had realized right away that with a loop
to cut up the victims, transportation would be radically
simplified. Consequently he contacted the manufacturer,
flew to Rouen and had the tool demonstrated, in halting
English, one misty morning inside a whitewashed cow-
shed in northern France. The loop consisted of a plain
handle shaped like—and the approximate size of—a banana furnished with a metal shield to protect your hand
against burns. The wire itself was as thin as fishing line
and ran into both ends of the banana, from which it could
be tightened or slackened with a button. There was also
an on-off switch that activated the battery-driven heating element and made the garrotelike wire glow white in
seconds. Mathias was elated; this tool would be useful for

more than carving up bodies. When he heard the price he almost burst out laughing. The loop cost Mathias less than the flight to Rouen had. Batteries included.

The publication of the Swedish study concluding that somewhere between 15 and 20 percent of all children had a different biological father from the one they thought reflected Mathias's own experiences. He was not alone. Nor was he alone in having to die a cruel, premature death because of his mother's whoring with tainted genes. But he would be alone in this: the act of cleansing, the fight against disease, the crusade. He doubted that anyone would thank or honor him. This he did know, however: They would all remember him, long after his death. For he had finally found what was to be his fame for all posterity, the masterpiece, the final flourish of his sword.

It was chance that set the ball rolling.

He saw him on TV. The policeman. Harry Hole. Hole was being interviewed because he had hunted down a serial killer in Australia. And Mathias was reminded of Gert Rafto's advice: "Avoid my beat." He also recalled, however, the satisfaction of having taken the life of the hunter. The feeling of supremacy. The feeling of power. Nothing later had quite compared with the murder of the police officer. And this Herostratically famous Hole appeared to have something of Rafto about him, some of the same offhandedness and anger.

Nonetheless, he might have forgotten all about Harry Hole had it not been for one of the gynecologists at the Marienlyst Clinic mentioning in the cafeteria the next day that he had heard that this to all outward appearances solid detective was actually an alcoholic and a nutcase. Gabriella, a pediatrician, added that she had the son of Hole's girlfriend as a patient. Oleg, a nice boy.

"He'll be an alcoholic then, as well," said the gynecologist. "It's in the damn genes, you know."

"Hole's not the father," Gabriella countered. "But what's interesting is that the man who's registered as the father, some professor or other in Moscow, is also an alcoholic."

"Hey, I didn't hear that!" shouted Idar Vetlesen over the laughter. "Don't forget client confidentiality, folks!"

Lunch carried on, but Mathias was unable to forget what Gabriella had said. Or, rather, the way she had expressed herself: "the man who's registered as the father."

Accordingly, after lunch, Mathias followed the pediatrician to her office, went in behind her and closed the door.

"May I ask you something, Gabriella?"

"Oh, hello," she said, and a flush of anticipation spread up her cheeks. Mathias knew she liked him; he supposed she thought he was handsome, friendly, funny and a good listener. She had even, indirectly, asked him out on a couple of occasions, but he had declined.

"As you may know, I'm allowed to use some of the clinic's blood samples for my research," he said. "And in fact I found something interesting in the sample of the boy you were talking about. The son of Hole's girlfriend."

"My understanding is that their relationship is now a thing of the past."

"You don't say? There was something in the blood sample, so I was wondering if there was anything in the family . . . "

Mathias thought he could discern a certain disappointment in her face. As for himself, he was far from disappointed by what she had to tell him.

"Thank you," he said, standing up and exiting. He could feel his heart pumping eager, life-giving blood, his feet propelling him forward without consuming any energy, his pleasure making him glow like a cutting loop. For he knew this was the beginning. The beginning of the end.

The Holmenkollen Residents' Association was having its summer party on a burning hot August day. On the lawn in front of the association pavilion the adults were sitting on camp chairs under umbrellas and drinking white wine while the children ran between tables or played football on the gravel field. Although she was wearing enormous sunglasses that concealed her face, Mathias recognized her from the photograph he had downloaded from her employer's Web site. She was standing on her own, and he went over to her and asked with a wry smile if he might stand beside her and pretend he knew her. He knew how to do this sort of thing now. He was not the Mathias No-Nips of old.

She lowered her glasses, scrutinizing him, and he established that the photograph had lied after all. She was much more beautiful. So beautiful that for a moment he thought Plan A had a weakness: It was not a foregone conclusion that she would want him; a woman like Rakel—single mother or not—had alternatives. Plan B had, to be sure, the same result as A, but would not be anywhere near as satisfying.

"Socially timid," he said, raising a plastic cup in an embarrassed gesture of greeting. "I was invited here by a friend living nearby, and he hasn't shown up. And everyone else looks as if they know each other. I promise to decamp the second he appears."

She laughed. He liked her laugh. And knew that the critical first three seconds had gone in his favor.

"I just saw a boy score a fantastic goal on the field down there," Mathias said. "I wouldn't mind betting you're related to him."

"Oh? That might have been Oleg, my son."

She succeeded in hiding it, but Mathias knew from countless sessions with patients that no woman can resist praise of her child.

"Nice party," he said. "Nice neighbors."

"You like parties with other people's neighbors?"

"I think my friends are worried I'm spending too much time on my own," he said. "So they try to cheer me up. With their successful neighbors, for example." He took a sip from the cup. "And with the very sweet house wine. What's your name?"

"Rakel. Fauke."

"Hello, Rakel. Mathias."

He shook her hand. Small, warm.

"You don't have anything to drink," he said. "Allow me. House sweet?"

On his return, and after passing her the cup, he took out his pager and looked at it with a concerned expression.

"Do you know what, Rakel? I'd love to stay and get to know you better, but the ER is short-staffed and needs an extra man immediately. So I'll put on my Superman outfit and make my way into town."

"Shame," she said.

"You think so? It's only for a few hours. Are you going to be here long?"

"I don't know. It depends on Oleg."

"Right. We'll see, then. Anyway, it was nice to meet you."

Again he shook her hand. Then left, knowing he had won the first round.

He drove to his apartment in Torshov and read an interesting article about water channels in the brain. When he returned at eight she was sitting under one of the umbrellas, wearing a big white hat. She smiled as he sat down beside her.

"Saved any lives?" she asked.

"Mostly scrapes and grazes," Mathias said. "An appendicitis. The high point was a boy who'd got a lemonade bottle stuck up his nose. I told his mother he was probably too young to sniff Coke. Sad to say, people in that type of situation don't have much of a sense of humor . . . "

She laughed. That refined, trilled laugh, which almost made him wish the whole thing were for real.

Mathias had already observed the thickening of his skin in various areas, but in the autumn of 2004 he noticed the first signs that the disease was entering the next phase. The phase he did not want to be a part of. The tightening of his face. His plan had been that Eli Kvale would be the victim of the year, then the whores Birte Becker and Sylvia Ottersen in the years that followed. The interesting part would be to see whether the police would pick up on the connections between the latter two victims and the lecher Arve Støp. But, as it turned out, his plans would have to be pushed forward. He had always promised himself that he would call it a day once the pain came, he wouldn't wait. And now it was here. He decided to take all three of them. As well as the grand finale: Rakel and the policeman.

Previously he had worked undercover, and now it was time to exhibit his life's work. To do that he would have to leave clear clues, show them the connections, give them the bigger picture.

He started with Birte. They agreed to talk about Jonas at her house after her husband had gone to Bergen in the evening. Mathias arrived at the appointed time and she took his coat on the porch and turned to put it in the closet. It was rare for him to improvise, but a pink scarf was hanging on one peg and he grabbed it as if by instinct. He wound it twice before going up behind her and placing it around her neck. He lifted the little woman up and positioned her in front of the mirror so that he could see her eyes. They were bulging; she was like a fish that had been hauled up from the deep.

After depositing her in the car, he went onto the lawn to the snowman he had made the night before. He pressed the mobile phone into its chest, filled the cavity and knotted the scarf around its neck. It was past midnight by the time he arrived at the garage of the Anatomy Department, injected fixative into Birte's body, stamped the metal tags, tied them on and put her on an unoccupied ledge in one of the tanks.

Then it was Sylvia's turn. He called her and rattled off the usual spiel, and they arranged to meet in the forest behind the Holmenkollen ski jump, a place he had used on previous occasions. But this time there were people nearby and he wouldn't take the risk. He explained to her that Idar Vetlesen, unlike himself, was not exactly a specialist in Fahr's Syndrome, and they would have to meet again. She suggested he call her the following evening, when she would be at home on her own.

The next evening he drove out, found her in the barn and set on her on the spot.

But it had almost gone wrong.

The crazy woman had swung her hatchet at him, hit him in the side, cut open his jacket and shirt and severed an artery, with the result that his blood had gushed out all over the barn floor. B-negative blood. Two people in a hundred's blood. So after he had killed her in the forest and left her head on top of the snowman, he returned, slaughtered a chicken and sprayed its blood over the floor to cover up his own.

It was a stressful twenty-four hours, but the strange thing was that he felt no pain that night. And over the subsequent days he followed the case in the newspapers, quietly triumphant. The Snowman. That was the name they had given him. A name that would be remembered. He would never have guessed that a few printed words in a newspaper could afford such a feeling of power and influence. He almost regretted having operated clandestinely for so many years. And it was so easy! There he was going around thinking that what Gert Rafto said was true, that a good detective would always find the murderer. But he had met Harry Hole and had seen the frustration in the policeman's frazzled face. It was the face of someone who comprehended nothing.

But then, while Mathias was preparing his final moves, it came like a bolt from the blue. Idar Vetlesen. He called to say that Hole had visited him asking questions about Arve Støp and pressing him for the connection. And Idar himself wondered what was going on; after all, it was unlikely that the selection of the victims was arbitrary. And, apart from himself and Støp, Mathias was the only person who knew about the paternities, since Mathias, as usual, had helped him with the diagnosis.

Idar was rattled, of course, but fortunately Mathias managed to calm him down. He told Idar not to say a word to anyone and to meet him in a safe place where no one could see them.

Mathias was nearly laughing as he said it; it was practically word for word what he told his female victims. He supposed it must have been the tension.

Idar proposed the curling club. Mathias hung up and pondered his options.

It struck him that he could make it seem as if Idar were the Snowman and at the same time procure himself some downtime.

The next hour he spent sketching out the details of Idar's suicide. And even though he appreciated his friend in many ways, it was an oddly stimulating, indeed inspiring, process. As the planning of the great project had been. The last snowman. She would have to sit—as he had on the first day of snow so many years ago—on the snowman's shoulders, feel the cold through her thighs and watch through the window, watch the treachery, the man who would be her death: Harry Hole. He closed his eyes and visualized the noose over her head. It glinted and glowed. Like a fake halo.

34

Sirens

Harry got into the car in the garage at the Anatomy Department. Closed the doors and his eyes, and tried to think clearly. The first thing to do was find out where Mathias was.

He had deleted Mathias from his mobile phone and now called directory assistance, which gave him the number and the address. He tapped in the number, noticed while he was waiting that his breathing was accelerated and excited, and tried to calm down.

"Hi, Harry." Mathias's voice was low, but sounded pleasantly surprised, as usual.

"Sorry to bother you," Harry said.

"Not at all, Harry."

"Ah, OK. Where are you now?"

"I'm at home. I'm on my way down to see Rakel and Oleg."

"Great. I was wondering if you could deliver the something to Oleg for me."

There was a pause. Harry clenched his jaw, making his teeth crack.

"Of course," Mathias said. "But Oleg's at home now, so you can—"

"Rakel," Harry interrupted. "We . . . I don't feel like seeing her today. Could I pop over to your place for a moment?"

Another pause. Harry pressed the receiver against his ear and listened hard, as if to pick up what his interlocutor was thinking. But all he could hear was breathing and fragile background music, minimalist Japanese glockenspiel or something like that. He visualized Mathias in an austere, equally minimalist apartment. Not that big, maybe, but tidy—that was obvious—nothing left to chance. And now he had put on a neutral light-blue shirt and a fresh bandage on the wound in his side. Because, when he had been standing on the steps in front of Harry, he hadn't held his crossed arms high to hide his missing nipples. It had been to hide the hatchet wound.

"Of course," Mathias said.

Harry was unable to decide whether his voice sounded natural. The background music had stopped.

"Thank you," Harry said. "I'll be quick, but promise me that you'll wait."

"I promise," Mathias said. "But, Harry . . . "

"Yes?" Harry took a deep breath.

"Do you know what my address is?"

"Rakel told me."

Harry cursed inside. Why hadn't he said he got it from directory assistance? There was nothing suspicious about that.

"Did she?" Mathias asked.

"Yes."

"OK," Mathias said. "Come right in. The door's unlocked."

Harry hung up and stared at the telephone. He could find no rational explanation for his foreboding that time was short and that he had to run for his life before darkness fell. So he resolved that he was imagining things.

That it didn't help, this type of fear, the terror that comes with the onset of night, when you can't see your grand-parents' farm.

He punched in another number.

"Yes," Hagen answered. The voice was toneless, life-less. The resignation-writing voice, Harry presumed.

"Drop the paperwork," Harry said. "You've got to call the chief constable. I need a firearms authorization. Ar-rest of suspected murderer on Åsengata 12, Torshov."

"Harry—"

"Listen. The remains of Sylvia Ottersen are in a tank at the Anatomy Department. Katrine is not the Snow-man. Do you understand?"

Silence.

"No," Hagen confessed.

"The Snowman is a lecturer at the department. Math-ias Lund-Helgesen."

"Lund-Helgesen? Well, I'll be damned. Do you mean the—"

"Yes, the doctor who was so helpful in focusing our attention on Idar Vetlesen."

Life had returned to Hagen's voice. "The chief is go-ing to ask if it's likely that the man's armed."

"Well," Harry said, "as far as we know, he hasn't used a firearm on any of the people he's killed."

A couple of seconds passed before Hagen caught the sarcasm. "I'll phone him now," he said.

Harry hung up and turned the key in the ignition while calling Magnus Skarre with his other hand. Skarre and the engine responded in unison.

"Still in Tryvann?" Harry shouted above the roar.

"Yes."

"Drop everything and get yourself in a car. Meet me at the intersection of Åsengata and Vogts Gate. It's a bust."

"All hell's broken loose?"

"Yeah," Harry said. The rubber screamed on the concrete as he let the clutch go.

He thought of Jonas. For some reason he thought of Jonas.

One of the six patrol cars Harry had asked the Incident Room for was already at Åsengata as Harry came down Vogts Gate from Storo. Harry drove up onto the pavement, jumped out and went over to them. They rolled down the window and passed Harry the walkie-talkie he had requested.

"Switch off the blender," Harry ordered, pointing to the rotating blue light. He pressed the TALK button and told the patrol cars to turn off the sirens well before they got to the scene.

Four minutes later six patrol cars were assembled at the intersection. The police officers, among them Skarre and Ola Li from Crime Squad, had crowded around Harry's car, where he sat with a street map in his lap, pointing.

"Li, you take three cars to cut off any possible escape routes. Here, here and here."

Li leaned over the map, nodding.

Harry turned to Skarre. "The caretaker?"

Skarre raised the phone. "Talking to him now. He's on his way over to the main door with keys."

"OK. You take six men and position yourselves by the entrance, back stairs and, if possible, on the roof. And you bring up the rear, OK? Has the Delta car arrived?"

"Here." Two of the officers, identical to the others from the outside, signaled that they were driving the regular vehicle for Delta, the Special Forces Unit trained particularly for this kind of operation.

"OK, I want you in front of the main entrance now. Are you all armed?"

The officers nodded. Some of them were armed with MP5 machine guns. The others had only service revolvers. It was a fiscal matter, as the chief constable had once explained.

"The caretaker says Lund-Helgesen lives on the second floor," Skarre said, slipping the mobile phone into his jacket pocket. "There's just one apartment on each floor. No exits to the roof. To reach the rear staircase he'd have to go up to the third and through a locked attic."

"Good," Harry said. "Send two men up the rear stairs and tell them to wait in the attic."

"OK."

Harry took with him the two uniformed officers from the car that had arrived first. An older officer and a young, pimply kid, both of whom had worked with Skarre before. Instead of going into Åsengata 12, they crossed the street and went into the building opposite.

Both young boys from the Stigson family stared wide-eyed at the two uniformed men while their father listened to Harry explaining why they had to use their second-floor apartment for a short while. Harry entered the sitting room, pushed the sofa away from the window and took a closer look at the apartment on the other side of the street.

"Light's on in the living room," he said.

"Someone's sitting there," said the older officer, who had taken up a position behind him.

"I've heard your eyesight deteriorates by thirty percent after you hit fifty," Harry said.

"I'm not blind. In the big chair there you can see the top of his head and the hand on the armrest."

Harry squinted. Shit, did he need glasses? Well, if the old guy thought he saw someone, then he must be right.

"You stay here and radio if he moves. All right?"

"All right." The older man smiled.

Harry took the kid along with him.

"Who's sitting inside?" the young officer said in a loud voice over the clatter of their feet as they raced downstairs.

"Heard of the Snowman?"

"Oh, crap."

"That's right."

They sprinted across the street to the other building. The caretaker, Skarre and five uniformed policemen stood ready by the front door.

"I haven't got a key for the apartments," the caretaker said. "Only for this door."

"That's fine," Harry said. "Everyone got their weapons ready? We make as little noise as possible, OK? Delta, you stay with me . . . "

Harry took out Katrine's Smith & Wesson and signaled to the caretaker, who turned the key in the lock.

Harry and the two Delta men, both armed with MP5's, strode soundlessly up the stairs, three steps at a time.

They stopped on the second floor outside an unmarked blue door. One officer laid his ear against the door, faced Harry and shook his head. Harry had lowered the volume of the walkie-talkie to the very minimum, and now he raised it to his mouth.

"Alpha to"—Harry had not allocated call names and couldn't remember first names—"the window post by the sofa. Has the target moved? Over."

He let go of the button and there was a low crackle. Then came the voice:

"He's still sitting in the chair."

"Roger. We're going in. Over and out."

One officer nodded and produced a crowbar while the other backed away and braced himself.

Harry had seen the technique used before; one man

prizes open the door so that the other can charge in. Not because they couldn't have broken it open, but because it is the effect of the loud bang, the power and speed, that paralyzes the target and in nine cases out of ten causes him to freeze on the chair, sofa or bed.

But Harry held up a restraining hand. He pressed the door handle and pushed.

Mathias hadn't lied; it was unlocked.

The door slid open without a sound. Harry pointed to his chest to say he would go first.

The apartment was not minimalist in the way that Harry had imagined.

It was minimalist in the sense that there was nothing there: no shoes in the hall, no furniture, no pictures. Only bare walls begging for new wallpaper or a lick of paint. It looked as if it had been abandoned for a substantial amount of time.

The living-room door was ajar, and through the gap Harry could see the arm of the chair, a hand on top. A small hand with a watch. He held his breath, took two long strides, gripped the revolver with both hands and nudged the door open with his foot.

He sensed the other two—who had moved into the edge of his vision—stiffen.

And heard a barely audible whisper. "Jesus Christ . . . "

A large illuminated chandelier hung above the armchair and lit up the person sitting there and staring straight at him. The neck bore bruising from strangulation, the face was pale and beautiful, the hair black and the dress sky blue with tiny white flowers. The same dress as in the photo on his kitchen calendar. Harry felt his heart explode in his chest as the rest of his body turned to stone. He tried to move, but could not tear himself away from her glazed eyes. The accusatory, glazed eyes.

Which accused him of not having acted; he had known nothing of this, but he should have acted, he should have stopped this happening, he should have saved her.

She was as white as his mother had been on her death-bed.

"Check the rest of the apartment," Harry said in a thick voice, lowering his revolver.

He took an unsteady step toward the body and held her wrist in his hand. It was ice-cold and lifeless, like marble. Yet he could feel a ticking, a weak pulse, and for one absurd moment he thought she had only been made up to look dead. Then he looked down and saw it was the watch that was ticking.

"There's no one else here," he heard one of the officers behind him say. Then a cough. "Do you know who she is?"

"Yes," Harry said, running a finger over the watch face. The same watch he had been holding in his own hand a mere few hours ago. The watch that had been left in his bedroom. That he had put in the birdhouse because Rakel's boyfriend was taking her out this evening. To a party. To celebrate that from now on the two of them would be as one.

Again Harry looked at the eyes, her accusing eyes.

Yes, he thought. Guilty on all counts.

Skarre had come into the apartment and was standing behind Harry, staring over his shoulder at the dead woman in the chair. Beside him stood the two Delta officers.

"Strangled?" he asked.

Harry neither answered nor moved. One shoulder strap of the sky-blue dress had slipped down.

"Unusual to wear a summer dress in November," Skarre said, mostly for the sake of conversation.

"She usually does," Harry said in a voice that sounded as if it came from a long way away.

"Who does?" Skarre asked.

"Rakel."

The policeman gave a start. He had seen Harry's ex when she used to work for the police. "Is . . . is . . . that Rakel? But . . . "

"It's her dress," Harry said. "And her watch. He's dressed her up as Rakel. But the woman sitting there is Birte Becker."

Skarre eyed the corpse in silence. It didn't look like any other corpse he had seen. This one was as white as chalk and bloated.

"Come with me," Harry said, directing his attention to the two Delta officers before turning to Skarre. "You stay here and cordon off the apartment. Call the Crime Scene Unit in Tryvann and tell them they've got another job waiting for them."

"What are you going to do?"

"Dance," Harry said.

The apartment went quiet after the three men had clattered down the stairs at a run. But seconds later Skarre heard a car starting and the scream of tires on the pavement of Vogts Gate.

The blue light rotated and lit up the road. Harry was sitting in the front passenger seat and listening to the phone ringing at the other end. Hanging from the mirror, two miniature bikini-clad women danced to the despairing lament of the siren as the police car slalomed between vehicles on the Ring 3.

Please, he implored. Please pick up, Rakel.

He looked at the metal dancers beneath the mirror, thinking he was like them: someone who danced impotently to another's tune, a comic figure in a farce in which he was always two steps behind events, always racing through doors a little too late and being met by the audience's laughter.

Harry cracked. "Fuck, fuck, fuck!" he yelled and slung the mobile phone at the windshield. It slid off the dashboard and down to the floor. The officer driving exchanged glances with the other officer in the mirror.

"Turn off the siren," Harry said.

It went quiet.

And Harry's attention was caught by a sound coming from the floor.

He picked up the phone.

"Hello!" he shouted. "Hello. Are you at home, Rakel?"

"Of course I am—you're calling the landline." It was her voice. A gentle, calm laugh. "Is something the matter?"

"Is Oleg at home, too?"

"Yes," she said. "He's sitting here in the kitchen eating. We're waiting for Mathias. What's up, Harry?"

"Listen to me carefully now, Rakel. Do you hear me?"

"You're frightening me, Harry. What is it?"

"Put the safety chain on the door."

"Why? It's locked and—"

"Put the safety chain on, Rakel!" Harry yelled.

"OK, OK!"

He heard her say something to Oleg, then a chair scraped and he heard running feet. When the voice was back it was trembling.

"Now tell me what's going on, Harry."

"I will. First, though, you have to promise me you won't let Mathias into the house under any circumstances."

"Mathias? Are you drunk, Harry? You have no right—"

"Mathias is dangerous, Rakel. I'm sitting here in a police car with two other officers on our way up to you now. I'll explain the rest later. Now I want you to look out of the window. Can you see anything?"

He heard her hesitate. But he said nothing further, just waited. For he knew with a sudden certainty that she trusted him, that she believed him, that she always had. They were approaching the tunnel by Nydalen. On the side of the road the snow lay like grayish-white wool. Then her voice was back.

"I can't see anything. But I don't know what I'm looking for, do I?"

"So you can't see a snowman?" Harry asked quietly.

He could tell from the silence that the whole thing was becoming clear to her.

"Tell me this isn't happening, Harry," she whispered. "Tell me this is just a dream."

He closed his eyes and considered whether she could be right. On his eyelids he saw Birte Becker in the chair. Of course it was a dream.

"I put your watch in the birdhouse," he said.

"But it wasn't there, it . . . ," she began, paused and let out a groan. "Oh, my God!"

35

Monster

From the kitchen Rakel had a view of all three sides from which a person might approach the house. At the back there was a short but precipitous rocky slope it was difficult to descend, especially now that the snow had settled. She went from window to window. Peered out and tested them to make sure they were firmly shut.

When her father had built the house after the war he had put the windows high in the wall, with iron bars covering them. She knew this had something to do with the war and a Russian who had sneaked into his bunker near Leningrad and shot all his sleeping comrades. Everyone apart from him, who had been asleep nearest the door, so exhausted that he hadn't woken up until the alarm was sounded and discovered that his blanket was strewn with empty cartridges. That was the last night he'd slept properly, he had always said. But she'd always hated the iron bars. Until now.

"Can't I go up to my room?" Oleg said, kicking the leg of the large kitchen table.

"No," Rakel said. "You have to stay here."

"What's Mathias done?"

"Harry will explain everything when he comes. Are you sure you've attached the safety chain properly?"

"Yes, Mom. I wish Dad was here."

"Dad?" She hadn't heard him use that word before. Except for Harry, but that was several years ago. "Do you mean your father in Russia?"

"He's not Dad."

He said it with a conviction that made her shiver.

"The cellar door!" she screamed.

"What?"

"Mathias has the cellar-door key, too. What should we do?"

"Simple," said Oleg, finishing his glass of water. "You put one of the garden chairs under the door handle. They're just the right height. No chance anyone could get in."

"Have you tried?" she asked, taken aback.

"Harry did it once when we were playing cowboys."

"Sit here," she said, heading for the hall and the cellar door.

"Wait."

She stopped.

"I saw how he did it," said Oleg, who had got to his feet. "Stay here, Mom."

She looked at him. God, how he had grown in this last year; he would soon be taller than her. And in those dark eyes of his the childishness was giving way to what for the moment was youthful defiance, but would, she could already see, in time become adult determination.

She hesitated.

"Let me do it," he said.

There was a plea in his tone. And she knew this was important for him; it was about bigger matters. About coming to terms with childish fears. About adult rituals. About becoming like his father. Whoever he thought that was.

"Hurry," she whispered.

Oleg ran.

She stood by the window and stared out, listening for the sound of a car on the drive. She prayed that Harry would come first. Wondered about how quiet it was. And had no idea where the next thought came from: how quiet it would be.

But then she did hear a sound. A tiny sound. At first she assumed it came from outside. But then she was sure that it came from behind her. She turned. Saw nothing, just the empty kitchen. Then there was that sound again. Like the heavy tick of a clock. Or a finger tapping on a table. The table. She stared. That was where the sound was coming from. And then she saw it. A drop of water had landed on the table. She slowly raised her face to the ceiling. In the middle of the white paneling a dark circle had formed. And from the middle of that circle hung a shiny drop. It let go and landed on the table. Rakel saw it happen, yet the sound made her jump, as if she had received an unexpected slap to the head.

My God, it must be from the bathroom! Had she really forgotten to turn off the shower again? She hadn't been on the second floor since she came home; she had started cooking right away, so it must have been running since this morning. And it *would* have to happen now, in the midst of all this.

She went into the hall, dashed up the stairs and headed for the bathroom. She couldn't hear the shower. She opened the door. Dry floor. No water running. She closed the bathroom door and stood outside for a couple of seconds. Glanced at the adjacent bedroom door. Slowly walked over. Rested her hand on the handle. Hesitated. Listened again for cars. Then she opened the door. She looked inside the room. She wanted to scream. But instinctively she knew that she mustn't—she had to be quiet. Perfectly quiet.

*   *   *

"Fuck, fuck, fuck!" Harry screamed and banged a fist onto the dashboard, making it quiver. "What's going on?"

The traffic had ground to a halt in front of the tunnel. They had been there now for two long minutes.

The reason came over the police radio that second. "There's been a collision on the Ring 3 by the exit of the westbound tunnel at Tåsen. No injuries. Tow truck's on its way."

On a sudden impulse Harry snatched the microphone. "Do you know who it is?"

"We know it's two cars, both with summer tires," the nasal radio voice drawled laconically.

"November snow always brings chaos," the officer at the back said.

Harry didn't answer, just drummed his fingers on the dashboard. He weighed the alternatives. There was a barricade of cars in front of and behind them; all the blue lights and sirens in the world could not get them through. He could jump out, run to the end of the tunnel and radio a patrol car to meet him there, but it was more than a mile.

It was quiet in the car now; all that could be heard was the low hum of idling car engines. The van in front of them nudged forward a yard and the police driver followed. Didn't brake until he was almost on its rear bumper, as if afraid anything but aggressive driving would cause the inspector to explode again. The sudden braking made the two metal bikini-clad women jingle cheerfully in the silence that followed.

Harry thought about Jonas again. Why, though? What had made him think about Jonas when he was talking to Mathias on the phone? There was something about the sound. In the background.

Harry studied the two dancers under the mirror. And everything clicked into place.

He knew why he had thought about Jonas. He knew what the sound had been. And he knew there wasn't a second to lose. Or—he tried to repress the thought—there was no need to hurry anymore. It was already too late.

Oleg hurried through the dark cellar corridor without looking left or right, knowing that the salt deposits on the brick walls were in the shape of white ghosts. He tried to concentrate on what he was going to do, tried not to think about anything else, not to let the wrong thoughts enter his mind. That was what Harry had said. It was possible to conquer the only monsters that existed, those inside your head. But you had to work at it. You had to confront them and fight them as often as you could. Minor skirmishes you could win. Then go home, bandage your wounds and try again. He had done it, he had been alone in the cellar many times, he had needed to be, of course, to make sure his skates were kept cold.

He grabbed the garden chair, dragged it after him for the noise to drown the silence. He checked that the cellar door was in fact locked. Then he wedged the chair under the handle and made sure it could not move. There we are. He stiffened. What was that? He looked up at the small window in the door. He couldn't hold back the thoughts any longer—now they flooded in. Someone was standing outside. He wanted to run away, but forced himself to stand his ground. Fought against the thoughts with other thoughts. I'm on the inside, he told himself. I'm as secure here as up there. He breathed in, felt his heart pounding like a runaway bass drum. Then he leaned forward and peered at the window. He saw the reflection of his own face. But above that he saw another face, a distorted face that was not his. And he saw hands, monster hands being raised. Oleg backed away, terrified. Bumped into something and felt hands close around his face and mouth. He was unable to scream. For he wanted to scream. He wanted to scream that this was not in his mind, this was the monster, the monster was inside. And they were all going to die.

"He's in the house," Harry said.

The other officers looked at him with incomprehension as Harry pressed the REDIAL button on the phone. "I thought it was Japanese music, but it was metal wind chimes. The kind Jonas has in his room. And that Oleg has, too. Mathias has been there all the time. He told me himself, didn't he . . . ?"

"What do you mean?" the officer in the back ventured to ask.

"He said he was at home. And that's the house on Holmenkollveien now, of course. He even said he was on his way *down* to see Rakel and Oleg. I should have known. After all, Holmenkollen is up in relation to Torshov. He was on the second floor on Holmenkollveien. On his way down. We have to get them out of the house now. Answer, for Christ's sake!"

"Perhaps she's not near—"

"There are four telephones in the house. He's just cut the connection now. I have to get there."

"We can send another patrol car," the driver said.

"No!" Harry snapped. "It's too late anyway. He's got them. And the only chance we have is the final pawn. Me."

"You?"

"Yes. I'm part of his plan."

"You're *not* part of his plan, you mean, don't you?"

"No. I am part. He's waiting for me."

The two policemen exchanged glances as they heard the bleat of a motorbike worming its way forward between the stationary cars behind them.

"You think he is?"

"Yes," Harry said, catching sight of the bike in the side mirror. Thinking this was the only answer he could give. Because it was the only answer that offered any hope.

Oleg struggled with all his might, but went limp in the monster's iron grip when he felt the cold steel on his throat.

"This is a scalpel, Oleg." The monster had Mathias's voice. "We use it to dissect people. And you wouldn't believe how easy it is."

Then the monster told him to open wide, shoved a filthy cloth in his mouth and ordered him to lie on his stomach with his arms behind his back. As Oleg didn't obey at once, the steel was thrust in under his ear and he felt hot blood coursing over his shoulder and down the inside of his T-shirt. He lay on his stomach on the freezing cement floor, and the monster sat on top of him. A red box fell beside his face. He read the label. Plastic ties, the kind of thin ties you saw around cables and on toy packaging, which were so irritating because they could only be tightened, not loosened, and they couldn't be pulled apart however thin they were. He felt the sharp plastic cut into the skin around his wrists and ankles.

Then he was lifted up and dropped and there was no time to wait for the pain as he landed with a crunch. He stared up. He was lying on his back in the freezer; he could feel the ice that had broken off burn the skin on his forearms and face. Above him stood the monster, with his head angled to one side.

"Good-bye," he said. "We'll meet on the other side before very long."

The lid was slammed down and there was total darkness. Oleg could hear the key being turned in the lock and swift steps fading into the distance. He tried to lift his tongue, tried to get it behind the cloth, had to get it out. Had to breathe. Had to have air.

Rakel had stopped breathing. She stood in the bedroom doorway knowing that what she saw was insanity. An insanity that made her flesh creep, her mouth drop and her eyes bulge.

The bed and other furniture had been pushed against the walls, and the floor was covered by an almost invisible surface of water that was only broken when a new drop fell on it. But Rakel didn't notice; the only thing she saw was the enormous snowman dominating the center of the room.

The top hat above the grinning mouth almost touched the ceiling.

When she finally recovered her breathing and the oxygen rushed to her brain she recognized the smell of wet wool and wet wood and heard the sound of melting snow dripping. A wave of cold surged toward her, but this was not what gave her goose pimples. It was the body heat of the man standing behind her.

"Isn't it beautiful?" Mathias said. "I've made it just for you."

"Mathias . . ."

"Shh." He placed a kind of protective arm around her throat. She looked down. The hand was holding a scalpel. "Don't talk, my love. There's so much to do and so little time."

"Why? Why?"

"This is our day, Rakel. The rest of life is so unbelievably short, so let's celebrate, not waste time explaining. Please put your arms behind your back."

Rakel did as he said. She hadn't heard Oleg come up from the cellar. Perhaps he was still in the cellar; perhaps he could get out if she could just detain Mathias. "I'd like to know why," she said and could hear emotion tugging at her vocal cords.

"Because you're a whore."

She felt something thin and hard tighten around her wrists. Felt his warm breath on her neck. His lips. And then his tongue. She gritted her teeth, knowing that if she screamed he might stop and she wanted him to go on, to waste time. The tongue worked its way around and up to her ear. A little nibble.

"And the son from your whoring is in the freezer," he whispered.

"Oleg?" she said, feeling herself lose control.

"Relax, my darling, he won't die of cold."

" Wo-won't he?"

"Long before his body has cooled down the son of a whore will have died from asphyxiation. It's simple mathematics."

"Mathema—"

"I did the calculations ages ago. It's all calculated."

A revving motorbike skidded up the winding roads of Holmenkollen in the dark. The roar reverberated between the houses and onlookers considered it madness in these snowy conditions. The rider should have his license taken away. But the rider didn't have one.

Harry accelerated up the drive to the black timber house, but in the sharp turn the wheels spun on the fresh snow and he felt the bike losing speed. He didn't try to correct the skid; he jumped off and the bike rolled down the slope, burst through a few low spruce branches before coming to a halt against a tree trunk, tipped onto its side and, spitting snow from the back wheel, breathed its last.

By then Harry was already halfway up the steps.

There were no footprints in the snow, neither to nor from the house. He took out his revolver as he bounded up to the door.

It was unlocked. As promised.

He slipped into the hall, and the first thing he saw was the cellar door wide open.

Harry stopped to listen. There was a noise, a kind of drumming. It seemed to be coming from the kitchen. Harry hesitated. Then he opted for the cellar.

With his revolver pointing in front of him, he sidled down the staircase. At the bottom he stopped to let his eyes get accustomed to the dark and listened. He had a sense that the whole room was holding its breath. He spotted the garden chair under the door handle. Oleg. His eyes delved further. He had decided to go upstairs again when his attention was caught by the dark stain on the brick floor by the freezer. Water? He took a step closer. It must have come from under the freezer. He forced his thoughts away from where they wanted to go and pulled at the lid. Locked. The key was in, but Rakel didn't usually lock the freezer. Images from Finnøy emerged in his brain, but he hurried, twisted the key and lifted the lid.

Harry just caught the glint of metal from the murky depths before a burning pain in his face made him throw himself backward. A knife? He had fallen on his back between two dirty-laundry baskets and a figure, speedy and nimble, was already out of the freezer and standing over him.

"Police!" Harry shouted and quickly raised his gun. "Don't move!"

The figure stopped with one hand raised over his head. "H-Harry?"

"Oleg?"

Harry lowered the revolver and saw what the boy was holding in his hand. A speed skate.

"I . . . I thought Mathias had come back," he whispered.

Harry got to his feet. "Where is Mathias?"

"I don't know. He said we would meet soon, so I assumed . . ."

"Where did the skate come from?" Harry tasted metallic blood in his mouth and his fingers found the cut on his face, which was bleeding profusely.

"It was in the freezer." Oleg gave a sly grin. "I was getting so much hassle for leaving the skates on the steps, so I keep them under the peas where Mom won't see them. We never eat peas, as you know."

He followed Harry, who was already on his way up the stairs.

"Luckily I'd had the blades sharpened, so I could cut the ties. The lock was impossible, but I managed to stab a couple of holes in the plate at the bottom to get some air. And I smashed the bulb so that the light wouldn't come on when he opened the lid."

"And your body heat melted the ice that ran out of the hole," Harry said.

They emerged in the hall, and Harry pulled Oleg over to the front door, opened it and pointed.

"See the neighbors' light? Run over and stay there until I come to get you. OK?"

"No!" said Oleg firmly. "Mom—"

"Shh! Now listen. The best thing you can do for your mom right now is to get away from here."

"I want to find her!"

Harry grabbed Oleg's shoulders and squeezed until tears of pain formed in the boy's eyes.

"When I say run, you run, you damn idiot."

He said it in a low voice but with such repressed fury that Oleg blinked in confusion and a tear rolled over his eyelashes and onto his cheek. Then the boy turned on his heel, rushed out the door and was swallowed up by the darkness and the driving snow.

Harry grabbed the walkie-talkie and pressed the TALK button. "Harry here. Are you far away?"

"We're by the stadium. Over." Harry recognized Gunnar Hagen's voice.

"I'm inside," Harry said. "Drive up to the front of the house, but don't enter until I say. Over."

"Roger."

"Over and out."

Harry went toward the sound he'd heard earlier in the kitchen. From the doorway he watched the thin stream of water falling from the ceiling. It had been tinted gray by the dissolved plaster and was drumming furiously on the kitchen table.

Harry took the staircase to the second floor in four long strides. Tiptoed to the bedroom door. Swallowed. Studied the door handle. From outside he could hear the distant sound of police sirens approaching. Blood from his cut dripped onto the parquet floor with a gentle plop.

He could feel it now, as pressure on his temples; this was where it would end. And there was a kind of logic to it. How many times had he stood like this in front of the bedroom door, at daybreak, after a night when he had promised to be at home with her, how often had he stood there with a bad conscience knowing she was inside asleep? Carefully he pressed the door handle, which he knew would creak halfway down. And she would wake up, look at him with sleepy eyes, try to punish him with her glare, until he slipped under the duvet, snuggled up to her body and felt its stiff resistance melt. And she would grunt with pleasure, but not too much pleasure. And then he would stroke her more, kiss and nibble at her, be her servant until she was sitting on him, no longer the queen in her slumbers, but purring and moaning, wanton and offended at the same time.

He closed his fist around the handle, noticed how his hand recognized the flat angular shape. He pressed with infinite care. Waited for the familiar creak. But it was not forthcoming. Something was different. There was resistance. Had someone tightened the springs? Gingerly, he let go. Stooped down to the keyhole and tried to peep in. Black. Someone had blocked the hole.

"Rakel!" he shouted. "Are you there?"

No answer. He placed his ear against the door. Thought he could hear a scratching sound, but wasn't sure. He held the handle again. Wavered. Changed his mind, let go and hastened into the adjacent bathroom. Pushed open the little window, forced his body through and leaned out backward. Light was streaming from between the black iron bars of the bedroom window. He wedged his heels against the inside of the frame, tensed his leg muscles and stretched out of the bathroom and along the outside wall. His fingers groped in vain to find a hold between the rough logs as the snow settled on his face and melted into the blood running down his cheek. He applied greater force; the window frame was pressing into his leg so hard it felt as if the bone would crack. His hands crept along the wall like frenetic five-legged spiders. His stomach muscles ached. But it was too far—he couldn't reach. He stared down at the ground beneath him, knowing that under the thin layer of snow there was pavement.

He felt something cold against his fingertips.

An iron bar.

Got two fingers around the bar. Three. Then the other hand. Let his aching legs swing free, dangled and hurriedly found a foothold to relieve the pressure on his arms. At last he could see into the bedroom. And he saw. His brain struggled to absorb the sight while it knew immediately what it was looking at: the finished work of art, the prototype of which he had already seen.

Rakel's eyes were wide open and black. She was wearing a dress. Crimson. Like Campari. She was "cochineal." Her head strained toward the ceiling as though she were standing by a fence trying to see over, and from this position she stared down and out at him. Her shoulders were pulled back and her arms hidden. Harry assumed her hands were tied behind her back. Her cheeks bulged as though she had a sock or a cloth in her mouth. She sat astride the shoulders of an enormous snowman. Her bare legs were crossed in front of the snowman's chest, and he could see her tensed leg muscles quivering. She mustn't fall. She couldn't. For around her neck there was not a gray, lifeless wire, as with Eli Kvale, but a white glowing circle, like an absurd imitation of an old toothpaste advertisement promising a ring of confidence, good fortune in love and a long and happy life. A wire ran from the black handle of the cutting loop to a hook in the ceiling above Rakel's head. The wire continued to the other end of the room, to the door. To the door handle. The wire was not thick, but long enough to have provided noticeably more resistance when Harry had begun to press the handle. If he had opened the door, indeed if he had even pressed the handle right down, the white glowing metal would have cut into her throat, right under her chin.

Rakel was staring back at Harry without blinking. The muscles in her face were twitching, alternating between fury and naked fear. The loop was too narrow for her to remove her head unscathed; instead she held her head down so that it did not touch the death-bringing glow that hung almost vertically around her neck.

She looked at Harry, down at the floor and back to Harry. And Harry understood.

Gray clumps of snow were already lying in the water covering the floor. The snowman was melting. Fast.

Harry got a good foothold and shook the bars as hard as he could. They didn't budge, didn't even offer a hopeful creak. The iron was thin but firmly attached to the timber.

The figure inside was swaying.

"Hold on!" Harry shouted. "I'll be there soon!"

Lies. He wouldn't even be able to bend the bars with an iron lever. And he didn't have time to start sawing them off. Fuck her father, the crazy bastard! His arms were aching. He heard the ear-piercing siren of the first car turning into the drive. He looked around. It was one of Delta's special vehicles, a large, armored beast of a Land Rover. A man dressed in a green flak jacket jumped out of the passenger seat, took cover behind the vehicle and held up a walkie-talkie. Harry's handset crackled.

"Hello!" Harry shouted.

The man, taken aback, looked left and right.

"Up here, boss."

Gunnar Hagen straightened up behind the vehicle as a patrol car swung up in front of the house with the blue light swirling.

"Should we storm the house?" Hagen shouted.

"No!" screamed Harry. "He's got her strung up. Just . . . "

"Just?"

Harry raised his eyes, stared. Not down to the city, but up to the illuminated Holmenkollen ski jump farther up the ridge.

"Just what, Harry?"

"Just wait."

"Wait?"

"I have to think."

Harry rested his forehead against the cold bars. His arms were aching and he bent his knees to put most of his body weight on his legs. The cutting loop must have an off-switch. On the plastic handle, probably. They could smash the window and poke a long pole in with a mirror attached so that they could perhaps . . . But how the hell would they be able to press the off-switch without everything moving and . . . and . . . ? Harry tried not to think about the ludicrously thin layer of skin and soft tissue that protected the carotid artery. Tried to think constructively and ignore the panic that was roaring in his ears, telling him to get in and take control.

They could enter through the door. Without opening it. Just saw away the panel. They needed a chain saw. But who would have one? Only the whole of fucking Holmenkollen. After all, they all had spruce forests in their yards.

"Get hold of a chain saw from the neighbor's house," Harry yelled.

Down below he heard the sound of running. And a splash inside the bedroom. Harry's heart stopped and he stared in. The snowman's whole left side was gone. It had sheared off and landed in the water. The snowman was collapsing. He saw Rakel's body tremble as she fought to maintain her balance to keep away from the white, tear-shaped gallows noose. They would never get back with the chain saw in time, let alone cut through the door.

"Hagen!" Harry heard the shrill hysteria in his own voice. "The patrol cars have a tow rope. Sling it up here and back the Land Rover up to the wall."

Harry heard a buzz of voices, the Land Rover's engine revving in reverse and a car trunk being opened.

"Catch!"

Harry let go of the bar with one hand and turned to see the coiled rope coming toward him. He lunged in the dark, caught it and held on as the rest unfurled and fell back down to the ground with a thud.

"Tie the end to the tow bar."

There was a carbine hook attached to his end of the rope. As quick as lightning he smacked the hook against the junction of the bars in the middle of the window and the lock snapped shut. Speed-cuffing.

Another splash from inside the bedroom. Harry didn't look. There was no point.

"Go!" he yelled.

Then he grabbed the edge of the gutter with both hands, using the bars as a ladder, and heard the Land Rover's revs increase as he swung himself onto the roof. With his chest on the roof tiles and his eyes closed he could hear the motor engage, the rev count fall and the iron bars groan. More groaning. And more. Come on! Harry was aware that time was passing more slowly than he thought. And yet not slowly enough. Then—as he was waiting for the auspicious crack—the rev count suddenly rose to a ferocious whine. Shit! Harry realized the tires of the Land Rover were spinning around helplessly.

A thought fluttered through his brain: He could say a prayer. But he knew that God had made up His mind, that destiny was sold out, that this ticket would have to be bought on the black market. His soul wouldn't be worth much without her anyway. The thought was gone that very same second, interrupted by the sound of rubber, a sinking rev count and an increasing groan.

The big heavy tires had spun their way down to the pavement.

Then came the crack. The rev count roared and died.

A second of total silence followed. And then a hollow crash as the bars hit the car roof below.

Harry pushed himself up. He stood with his back to the yard on the edge of the gutter and felt it give way. Then he bent down, grabbed the gutter with both hands and kicked off. Swung like a pendulum from gutter to window. Jack knifed. The moment the old, thin window-pane gave with a tinkle under his boots, Harry let go. And for a few tenths of a second he had no idea where he would land: down in the yard, on the jagged glass teeth of the window or in the bedroom.

There was a bang, a fuse must have been blown, and everything went black.

Harry sailed through a room of nothing, felt nothing, remembered nothing, was nothing.

And when the light came back on his only thought was that he wanted to return to that space. Pain radiated from all over his body. He was lying on his back in icy-cold water. But he must have been dead because he was look-ing up at an angel dressed in blood red, seeing her shin-ing halo glow in the dark. Slowly sound returned. The scratching. The breathing. Then he saw the distorted face, the panic, the gaping mouth stuffed with the yel-low ball, the feet scrambling up the snow. He just wanted to close his eyes. A noise, like low moaning. Wet snow crumbling.

In retrospect, Harry couldn't really account for what happened; he could remember only the nauseating smell as the cutting loop burned through flesh.

At the very moment the snowman collapsed he stood up. Rakel fell forward. Harry raised his right hand as he fastened his left arm around her thighs to hold her up. He knew it was too late. Flesh sizzled, his nostrils were filled with a sweet, greasy smell and blood ran down his face. He looked up. His right hand was situated between the white glow of the loop and her neck. The weight of her neck forced his hand down against the white-hot wire, which ate through the flesh of his fingers like an egg slicer through a hard-boiled egg. And when it was right through it would cut open her throat. The pain came, delayed and dull, like an initially reluctant then insistent steel hammer on an alarm clock. He fought to stay upright. Had to have his left hand free. Blinded by blood, he hauled her up onto his shoulders and stretched his free hand over his head. Felt her skin against his fingertips, her thick hair, felt the loop burn into his skin before his hand found the hard plastic, the handle. His fingers found a flip switch. Moved it to the right. But stopped as soon as the noose started tightening. His fingers found another switch and pressed. The sounds disappeared, the light flickered and he knew he was on the point of losing consciousness again. Breathe, he thought, the important thing was to get oxygen to the brain. But his knees were giving way, nevertheless. The white glow above him changed to red. And then gradually to black.

At his back he heard the sound of glass being crushed under several pairs of boot heels.

"We've got her," a voice said behind him.

Harry sank to his knees in the blood-tinged water, with clumps of snow and unused plastic ties floating around him. His brain engaged and disengaged as if the power supply to it were failing.

Someone said something behind him. He caught fragments of it, inhaled air and groaned, "What?"

"She's alive," the voice repeated.

His hearing stabilized. And sight. He turned. The two men clad in black had laid Rakel on the bed and cut the plastic ties. The contents of Harry's stomach came up without warning. Two heaves and it was all out. He stared down at the vomit floating in the water and felt a hysterical urge to laugh out loud. Because the finger seemed to have been spewed up with everything else. He lifted his right hand and looked at the bleeding stump as confirmation. It was his finger floating in the water.

"Oleg . . . " It was Rakel's voice.

Harry picked up a plastic tie, wrapped it around the stump of his middle finger and tightened it as hard as he could. Did the same with his index finger, which had been sliced through to the bone but was still firmly attached.

Then he went to the bed, spread the duvet over Rakel and sat beside her. The eyes staring up at him were large and black with shock, and blood ran from the wounds where the loop had come into contact with the skin on both sides of her neck. He took her hand with his uninjured left.

"Oleg," she repeated.

"He's OK," Harry said and responded to her hand pressure. "He's with the neighbors. It's over now."

He saw her trying to focus her eyes.

"Promise me?" she whispered, barely audible.

"I promise you."

"Thank God."

She sobbed once, buried her face in her hands and began to cry.

Harry looked down at his injured hand. Either the ties had stopped the bleeding or he was empty.

"Where's Mathias?" he said quietly.

Her head bobbed up, and she gaped at him. "You just promised me that—"

"Where did he go, Rakel?"

"I don't know."

"Did he say anything?"

Her hand squeezed his. "Don't go now, Harry. I'm sure someone else can—"

"What did he say?"

He could tell by the way her body recoiled that he had raised his voice.

"He said that it was finished now and he would bring it to a conclusion," she said as tears welled in her dark eyes again. "And that the end would be an homage to life."

"An homage to life? Those were the words he used?"

She nodded. Harry loosened his hand from hers, stood up and went to the window. Scoured the night sky. It had stopped snowing. He looked up at the illuminated monument that could be seen from almost everywhere in Oslo. The ski jump. Like a white comma against the black ridge. Or a full stop.

Harry went back to her bedside, bent down and kissed her on the forehead.

"Where are you going?" she whispered.

Harry raised the bloodstained hand and smiled. "To see a doctor."

He left the room. Stumbled down the stairs. Came out into the cold, white darkness of the yard, but the nausea and giddiness would not release their grip.

Hagen stood beside the Land Rover talking on a mobile phone.

He broke off the conversation and nodded when Harry asked if they could drive him.

Harry sat in the back. He was thinking about how Rakel had thanked God. She couldn't know, of course, that someone else deserved her thanks. Or that the buyer had accepted the offer. And that payback time had already started.

"Down to the city center?" the driver asked.

Harry shook his head and pointed upward. The right index finger looked strangely alone between the thumb and the ring finger.

36

The Tower

It took three minutes to drive from Rakel's house to Holmenkollen ski jump. They drove through the tunnel and parked on the viewing promontory among the souvenir shops. The slope looked like a frozen white waterfall that plunged down between the stands and broadened into a flat out-run a hundred yards below.

"How do you know he's here?" Hagen asked.

"Because he told me he would be," Harry said. "We were sitting by a skating rink and he said the day his life's work was over and he was so ill he wanted to die he would jump from that tower there. As an homage to life." Harry pointed to the illuminated ski tower and the in-run soaring up against the black sky above them. "And he knew I would remember."

"Insane," whispered Gunnar Hagen, peering up at the darkened glass cage perched on the top of the tower.

"Could I borrow your handcuffs?" Harry asked, turning to the driver.

"You've already got some," Hagen said, nodding toward Harry's right wrist, where he had attached one cuff. The other hung open. "I'd like two pairs," Harry said, taking the leather case from the driver. "Can you help me? I'm a couple of fingers short here . . . "

Hagen shook his head as he attached half of the driver's handcuffs around Harry's other wrist.

"I'm not happy with you going on your own. It frightens me."

"There's not a lot of room up there and I can talk to him." Harry produced Katrine's revolver. "And I've got this."

"That's what frightens me, Harry."

Inspector Hole sent his boss a quick glance before twisting around and opening the car door with his healthy hand.

The police officer accompanied Harry to the entrance of the Ski Museum, which he had to pass through to get to the tower lift. They had taken along a crowbar to smash in the door. But as they approached, the flashlight caught fragments of glass glinting on the floor over by the ticket counter. A distant alarm from somewhere inside the museum was inhaling and exhaling with a howl.

"OK, so we know our man's here," Harry said, making sure his revolver was in position at the back of his waistband. "Place two men by the rear exit as soon as the next patrol car arrives."

Harry took the flashlight, stepped into the dark building and hurried past the posters and pictures of Norwegian ski heroes, Norwegian flags, Norwegian ski grease, Norwegian kings and Norwegian Crown princesses, all accompanied by succinct texts proclaiming that Norway was one hell of a nation, and Harry remembered why he had never been able to stomach this museum.

The elevator was right at the back. A narrow, enclosed space. Harry studied the elevator door. Felt the cold sweat on his skin. There was a steel staircase next to it.

Eight landings later he regretted his decision. The

dizziness and nausea had returned and he was retching. The sound of footsteps on metal echoed up and down the flight of stairs, and the handcuffs dangling from his wrists played iron pipe music against the handrail. His heart ought to have been pumping adrenaline and preparing his body for action at this point. Perhaps he was too drained, too spent. Or perhaps he knew it was all over. The game was up, the outcome obvious.

Harry went on. Set his feet down on the steps, didn't even bother to try to be quiet, knew he had been heard ages ago.

The staircase led directly to the dark cage. Harry switched off his flashlight and felt a cold current of air as soon as his head appeared above the floor. Pale moonlight fell into the room. It was about forty square feet with glass all around and a steel railing that tourists clung to with a mixture of terror and joy as they enjoyed the view of Oslo or imagined what it must be like to set off down the in-run on skis. Or fall off the tower, sink like a stone toward the houses and be smashed between the trees far below them.

Harry climbed to the top step, turned to the silhouette outlined against the blanket of light that was the town beneath. The figure was sitting on the railing, by the large open window from where the cold air was flowing.

"Beautiful, eh?" Mathias's voice sounded light, almost cheerful.

"If it's the view you mean, I agree."

"I didn't mean the view, Harry."

One of Mathias's feet was dangling outside, and Harry was standing by the stairs.

"Did you or the snowman kill her, Harry?"

"What do you think?"

"I think you did it. After all, you're a clever guy. I was counting on you. Feels dreadful, doesn't it? Of course, it's not so easy to see the beauty then. When you've just killed the person you love most."

"Well," Harry said, taking a step closer, "I don't suppose you would know much about that, would you."

"Wouldn't I?" Mathias leaned his head back against the frame and laughed. "I loved the first woman I killed more than anything else on this earth."

"So why did you do it?" Harry felt a stab of pain as he moved his right hand behind his back and around the revolver.

"Because my mother was a liar and a whore," Mathias said.

Harry swung his hand around and raised the revolver. "Come down from there, Mathias. With your hands in the air."

Mathias eyed Harry with curiosity. "Do you know there's a twenty percent chance that your mother was the same, Harry? A twenty percent chance that you're the son of a whore. What do you say to that?"

"You heard me, Mathias."

"Let me make it easier for you, Harry. First, I refuse to obey. Second, you can say you couldn't see my hands, so I could have been armed. Fire away, Harry."

"Get down."

"Rakel was a whore, Harry. And Oleg's the son of a whore. You should thank me for letting you kill her."

Harry switched the gun to his left hand. The loose ends of the handcuffs banged against each other.

"Think about it, Harry. If you arrest me I'll be declared of unsound mind, pampered in some psychiatric ward for a few years before being released. Shoot me now."

"You want to die," Harry said, moving nearer. "Because you're going to die of scleroderma."

Mathias smacked a hand against the window frame.

"Well done, Harry. You checked what I said about antibodies in my blood."

"I asked Idar. And afterward I researched scleroderma. If you've got the disease, it's easy to choose another death. For example, a spectacular death that would appear to crown this so-called life's work of yours."

"I can hear your contempt, Harry. But one day you'll understand, too."

"Understand what?"

"That we were in the same business, Harry. Fighting disease. But the diseases you and I are fighting can't be eradicated. All victories are temporary. So it's just the fight that is our life's work. And mine finishes here. Don't you want to shoot me, Harry?"

Harry met Mathias's eyes. Then he turned the revolver around in his hand. Held it out to Mathias, butt first. "Do it yourself, you bastard."

Mathias frowned. Harry saw the hesitation, the suspicion. Which gradually gave way to a smile.

"As you wish." Mathias stretched across the railing and took the weapon. Caressed the black steel.

"You made a great error there, my friend," he said, pointing the revolver at Harry. "You'll make a nice period at the end of the sentence, Harry. The guarantee that my work will not be forgotten."

Harry stared into the black muzzle, watching the hammer raise its ugly little head. Everything seemed to move slower and the room began to revolve. Mathias took aim. Harry took aim. And swung his right arm. The handcuff made a low whine through the air as Mathias pressed the trigger. The dry click was followed by a metallic smack as the open cuff struck his wrist.

"Rakel survived," Harry said. "You failed, you satanic bastard."

Harry saw Mathias's eyes widen. Then narrow. Saw them stare at the revolver that had not fired, at the iron around his wrist binding him to Harry.

"You . . . you removed the bullets."

Harry shook his head. "Katrine Bratt never had bullets in her revolver."

Mathias looked up at Harry and leaned backward. "Come on."

Then he jumped.

Harry was jerked forward and lost his balance. He tried to hold on but Mathias was too heavy and Harry a diminished giant, weakened by the loss of flesh and blood. The policeman screamed as he was dragged over the steel rail and sucked toward the window and the abyss. What he saw as he threw his free left arm above his head and behind him was a chair leg and himself sitting alone in a filthy, windowless Chicago apartment. Harry heard the sound of metal on metal, then he tumbled through the night in free fall. The game was at an end now.

Gunnar Hagen stared at the ski jump tower but the swirling snow flakes that had started again obscured his vision.

"Harry!" he repeated on his walkie-talkie. "Are you there?"

He released the button, but again the answer was intense, rustling nothingness.

There were four patrol cars in the open parking lot by the jump now, and total confusion had reigned when they had heard the scream from the tower a few seconds before.

"They fell," said the officer beside him. "I'm sure I saw two figures falling out of the glass cage."

Gunnar Hagen lowered his head in resignation. He didn't quite know how or why, but for a moment it seemed to him there was an absurd logic in things ending this way; there was a kind of cosmic balance.

Nonsense. What utter nonsense.

Hagen couldn't see the police vehicles in the drifting snow, but he could hear the lament of the sirens, like wailing women; they were already on their way. And he knew that the sound would attract the scavengers: the media vultures, the nosy neighbors, the bloodthirsty bosses. They would come to get their favorite tidbit off the body, their delicacy. And this evening's two-course meal—the repugnant snowman and the repugnant policeman—would be to their liking. There was no logic, no balance, just hunger and food. Hagen's walkie-talkie crackled.

"We can't find them! Over."

Hagen waited, wondering how he would tell his superiors that he had let Harry go alone. How he would explain that he was only Harry's superior, not his boss and never had been. And that there was a logic there, too, and that actually he didn't give a damn whether they understood or not.

"What's going on?"

Hagen turned. It was Magnus Skarre.

"Harry fell," Hagen said, nodding toward the tower. "They're searching for the body now."

"Body? Of Harry? No chance."

"No chance?"

Hagen turned to Skarre, who was squinting up at the tower. "I thought you'd have known the guy by now, Hagen."

Hagen could feel that despite everything he envied the young officer his conviction.

The walkie-talkie crackled again. "They're not here!"

Skarre turned to him, their eyes met and Skarre rolled his shoulders in a *What did I tell you?* shrug.

"Hey, you!" Hagen shouted to the Land Rover driver and pointed at the searchlight on the roof. "Shine it on the glass cage. And get hold of some binoculars for me."

A few seconds later a beam cut through the night.

"Can you see anything?" Skarre asked.

"Snow," Hagen said, pressing the binoculars against his eyes. "Shine a bit higher. Stop! Wait . . . my God!"

"What?"

"Well, I'll be damned."

At that moment the snow retreated like a theater curtain being drawn. Hagen heard several policemen shout. It looked like two men shackled together were dangling from the rearview mirror of a car. The lower of the two held a hand above his head in a kind of triumphant flourish; the other had both arms stretched out vertically as if he were being crucified sideways. And both were lifeless, with sunken heads as they slowly gyrated in the air.

Through the binoculars Hagen could see the handcuff holding Harry's left hand to the railing on the inside of the glass cage.

"Well, I'll be damned," Hagen repeated.

As chance would have it, the young officer from the Missing Persons Unit, Thomas Helle, was crouched down by Harry Hole when he regained consciousness. Four policemen had hauled him and Mathias Lund-Helgesen back up into the glass cage. And in the years to come Helle would tell the story of the infamous inspector's strange first reactions again and again.

"He was all wild-eyed and asked if Lund-Helgesen was still alive! As though he was terrified the guy had died. As though that was the worst thing that could have happened. And when I said yes and that he was being taken away in the ambulance he yelled that we had to remove Lund-Helgesen's shoelaces and belt and make sure he didn't commit suicide. Have you ever heard anything like it? Showing that much care for a guy who'd just tried to murder your ex?"

37

Dad

Jonas thought he had heard the metallic jangle of the wind chimes, but had gone back to sleep. It was only when he heard the choking sounds that he opened his eyes. There was someone in the room. It was Dad; he was sitting on the edge of his bed.

And the choking sounds were him crying.

Jonas sat up in bed. He placed a hand on his father's shoulder and felt it shaking. It was odd; he had never noticed that his father had such narrow shoulders.

"They . . . they've found her," he sobbed. "Mom's . . . "

"I know," Jonas said. "I dreamed it."

The father swiveled around in surprise. In the moonlight seeping through the curtains Jonas could see the tears running down his cheeks.

"It's just us now, Dad," he said.

His father opened his mouth. Once. Twice. But nothing came out. Then he stretched out his arms, wrapped them around Jonas and drew him close. Held him tight. Jonas laid his head against his father's neck, felt the hot tears wetting his scalp.

"Do you know what, Jonas?" he whispered through

the tears. "I love you so much. You're the dearest thing I have. You're my boy. Do you hear? My boy. And you always will be. We'll manage, won't we? Don't you think?"

"Yes, Dad," Jonas whispered. "We'll manage. You and me."

38

DECEMBER 2004

The Swans

It was December and the fields outside the hospital windows lay bare and brown under a steel-gray sky. On the highway, studded tires crunched on dry pavement and pedestrians scuttled across the footbridge with coat collars turned up and faces closed. But inside the walls of the building people huddled closer. And on the table in the ward the two candles marked the second Sunday of Advent.

Harry pulled up in the doorway. Ståle Aune was sitting up in bed and had obviously just made a joke because the head of the Forensics Unit, Beate Lønn, was still laughing. On her lap sat a red-cheeked baby, looking at Harry with big round eyes and an open mouth.

"My friend!" Ståle growled as he caught sight of the policeman.

Harry walked in, stooped, gave Beate a hug and offered Ståle Aune a hand.

"You look better than when I saw you last," Harry said.

"They say I'll be discharged before Christmas," Aune said and turned Harry's hand in his. "That's some fiendish claw. What happened?"

Harry allowed him to study his right hand. "The middle finger was chopped off and couldn't be saved. They sewed together the sinews in the index finger, and the nerve endings will grow a fraction of an inch a month and try to find each other. Though the doctors say I'll have to live with permanent paralysis on one side of it."

"A high price."

"No," Harry said. "Small beer."

Aune nodded.

"Any news about when the case is due to come up?" asked Beate, who had got to her feet to put the baby in the stroller.

"No," Harry said, watching the forensic officer's efficient movements.

"The defense will try to have Lund-Helgesen declared mad," Aune said, preferring the demotic form "mad," which, in his opinion, was not only a suitable description but also poetic. "And not to achieve that would take an even worse psychologist than me."

"Oh, yes, he'll get life anyway," Beate said, angling her head and straightening the baby's blanket.

"Just a shame life isn't life," Aune growled and put out a hand for the glass on his bedside table. "The more aged I become, the more I tend to the view that evil is evil, mental illness or no. We're all more or less disposed to evil actions, but our disposition cannot exonerate us. For heaven's sake, we're all sick with personality disorders. And it's our actions that define how sick we are. We're equal before the law, we say, but it's meaningless as long as no one is equal. During the Black Death seamen who coughed were immediately heaved overboard. Of course they were. For justice is a blunt knife, both as a philosophy and as a judge. All we have is fortunate or less fortunate medical prospects, my dears."

"Nevertheless," Harry said, staring down at the still-bandaged stump of a middle finger, "in this case, it'll be for life."

"Oh?"

"Unfortunate medical prospects."

The silence filled the room.

"Did I say that I was offered a finger prosthesis?" Harry announced, waving his right hand. "But basically I like my hand as it is. Four fingers. Cartoon hand."

"What did you do with the finger that was there?"

"Tried to donate it to the Anatomy Department, but they weren't interested. So I'll have it stuffed and put it on my desk, just like Hagen does with the Japanese little finger. Thought an upright middle finger might be a suitable Hole welcome."

The other two laughed.

"How are Oleg and Rakel doing?" Beate asked.

"Surprisingly well," Harry said. "Toughies."

"And Katrine Bratt?"

"Better. I visited her last week. She starts work again in February. Going back to her old unit in Bergen."

"Really? Didn't she almost shoot someone in her excitement?"

"Wrong call. Turns out she was walking around with an empty revolver. That was why she dared to press the trigger so far back. And I should have known that."

"Oh?"

"When you move from one police station to another you hand in your service revolver and get a new one with two boxes of ammo. There were two unopened boxes in her desk drawer."

A moment of silence followed.

"It's good she's well again," Beate said, stroking the baby's hair.

"Yes," Harry said absentmindedly, and it occurred to him that it was true; she did seem to be getting better. When he had visited Katrine in her mother's apartment in Bergen she had just had a shower after a long run on Sandviken Mountain. Her hair was still wet and her cheeks red as her mother served tea and Katrine talked about how her father's case had become an obsession. And she apologized for having dragged him into the matter. He didn't see any regret in her eyes, though.

"My psychiatrist says that I'm just a few notches more extreme than most people." She had laughed, and then shrugged. "But now I'm done with all that. It's pursued me from my childhood. Now he's finally had his name cleared and I can move on with my life."

"Shuffling papers for the Sexual Offenses Unit?"

"We'll start there, then we'll see. Even top politicians make comebacks."

Then her eyes glided toward the window, across the fjord. Toward Finnøy, perhaps. And as Harry left he knew the damage was there and always would be.

He looked down at his hand. Aune was right; if every baby was a perfect miracle, life was basically a process of degeneration.

A nurse coughed by the door. "Time for a few jabs, Aune."

"Oh, please let me off, sister."

"No one is let off here."

Ståle Aune sighed. "What is worse? Taking the life of a person who wants to live or taking death from a person who wants to die?"

Beate, the nurse and Ståle laughed, and no one noticed Harry twitch in his chair.

Harry walked up the steep hills from the hospital to Lake Sognsvann. There weren't many people around, only the loyal throng of Sunday walkers doing their fixed circuit around the lake. Rakel waited for him by the roadblock.

They gave each other a hug and started the circuit in

silence. The air was sharp and the sun matte in a pale blue sky. Dry leaves crackled and disintegrated beneath their heels.

"I've been sleepwalking," Harry said.

"Oh?"

"Yes. And I've probably been doing it for a while."

"It's not so easy to be fully present all the time," she said.

"No, no." He shook his head. "Quite literally. I think I've been up and walking through the apartment at night. God knows what I've been up to."

"How did you find out?"

"The night after I came home from the hospital I was standing in the kitchen looking at the floor, at some wet footprints. And then I realized I didn't have a stitch on, except for my rubber boots, it was the middle of the night and I was holding a hammer in my hand."

Rakel smiled and looked down. Skipped a pace so that they were walking in rhythm. "I started sleepwalking for a while. Right after I became pregnant."

"Aune told me adults sleepwalk at times of stress."

They stopped at the water's edge. Watched a pair of swans float past, calm and noiseless, on the gray surface.

"I knew from the very first moment who Oleg's father was," she said. "But I didn't know that he and I were having a child when he was informed that his girlfriend in Oslo was pregnant."

Harry filled his lungs with the sharp air. Felt it bite. It tasted of winter. He closed his eyes to the sun and listened.

"By the time I found out, he had already made his decision and left Moscow for Oslo. I had two options. To give the child a father in Moscow who would love and look after him as if he were his own—so long as he thought he *was* his own—or for the child to have no father. It was absurd. You know how I feel about lying. If someone had told me that I—*I*, of all people—would one day choose to live the rest of my life based on a lie, I would of course have denied it vehemently. You think everything is simple when you're young; you know nothing about the impossible decisions you may have to face. And if I'd only had myself to consider, this would have been a simple decision, too. But there were so many things to take into account. Not only whether I would crush Fjodor and affront his family, but also whether I would destroy things for the man who had gone to Oslo and his family. And then there was Oleg to take into account. Oleg came first."

"I understand," Harry said. "I understand everything."

"No," she said. "You don't understand why I haven't told you this before. With you there was no one else to take into account. You must think that I've tried to appear to be a better person than I am."

"I don't think that," Harry said. "I don't believe that you're a better person than you are."

She rested her head on his shoulder.

"Do you believe it's true what they say about swans?" she asked. "That they're faithful to each other until death do them part?"

"I believe they're faithful to the promises they've made," Harry said.

"And what promises do swans make?"

"None, I would assume."

"So you're talking about yourself now? In fact, I liked you better when you made promises and broke them."

"Would you like more promises?"

She shook her head.

When they started walking again she hooked her arm under his.

"I wish we could begin afresh," she said with a sigh. "Pretend nothing had happened."

"I know."

"But you also know that that's no good."

Harry could hear that the intonation implied this was a statement; however, hidden somewhere there was still a tiny question mark.

"I've been thinking of going away," he said.

"Oh, yes? Where?"

"I don't know. Don't come looking for me. Especially not in North Africa."

"North Africa?"

"It's a Marty Feldman line in a film. He wants to escape and be found at the same time."

"I see."

A shadow flitted across them and over the gray-yellow leached forest floor. They looked up. It was one of the swans.

"How did it work out in the film?" Rakel asked. "Did they find each other again?"

"Of course."

"When are you coming back?"

"Never," Harry replied. "I'm never coming back."

In a cold cellar in a Tøyen high-rise two worried representatives of the residents' committee were looking at a man in overalls wearing glasses with unusually thick lenses. The breath was coming out of the man's mouth like white plaster dust as he spoke.

"That's the thing about mold. You can't see it's there."

He paused. Pressed his middle finger against the wisp of hair that was stuck to his forehead.

"But it is."